FATE OF ALANDRIA

Book One of the Fate of Alandria Series

Ashley Eileen

Fate of Alandria Copyright © 2024 by Ashley Eileen

All rights reserved. No part of this publication may be reproduced, stored or transmitted in any form or by any means, electronic, mechanical, photocopying, recording, scanning, or otherwise without written permission from the publisher. It is illegal to copy this book, post it to a website, or distribute it by any other means without permission. This Book may be used in brief quotations embodied in critical reviews or articles.

This novel is entirely a work of fiction. The names, characters and incidents portrayed in it are the work of the author's imagination. Any resemblance to actual persons, living or dead, events or localities is entirely coincidental.

First Edition: September 2024

For information contact:
https://www.authorashleyeileen.com/

Formatting and Interior Design by Ashley Eileen
Cover Illustration and Design by Ashley Eileen

Hardcover SE ISBN: 9798329046939

Content Warnings

Arranged Marriage, Depression, Mentions of alcohol, Mentions of a dying race, Gore, Manipulation, Cheating, Necromancy, Necrophilia, Death of a Child, Mentions of Complications with Birth, Murder, Tattoos, Physical Abuse, Forced Consent, Blood Magic, Blood, Mentions of Child Abuse, Sexual Content

I do my best to include all potential triggers, I deeply apologize if I missed any. If you find something that may be difficult for someone to read, feel free to reach out to me to update the list.

Book Playlist

For a curated Spotify playlist for this book, scan the code below.

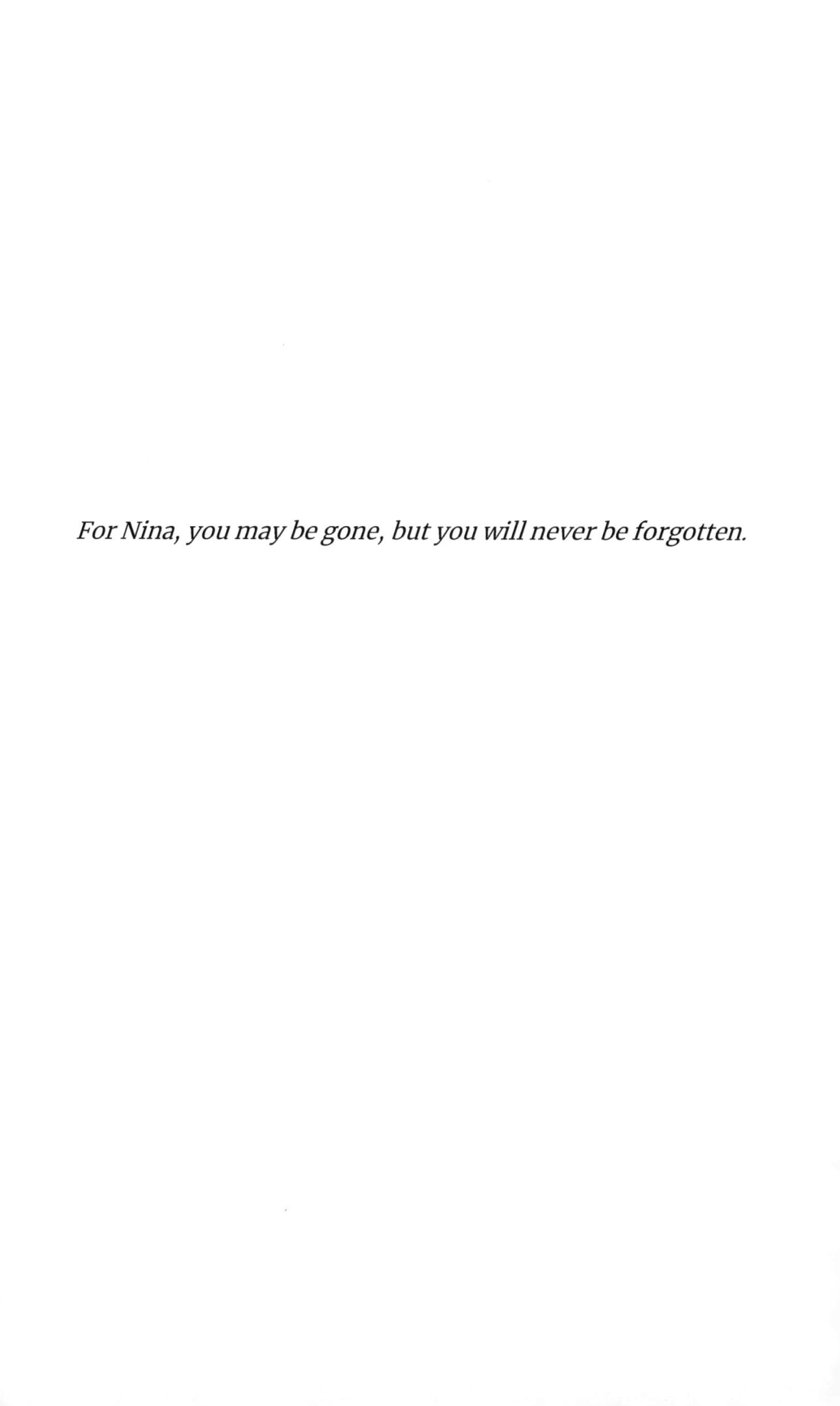

For Nina, you may be gone, but you will never be forgotten.

Pronunciation Guide

Characters:
Sage Torrin - SEYJ TORR EN
Kira - KIER RAH
Hassian - HAH SEE EN
Idril - EE DRILL
Gildor - GIL DOOR
Thranduil - TH RAN DO ILL
Gaiwen - GUY WEN
Thalia - TAL EE AH
Anton - ANT ON
Auhdaye - AWE DAY
Keevah – KEY VAH
Kamira - KAH MERE AH
Iolta - I OHL TAH
Sebille - SEH BILL
Aurora - UH ROAR UH
Meera - MERE UH
Thevin Brawnmire – THE VIN BRA ON MIRE
Modey - MOH DAY
Hinley - HIN LEE
Agene - UH GEEN
Merellee – MAIR AH EL EE

Places:
Alandria - UH LAWN DREE UH
Aliria - UH LEER EE UH
Alacarin Forest - AL CAH RIN
Drifton - DRIFT IN
Halaris - HA LAR ESS

Chapters

Prologue 1
Chapter One 7
Chapter Two 15
Chapter Three 21
Chapter Four 29
Chapter Five 35
Chapter Six 43
Chapter Seven 50
Chapter Eight 57
Chapter Nine 65
Chapter Ten 75
Chapter Eleven 83
Chapter Twelve 91
Chapter Thirteen 103
Chapter Fifteen 123
Chapter Sixteen 129
Chapter Seventeen 139
Chapter Eighteen 145
Chapter Nineteen 155
Chapter Twenty 165
Chapter Twenty-One 171
Chapter Twenty-Two 177
Chapter Twenty-Three 183
Chapter Twenty-Four 189
Chapter Twenty-Five 195
Chapter Twenty-Six 203
Chapter Twenty-Seven 215
Chapter Twenty-Eight 225

Chapter Twenty-Nine 231
Chapter Thirty 241
Chapter Thirty-One 251
Chapter Thirty-Two 259
Chapter Thirty-Three.. 267
Chapter Thirty-Four 279
Chapter Thirty-Five... 291
Chapter Thirty-Six 305
Chapter Thirty-Seven 317
Chapter Thirty-Eight 327
Chapter Thirty-Nine.. 333
Chapter Forty.. 341
Chapter Forty-One 349
Epilogue 353

REALM OF ALANDRIA

- TRESSIAN SEA
- AERIS ACADEMY
- HALARIS
- ???
- TAZZIAN SEA
- ACCARIN FOREST
- SHIMMERINE LAKE
- SCOURGE LAKE
- GAWEN'S FOREST
- ASTAVOR — HOME OF THE HIGH KING
- NINAGA FOREST
- DRIFTON
- HIGHLAND SEA
- REALM DOCKS

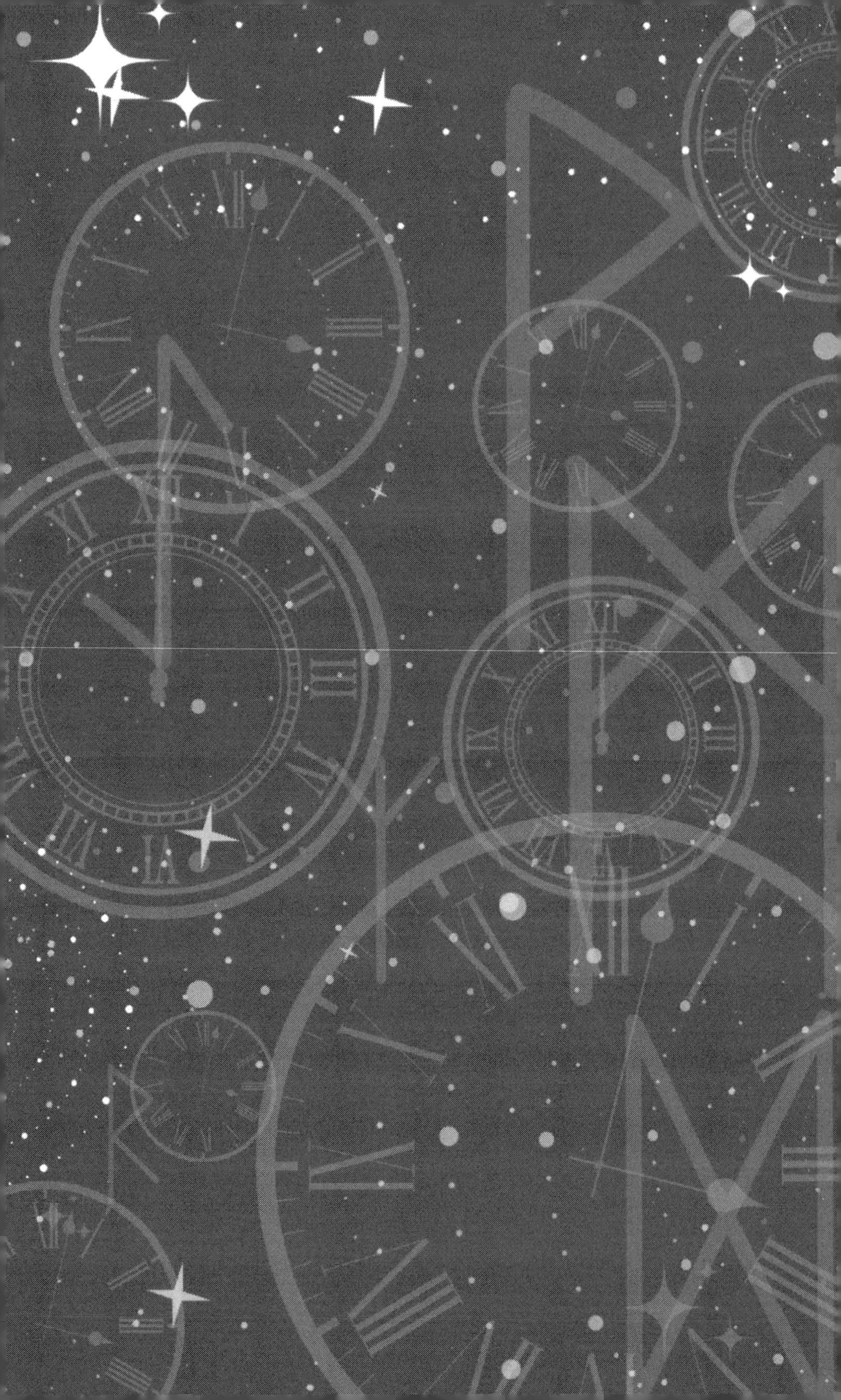

Prologue
Idril

18 years ago

The sun is shining through the large windows of my bedroom. I am lying in the bed I share with my husband. *My husband.* By The Nines. I wonder if I will ever get used to saying that. We have been married for a year and are now with child—one that will be coming very soon, just a few weeks.

My husband, Gildor, begins to stir, a smile creeping across his face. "Are you watching me as I sleep again, wife?"

I laugh, running my fingers through his long red hair, "Me? I would never."

"Liar," he mumbles before rising to place a tender kiss on my belly. I feel a flutter in response to his presence. "Well, good morning to you, too, little one. I cannot wait until the day you are born so I can teach you how to wield a sword and be a great warrior, just like your father."

"Love, we've talked about this; you can't teach a baby how to sword fight. She needs to grow a few seasons first."

He lets out an exaggerated sigh. "Fine." He gives my belly one more quick peck before coming up to kiss my lips. "What's on the agenda today, my beautiful wife?"

"Well, I-" time begins to slow around me as a sensation I am much too familiar with begins to take root. My vision clears, and so does the figure before me, the Goddess of Fate and Wisdom. "Kamira?" I ask with question, even though I know it's her. My connection has only ever been with her.

"Hello, my child. I am sorry that I must disturb you on what was looking to be a beautiful morning. Please sit with me," she motions for me to sit on the ledge of the water fountain.

"You are never a bother, Goddess Kamira."

"I'm afraid you will not like the news I must give." She takes my hands in hers. "There is a future written in the stars, and many paths lead to this destiny, but they all end the same. You will live long enough to see your child come into this world. That is all. The child must leave with the one whose hands are covered in blood. You cannot go with for your death is tied together with Gildor."

My heart begins to fill with the grief of her words, "I must give up my child, but why?"

Kamira nods solemnly, "A gift must be passed from a blessing bestowed. A child born from love and great sacrifice."

"Kamira, speak plainly, I beg of you. I wish to know if I do not see my child grow up. Please."

Kamira rests her head against my forehead, tapping into our connection; she shares her vision with me. Flashes of images play in my mind. The future that cannot be changed has made itself clear to me, and I know it must be done. I will give birth to the child of the prophecy told long ago: a child born of both life and death destined to be the savior of the realm or its undoing. "Do you understand now?"

"I do."

"Iolta will make the path you must take painless when the time comes. You will know love in death just as you have in life. Farewell, my child." Kamira pulls away from me until we are no longer touching. The scene around me changes back to that of my room, and time begins once again. "Well, dear husband, it looks like we will be planning for our little one's future today.

Part One

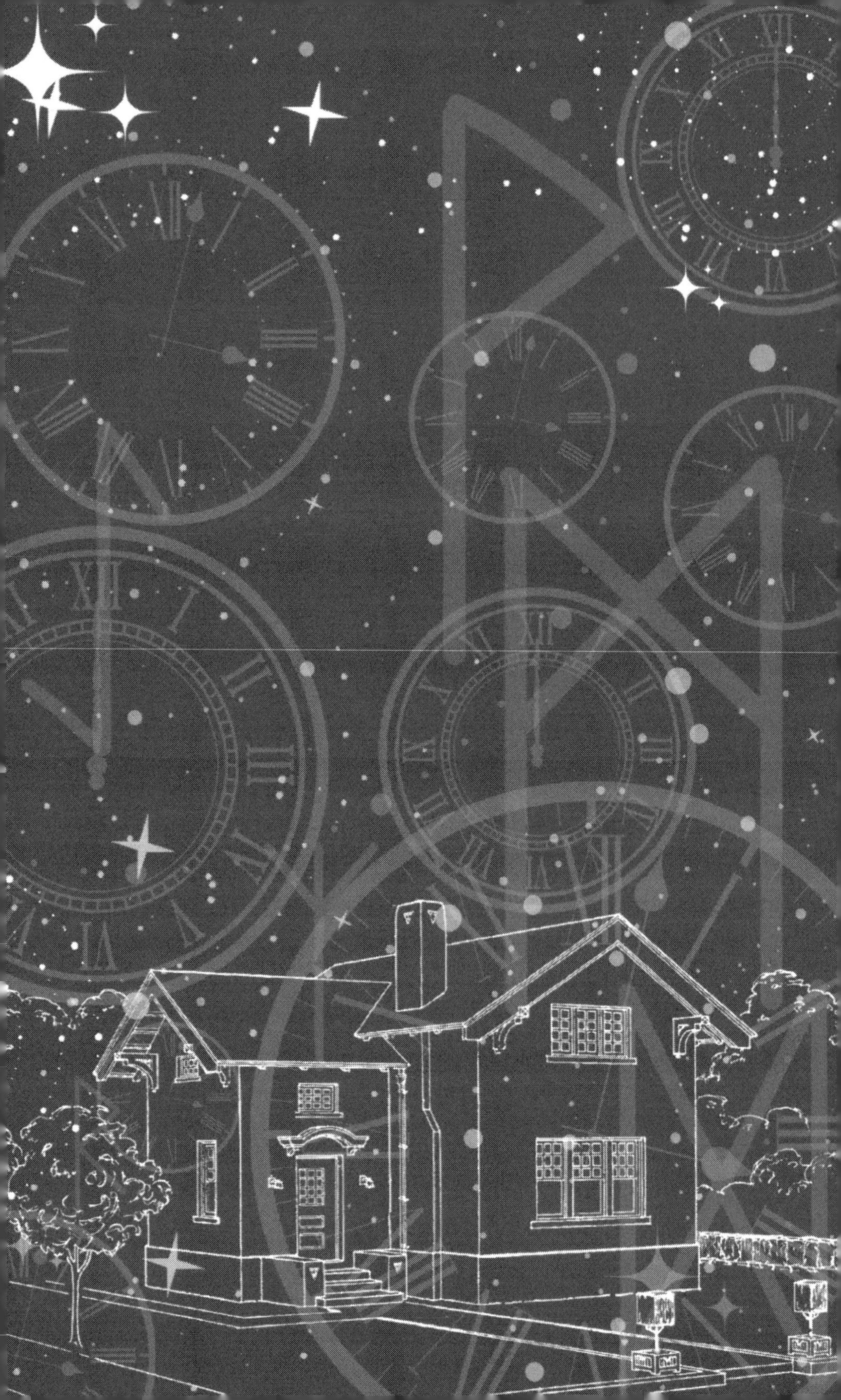

Chapter One.
Wren

Present day

I should stop checking social media. All it gives me is the overwhelming sense that I don't fucking know what I'm supposed to be doing with my life. It doesn't matter that I only just graduated high school two weeks ago; that doesn't make me feel any less of a failure. Some of my friends knew what they were going to do with their lives going back as far as middle school; however, that is not the case for me. I have scoured many brochures and visited many campuses, but everything just feels wrong.

    I'll be the first to admit that I wasn't the brightest person in my class, but I wasn't at the bottom of the barrel either. How is it that every avenue I try to explore feels wrong? I set my phone down atop my vanity; maybe going out and doing something today will help. I take a deep breath and look in the mirror; my auburn hair has gotten too long and unruly. Maybe I should get a haircut? *No, Wren, that's just the mental breakdown in you trying to encourage drastic change. You like your long hair.*

    I stretch my fuzzy headband over my head to pull my hair back and out of my face. My face is more angular than the girls I went to school with, and honestly, it's made me a little insecure over the years. Well, that and the fact that I tower over most of them. Don't get me wrong; I enjoy not needing stools to reach for everything like my mother does; however, things like prom group photos really sucked. The number of times I heard the line, can you squat down some more, Wren? You are towering over the other girls. Well, quite frankly, it got old fast. I do some of my skincare; mainly, it's just a cream with a decent amount of SPF. I spend much of my free time outside, so I'd rather be safe than sorry. Lately, I've been enjoying sitting in my mother's garden out back; there's just something about nature that calls to me.

Once I finish that, I figure out what to do with my hair. If I'm being entirely honest with myself, I have no idea what the hell I am doing in that department, either. My mother, Kira, wasn't exactly helpful with that. She always looks like she just crawled out of some tree in the forest, her hair going this way and that, and our hair texture is not even in the same atmosphere. Where my hair is long and wavy, my mom's looks short but is super curly. Usually poofy, and I kid you not, I am constantly plucking a leaf or a twig from her hair.

Sometimes, I wonder if she's actually my mother, a thought I shouldn't be thinking, but I cannot help but notice the differences between us. Maybe I get my ginger genes from my father. I wouldn't know because he's not in the picture, and we don't talk about him.

I brush out my hair until I am sure all the tangles are gone and stare at myself in the mirror while I debate how I want to approach it today. I take a good section of hair from the right side of my head, braiding it to pin it behind my ear. I pick up the pin and go to the other side of my pointed ear. My pointed what? I drop the pin in my brief state of shock and look at my ear again—my normal human-shaped ear. Maybe I didn't get enough sleep last night. I pick up the pin I dropped and finish styling my hair to the best of my ability, which isn't great.

As I ponder what I want to do today, I decide to spend my day browsing the local bookstore and swinging by the plant nursery next door. I grab my thin-strapped orange dress with a floral pattern from my closet, put it on, and head downstairs.

My mom is in the kitchen in her gardening apron. Dirt covers her cheeks and arms as she cleans up yet another rescued plant. "Where'd that one come from?" I ask, pulling a leaf from her hair.

"The neighbors saw me cleaning the garden bed again and figured I would appreciate a little project." She smiles up at me while trimming the dead bits of the plant. "You look nice today. Where are you off to?"

"I figured I would go check out the bookstore, then the nursery. Abigail just posted her latest acceptance letter."

"Oh, it's one of those days. Just how many colleges did she need to apply to? This makes what five now?"

"Seven."

"Nines," my mother exclaims with her hand on her chest. My mother isn't religious, at least not in the way people around here are. She believes in nine goddesses, and I hope no one ever asks me all the names because I can't remember half of them.

"She comes from a well-off family; I think she's collecting acceptances like trophies."

"Hmm. I think that's ridiculous but to each their own. Well, have fun, and if you see any good ones at the nursery, please bring them home. I have plenty of room in my garden." The good ones, as my mother calls it, are the plants nearing their death bed. She has this odd urge to save things she sees dying in nature and is almost always successful. She was so distraught the few times she failed and vowed never to repeat the same mistake. As for her garden, who knows which she is referring to? My mother has an outdoor one, a giant greenhouse, and a whole room inside the house dedicated to her plants. This does not even include the various ones she has sitting in random places in the house.

I give my mother a small peck on the forehead before replying, "Will do." I head toward the front door, glancing at my mother as she makes her way out the sliding door to pot her new plant, and I let out a chuckle. There's a stick protruding from the back of her hair.

"Good afternoon, Wren," Lana, the owner, shouts from her register. "Are you looking for anything particular today or just browsing?"

I move closer so we're not yelling at each other from afar. "Just browsing today, hoping to pick up a new book or two. I brought my tote just in case," I say as I hold it up. The tote doesn't give a special kind of discount or anything, but it does mean I can walk home with my possible loot and not risk dropping things.

"Well, I'll let you get to it. Want a coffee or anything today?" She asks.

"Coffee would be great," I say.

"Iced with a shot of espresso, oat milk, caramel syrup, and a hearty heaping of caramel drizzle, right?" she asks me, squinting her face in recollection.

"You nailed it!"

"Alright, it'll be just a moment, and that'll be four dollars and twenty-five cents today," she says as she types my order into her register. "Do you have your loyalty card on you so I can stamp it?"

"I sure do," I hand her the card and the cash.

"Double stamps Wednesday," she says as she punches two more holes into my card, leaving me one stamp away from a free coffee.

"Thank you," I say as she hands me back the card. As she walks away to make my drink, I stuff a couple of dollars into her tip jar.

She's back in less than three minutes with a mason jar filled with my coffee order. "Here you go, Wren. Have fun browsing.

I hope you find something to your liking today," she says, giving me a wink before going to help the next customer with their order.

I turn around and let my eyes wander to the display setup she has going on. Only one aisle interests me, and that's the fantasy section. Many of my friends are big into contemporary romance, but I've always been a give me some mythical creatures and a battle to be won type of girl. Plus, romance isn't my thing as someone who has never really shown interest in any kind of relationship. However, I will read a fantasy romance here and there.

I'm reading a book where a whole kingdom is cursed, and it's up to the princess to save everyone when the tickle of a soft voice whispers in my mind. *Wake up, Sage. It's time to wake up.* The voice is like velvet in my mind. I feel like my body is being torn from itself, not in a painful way, but like I am about to have an out-of-body experience, and there is no way this is happening right now. I shake my head and put the book back on the shelf. Maybe I should go home. I feel sweat drip along my spine, and I get the chills. Maybe going out today wasn't such a good idea.

I walk up to Lana to give her my almost full cup of coffee. "Did I mess it up?" she asks, her face lacing with concern.

"No, I'm just not feeling too well right now and think I should head home and rest."

"Let me put that in a to-go container for you in case you want to drink a little on your walk back home. Are you going to be okay walking? We can call your mother if you need a ride." She shuffles to the back, grabs a paper cup from the counter, and transfers my drink.

I tap my cell phone to remind her I have one. "I'll be fine to walk; Mom might be a little disappointed I didn't bring her home a new plant to love, though," I say with a laugh. Laughing might have been a bit of a mistake because the room begins to spin on its axis, and the next thing I know, my body is falling to the floor. I don't feel the impact. When I fall, it feels like I'm passing through the floor, only to land on my feet in a room full of stars.

I take a moment to adjust to my surroundings. Obviously, I just fainted in the coffee shop, and I am having a weirdly vivid and self-aware dream right now. Looking down at my feet, I am standing on a white-colored pathway. My eyes trace along the path and see it leads to a beautiful large water fountain. Sitting upon the ledge of the water fountain is a slender-looking woman with brown hair that's pinned up. Curtain bangs frame her face in delicate curls. I find myself walking toward her, wanting to see the rest of her. She's familiar to me, but not.

She motions for me to sit beside her on the fountain's ledge, and I do. I feel like I can trust her, and I feel as if she is safe. I situate myself beside her, close enough that if I extended my fingers, we would be touching. I look at her face now that I am close enough to her. She has deep brown eyes, and they exude kindness from them. Her skin is pale like mine, possibly with a warmer undertone. It's hard to tell because her skin looks as if it's shimmering. Almost like the stars that are above us. Who is this woman?

"Hello, little Sage," she says with a smile. Her smile is inviting and trusting.

"I'm sorry, but I think my name is Wren," I say. My name is Wren. Right? Somehow, saying that here doesn't feel correct.

"Wren is but the name you grew up to call yourself. You are Sage Torrin, and it is time for that which has been dampened and dulled in you to wake up. Your fate awaits you in Alandria."

"Dampened and dulled?" I ask. She only nods but does not elaborate.

"There is a future written in the stars, and many paths lead to this destiny. This path is yours to choose. One shall lead to a future bright, the other dark."

"I don't understand what you are trying to say."

"You will. The woman you grew up believing to be your mother will have much to share. Listen close, listen well. Change is coming; accept it into your heart." She places her forehead on mine and whispers, "Wake up, Sage."

The world around me begins to whirl and spin. I no longer feel the pressure of her forehead against mine, and the room is familiar to me once again. I am back in the bookstore. No, not the bookstore, our couch. I'm home. Maybe I didn't go out today; perhaps I fell asleep reading.

"Oh, wren," my mother says as she runs over to me and rubs my forehead, tears glistening in her eyes.

"I don't think my name is Wren," I say, and my mother closes her eyes slowly and nods.

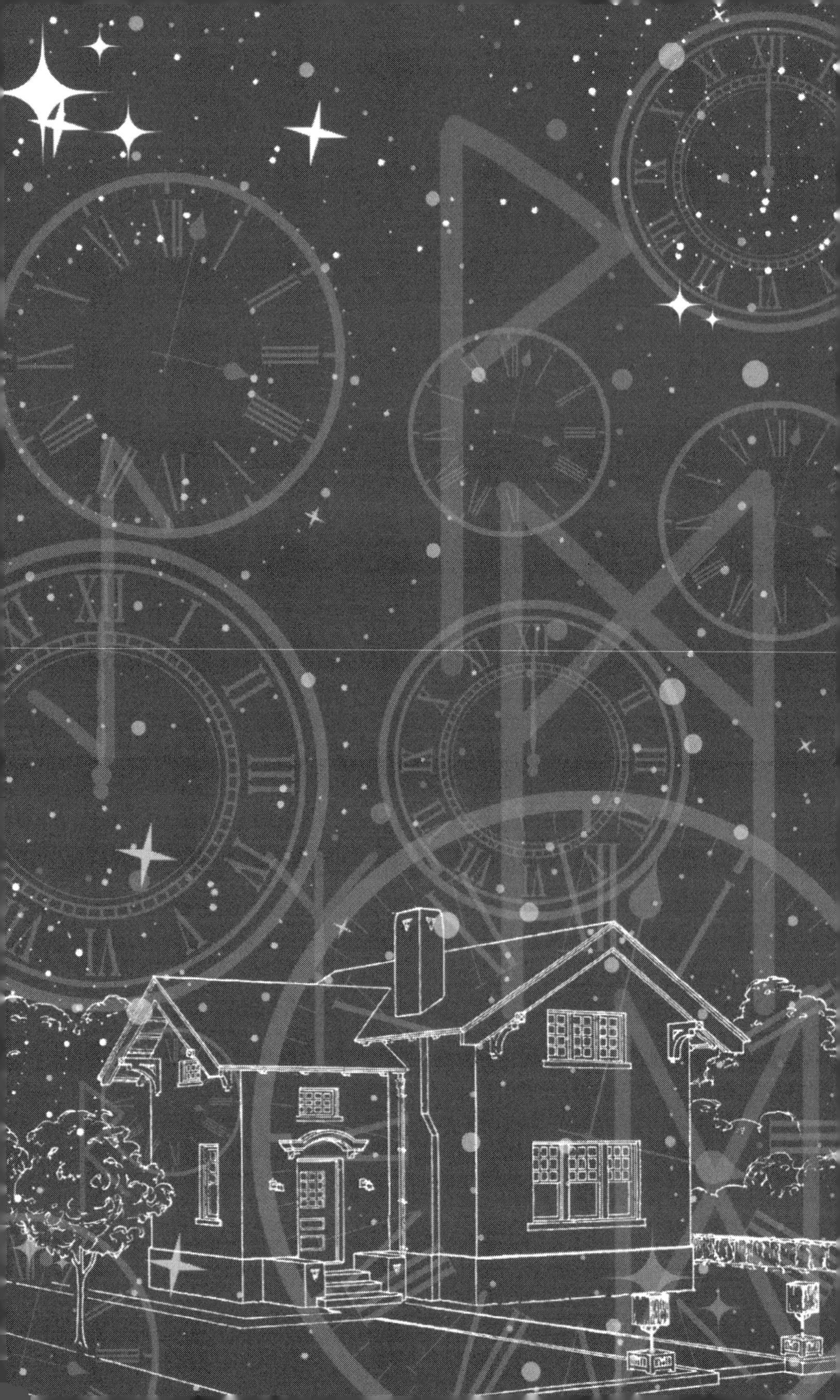

Chapter Two.
Not Wren But Sage.

"This is the part where you are supposed to say, no, Wren, you just fell and hit your head at the bookstore," I joke, letting out a really uncomfortable laugh.

"Oh, how I wish I could, but from the look on your face, I think you just had a conversation with Kamira."

"Kamira?"

"Kamira is the goddess of Fate and Wisdom. Your mother had a special connection with her, which allowed them to speak. Your mother was said to have the gift of foresight, but she was more of a messenger."

"So, when this, Kamira, person-"

"Goddess," my mother, not mother, corrects me.

"-goddess said you weren't my mother then, that was true?" She nods solemnly. "So, what do I call you if you are not my mother?"

"Kira. Just as the neighbors and everyone else call me. That was always my true name. Kira Maye if you want to get into specifics."

"And who was my mother? My father?" So many questions are racing in my mind, and I don't know where to begin.

"Your mother's name was Idril, and your father was Gildor. Their last name was Torrin. She is, er, was the daughter of the High King, Thranduil."

"Was?" I ask, feeling this sad pit in the center of my being.

"Yes, she died, ensuring that you lived when you were born."

"How do you know all of this? How do you know them? What is a High King?" I let out in almost a single breath. As I said, I have many questions forming in my mind.

"I was there. I was tasked with," Kira paused, and I could tell she was searching for the right word, "removing you from your mother and raising you in a different realm."

"When you say removing me, what do you mean?"

Kira blanches. "Well, the way you were positioned in your mother, you weren't going to survive, and neither was she. We don't have the same advancements in medicine, and we didn't have the time."

"Kira, what did you do?" My voice cracks.

"Your mother ordered me to cut you from her body."

"You cut open my mother? What about the amount of pain?" I can feel my face getting wet with tears. My heart picks up pace as I feel my body temperature rising. I don't know why I thought asking questions was a good idea. I've always sucked with change, and now everything it's all happening at once. I feel sick, teetering on the edge of vomiting. I dig my nails into my thigh to try and ground myself. Just get the truth over with and make it through this step.

"I didn't want to. She took my hand and forced the blade in. I had to finish. I promise your mother felt no pain outside of heartbreak. She was goddess-blessed; they helped her through it. She used the last of her strength to glamour us and lock your magic until sometime after you reached adulthood. There's no perfect science to magic."

"Why would I need my magic locked away? Hold that thought," I raise my hand to pause the conversation while I rush over to grab the trash bin near the couch and begin to throw up. My nerves were at an all-time high. I always had suspicions Kira wasn't my mother, but learning the truth is a lot to process. After hunching over the bin for what felt like a lifetime, I was fairly certain nothing else would come out, so I nodded my head for Kira to continue.

"Your mother locked your magic away because magic works like a beacon, which, in your situation, we needed to not have. A very dangerous man wants you and the magic you are foretold to have."

"Why suppress my magic into adulthood? Why not until I was just old enough to start learning? Couldn't you have protected me with yours?"

"In Alandria, you don't begin learning to hone your magic until college. The teaching of basic magic is intended for the parents. There are a few reasons why they chose to suppress your magic into adulthood. The first is that when you are an adult, you get to attend the academy, which is protected by wards. It's a safe place to learn because it can defend itself from threats. The second is that I am a braacea or, as some would call me, forest fae. I am a lesser fae and don't have as much magic as the high fae. My magic comes from my bond with nature. I can communicate with plants and animals and do small element manipulation. I can protect our home, but not for long periods."

"Is that why we have so many plants because you can draw power from them?"

"A little bit of yes and no. They do make me stronger. Enough to keep a small field of protection around the home and alert me of unwanted visitors, but also because they give me a sense of home. My kind does best living within the forest."

"Wait, is that why you always have leaves and sticks in your hair? Have you been sleeping outside all this time?"

Kira shrugs. "I'm comfortable there. Oh, and to answer your question about what a High King is, that is just speak for the very top of fae royalty. They preside over everyone in the realm."

"Wait, so am I like some kind of royalty or something?" I let out a laugh, but my insides are screaming what the fuck over and over again.

"Yes."

"How will this college know I'll be attending?" I ask.

"Well, as soon as the suppression spell is completely worn off, it will send a magic beacon. The school has a book of names in the headmaster's office. Your name is probably already there, but it will give a location, and a creature will be tasked to deliver it to you. It's usually a fox; they do many of our realm-to-realm communications."

"Wait, so are all foxes working for the fae?"

"Foxes are fae, but to answer your question, yes. All foxes work with the fae."

"So, people that take in foxes as pets-" I start.

"Are carrying around fae that are shapeshifted as such. They just let it happen, usually because the person in question is a changeling, and it's their way of watching over them. The fae don't take changelings back anymore, well, not usually."

"Right," I am completely overwhelmed right now.

Kira takes notice, "We will stop there. They will go over so much of this when you get into the school. I probably just dumped way too much information on you. It's been a long time since I could discuss our realm with anyone." Kira looks at her watch to check the time. "It's getting late. I'll order some dinner for us, and we can watch a show together or something. Does that sound okay?"

"That sounds perfectly normal. Yes, please," I say.

"Great, go wash up, and I'll order your favorite. Oh, and let me grab this just in case," Kira walks over to the kitchen pantry and pulls out a fire extinguisher.

"What's that for?"

"Your father had an affinity for fire, and well, I don't know what one you will get. I would rather be safe than sorry," she shrugs.

I laugh because I'm hysterical at this point. "What about my mother? What was hers?"

"Earth," Kira waves around the room. "I think we have that one covered. Now go! Go wash up, and we can enjoy chicken fajitas with the crunchy shell."

"Don't forget to add extra guac. Oh, and can we get some cheesecake, too?" My stomach growls as if it's begging for it, too.

"Of course, I'll even order the strawberry lemonade. Now hurry up!" Kira laughs as she starts putting our order into the delivery app.

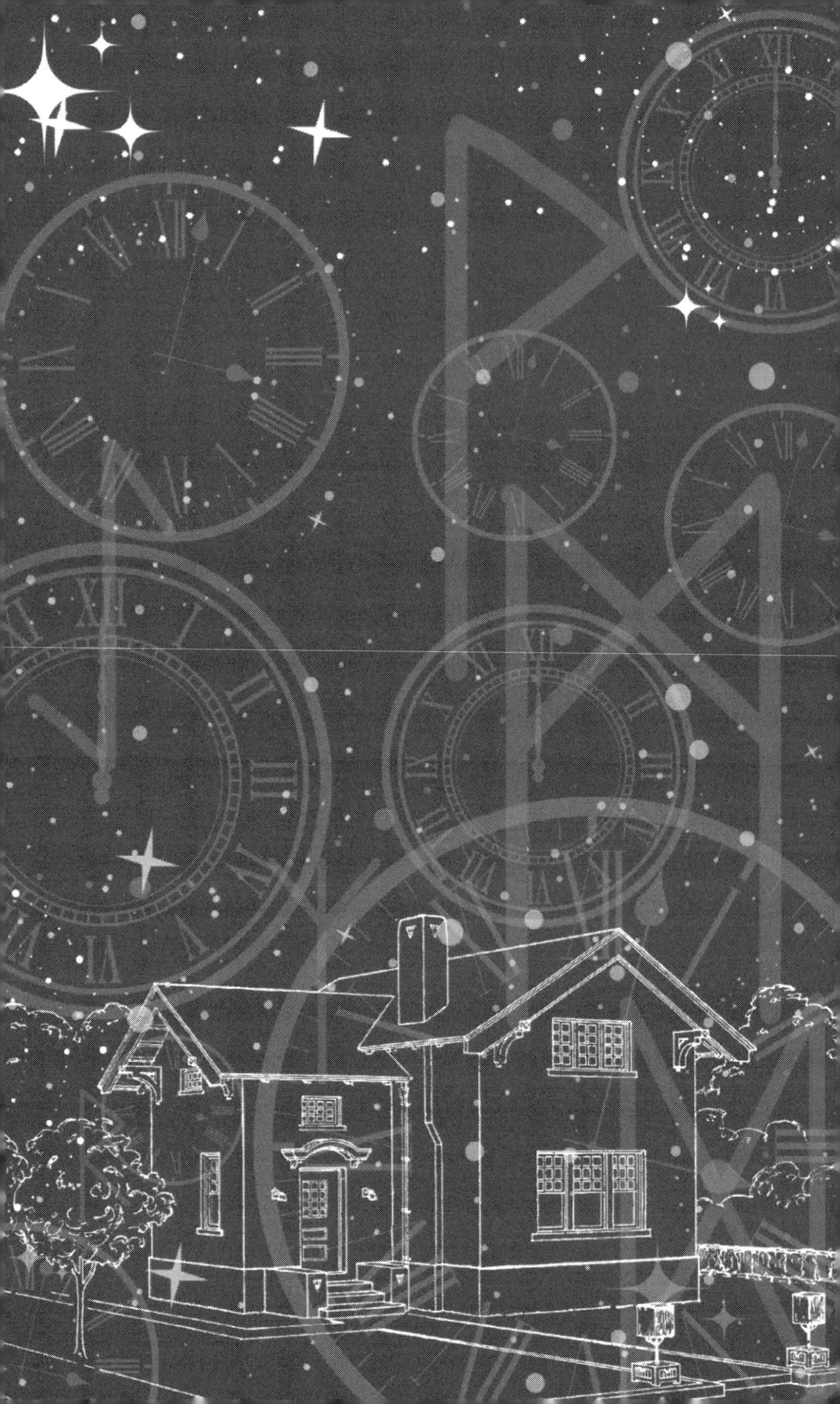

Chapter Three
Sage

I am helping Kira out in her garden today. She was up bright and early this morning and ran to the plant nursery. I swear she filled every available space in the car with a plant. I don't know where Kira gets the money to afford any of this because I cannot say I have ever seen her work an actual job. I guess the local law enforcement or the government never showing up is a good sign that whatever she's doing is legal in some way.

"Kira, what happens to all of this stuff when we have to leave, to-" I pause, trying to recall the name.

"Alandria," Kira finishes for me. I nod. "Well, you see this trinket here?" She points to a necklace I always see her wearing. It is shaped like a cube and has a clear crystal inside. "This is called an omni-vessel. I tap it three times while thinking of my intent inside my head. It'll hold everything here inside it, and I can bring it with us and relocate. All the plants and stuff will be stuck in suspended animation until I release them."

"Can people get stuck inside that? Speaking of people, won't people realize our house is gone?"

"No, it cannot hold living souls like that. They'll appear on the ground nearby. As to our neighbors, your friends, they'll forget about us when I use this." She holds up a pouch and opens it to show a shimmering dust-like powder as to where she was carrying that I have no idea. "The dust is already imbued with what needs to be done, another gift from your mother. It'll make the humans forget us, and in place of the open lot will be a community garden. That, of course, was my idea."

"My friends will forget me?"

"I'm sorry. This change isn't going to be an easy thing." Kira rubs my back in a comforting gesture.

"How did you get this house anyway?" I ask.

"Oh look, Sage, the roses are all bloomed!" Kira exclaims. I know she's trying to change the subject, but they can't be. There were no blooms just a moment ago.

I spin around in a circle and see all the flowers have bloomed—every single one. The seeds we planted last week are in full bloom. "But how?"

Kira cheers and spins as the garden grows, more flowers sprouting from the ground in glorious blooms and it's like they are singing to us only a melody the both of us can hear. "I think you have an Earth affinity just like your mother," Kira giggles as she twirls around. That's when I first notice that Kira isn't as I have seen her all these years. Now standing before me is a woman completely green from head to toe with pointed ears. Somehow, she's even shorter, standing at a height below my hips.

"Kira, you're-" I pause, not knowing how to say the words.

She looks up at me, her eyes shining with delight. She reaches into her pockets and pulls out a cloth, angling it toward me. "For your nose; Sage, you are just as perfect as the day you were born." Her grin is so bright; I swear she could light up a whole night sky with its brilliance.

I accept the cloth, bringing it to my nose, dabbing at whatever Kira saw. I examine the fabric and realize it has blood on it. My nose is bleeding. I have probably been standing outside for too long. I keep blotting my nose until I am confident the bleed has clotted. I observe Kira as she frolics about the garden, sniffing all the blooms and whispering words too faint for me to hear. It dawns on me that if Kira looks different, perhaps I do too, especially considering what I thought I saw the morning before I went into town.

I pull out my phone and open up the camera app, taking a quick look in Kira's direction to see if she's watching me. Something about doing this feels intimate, and I'd rather not have anyone see. Especially in the off case I am wrong and look the same. My hands are shaking from the anxiety building. *Just get it over with; you're just looking at your reflection—no big deal.* I let out a deep breath and look at my screen. My eyes are more angular than what I grew up believing, and I have pointed ears. Although they differ from Kira's, mine are more extended and slender, whereas hers are short and wide. Thankfully, no green skin, so whatever she is, it's different than whatever I am.

"Excuse me," a muffled voice says. I search around for the sound of the voice until I eventually spot it. A fox pokes its head out of the blooms, holding a letter in its mouth. A letter I can see is addressed to me. It motions its head upwards, and I take the letter before it trots off and out of sight.

Kira returns to my side, "Well, open it already, Sage. We've been waiting a very long time for this."

You would think that for someone who had only just heard of this school, I wouldn't be filled with as much excitement as I am, but everything that I just experienced at this moment is hitting me like an adrenaline shot. I hold the dark green envelope in my hand, staring at the wax seal of the letter A. Sweat trickles down my spine as I carefully lift the wax seal from the envelope. I pull out a sheet that looks like the letter, leaving the rest inside.

Ms. Torrin,

As the headmaster of Aliria Academy, I am honored to extend an official notice of acceptance into our fine school. We recognize and celebrate the unique talents and potential of each fellow student who steps through our door.

At Aliria Academy, we are not merely a place of academic pursuit; we are a place of sanctuary and have been such since the day our doors opened. Rest assured, precautions have been taken and remain that way, as we are aware of your particular problem.

I have enclosed a list of all necessary books and miscellaneous items you will need throughout your first year at the academy, as well as a travel itinerary showing where the nearest portal is to your location.

Term begins during the start of the autumn season. We look forward to having you attend.

Signed,
Headmaster Thevin Brawnmire

I look at Kira, "How long will it take to get there? If school starts in the autumn and it's summer, won't we be early if we leave now?"

"Perhaps a little early. May I see the itinerary?" I hand her over all the contents of the letter. "Hmmm, well, we have a bit of traveling to get the portal, plus flight time. It may take us a month to reach Halaris." Kira mumbles some as she reads over the paper to herself. "We will have to gather ingredients. I guess I can show you around the capital." more mumbling. "We stay at," she becomes so inaudible I cannot understand anything she is saying. Eventually, she hands the papers back to me. "We will make it work. If we get there early, there's plenty we can do to pass the time. The mountain city was pretty well fortified the last time I was there. I doubt it'll be too dangerous to spend some time getting to know the city a bit before the school season starts."

"What do we do now?"

"Well, now you go upstairs to your room and pack a bag, and I will do the same. Meet me out front, and we will pack up the house and be on our way. I don't want to linger here too long now that your magic is no longer suppressed. Unfortunately, I have to glamour us a little longer, so come over here while I tap into some of these plants, please." I crouch down next to Kira, and she places a hand on my shoulder while she digs her other hand into the soil of the earth. I can hear a soft humming sound as she closes her eyes. Her figure begins to blur before me as the green version of herself disappears back into the woman I grew up with. I run a hand through my hair to feel for the point of my ears that is no longer there. They are round and human. I feel an odd sense of longing for them to be back, a part of me I had just met. I tell myself this is just until we cross through the portal.

Kira loads my bag into the back of the car before closing the trunk. She hurries to the steps of the front door, where she left a few potted plants before putting them in the back seat of the car. "Just in case I need to use some magic along the way." Even though my magic is available, I don't know how to use it, so it's a good idea that she brings something along that might help us if we encounter anything. "Right, well, go ahead and sit in the car while I take care of this," she motions to the house.

I watch as Kira closes her eyes and taps the omni-vessel three times. A flash of light envelops the house as it shrinks and swirls toward her like a tornado until it's out of sight. I feel like I'm being watched, but as I look around, none of the neighbors are even turning an eye our way. It's almost like they are not seeing any of this.

I look back at Kira, and she has the bag of shimmering dust in her hand. She pours some into her palm and blows. The dust expands and floats across where the house was and keeps going and stretching until it is far beyond what my eyes can see. When it eventually fades, I can see the changes. Where our house once stood lays a fenced area with growing flowers and vegetables. A sign reads, 'Community Garden, take what you want.'

Nobody looks in our direction, even as Kira starts up the car. I still have so many questions for her, but for now, those can wait. This is potentially my last moment in the human realm, and I'd like to take the time to admire it. Things are going to be so much different than what I am used to.

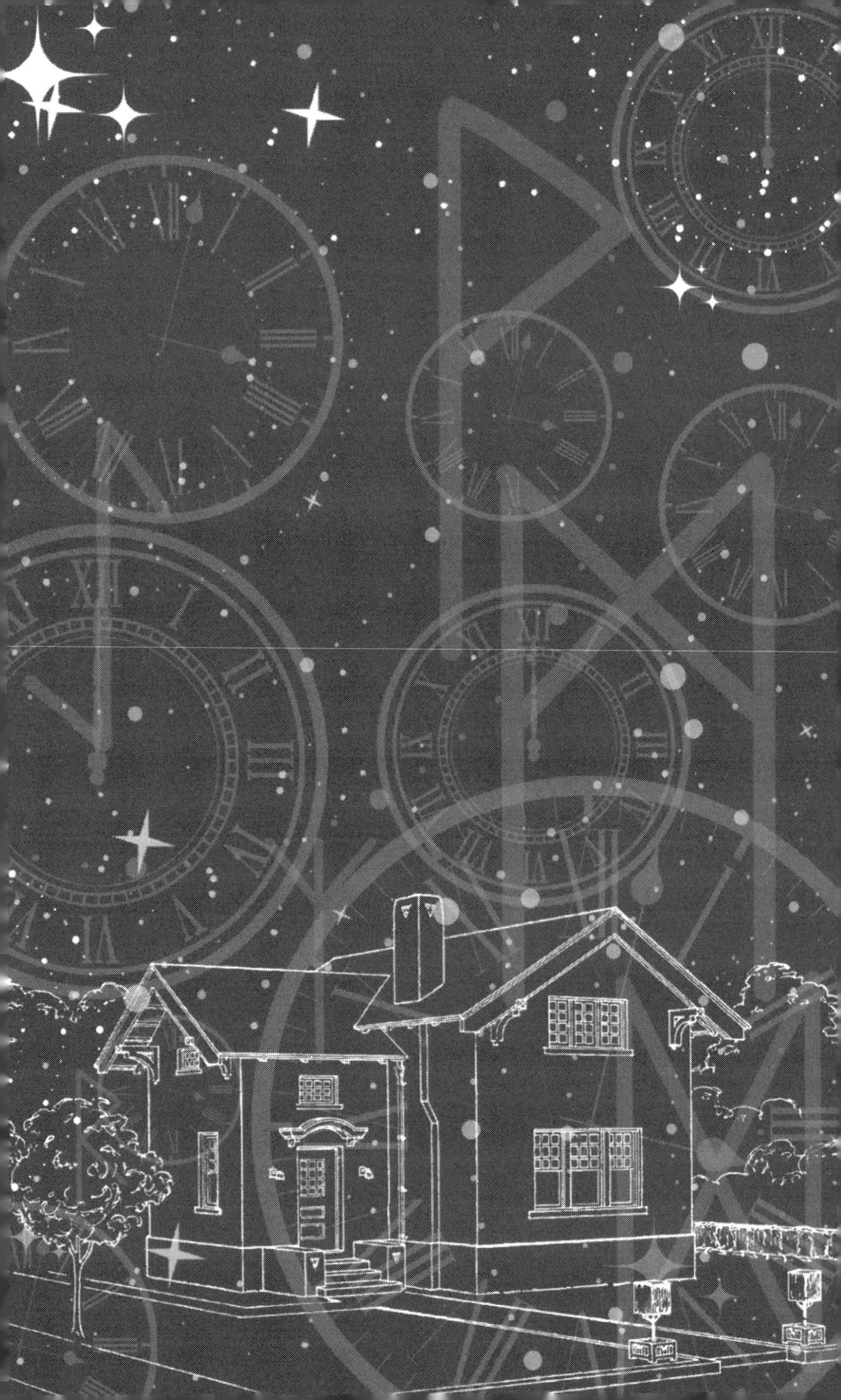

Chapter Four
Sage

Kira explained how we ended up where we were and that my mother had created a one-time portal for us. My mother had it all planned out before she ever retrieved Kira, knowing that she would have done everything in her power to make them come with us. I believe that whatever she saw and had to do back then was unbelievably hard on her. She raised me with a constant smile and a big heart, but there was always a haunting look in her eyes. I have no doubts that she's seen more than just what she's told me.

  We weren't far from the portal; my mother's portal landed in Michigan, and we had to travel north to an island up in Canada. This meant Kira had to tap into some of the plants she brought to glamour some papers to look like passports and again to make it look like they were real despite nothing coming up on the devices. Once we passed through the border patrol, we headed toward Port Nelson. According to our GPS, the drive was intended to take a little over 7 hours, but Kira missed a few turns, adding at least an hour, maybe more. I cannot say for certain because I fell asleep at some point. I'm pretty sure Kira was talking about all the different species of hibiscus around the world, but I had never met the back of my eyelids so fast before. I took a little time during the drive to research places like the island we were headed to next, and according to the internet, there isn't much of anything there.

Once we reached the port, Kira unloaded our belongings from the car and deposited the car keys and phones into a metal container per the instructions in the letter. We won't be coming back for them either. The vehicles in this realm, the Other Realm, differ from what operates in Alandria, and phones do not work there. I imagined as much. If wiping our existence from anyone who ever knew us was necessary, then I doubt inter-realm communications through my cell phone carrier is either. I will miss my friends. We may have already started to drift apart in senior year, but they still mean a lot to me. We knew each other our whole lives. They get to forget about me, but I have to live with this ache in my heart.

Kira and I begin to make our way down a very long pathway. The strap of my bag digs into my shoulder, and I realize I probably shouldn't have brought so much clothing. I was unaware of how long this trip would take, and I didn't know I would be stuck carrying it around. Kira and I had been walking for about twenty minutes before coming across a small docking area with many rowboats. Other people are loading up into the boats, and judging by their ears, they are fae, too. Kira hands one of the dockworkers two small tickets, and we get loaded onto one of the rowboats.

I can prepare myself for many things, but I don't think I could have prepared myself for this. According to the two men rowing our boat across the Hudson Bay, this type of travel is typical to get to the island we are headed to, and fae folk alike enjoy the quiet of the journey. I, however, am about 10 seconds from vomiting overboard because the rocking of the boat is possibly one of the worst experiences of my life.

"Just hang on, girl, we're almost there," laughs the man rowing furthest toward the front of the boat. With the acknowledgment of my predicament, I cannot hold it in any longer, and I proceed to vomit all over into the bay. The men laugh, and one reaches over and flips a bead to the right on a counter, which they have stashed away. There are three beads on the right. Only two others have vomited during the journey, lovely.

It's not much longer after that when we dock on Coats Island. My paperwork from the headmaster says this is the last stop before we cross into Alandria. I have to say the internet appears to be correct because the closer we row to the island, there's a whole lot of nothing to see outside of large rocks up near the shoreline, some mountains with fog rolling down them, and some open fields.

"Right, well, here you are."

"I don't understand," I say. "There's nothing here."

"That's cause you got about another hour wait, girl," says one of the scruffier men on the boat. "Just remember, don't stand on the dirt; ain't no grass growing there for a reason. Now go find you a spot to wait; it's packed up there already." The man stares off toward an empty field, and I cannot help but question what Kira and I are getting into as we stand on the shoreline. I turn my head back toward him to say just that, but they are already silently rowing away.

"Kira, is this normal?" I ask.

She shrugs as she replies, "Not sure, Sage. I've never done realm travel before outside of the portal your mother made. It's always been a thing, just not common. The Order were the primary users of portals, more for cross-resource trade and things like that." With the last remaining plant and her bag in the other, Kira looks over to me and asks, "Shall we?"

I nod, and we walk closer to the large dirt patch before us. The closer we walk, the more I can hear a faint hum until, eventually, there is a whoosh sound and a gust of wind, and I am not standing in a field I thought to be empty. There are dozens, if not hundreds, of varying fae, all holding luggage and talking among themselves. I also note that not a single foot is touching the dirt. The chatter of the waiting fae is so loud that whatever barrier prevented me from seeing them must also muffle the sound. I wonder how the men from the boat could see them when we could not.

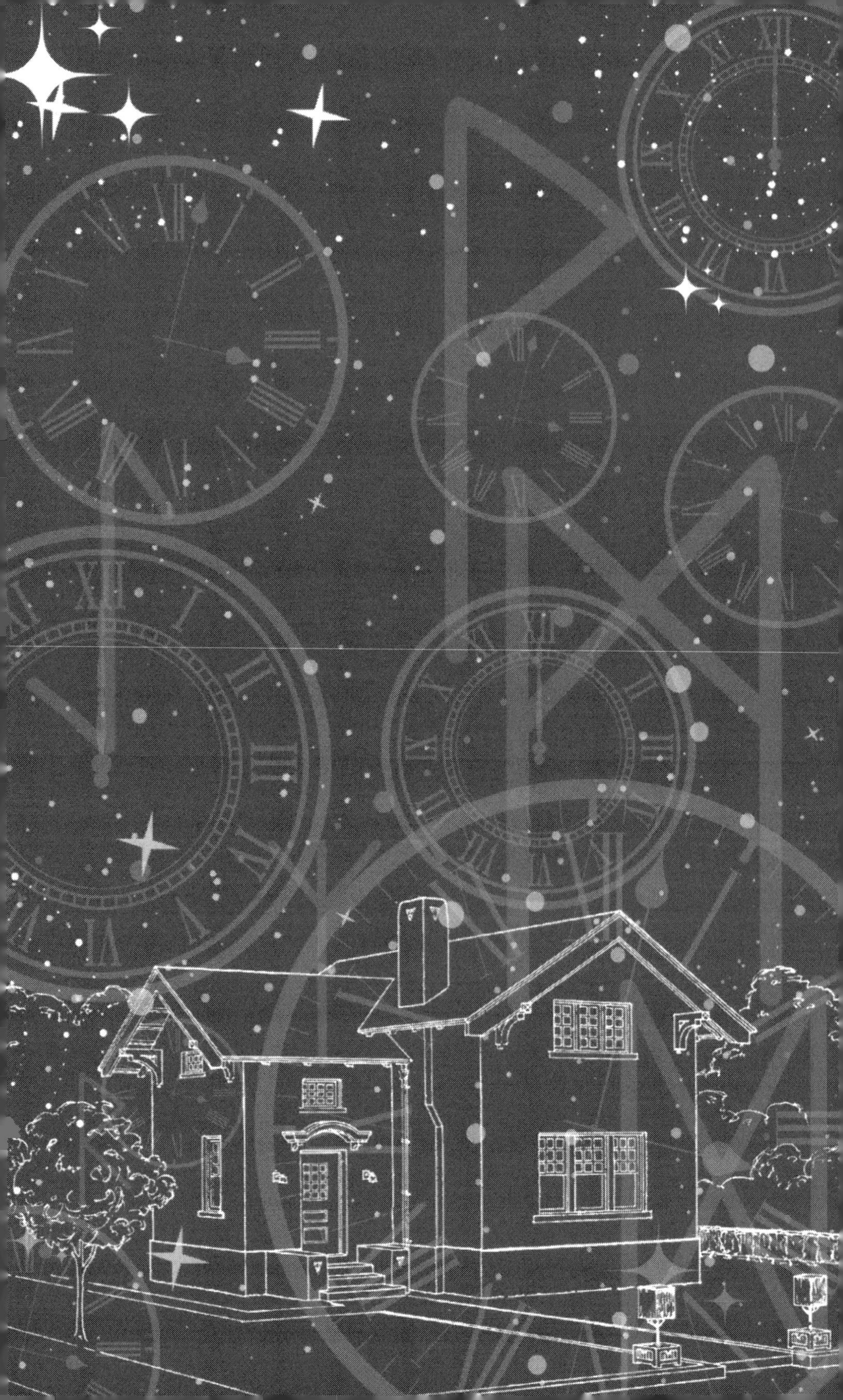

Chapter Five
Sage

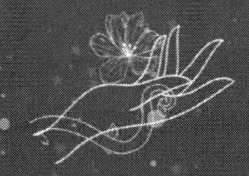

It's exactly one hour from when the man said that the wind starts to pick up. Everyone begins to hold onto their belongings for dear life as a small blue circle appears in the dirt and gets progressively larger until it breaks out of the orb shape it appeared in. The wind stops, but I can hear a soft humming sound. A slender man with blond hair and a full beard emerges from the blue wall that now appears on the dirt. "Alright, if you will all please follow me. Let's get you all to your destinations then, shall we?" He says as he quickly turns back from where he came, disappearing into the blue light.

Movement breaks out from all around as everyone begins to march into the blue light. "Well, you heard the man, let's go on in." Kira laughs as she begins making her way toward the light. I quickly jog to catch up after being stunned by how weird everything is.

Walking through the blue wall of light didn't feel any different than just walking. Maybe the air is a little cleaner? The only thing that changed was it went from the sound of fae talking among themselves and the quiet of the island to the continued chatter and the sound of engines replacing the quiet.

I look around, and we are standing on a sandy beach. Nearby is a large pier filled with people. There's a giant metal-like building with lots of windows at one end of the dock. I assume it's possibly to get tickets if you don't have any for the giant floating ships that are all around us. Kira and I make our way toward the pier, climbing steps that feel so steep my thighs are burning afterwards.

"Hold this, please," Kira says as she hands me over the plant to pull out the envelope from the headmaster again. "Oh good, we have tickets already for here too. Let's see, we are on ship A07. Let's see if we can find that." I follow Kira, struggling to balance holding her plant, as she looks around and searches for the correct ship.

A woman in a soft yellow uniform and peaked cap approaches us. "Can I help you at all?" Her voice is kind.

"Why, yes, actually. We are looking for ship A07. Can you point us in the right direction?" Kira smiles warmly at the woman.

"I sure can. I am heading that way myself, as that's my ship. I'm Captain Devin Nashport. Who might the two of you be?"

"I'm Kira, and this is my ward, Sage." She shakes hands with the captain, "Thank you very much for your help." Kira says as we follow Devin through the bustling crowd.

"Oh, it's not a problem at all. You look like you are about academy age. Is that where you all are headed?" She nods in my direction.

"Yes, it's her first year," Kira replies. I listen in on the conversation as they talk all about how exciting it is when you first walk through the academy doors. Considering why I was hidden away, I'm unsure what I can share and what must be kept private. On top of that, my stomach is still uneasy from all the stress, anxiety, and the very shaky boat ride. If I open my mouth in the next few minutes, I will lose whatever food is left in my system.

Many people are just brushing past one another, and I cannot help but wonder where all these ships are going. We will be boarding the one to Halaris, which, as Kira explained, is the capital city built high in the mountains. Eventually, we make it to the ship's loading dock, and Devin leaves us as she is cleared to board the vessel due to her status as the captain while Kira and I stand in line. Despite there being at least a dozen other ships, the line is packed with fae. I just know we are going to be here for a while.

As I stand in line waiting, I watch as a platform raises clusters of fae that have already been cleared onto the airship deck. The airship in itself is a sight to behold. It has the body of a galleon ship with windows that are scattered throughout the top part of its body. Intricate metal patterns are spread throughout the wood of the vessel, which look like they provide both support and add to the overall beauty of the ship. Along the side, I can see a smaller metal arm tucked inward toward the ship. At the end of the arm is a fabric that has wire running through various parts. It reminds me of a dragonfly or perhaps a butterfly wing. Wings. It looks like a wing; it must also be like that on the other side. Near the ship's rear is another large metal attachment with blades. It almost makes me think of a fan. Well, if a fan didn't have the protective covering on it. Above the entire body of the ship is a giant elongated balloon. The inner section is made of some type of fabric, but it's encased in a metal cage. It's like nothing I have ever seen before. Considering how I felt on the small motorboat, I wonder if I will feel as sick on this ship. Perhaps not, since we will be sailing through the skies, at least, I hope.

Kira and I continue to press forward as the line shrinks down. I'm still holding onto her plant while she tends to our paperwork. It's not long before we are called forward. "No glamour permitted beyond this point. It's the rules." Kira nods as she uses the last of the plant's essence to turn us back to our fae forms. The plant isn't dead but smaller, like it's a baby once again. "Forest fae huh, well I'll be. We ain't seen one of you since-"

Kira interrupts, "I'd rather not go over that part of our history right now, if you don't mind." Kira has always had a kind and calm demeanor, so the approach to the casual conversation is a bit concerning. I won't press her on the matter. If it's something she thinks I should know, I have no doubt she will tell me.

"I understand, I apologize. May I see your ticket, please?" If Kira's reaction was insulting in any way, the older woman did not let on. Kira hands over the tickets, and the woman looks them over before tearing off the bottom section of each one and passing them back to Kira. The woman takes the plant from me before saying, "Looks like you are good to go. Go ahead and stand on the platform up ahead and wait to be lifted to deck level." Kira says a quick thanks before the woman calls over the next group of people.

As Kira and I step onto the platform, I can feel a slight tremor in her hand. I reach out and give her hand a quick squeeze to let her know I am here for whatever she needs, and I do not let go of her hand while we wait for the platform to rise.

A group containing four more fae board the platform before the operator slides a metal gate closed over the open area and pushes the lever upward. The platform whirs as the gears begin to turn, and we begin to ascend. The smell of hot steel permeates the air as the gears work to move the platform. It's not a smooth process, and I can feel how each gear grinds in my bones. Thankfully, it takes only a few moments before the platform comes to a jerking stop, and the operator moves the lever to the center position. He motions for the group to clear the other side of the platform so he can cross through. He unlatches the gate and slides it open before bending down and grabbing a rectangle shape on the platform's flooring, flipping it out toward the new opening, creating a small bridge where a gap once stood. "Alright, go ahead and board." He waves everyone off the platform.

The ship's deck is a hubbub of activity as workers walk around inspecting the lines leading up to the elongated balloon and look over the gauges on anything looking remotely mechanical. We can see Captain Nashport as she speaks with several of the crew, nodding at whatever they discuss. She glances our way and waves us over.

"Welcome aboard, my new friends! Your tickets should have a room number listed if you want to hurry and go and store your belongings before launch. The ascending is one of my favorite parts and a sight to behold. It's a few days' flight until we touch down in the capital city, so you might as well make yourselves comfortable. Just head through that door over there and go down the set of stairs. You'll have the choice of going left or right. Go right. That's the living quarters section, to the left is the common area where everyone gathers to eat and there's a shower area." A look of relief washes over me. I didn't even think about what type of technological differences there would be between realms. It's good to know some form of plumbing exists.

"Pardon me asking, but how is the ship capable of having showers?" I ask.

"We have several staff aboard the ship, with varying affinities to help make the travel as seamless as possible, including a few who hold the water affinity. They draw water from the sky and funnel it into a port located on the side of the ship. The water used in the showers then runs through some framework where it's turned into steam and helps operate this ship. Instead of just constantly pulling fresher water, we have kind of a recycling system going on. Same thing if it rains, we have grates collect the water. We check to see if it's usable, and if it is, then we utilize that. Sometimes the water gets contaminated, and it's a whole process of disinfecting the grates and all that."

"How would water get contaminated?" I ask.

"We will just pray to The Nines that you will never have to know that reason." The reply is so ominous to previous conversations that it sends a chill down my spine. "Now hurry along so you don't miss this part!"

Sage ◆ 41

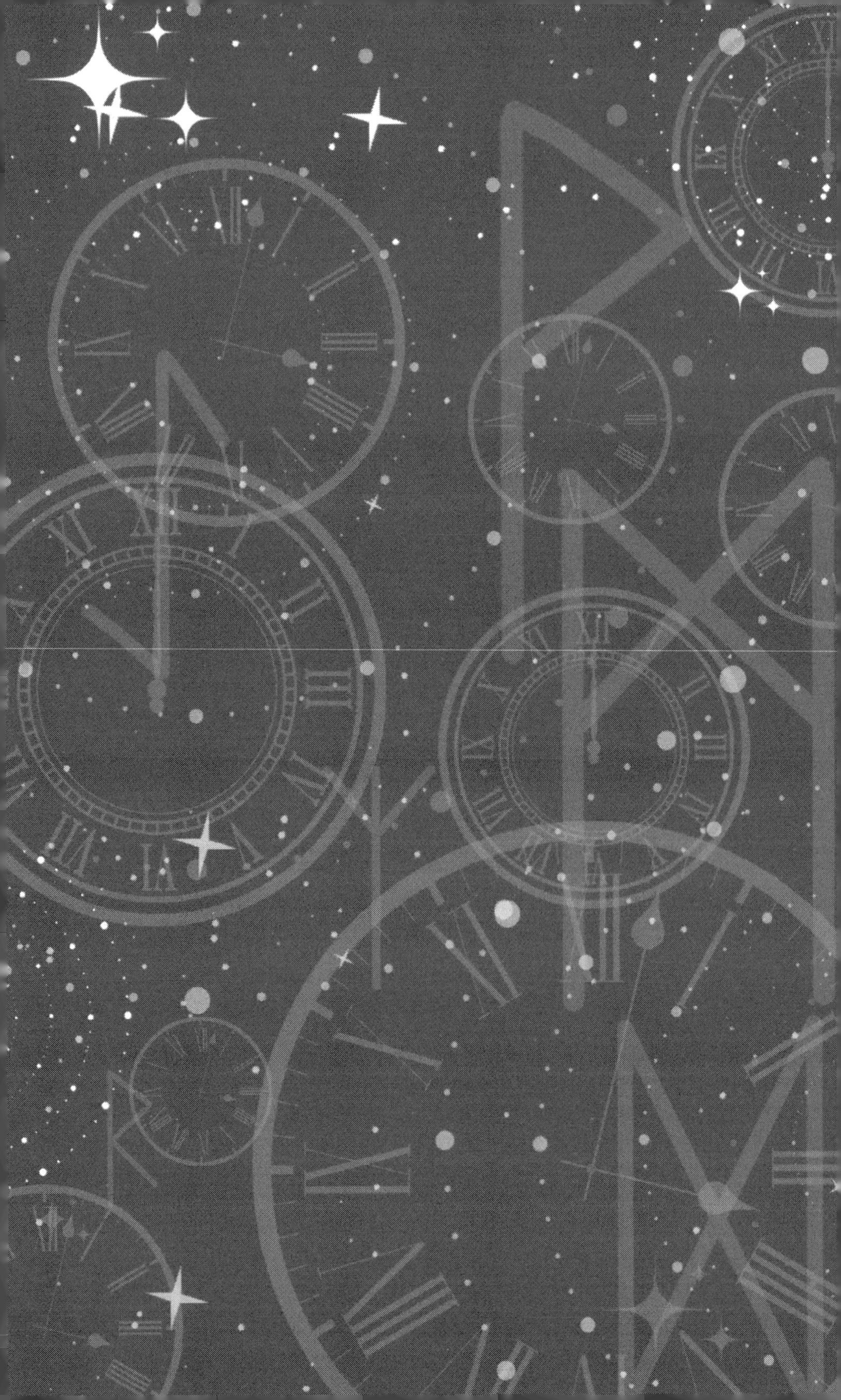

Chapter Six
Sage

I don't know what I expected to see after we descended the stairs, but the sight before me is breathtaking. The below deck has wood paneling, but it's different than anything I have ever seen. The walls emit a glow on every surface. It's enchanting but not the only thing capturing my eye as we walk down the hall. The lower half of each panel has been etched with intricate drawings of creatures—some I have seen before in fantasy movies and others I haven't. I wonder if this was carved using someone's affinity or if someone took the time to carefully carve the design. The attention to detail is impressive.

"Kira, how is the wood glowing?" I ask, running my fingers along the detail of the wood.

"It looks like they used wood from the Alcarin Forest to build the ship's interior. I hope that means they're planting more than they are taking. I'd hate to see another forest destroyed." I want to ask what she meant by another, but I think better of it and choose to listen. "This might be their way of enhancing defense against the dark creatures."

"Dark creatures?" I ask. "Kira, what kind of a realm are we in?"

"The creatures didn't always exist. They were," she pauses for just a moment, "created."

"Created how?"

"That I am unsure. Forbidden magic exists, and it comes at a great cost. They are the result of someone who paid that cost. The very person, the very reason I had to flee with you. There's not much I can say about what happened after we left. It is best to leave that to your school studies. It should be in your curriculum."

"So how does this wood help with defense?"

"The light can't be snuffed when magic is suppressed. There is something in its properties that makes it immune. Some dark creatures, at least those I have seen, can cause total darkness, and something in their shadows cuts off access to magic, and seeing anything around you can be difficult. It's like being in a dense fog. I don't think this would stop the magic suppression, but it would help with being unable to see so you can get somewhere safer." Kira suddenly stops and points to a door. "This is our room. Let's hurry, get our stuff set up, and get back up deck."

Kira and I open the door to our room. It has two twin-sized beds on either side of the room, with little space between them, but big enough for a small circle table with a glass jar containing a floating fire source to be nestled between them. I approach the fire and touch the jar, surprised at the lack of heat.

"That's everflame. The fire is meant to last forever and doesn't create a heat source, making it completely harmless. That won't be immune to the dark creatures, which is probably why they used Alcarin wood as well." Kira points to the end of each bed. "There looks to be some storage area where we can put our duffle bags. Grab the key from the table, will you? We will do manual locking since you don't know any spells, and I am fresh out of magic sources. I'm not worried anyone will go snooping about our things, but better safe than sorry." I grab the key and toss my bag into the space at the end of the other bed. Kira chose the one that sits right next to the window. I hand the key over to Kira, and we make our way back to the deck.

 Despite me taking way too much time to gawk at the walls when we were below deck, we weren't late to witness the takeoff. From the looks of it, a lot of the passengers are still below deck. Judging from the sounds we heard coming from the ship's common area, most are just interested in some grub and watching it from the windows. I will admit, that is a bit of a relief. So many people are aboard this ship, and I have never done well with crowds. It wouldn't have been shoulder-to-shoulder, but it was still too close by my standards.

 The captain nods in our direction in the form of a welcome before addressing her crew. "Alright, let's get this ship in the skies. Fire her up!" she shouts.

 A man dressed in yellow attire similar to the captain's but with red embroidered along the edges walks toward the center of the ship, where an outline of a square resides. They pull back on a lever among a group of them, and the space opens up. A decently sized circular pit rises filled with coal or some stone. It's hard to tell. There's metal piping work connected to the bottom of the circular pit. The man walks toward the pit with glowing red hands and places them above whatever fills the inside, and it begins to glow. Steam emits from the metal piping along the bottom. That must bring the water up from the reservoir. After he checks to ensure that steam is coming from all the pipes, he walks back over to the levers and pulls down on another. This causes a cylindrical shape to encase the pit, connecting it to the balloon above. The balloon puffs up in response, and the ship begins to rise.

 "Add wind!" the captain shouts.

 Another person in similar attire, differing only in the sleeves having white thread, walks toward where the fan-like mechanism is, and it starts to spin; this causes the ship to begin picking up pace.

"Wings!"

Two people on each side of the ship begin to crank levers, and the fabric I saw earlier starts to pull away from the ship as the metal arm opens up. When it's fully expanded, the fabric billows out, which also adds to the speed.

"Would you look at that," the captain says as she walks toward the wheel of the ship, and the crew claps. I begin to wonder how the ship turns, but I see the captain spin the wheel to the right to turn us away from the large body of water we are floating above and toward the land. All the attachments seem to turn in time with the wheel; it's a smooth system, and I cannot even begin to grasp how any of this is possible. I suppose a lot is possible when you mix magic and science.

I walk over to an open railing that's out of the way of the workers and watch as we fly above everything. I see a fast movement underneath us but don't get a quick enough glance. The movement is followed by a roar, and I look around. No one is panicking. What the fuck was that? I lean over the railing, trying to get a better look and catch a glimpse of it again, only to be covered in a shadow. I look up and nearly topple overboard from shock as I am looking up at a fucking dragon.

"It's okay, Sage," Kira laughs. "They aren't like the stories you read or the movies you watch. They're harmless." She says as she grabs onto my arm and pulls me further from the edge of the ship.

"How is something of that size harmless, Kira?" If my eyes get any wider, I swear they are going to plop out of my skull.

"Well, they don't eat meat, at least not on purpose."

"Not on purpose? Kira, are you even hearing yourself right now?"

She playfully slaps my arm. "Don't be so serious. They graze on the trees. The not-on-purpose bit is they may have accidentally eaten some of my people. They don't mean to. I mean, not that it's not tragic. All I'm saying is the only being that needs to fear them is me, and last I checked, I'm not resting in a tree."

"They ate your kind?"

"Sage, I am literally green all over. I'm a lesser fae for a reason. My power comes from nature itself because I am in part nature, just with some more living aspects to me."

"Are you telling me I was essentially raised by a plant?"

"If you want to put it that way," she shrugs. My lip quivers as I do my best to suppress a laugh. "What I am saying is they are harmless. They are naturally curious, and these ships that are taking to the sky are probably a bit of a curiosity to them. The only thing that will happen is they might chase the ship for a few hours before moving on to the next interesting thing. They're like what the realm we just came from calls puppies."

All my life, I never imagined hearing the comparison of a dragon to a puppy. "Alandria is," I pause, "interesting."

"You are only just learning the beginning," she says with a smile. "Now, you can go back and watch the landscape as we fly over it again. Please remember we are really high above the ground right now, and I would rather you not fall overboard to your death."

"I'll be more mindful of my shock," I say as I walk back up to the railing. We are flying above a forest now and what looks like to be a village. Although I don't see any activity. "What's that village called?"

"That's Drifton. That was the first village attacked during the war. I don't know why it was the first, but the rumor was Gaiwen, the man after you; the rumor was that his wife cheated on him with some noble in that village. They say he made her watch as he killed him. He likes to make people suffer. He slaughtered that whole village because he wanted to. Well, not all; a few managed to escape to tell your grandfather what was happening."

"That's awful. How is one man able to do all that?"

"Well, he kind of has an army of undead creatures that heed his call."

"Wait, can the fae have powers like that? That all just seems too dark to be something that someone is born with."

"Because no one is born with that. It's not a power someone should have. When you mess with the balance, a price must be paid. Not only was his essence corrupted from being born of the light affinity, but he also lost a lot of his humanity. He doesn't see reason. The light affinity is a gift born only to light fae, and he was the last of his kind, to corrupt his magic like that--I have no idea why he wants you, and I don't plan on any of us ever finding out the answer to that. We will stop him and right the wrongs he made like that over there." Kira points to nothing but black death below us.

"What was that? How-"

"That is a blight that is expanding across the land. That was my home. Those were my people." Kira says that last part with such a fierce bite, and I realize she's crying. "I am the last of my kind, and I only survived because I wanted to learn more about those with magical affinities. I left my people to work at the academy where I met your mother. Do I regret doing so? No, because I made the dearest friend whom I will treasure forever, but survivor's guilt, I would not wish that upon anyone."

"I am glad you are here with me, Kira. I'm sorry for your loss; that's a heavy burden."

"I wouldn't wish this feeling upon anyone. I hold onto hope that some of us survived, but the war went on for years, and no one had come forward before we went through that portal. I have no idea where they would have gone if they had survived. You will find that a lot of races here in Alandria are dying, and it's not something you will be able to fix. Don't let that burden fall onto your shoulders when the time comes. We are not responsible for the crimes of those before us. It's been a long day. Why don't we see if they have some food in the common area and get ready for bed?"

Even though I'm not tired and want to continue seeing the land from this view, I nod. I know she needs an excuse not to talk about this right now. "Absolutely, I'm famished."

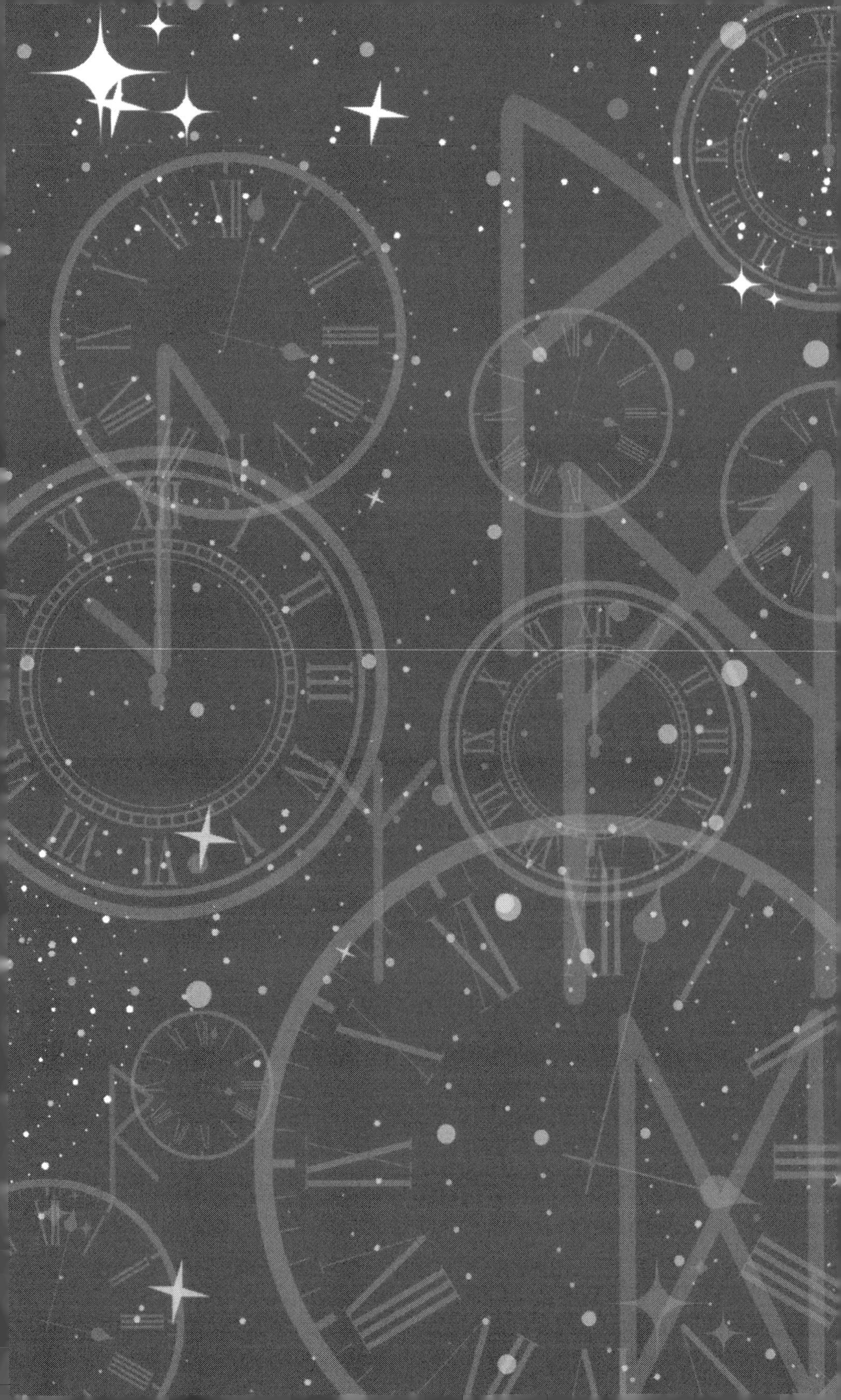

Chapter Seven
Sage

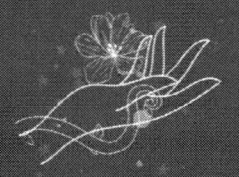

I don't know how long I was asleep, but the window above Kira's bed is dark. I try to move quietly to my bag so as not to wake her; I fail in that regard. "How long have we been asleep?"

"I don't know, but maybe a few hours. It's still dark out. I was going to use the showers. I feel gross after all the traveling."

"I'm a little peckish. I'll see if I can locate some food and meet you back here. Deal?"

"Deal." Kira slips on her shoes and goes to exit the room but stops when she finds a letter that was slid under our door. "Whose it from?"

"The captain. We slept through the whole day. She wanted to let us know that we passed Scourge Lake and are one day out from Halaris. By The Nines, this is great!" Kira exclaims.

"What is?" I ask.

"She also wrote that there is always food available in the commons since they work on a rotating shift and to help ourselves to it when we wake. I have suspicions about her and her friendliness. Not bad ones, but I think she might know who you are. In either case, she's been very kind and helpful. Go on and shower. I'll be back soon." Of course, Kira would want to seek food as soon as she woke. If there is one person that enjoys food more than me, it's her.

When Kira exits the room, I sniff myself and see how bad I've gotten. Horrible would be the answer. There is not an ounce of deodorant left to mask my scent. I go to grab clothes and everything I'll need to clean myself. I quickly find a new set of clothes, but, in our haste, we didn't grab anything else. I mean, sure, Kira has the house in her necklace, but it's not like we can do anything with it here. I hope they have something that'll help with washing. I lock the door from the inside since Kira has the key with her and make my way down the hall toward the common area.

I look for the showers for the women, but it appears there is only one common area shower. When I walk through the doorway, it's like I am completely transported into nature. There's a circular pit similar to the one they used for the stones on the deck, but this one isn't filled with anything. It's smooth stone, with small grates to drain the water scattered about. Around the circle, it almost looks like a fence, but I'm unsure what material it is. It's covered in growing vines that extend all around the room. Kira mentioned that some magic stems from nature, so I wonder if it helps with something in the room. Above the fencing are similar to shower heads all around the circle. I don't see any buttons or levers to operate it, so this will be interesting.

I look around and don't see anything to help wash my body or dry myself, for that matter. No one is in here, so I guess this gives me a chance to figure it out in peace. I strip out of my old clothes and fold them neatly before setting them along the outer wall where there is a paved walkway. I do the same with the clothes I will be changing into. I think this helps keep the wood part of the ship from getting damp. This is all guesswork; I have no idea how this stuff works.

I look around for some button or lever, but I can't find anything. I walk into the pit and make my way toward one of the shower heads, and to my surprise, it turns on all by itself.

The water isn't scalding or cold; in fact, it is the exact temperature I would wash under normally.

I wet my hair and body under the water, feeling grimy still as I don't have anything to cleanse myself with. One of the vines begins to move toward me as I step away from the water with a gelatinous glob; like it's offering it to me. Another vine moves toward me to tap my head before it moves down my arm and taps again as if to say it's for my hair and body. The vines pull away after I accept the pile of goo. I give it a slight sniff, and I cannot place the smell, but it's divine. I lather my hair before using the rest to cleanse my body. Once I am thoroughly soaped up, the spout turns back on and I rinse it all out. Once everything is rinsed, the water cuts off again.

Now, onto my next problem: I am sopping wet, and I didn't pack a hair brush. I reach up to at least comb my fingers through my hair; to my surprise, it's not even tangled. It's as if I brushed my hair already. I step back onto the pathway, and as soon as both my feet are planted down, the leaves on the outer wall begin to stir. A warm breeze comes up from the stones along the path, wrapping my body in a gentle gust of wind. My hair twirls softly as the water from my skin and hair begins to dry; another curiosity noted about Alandria. I will have to ask Kira if it's like this everywhere. Once both my body and hair are dry, the wind settles. I go over to retrieve my clothes; looking back at the shower area, I whisper a soft thank you. The leaves rustle in acknowledgment before I slip out and back to my room.

I practically skip back to our room. When I reach the door, I quietly knock to check and see if Kira made it back yet. "Come in, Sage."

I open the door and waltz in, plopping my dirty clothes near the floor of the bed. "That shower was incredible. Are all showers like that here? What is the gelatinous goop the vines gave me to wash my hair? I didn't bring deodorant," I sniff my armpits, so divine, "but I smell great."

"Slow down with the questions, Sage," Kira laughs. "To answer your first question, no, not all showers, mainly communal ones, to save resources. Here, take this." She places a sloshing bowl of stew in my hands. "Water and a roll are on the table. Eat. To answer your second question, it is like 3 in 1 shampoo. It cleanses and conditions your hair but can also be used for your body. Magical plants produce it naturally, so it's not harmful and very beneficial. You will notice nature here often knows what you need and is willing to help, partly due to the special bond we fae have with it. You probably don't need deodorant because that stuff works great, but you might also desire to pick something up at the apothecary shop in town."

"I was wondering, how will we afford anything when we get to the capital? You've been gone 18 years, and it's not like anyone knows who we are."

Kira starts digging through her bag, "That reminds me. Oh, where did I put it? AHA! Here is it!" She extends a small black box to me. I set my nearly empty stew on the table and open it up.

"A stone necklace? What stone is this? It looks so peculiar." I ask.

"That is a stone of power. It was your mother's and was passed down from her mother and so on. It will identify you as part of the Torrin family."

"What exactly will that do?"

"Give you access to their coffers. The stone can do so much more than that, but for now, it will help us with getting you sorted for school."

"How will they know I am not impersonating someone, that it isn't stolen?"

"Because," she takes the necklace and tries to put it on herself, but it immediately unclasps, falling into her prepared hands. "Only a female member of the Torrin family can wear it. Go on and put it on. It's enchanted, so it won't ever fall off or break."

My hands are shaking as I bring the chain up and around my neck. For some reason, I am fearful it will unclasp just like it did for Kira. That perhaps somehow, I am not the child she claims I am, but when I link the clasps together, and it stays, a sense of relief hits me.

"There, now finish your dinner. I'm not sure when the captain wrote that letter. but there might still be time to catch a good glimpse of the Alcarin Forest." I scoop up the remaining liquid from my soup using my roll and drink the remainder of my water.

Kira and I return the dishes to the common area and rush up to the ship's deck. We are too far past the forest to see it from the sides of the ship, so we go to the back. It's not the best view, but I can see off in the distance the faint glowing of the trees. It may be blurry, but I can tell it is beautiful. Kira and I stay there for the next few hours, watching as the light from the forest grows more faint.

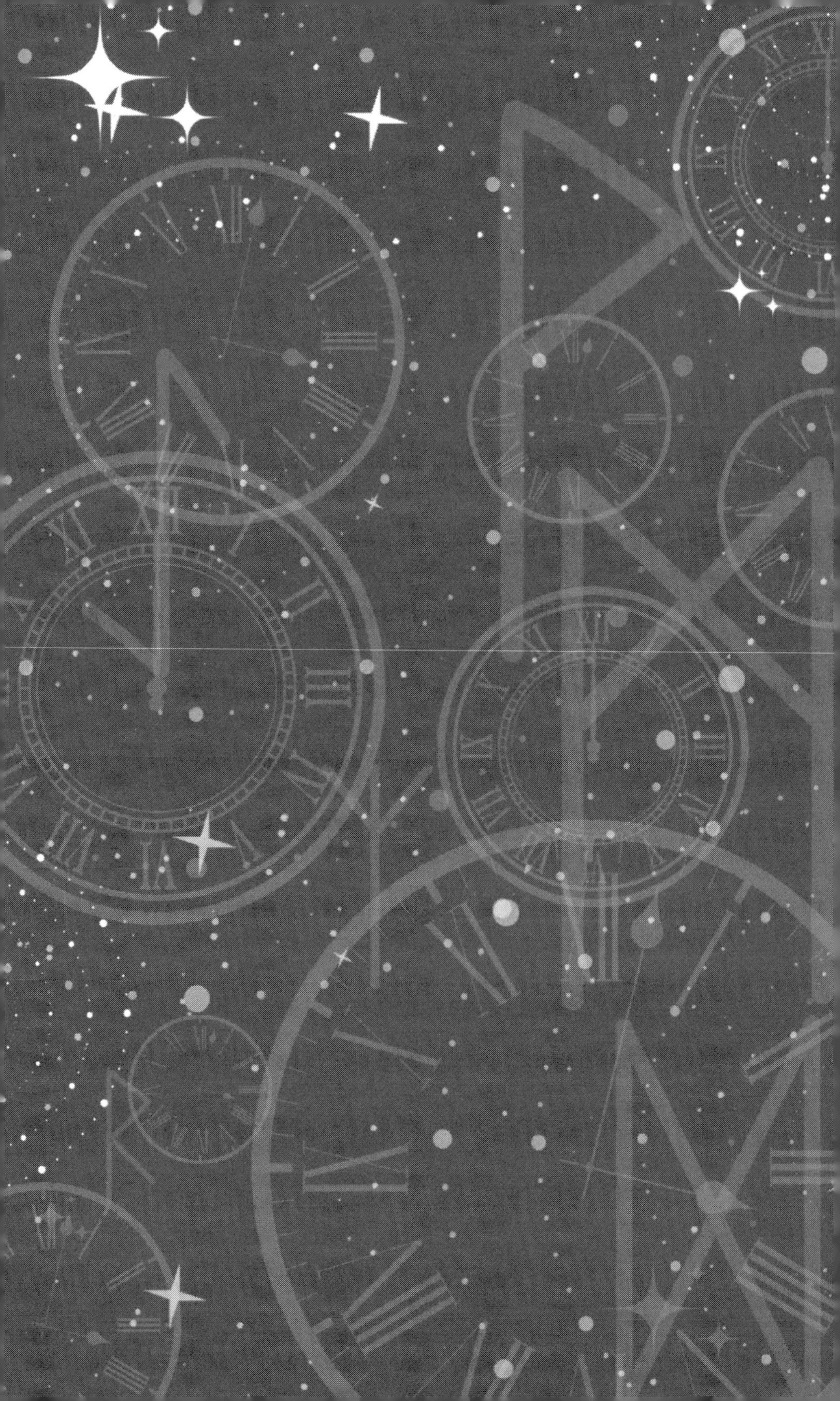

Chapter Eight
Sage

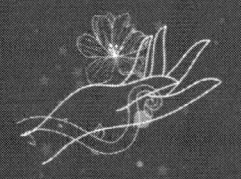

The journey has been going fairly smoothly. As it turns out, I handle airships much better than a rowboat. Currently, we are passing through the valley of the mountains and are close to finally reaching the capital city, Halaris. It's accessible only through a flyer; you could find an alternate route if you were extremely determined, but the journey would be arduous. Kira and I have made it our mission to spend the waking hours between mealtime and sleep watching the view from the deck. We are at the front of the ship, eagerly waiting to catch sight of the capital city.

I can see the lights reflecting from the city before I see the city itself. Even up here, I can see that Halaris is very industrially designed. I wonder if it was always like this or if these were changes, they implemented after seeing what Gaiwen did to that village and the forest.

One of the crew members pulls a lever down, and the blades of the engine fans come to an agonizingly slow pace, decreasing the ship's speed as we draw closer to a large platform with a hollow center. Similar platforms are scattered around, but most are occupied with ships already. When we reach a close enough distance, another crew member pulls slowly on another level as it raises the cylinder tube that was helping keep the steam at a steady current, while another with a water affinity cools down the pit of stones. This causes us to descend lower and lower until metal-like arms reach up from the platform and grip the ship's body. Slowly, the arm carries the ship the rest of the way to the center of the platform until the deck is level with it.

The captain unlatches a section of railing and slides it open as she reaches down and flips up a rectangle-shaped piece of metal attached to the deck. When it connects with the platform, locking mechanisms come up and hold it in place, creating a bridge. "Welcome to Halaris, and enjoy your stay!" she shouts at the passengers, wiping sweat from her brow.

The passengers say their thanks as they descend onto the platform toward what looks like a trolly train attached to sliders from above. Before stepping onto the ramp, I want to thank Devin for the care she took in our journey. I find her speaking with some crew members, and their laughter fills the air as I approach. "Hey, I just wanted to thank you for your attentiveness toward Kira and me. I appreciate it."

I turn to leave, and she grabs hold of my arm to stop me. "Even if I didn't know your status in the fae hierarchy," surprise laces my face, "Yes, I knew, you look just like your mother. Even if I didn't know, I would have looked out for you two. There's a light about you that I haven't seen in a long time, and I believe in what you can do. You may fall off the path, who knows, but I believe in the end, you will prevail for all of us. Take care, Sage."

I walk off the ship and catch back up with Kira. "Let me guess, she knew who we were?"

"Yeah, she did."

Kira and I load up onto the trolley and make our way into the heart of the city.

The ride was a smooth one when we made it to our stop. I would say that I almost enjoyed the ride, but I am not one hundred percent into the screeching sound of metal when any of the trolleys hit their breaks.

Kira and I make our way toward the bustling sidewalk as we look around for the first stop on our very long list. "I must admit, Kira, this city is different from what I thought it would be."

"Did you think it was like the books you were always reading? All dirt paths and no plumbing?" she jokes.

"Honestly, yeah. I didn't think it would be so-"

"Steam punky? As the people of the Other Realm call it."

"Yeah, exactly that."

"We were like that long ago, but since Drifton, we have adapted our technologies and fortified buildings better. The metal structures are thanks to some of those blessed with the earth affinity. Yours looks to be more geared toward plants, but some can work metals." Kira points to a building just a little way ahead. "There's our first stop. The treasury, we have to get some funds for supplies."

We walk past three businesses until we stop in front of one of the larger buildings nestled at a slight angle compared to the rest. I think it was meant to be a street corner type of thing, but the road leading away from the trolley that took us here is curved. The building is at least three times the height of the surrounding shops and homes, and there are three different entrance doors leading into the building. When we walked through the door, I was surprised to see that the room was spacious and open. There are teller booths similar to how banks in the Other Realm look. The only difference I note is that small carvings are scratched along the glass's sides. I wonder what those are for. I am about to ask Kira, but I think better of it. I have been bombarding her with question after question the whole journey.

"We need to head down that way," Kira says, pointing to a counter near the end of the building. "That's going to be where the person in charge of accounts will be. Since you haven't been here before, we must verify you. They will have access to your family's vaults and can get us what we need."

Our feet squeaking across the floor feels incredibly loud as we approach the counter. I don't understand why I feel so nervous. It's almost like the idea of being judged about who I am, who Kira says I am, is scary, but it's not. "Name, please."

"This is Sage Torrin; I am her ward. We are here to get access to her family's accounts for necessary supplies for first-year academics and a little extra."

The fae looks down at us from her counter. "I know who you are, Kira—my condolences about your family. Sage looks just like her mother; the resemblance is uncanny. I, however, cannot just give access freely, so does she have a proper form of identification on her?" The fae directs her conversation toward Kira, which I find odd because it makes me feel like I am not in the room or that I am not some person with thoughts of my own; perhaps it's just the familiarity of the two.

"Thank you. Sage, go ahead and show her the necklace." I pull the chain up, lifting the stone that I have hidden under my top, and flash it to her, long enough for her to verify it is the stone of power before slipping it back under my garments.

"Very well, everything looks good. Follow me, and you can take what you need. It's been a long time since anyone has come to pick up any funds. Even the High King doesn't visit the coffers. He has stayed holed up in that castle since Idril."

The woman walks around her counter and motions us to follow as she slides a key into the door behind her and pushes it open. We walk down a long corridor that curves in various directions; each side of the room has a different door. Eventually, we reach the end and are standing in front of a much larger door. She slides another key into the lock and places her hand on the door. There is a hissing sound, followed by some clicks as the locking mechanisms release and the door rolls to the side. The room is filled with varying crowns, jewels, and stacks of coins. Kira pulls out a small-looking pouch and fills it with some coins.

"Kira, I know that I need money for school, but can we take a little extra for you so that you may be comfortable and taken care of while I am attending?"

"It's not necessary, Sage. I worked for your family for a long time and have my own coffers. Thank you for thinking about my well-being, though," her cheeks turn a darker shade of green as she blushes. "Why don't you pick out one of the crowns before we go? Your mother would have taken you here to choose your first one, but seeing as she can't. There are a few dances at the academy, and the headmasters tend to request nobility to dress the part."

"I don't want to feel more out of place than I already do."

"If it will ease your mind, then alright. I assure you; you won't be the only fae girl wearing a crown; there will no doubt be other members of the fae noble houses attending. Oh, perhaps you will meet who you were to be betrothed to. What was his name again?"

"Hassian Blackwell," says the woman that brought us to the vault.

"Ah yes, that was it!"

"My, what now?" I ask.

"He's quite the looker, he is."

"I suppose that's another thing I forgot to mention. Arranged marriages are common among fae nobility. You were promised to another before you were even born. Of course, with your disappearance over the last nearly two decades, the contract might not be in play anymore."

"I'm not marrying someone because someone promised that without my consent," I say.

"Oh, I would never force you to. As long as your grandfather doesn't force you, your decisions are your own to make."

"I will tell him just the same."

The woman lets out a short laugh, "Good luck. Not to speak treason, but your grandfather can be a tyrannical man to say no to what he wants, well, it's next to impossible."

I look over to Kira for confirmation and she doesn't say anything. She looks down and chews on her lip. If there is anything I am sure of now, it's that I do not look forward to meeting my grandfather.

We don't spend much longer in the vault. Much to my chagrin, Kira got me to take one of the crowns. I chose one with green-colored gems and leaf designs. It felt fitting, seeing as my element is associated with the earth. Kira told me it was the same one my mother first picked when she was brought to these very vaults. I wish I had gotten to know the woman that I am similar to in so many ways. Knowing of a mother I never got to meet, grow with, and love, but carrying all these similarities to, is starting to feel like I am walking around carrying the ghost of someone.

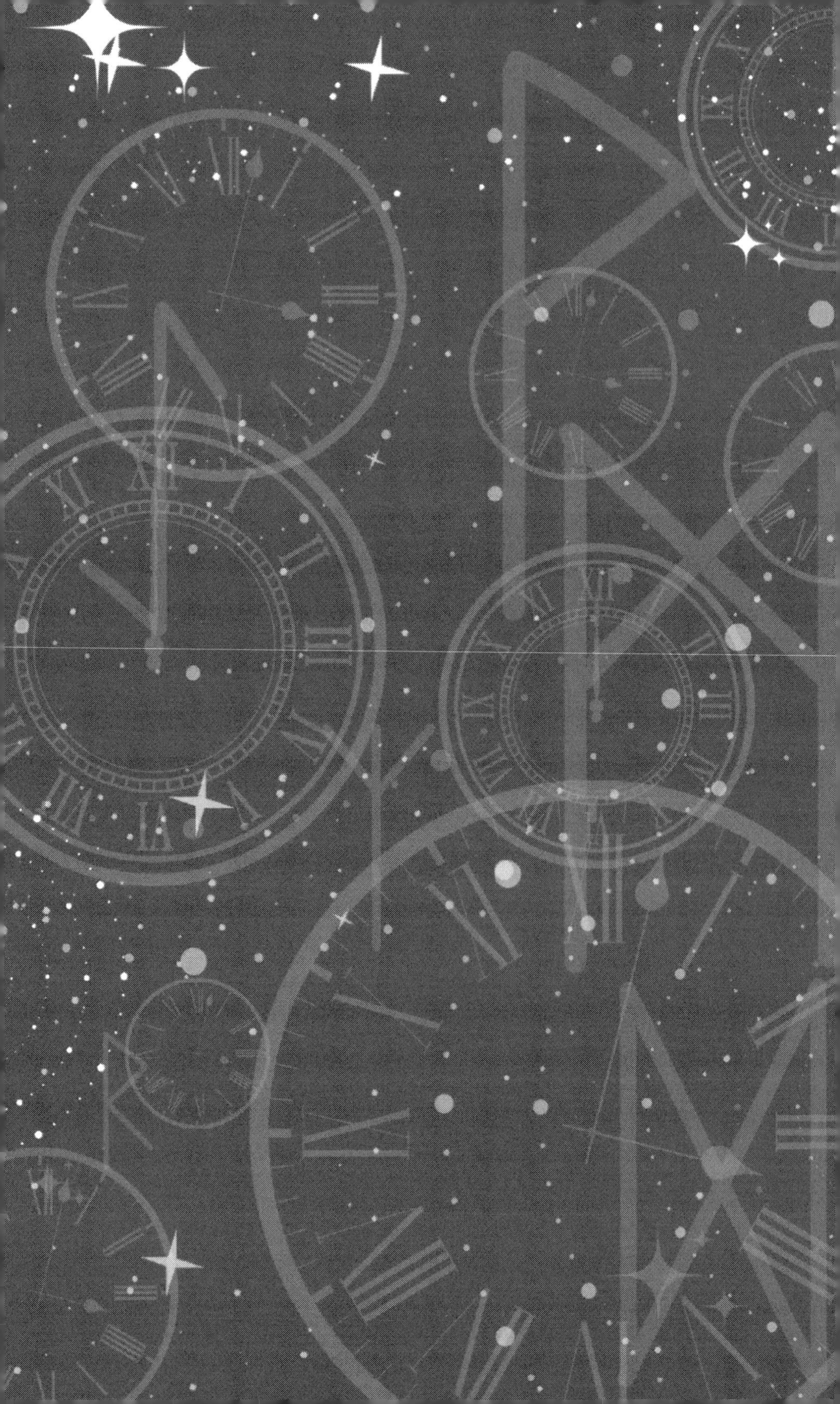

Chapter Nine.
Sage

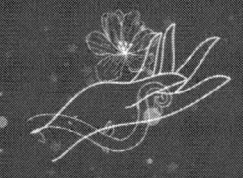

Getting what we needed from the treasury didn't take too long, and the next place on our list to stop was across the street. Bevel's Bookstore was nestled between two other shops: Agene's Apothecary and The Curiosities Shoppe. I was interested in visiting all of them, but Kira assured me that I would have time over what I have now come to learn to be a very long life to visit and explore all of Halaris.

The inside of the bookstore looked like a bit of a disaster. There were tons of unshelved books stacked in piles around the room. The floor had crinkled pieces of paper nearby where a stack of parchment lay on a table. "Welcome in!" A muffled voice shouts from somewhere above; this is followed by the sound of clamoring until a short, stubby man descends the ladder. "I'm Elwin Bevel at your service ma'ams." He gives an attempt at a curtsy. "Can I help you find anything in particular?"

"Yes, we need these books if you have them in stock. It's my ward's first year so we are off gathering everything. Oh, and if you have some blank journals, too."

He takes the list from her before looking us over. "This is quite a bit of books and your arms seem rather burdened already." He gestures to the luggage we have been lugging around with us since the ship. "I have been working on a little something that might help you with that. Let me go get it from my workshop, and then I'll help you with the books. The journals, I'm afraid I cannot help you with; you might get them at the scriptorium, though." The man wanders off while Kira and I wait.

"Before you ask, yes, that was a dwarf. The mountains were their home first. They are a very friendly bunch, very creative, designing some of the best quality things. In fact, the crowns your family had commissioned are dwarven-made. I'm sure, like a lot of their craftsmanship, they can withstand a lot."

"How many different types of races are there in Alandria?" I ask.

"Quite a lot. You will likely be trying to learn all that information for a very long time."

Elwin returns from his workshop in the back with what looks to be a wagon in tow. "I made her myself. It should be able to carry a decent amount of weight, and the wheels are made from some material I'm experimenting with at the moment. They won't lock up, and you will find they glide nicely on any terrain."

"How much would you like for it?" Kira asks.

"Not a coin. If someone asks where you got it, maybe pass along my name. Word of mouth is good for business. Now let me fetch those books for you so you can be on your way." Kira accepts the wagon, and we set our bags in the cart while we wait for Elwin to return. It doesn't take long before he's back with five books in tow.

"How much for the books?" Kira asks.

"Let's see History of the Dark Ascension, that's one silver. Healing Plants and a Dive into Fae Lore: she's a lot heartier so that she will be one gold. This one here, the Sensation and Perception: A Guide to Mastering Your Affinity. She's thick, but she's a standard material that is 3 bits. This guide on glamour and transmutation has a little scuff here on the corner, so I'll give you a discount on that, so one copper for her. Finally, we have Intro to Beasts; that one is slightly more expensive, so it's two gold. Let me add this up. Give me one moment." The sound of his quill scratching on parchment fills the room as he adds up our total. "Your total for all the books is three gold, one silver, one copper, and 3 bits."

Kira hands over four gold pieces. "Sorry, I don't have any smaller currency. We only just left the treasury."

"No worries, ma'am. I have plenty. My brain isn't the best with numbers, so give me a moment while I calculate your change." He continues to scribble on the parchment. "Ah, two bits is your change. That's not so bad." He hands over the bits, and Kira drops them into the pouch before retrieving the books and loading them onto the cart. "Thank you for your business, and enjoy your first year at the academy!"

We start to head down the walkway in the direction of the scriptorium. "Oh shoot, we do actually have to go to the apothecary. You need a cauldron and some crystals. I don't know why I was thinking we could get those at the herbalist shop. I'm glad we didn't get too far."

"Me too. This city is massive. I have a feeling my feet are going to be aching fiercely by the time we are done."

"I would deny that to give you some form of comfort, but lying is wrong."

I let out a loud groan before we walk into the apothecary shop. The ache in my legs is immediately forgotten when the scents in the apothecary reach my nose. It smells delightful. The walls are loaded with bottles and tinctures of various sizes, and I cannot help but wonder what each one is for.

"Greetings!" the shopkeeper calls to us as she emerges from a room behind the counter. They take a glance at the books in the wagon. "First year, I see. You'll need a cauldron, some crystals, maybe some rune stones?" they ask.

"The first two, yes, rune stones aren't on the list, but go ahead and add those too."

"What are rune stones?" I ask.

"They are used for all kinds of things like predicting the future; some can help protect others from misfortune. If you become talented enough, you can learn to put runes on objects, which helps with casting and other means," the shopkeeper replies.

"That's right. You aren't limited to just the magic you are born with. That is how the omni-vessel is made. If you look closely enough, you can see the small etchings." Kira holds out the necklace to me.

"You have an omni-vessel? That's some really powerful magic. How ever did you get one?" They don't bother asking if she made it herself, as Kira had explained to me that despite there being a plethora of ways to create new forms of magic, the forest fae are limited to their nature bond. However, they can use what other people create; they just cannot create on their own. The power source from plants isn't strong enough to create magic of that magnitude. She can do simple spells like glamour, detection, and minor healing, but her power does not extend beyond that.

"It was a gift from a dear friend to help care for my ward." The shopkeeper takes the hint not to press the topic further.

"Let me go fetch those supplies. I even have a guide on basic rune understanding I will add with the runes." They begin wandering around the shop, collecting various items. "Cauldron prices are a little hefty, so I apologize for that. Everything together is one platinum, two gold, one silver, and 3 bits."

Kira reaches into the pouch, pulls out eight gold pieces, and hands them over. The shopkeeper counts them out and hands her back some change, and with that, Kira and I are back on our way toward the scriptorium.

"You are so going to have to teach me how currency works here," I mumble as we exit the shop.

"It's quite simple. Think of platinum as a hundred-dollar bill, gold as equal to twenties, silver as ten, copper as five, and bits as one. We don't have what the Other Realm would call change, so it's always one solid number."

"Wait, so that cauldron was a hundred dollars?" I practically yell the question.

Kira nods. "It's going to be with you for a very long time, so the investment is worth it. It's not something that's made cheaply with poor materials. It has to withstand increasingly high temperatures and sometimes dangerous ingredients."

"I guess that makes sense. What do we have to get at the scriptorium?"

"Well, you need some blank journals for taking notes, and maybe if you choose to just write some personal notes. You will also need parchment for sending letters, like sending them to me, for example, if you need anything or just desire a chat. You also need a quill and ink. Come to think of it, you are going to need to take a little lesson on how to use that. It can be a bit tricky."

We rush through the scriptorium and the clothier, with the lunch hour quickly approaching. I collect more than enough writing material from the scriptorium and clothing suitable for my classes. According to Kira, the academy likes students to wear the color for their primary affinity, so my wardrobe will consist of a lot of green. I am very grateful that green looks good with my complexion and a little glad I didn't get my father's fire affinity. Red isn't the most flattering color on me.

We stop at one of the more prominent taverns in town for lunch, which is jam-packed, so we have to wait a bit for a seat to open up. Kira insists it has the best food in all of Alandria and is well worth the wait. My stomach growls in protest multiple times, but a woman with green skin and tusks eventually brings us to a table. Kira orders for both of us some grilled bird that I cannot recall the name of, with some roasted veggies paired with some of the house ale. The drinking age is 18 in Alandria. If you are old enough to attend the academy, you are old enough to partake in all the city has to offer. Mel, our waitress, tells us to ask for her if we need anything else as Kira hands her the coin for our meal.

    The tavern itself is breathtaking. There is an assortment of oval-shaped tables scattered all about the room with dazzling glass jars filled with everflame. The air is thick with the smell of all the various stews and dishes various patrons are eating, paired with whatever aroma this house ale is putting off. I never want to leave this atmosphere. It smells so unbelievably delicious. Through the sounds of chatter, I can hear someone softly singing, accompanied by the sound of an instrument of which I do not know the name. It looks similar to a lute. I think it is, but I am unsure of the differences between the Other Realm and this one. I would ask, but I wish to enjoy a good meal in a beautiful atmosphere alongside someone I care about most in any realm.

    I take a sip of the ale, testing out its flavor. It's fruity and sweet; it reminds me of one of my favorite coffee drinks back home but without the bitter aftertaste of the coffee beans. It's delicious, and I know I will need to pace myself before someone tries to give me a refill, and I become drunk before we finish the day's activities. The bird that Kira ordered for us tears off the bone easily. It's juicy but not overly greasy like the chicken back home. It does have a very similar taste. My favorite part has to be the grilled vegetables, though. They have a slight crunch, and whatever seasonings they add packs such a favorable punch. I could live on the vegetables alone. After Kira and I finish eating, we decide to just sit for a little while and enjoy the music as we rest our legs a little longer.

"Where will you stay while I am at the academy?" I ask.

"I might rent one of the available homes that are closer to this tavern. I will be spending a lot of time here. It has always been one of my favorite places in the city. There's just so much joy here. It's very untainted by some of the darker forces. However, if there is an open plot, I might use this; she points to the omni-vessel. I fear that I am missing my plants already."

"I'm sure you will be picking up more from one of the shops in town."

"Oh, absolutely, whether I can release this house or not. I might even have a few new babies grown by the time I see you next!" I adore the way Kira's face lights up when she gets to talking about plants.

"Not to damper the mood or anything, but I fear I will miss not seeing you every day while I attend the academy. I cannot recall a time we've been apart for more than me just staying at a friend's house for the night."

"We've got plenty of parchment, letters will have to do for now. I will miss you so much, too. Even though you are not of my kin, I raised you as such. You will always be like a true daughter to me. There will be opportunities to see each other while you are attending school. I will look forward to those days the most."

Kira and I break into conversation about the various shops that Halaris has. There's a beast shop where you can find animal companions and various mounts. There's a large shrine designated for worshiping the nine Goddesses that created the realm. I might visit there one day to learn more about my connection with Kamira. The Orders headquarters are across the street from the temple. Kira explains The Order to be like the military of Alandria. They recruit those willing to fight to protect the realm and deal with serious threats. Where we traveled on the public transit ships, there are also vessels purely designed for fighting excursions.

The last place on the list and what will probably be Kira's favorite shop is the Herbalist shop, which is also the city's primary healer. Her shop is filled with growing plants of all types, both for shop purposes like restocking the tinctures of herbs and selling to patrons to develop their own supply. Kira marvels at every plant she passes, and I swear she is having a secret conversation with all of them. According to the list, all I need now is some protective gear like gardening gloves and eyewear, some seeds, and some soil.

"I think you will enjoy your Herbology class and not just because it deals with plants and growing your own herbs for potions and salves. I think you will enjoy it because it connects really well with your affinity." Kira says as we are paying for the last of the supplies I will need.

As we got ready to leave the shop, another group of people walk in. Two fae that look about the same age as me, carry similar items to the ones I picked up today. The girl in the group gives me a wave before bounding over. "I'm just going to go ahead and introduce myself because it looks to me like you are also preparing for your first year. I'm Thalia. Thalia Day. That loaf standing by my parents is my twin, Anton." She peeks over at the bundles in our wagon, her tight curls bouncing as she tilts her body this way and that to get a better angle. She's a little nosy. "Green? You must have earth-based magic. My family has always had water. That's okay; we will still be great friends."

"That's bold, assuming we will be friends," I say. I don't know if she intended it that way, but her attitude came off as this is how it's going to be, and it just rubbed me in a weird way.

Her smile quickly fades. "I'm sorry. I didn't mean to sound so, well, how I sound. My brother's always telling me to mind my personal space." She turns to leave.

"Wait–" I say. "Let's start the conversation over, shall we?" She nods.

"I'm Thalia; it's nice to meet you."

"Hi, Thalia. I'm Sage, likewise."

Thalia and I continue talking while her parents collect what they need for her and her brother. I catch Kira from the corner of my eye smiling, knowing that I am already making a friend.

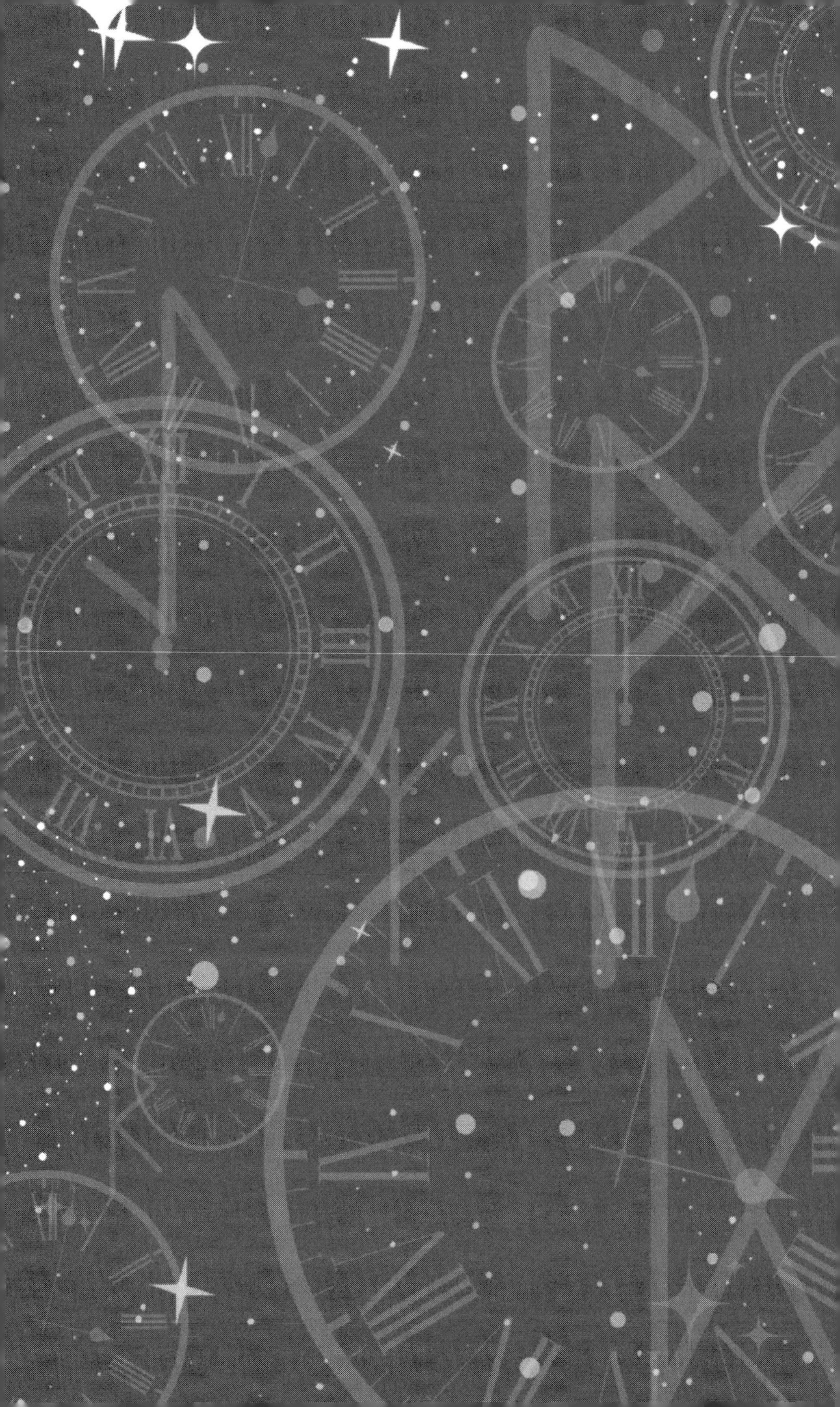

Chapter Ten
Sage

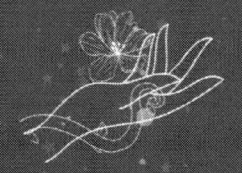

K ira and I are standing in the tavern after we have finished up all our shopping. Thalia and her family offered to let us stay with them, but Kira and I insisted otherwise. Kira knows how I deal with change, and I may have been putting on a strong front all day, but the breakdown is coming soon. We rented one of the rooms in the tavern for the night, we may stay longer depending on how lucky we are in securing a home or some land for Kira. We would be up in our rooms already, but Kira persisted that I have some dessert.

It would seem that this place is always lively, no matter the time of day. I wonder how I will be able to sleep through all of this if I even can. Since meeting Thalia I haven't been able to stop thinking about my friends back in the Other Realm. Even if we stopped talking as much when senior year began, that doesn't change my feelings about them. Everyone was planning for different futures; Kaylee wanted to be a film director, Hadley dreamed of being an animator or going into video game design, and Abigail was undecided. One day, she wanted to be a physical therapist, and the next, a fashion designer. It's funny how the smartest person I know can get all these acceptances and still not know what she wants to do. I guess I will never know what she chooses now that they don't even know who I am. I feel the wetness of a tear falling down my cheek, and I realize I'm crying.

"Here you go," the waitress hands Kira the desserts, and I catch her taking a glance at me. She looks like she is about to say something but thinks better of it and walks away.

"Oh, Sage, I'm sorry. I was anticipating this happening. I just wanted you to have some comfort in the form of food. Come now, let's go to our room." We pick our bags off the floor; there's no need to worry about the school supplies. They've been stored in the back room of the tavern for safekeeping. I follow Kira up the steps and down the hall to our room.

As soon as the door shuts behind us, the sounds of the tavern come to a halt. That's when I break. I crumble to the floor as I cry about everything I already miss, everyone that forgot, the lies, the destiny that I am supposed to follow, and just the general shit show that is now my life.

Kira sets the dessert on the table before running over to me and rubbing her hand in gentle circles on my back. "I'm so sorry, Sage. I should have told you the truth sooner. I let you form attachments. I just wanted you to have a good life and not worry."

I love Kira, I do, but it's hard not to be upset with her. Would it have been easier if I had grown up with the truth? I don't know. All I know is that my heart hurts so fucking much. I lost so much in a single moment. I don't deserve to have these burdens placed upon me. Why should I be responsible for saving a realm? Why did my parents have to die? "I'll be fine, Kira. Just give me a moment, please." Her comforting circles feel like pinpricks now on my back. I'm overstimulated, beyond overstimulated.

Kira lifts her hand from me and fetches me a cup of water. "I understand you want some space right now, so I will go downstairs for a while to give you that. You need a moment; take it. Please drink this. Go ahead and eat some of the dessert if I am not back by the time you're ready. I love you, Sage. I always have, and I always will." I take the cup from Kira and she exits the room.

I can't say I feel any better now that she's not in the room, but this gives me time to compose myself. I don't know how long I sit there crying on the floor, sipping my water, but my head hurts, my eyes are dry, and my skin is raw from continuously wiping away the tears. I miss the comforts of pulling out my phone for simple things like checking the time or watching silly videos when I'm upset. I look around the room, similar to a hotel room but without all the electronic amenities. There are two decent-sized beds, a table, two chairs, and a bathroom.

I head into the bathroom to clean myself up. This one is private, so it doesn't have the vines or the stones. There's cloth to dry with and various vials of serums that, upon a sniff inspection, smell good. I am sure I would enjoy them a lot more if I didn't just give myself a searing headache from my breakdown. Much like the showers on the ship, there are no knobs. I undress and step under the shower head, and water begins to flow immediately. I take some time to enjoy the warmth of the water while I read over the various labels of tinctures. I opt for something that smells similar to lavender. It probably is, but I don't know how different the plant life is between realms. The shower stays running even after I have rinsed off my hair and body. It's as if it knows I need this comfort for a little longer.

After what feels like a decent amount of time, and my headache has dulled significantly, I decide I am ready to get dressed. The water cuts off, and I grab one of the drying cloths from the shelf and wrap it around my body as best I can before exiting the bathroom. Kira returned while I was in the shower, and she is currently serving the dessert on some plates.

"Do you feel better, love?" she asks.

"Much. I'm sorry. I didn't mean to react that way to you. I was just-"

"Overwhelmed?"

I nod. "This is a huge adjustment. On the one hand, I am glad we left early so I can adjust too, but it would have been nice to have one more good day with my friends."

"I'm sorry."

"You were excited to return home. I cannot fault you for that. You had to go through a similar thing when you were burdened with the task of raising me," I say as I search through my clothes for pajamas.

"Sage, you were never a burden to me. I will admit I was overwhelmed at times, but the house helped. The only thing I would change about the past, if I could, would be losing your parents."

I slip on my nightgown, hang my damp towel in the bathroom, and return to Kira. "Enough of that sad talk. What kind of dessert is this?"

Kira perks right up, "Brumbleberry Puff. Think of it like a blueberry puff pastry, if the blueberries also had a hint of marshmallow taste."

"That's interesting," I say with hesitation.

"I promise it's an absolute delight. It's very sweet, though, so I didn't ask for the ale."

"Kira, I like having my teeth. If we keep eating these sweet things-"

"Oh shoot, I forgot to pick up paste when we were at the apothecary. I will make sure we get you some. I'm sure there isn't much left in our house even if we get a plot, and I'd rather put you on the good stuff anyway. Now, please eat up. Foregoing brushing your teeth another day won't be the end, I promise."

She scoots the plate close to me, and I pick up the fork. When I stab into the flakey bread, a purple jam-like substance seeps out, and with it, the smell of the berries. At the top of my head, I can't place it with anything back in the Other Realm, but it has my mouth watering. I load the fork up with a small bite at first, just to try. The moment it hits my tongue, the flavor is incredible. Kira was right, it's got the breaded and fluffy texture of a puff pastry, but the fruit portion is like blueberries and marshmallows. I would have never guessed that mixing the two would be so delightful.

"Kira, this is amazing!" She grins in response, a streak of the purple-colored jam sitting on the top of her lip. I grab a cloth folded on the table and hand it to her.

Kira chuckles as she dabs away the jam from her lip. "I forget how messy of an eater I can be." The green in her cheeks goes a darker shade.

"I like that you are still so very much you. My life may be different, but your personality is the same. It's a comfort to me. I will admit, it's hard to call you Kira."

"I did enjoy you calling me mom. You will always be a daughter to me, but in this realm, it's important I remain just Kira, your caretaker. I dare not think of what your grandfather would do to me if he knew I raised you as my daughter and not my ward."

"He wouldn't hurt you, would he?"

"There's no telling what that man would do. He wasn't the kindest. It's hard to believe he is your mother's father. Their hearts are so much different. He was never kind to the staff; often, I thought not a genuine kind to your mother either."

"How soon do you think until he will come to see me?"

"I'm surprised he hasn't stormed the city already. Granted, it's a few days' travel from his castle, but you've been missing for 18 years. I don't see why he wouldn't prioritize it."

I rub my eyes as the exhaustion settles in. "Well, I personally hope he doesn't come around for a very long time.

If he is even a fraction of the impression, I got from everyone today, I'm not interested in meeting him." I stifle a yawn.

"Come, Sage, off to bed."

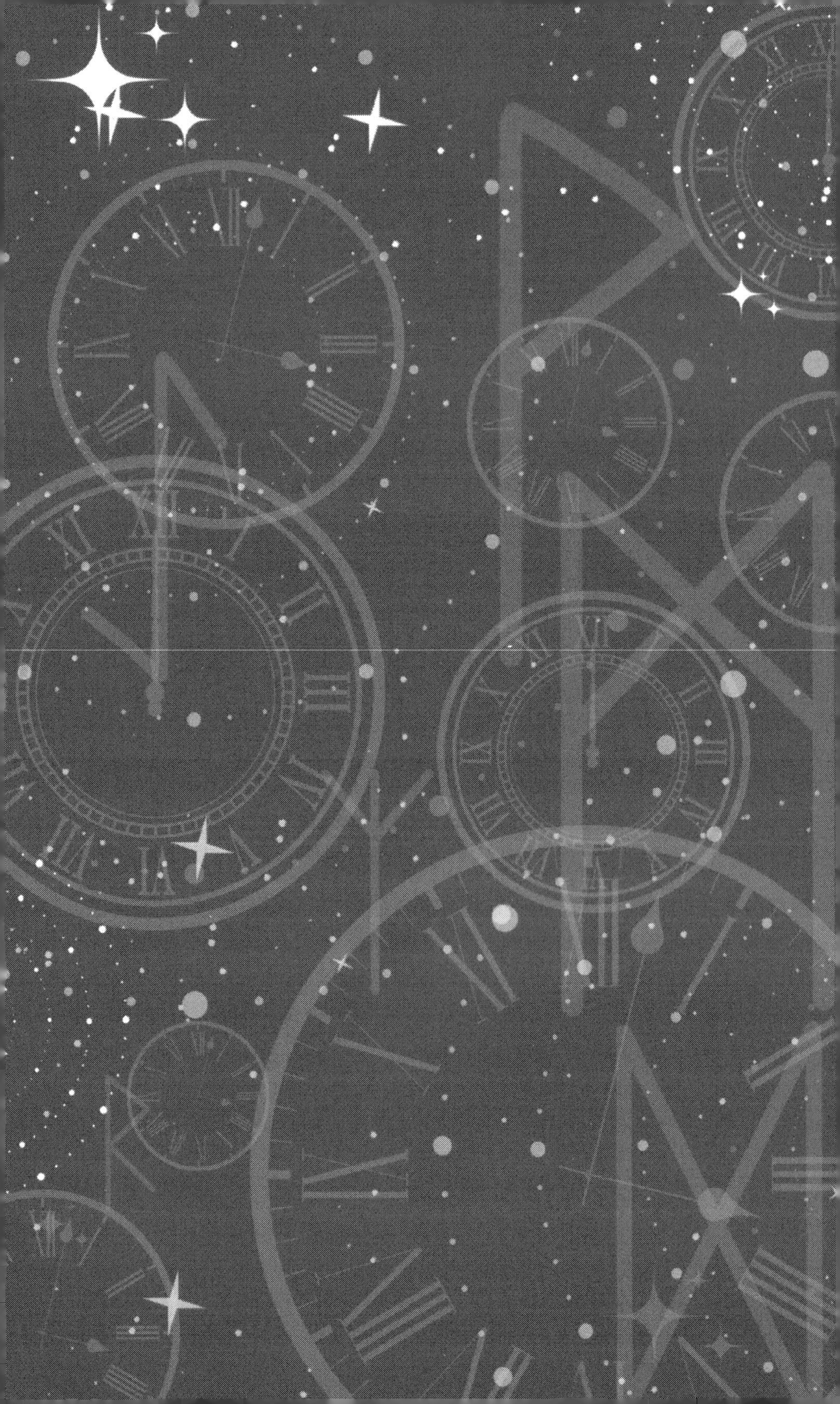

Chapter Eleven
Sage

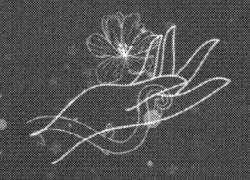

"Oh, this is perfect," Kira exclaims. We have been looking and viewing real estate all morning, and I swear I have blisters on my toes from all the walking.

"Good. We'll take this one." I turn to, I guess, what you would consider a real estate agent in a fantasy world. I hand over a considerable amount of coin to them, probably more than what this plot of land is worth. I won't risk Kira changing her mind again and having to walk around more. I am eager to revisit my childhood home again.

"Very well. I will draft the paperwork and bring you the deed by the afternoon. In the meantime, consider this land yours."

I watch the man as he walks away, and as soon as he is out of my line of sight, I turn to Kira and say, "Well, hurry up."

She grins as she taps the omni-vessel three times, and I watch as my childhood home appears perfectly intact on the newly acquired plot of land. Kira grabs my hand and practically drags me across the lawn into our home. There's something so unbelievably relieving about standing in this house again. All this change might be happening around me, but I will continue to have this one thing that keeps me genuinely connected to my past.

"I'm going to go check out my garden," Kira practically yells as she releases my hand and runs to the backyard.

I run up to my room to see if the magic affected anything since it was in the omni-vessel when the powder was released. Once I get to the door, I am almost afraid to turn the knob. What if it isn't there? What if it is? Will it hurt to still have memories to look back on? I close my eyes and breathe, slowly turning the doorknob until I can push the door open. I step inside, looking where I hang my photos on the wall. They're all there—all of my friends and the adventures we had together.

As I shuffle through the photos of my friends and I, I cannot help but pause at a particular one with my friend Kaylee. I remember the night so fondly. She and I didn't go to bed that night. She had an English quiz on Romeo and Juliet that week and couldn't focus on reading it. As the ever-helpful friend, I recited the whole thing to her and used a different voice for each character. I did not have a voice the following day, but I was paid in pizza rolls, and we spent the next day reading over the ridiculous teen magazines. I wonder if they could have gone on carrying the memories of us together. Would it have been that dangerous if they remembered?

I pull out one of my many photo albums and situate myself on the beanbag in the corner of my room. I spend the next few hours flipping through the pages, laughing and smiling at all the memories.

I don't know how much time has passed, but Kira comes knocking at my door. "It's time for dinner, Sage."

"I'll be right down," I say as I move to return the album to its rightful place. There's something about having the chance to look at those photos and remember for all of us that makes me feel a whole lot better.

I wander downstairs, and a familiar and favorite scent of mine hits my nose. I guess food stays good in the omni-vessel because I know that smell anywhere. Pollo Asado and yellow rice. I hope we can have something similar to my favorite foods here, or maybe we can have someone get my favorites from the Other Realm. Does having food imported from another realm hurt the balance somehow?

"I figured this would be okay for dinner tonight. I know how much you have taken a liking to it recently."

"This is perfect. I can't believe we had the ingredients still in the house."

"I didn't think we did actually. It could be the house sensed you needed the familiarity of home and things that bring you comfort. It was able to conjure milk when you were a baby."

I decided to test out the theory, putting out in the universe of my mind that I wanted some cheesecake to go with dinner. I nearly choke on my chicken because the house conjures up a cheesecake. "I guess you would be right. I wonder how all this works, the conjuring from nothing. It feels like it would upset the balance somehow," I say as I jab my fork and steal a bite of cheesecake. Kira swats my hands for my lack of manners.

"The house pays a cost. It's pretty minimal. I'm quite surprised you never saw it before. The fuse box doesn't have switches. There's a stone in there, and each act of magic takes a little away from it.

"How much longer does the house have?" I ask. Now, I feel incredibly guilty for asking for some cheesecake.

"Oh, don't worry about that. The stone has enough magic energy to fuel the whims and needs of its residents for a very long time. Well beyond our lifespan. The stone is not nearly as powerful as your necklace, but enough."

"You mentioned my necklace is called the stone of power. Why is that? What is it meant for?"

Kira sets her fork down. "Unfortunately, I cannot tell you that. It was another one of your mother's wishes that you learn what it can do on your own. I don't know if that was a her thing or if the stone requires the user to do so. It's not common knowledge, and the information is only passed down between the women in your family."

"Interesting," I say as I roll the stone between my fingers.

"The flowers are still in full bloom in the back garden, by the way."

"Really?"

Kira nods. "You have some really powerful magic in you. I cannot wait to see what you can do when you reach your full potential."

"Does the academy allow us to leave freely?"

"They used to allow the students to leave on the weekends, back when I worked there. I assume since Gaiwen that they tightened the leash on that a bit and it might just be for holiday breaks."

"That's a shame. I am still happy I will get to visit you, even if it's longer than I was hoping for."

"We will make it work. I have confidence you will make some new friends; I mean, look at how you made quick friends with that Thalia girl. You've always been charismatic. I think you get that from your mother. She was always good with words; it's why I took a liking to her so fast when she started at the academy."

"Kira, can I be open with you for a moment?"

"Of course, dear."

"It hurts sometimes when people compare me to my mother. I never got the chance to meet her, yet every person who knew her or of her seem to constantly be making the comparison. It's hard being compared to someone everyone says was so great. It just feels like the bar has been set so high and when the disappointment hits that I am not who they think I am; the outcome is going to be so much worse. I didn't ask for this."

"I'm sorry. I didn't realize it was bothering you so much to be compared to your mother."

"It's not the end of the world if it happens, but I'm still me. I am my own person, and I don't want people to think I will be a certain way if that's not me."

"I understand. I don't expect you to be someone you are not, Sage. I'm sorry I didn't tell you about everything sooner; I admit my failure in that part. I was put in a situation I didn't know how to handle or what to do."

"Am I mad at you for lying to me? Yes, but I am also grateful to you. You allowed me to live carefree for eighteen years. You never put me in a situation where I felt unwanted or unloved. I'm just confused and overwhelmed. I miss my friends, but we were parting ways. I just wasn't ready to lose everything. I am also struggling with living with the knowledge that they don't remember me."

"I'm sorry I had to do that. It was a precaution. I couldn't allow them to live with the knowledge magic was real. The house couldn't stay because it's powered by magic. Your friends couldn't remember. This is not because I believed they would betray you, but we don't know what level your enemies would go to extract information about you from them."

I move my food around on my plate. Did she really believe someone would cause harm to my friends if they hadn't for eighteen years? Is she just saying that to justify her actions? I want to trust Kira, I do, but I am struggling. I am expected just to be agreeable with everything. I've been agreeable all my life. I trusted Kira, and she lied to me my whole life.

"I'm feeling a little exhausted, Kira. I'm going to go to bed if that's alright."

"You don't want to watch a movie? We still have DVDs. We still have some of the perks from the Other Realm."

I shake my head. "Not tonight. I just want to sleep in my bed. It's been far too long since I have done that."

"Alright. I'll clean up here. You go off to bed then."

"Thanks," I fake a yawn before heading up to my room. Despite not being tired, I force myself to get some rest anyway. I fall asleep thinking about old memories.

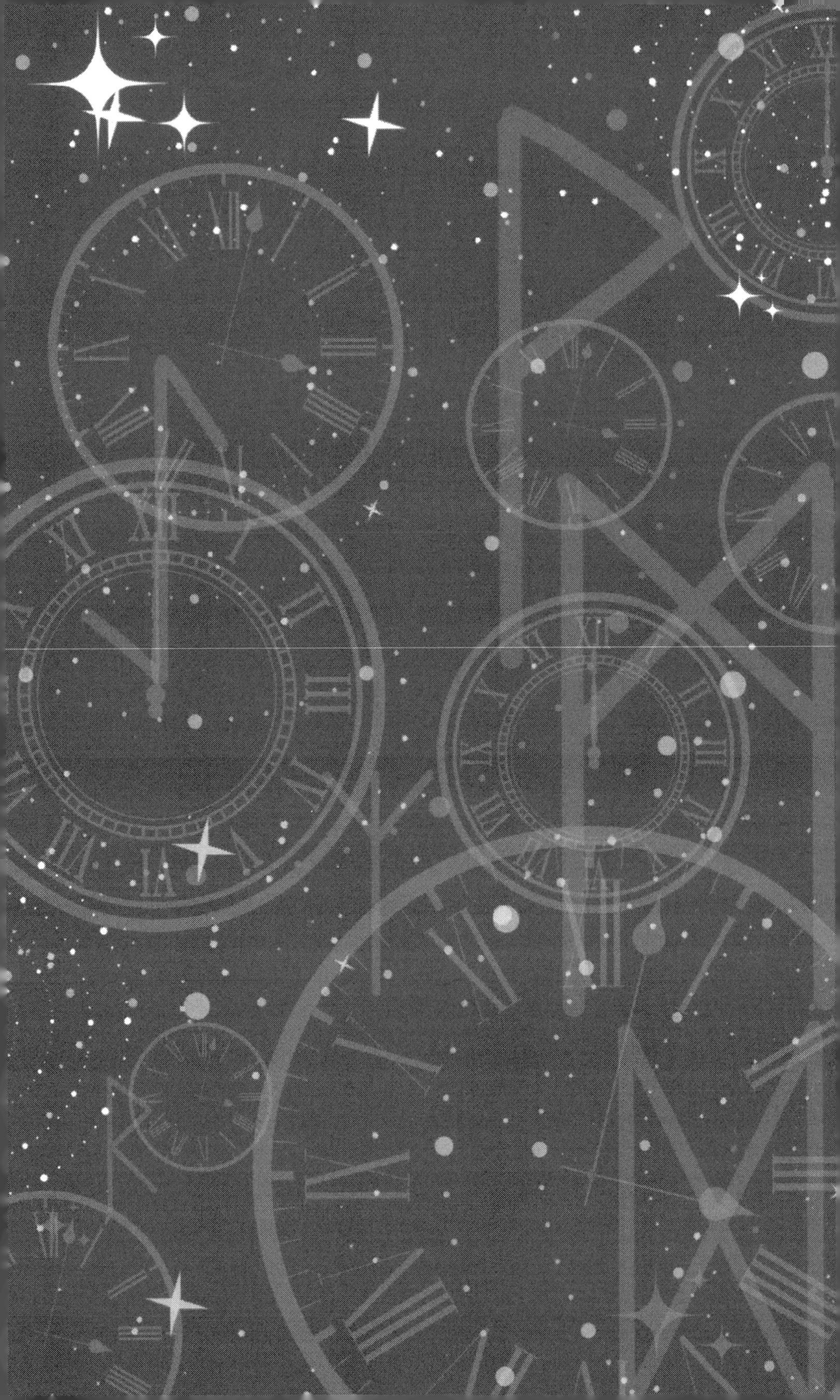

Chapter Twelve
Sage

Summer has come and gone, and we are now in the autumn season. Things got better between Kira and I again. They are not perfect, but I understand her more. I don't believe it's going to be the last of my emotional breakdowns, but I think that I can handle things better now. I can make new friends; it was always bound to happen. I feel like it's common for people to drift away if they go to different colleges anyhow. As a bonus, I met Thalia and her brother, Anton. Kira made fast friends with their parents, and I had a cool set of twins with whom I could hang out.

Her family was so welcoming and kind; it was a relief to spend the summer days just getting to know them. Plus, they have the sweetest griffin name Griyf. I learned all about how they came to have one in their family; it was quite an endearing story. Baby griffins often imprint onto a fae they deem worthy. It's not something that happens over time; it's an instant thing that takes place when you meet for the first time. The parents of the griffin become aware of the bond, and if it's old enough to thrive without its parent, they send it off with you. If the baby is still too small at the time of the imprinting, the parents will seek the fae out later. The learning to fly and all those life milestones are in the capable hands of the bonded. Thalia's parents are firm believers that griffins can see the future and know that the fae they chose will provide them with a good life.

Griyf is imprinted on Thalia, which means we are loading up three students' worth of first-year supplies onto the vehicle the school sent over while also trying to fit a child Griffin. Griyf isn't as large as he could be, but he's also not very small. He's about the size of a large breed dog in the Other Realm, and he's currently being very disagreeable.

"Come on, Griyf, get in the cart," Thalia whines. Griyf is whipping his head back and forth, eyeing up the cramped space where the luggage is. The cart has seating similar to a horse-drawn carriage, and behind that is a decent-sized metal container for storing items and, in this case, a child griffin. The carts are designed to show up at a location and take you to the academy; no one steers them, and nothing pulls them along.

Anton is sitting in the front of the wagon with his feet lounging up on the ledge. "If you can't get him to listen to this, how do you expect to teach him to fly? You need to be more assertive, sister."

"I'm trying," she bites.

"Yes, because whining as you make demands to your griffin is being assertive."

I smack his arm as I load up into the carriage. "Hey, be nice to her!" He laughs, rolls his head back, and closes his eyes.

"There we go, Griyf! Now who's a good boy," Thalia says in the weird baby voice she uses when he finally listens. "Now I have to close the door, but I opened the window for you so you can get some air." I turn my head and watch Thalia quickly close the door and slide the lock as Griyf protests with loud chittering and wide eyes. She bounds her way into the carriage seat beside me. "Everyone ready?"

"We've been ready Tal," Anton says as he taps three times on the carriage and it rolls away from their home. I am quickly learning a lot of magic works with the number three.

The academy is a decent distance from the bustling city below, up winding hills and steep slopes. You would think that

Halaris, being already high in the mountains, you couldn't get any higher. You would be very wrong. The academy rests at the very peak of the mountains. When you are in the city, you can see the academy from there, albeit it looks small, the closer you get, the more you can see how grand it is. My legs ache at the thought of how much walking I will have to do there; just walking around Halaris was rough. The size of the academy takes the cake.

We are about 10 minutes more of a ride up the mountains until we reach the gate to the academy, and from this distance, I can see jutting towers. I'm aware that this academy has a lot to offer its students, from living accommodations to core classes and optional ones. Judging by all the carts also making their way up the academy, there are a lot of students. I know that not all of these students live in Halaris; some dwell in the Other Realm, and some are from around Alandria, the inhabitable bits at least. They believe I can fix a lot of corruption in this realm. I hope that I can be who they think I am.

The carriages line up outside the gate, meaning we must walk the rest of the way with our belongings. Griyf is ecstatic to be out of the carriage finally, and he makes so many noises that it's getting us weird looks from the other students arriving. It's uncommon for a first-year to arrive with a future mount. Since the first year is beast studies, most students wait until their second year, but you can't exactly stop imprinting.

Anton grabs his belongings and marches through the iron gates. I have a strong feeling he is going to try to avoid Thalia and me when he can. I guess twin love only extends so far. Thalia and I break out in a good sweat by the time we have our belongings sorted and out of the carriage. The carriage drives off as soon as it's empty, leaving us with no way to go but forward.

"I know you grew up in Halaris and haven't traveled to the Other Realm, but we have movies there, and now I realize how unrealistic they are when it comes to magic schools. They never show them struggling to carry around a ridiculous amount of school supplies."

"I'm sure there is some method that makes this easier, but they will say it's character-building to do it on your own."

"The only thing I am building is a leg cramp and a ridiculous amount of sweat."

Thalia and I continue complaining about how agonizing and brutal it is as we cross the courtyard. The courtyard truly is beautiful, with lush green hedges lining the various walkways and a fountain that is so similar to the one that I saw when Kamira spoke to me. There are little floating balls of light that Thalia explains to me are called Devas. They are lesser fae that are attracted to thriving plant life.

Tending to all the things greenery are brownie fae. They are not much taller than the shrubbery surrounding the walkways. Their bottom half is like that of a minotaur and the upper torso of a human. They have dragonfly-like wings attached to their back, and their faces make me think of a deer. They are pretty cute and, as I was informed, very friendly. They choose to work at the academy because it's one of the safest places in the realm, and they do not like any form of violence. Thalia and her family spent a lot of time teaching me on what to expect to see while I was at the academy. I am seriously so grateful for everything they taught me beforehand.

Despite my exhaustion, the walk through the courtyard to the academy's entrance didn't take that long. An older woman with gray hair and glasses ushers students along, telling us which direction to head to find our rooms. "Name, please?" she asks me.

"Sage Torrin."

"Ah, the High King's granddaughter. I'm sorry to inform you everyone's rooms will be the same across the board. There will be no special treatment for anyone despite their status," she eyes me like I am about to object. "Each student at the academy is expected to room with the three other elements. One cannot thrive without the other and we like to instill that lesson starting in your first year. Are we going to have a problem?"

"No. I am okay with the rules you have in place," I say. I don't know what I did to already have a professor in a sour mood toward me.

Good. According to our records, you are an earth fae. Is this correct?"

"Yes."

"Good. You will be in the North Tower with the rest of the first-year students. Just keep walking this corridor until you reach the green door. Your advisor will direct you to the correct room. Place your cauldron, class-assigned books, and Herbology supplies over to that pile there. They will be brought to the correct classrooms." She snaps her fingers and my name appears on all my items.

I guess that's how I will know what belongs to me. I wait for Thalia to set her things on the pile, and we start walking down the corridor.

"Well, she already doesn't like me," I tell Thalia as soon as we turn the corner.

"I'm not sure what professor she was, but I hope we don't have her anytime soon. She might be comparing you to your grandfather, which isn't fair."

"My grandfather is that bad, huh?"

"Well, let's just say I've only ever heard of how rude he is to those not of nobility, and he doesn't seem to care for anything lesser. Your grandfather isn't ruler because of blood; it's by marriage. Technically, once you wed and produce an heir, the line of succession must pass to you."

"I don't want children any time soon."

"Honestly, I think that's the most outdated rule. I get that they need an heir from your bloodline, but it forces you to try and conceive right away to claim what is rightfully yours."

"Why does it have to be my bloodline? What can't I adopt?"

"Your bloodline is unique. When The Nines created the realm, they made your family first, bestowing you all with special abilities."

"Like my mom being able to speak with Kamira?" I ask.

"Yeah, you could get that gift too, but you can also have something unique on top of it. Since it would be a gift inherited, not the gift bestowed."

"I have spoken with Kamira before."

Thalia stops walking. "We spent practically all summer together, and you kept that from me the whole time. I'm wounded."

"I'm sorry, I was a bit busy trying to enjoy my first summer in Alandria with my new friend. Have we passed the green door?"

"You're forgiven this time, and nope. We passed red and brown. They used to separate us by element back in the day."

I let out a groan. "My legs are so sore."

"You're going to love the bathing room. How are you so sore? We walked around the city all summer."

"What's special about the bathing room? Not enough. My body always feels so achy."

"It shouldn't. Maybe living in the Other Realm affected you somehow?" I shrug. "The bathroom has healing properties in the water. Something with the rune system. It will help if you get injured or, in your case, feel stiff and sore."

"I will be using them as soon as I can then."

"Here we are!" She reaches her arm back to stop me from walking, which is probably smart. I am in automation mode right now. Thalia swings the door open, and we are greeted by an open area filled with students lounging about while others are waiting in line. That must be to speak with the advisor because Thalia pulls me in line with her. The line moves insanely fast, and before we know it, we are up next.

"Greetings, new blood. I am Meera. Here's your quick rundown. I am the advisor for everyone who stays in this tower. Two other advisors are floating about for this tower. They are Jake and Brin. Right now, they are helping prepare the hall for everyone's arrival. You will meet them later. If you have any questions or concerns, please let us know, but please respect the fact that we are also students. Be mindful of what time those concerns are and that if it's a dangerous concern to speak with Professor Auhdaye, you should have just met her at the entrance. You can find your advisors in that room back there during the evenings and early mornings," she points to the door behind her. "We have individual rooms in there; that's only because we are third years, and we need to be accessible to you. As Auhdaye may have informed you, these are not typical living arrangements. Male and female rooms are in separate sections of the tower, but we do share a shower room. She is also assigned to our tower, given she is the Herbology teacher, and this used to be the Earth Tower. Great. Now that we have that out of the way, may I please have your name?"

"Sage Torrin."

She flips through her stack of papers. "Ah, there you are. You are going to be on the second level. Just go up those steps over there," she points to the stairwell near the fireplace. "You will be the second doorway you pass. A number two will be carved on the door so you won't miss it. Each living area is divided by male and female. Showers are back from where you came between this tower and the first one you passed. There's another one between the other two towers. You will be sharing with third years."

"I'm so tired of stairs," I say more to myself than her.

"You do get used to it. The first few weeks are the hardest. I recommend using the showers frequently. The water has restorative properties. You just have to get used to being open to all genders; that's always the hardest part, with everything being so public."

I am getting used to that being the case with most things in Alandria. Thalia stays behind to discuss something with Meera. It doesn't take long until I am at the door leading to what will be my room throughout my first year here. I push open the door, and what I see is quite surprising. I was expecting cramped quarters and limited space. Instead, I find a living area with enough seating for four, everflame dances around the ceiling, and many varying potted plants. On either side of the room are two sets of bi-folding glass doors. One is open, and I see a blonde woman folding white-toned outfits on her bed.

"Hey," I say. I might as well bite the bullet and meet one of my roommates.

"Oh hey! Are you looking for your bed? If you are Sebille, you are in here; if not, you are through the other doors."

"Not Sebille."

"Well, not Sebille, do you have a name?"

"Sage."

"Nice to meet you, Sage. My name is Aurora. If you didn't guess by my wardrobe, I'm an air elemental."

I glance down at my casual sundress. I didn't wear my elemental color. We were told we could pack a few different colors on non-school days and that we didn't have to wear our colors. I am, funnily enough, wearing a white slip midi dress that ties with bows on my shoulders. "I'm obviously not an air elemental, just choosing to dress casually for move-in. From what I can tell so far, I am earth, though, leaning more toward plant-based magic."

"I totally get it. I have my casual clothes stowed away already. Your name and the itinerary for today should be on some parchment. Basically, just unpack and settle in, get to know your new roommates, while we wait for dinner. The headmaster will do general introductions, and then class starts tomorrow."

"I'm actually really looking forward to this; you seem really nice." I turn to walk toward my room, and I crash into a girl with long black hair.

"Watch it," she snarls at me.

"I am so sorry. I didn't hear anyone come in or you approach," I say.

"Yeah, whatever. What's the name for the bed over there?" she directs the question to Aurora.

"Sebille," Aurora says.

"Great," the girl slams her shoulder into me as she brushes past. Apparently, that's Sebille.

I collect myself, worried about who the final roommate will be, when Thalia walks in the door. "Thank The Nines," she exclaims when she sees me.

"Tal!" I hug her. "What took you so long?"

"I was getting to know Meera. She's fascinating."

"Look you're already making more friends. Should I be concerned for my spot as best friend?"

Thalia blushes. Oh, she totally likes Meera as more than a friend noted. "Of course not, Sage. I didn't spend the summer confiding my darkest secrets with you to replace you so soon."

Aurora comes bounding out of her room. "Hi! I'm Aurora. You are the last roomie for me to meet," she says, extending her hand in welcome.

"Pleasure to meet you, Aurora. I am Thalia. My friends call me Tal."

"Noted. Well, you two better go unpack." Aurora returns to her room and Thalia and I go to inspect ours.

I didn't peek too far into Aurora's side to see what the layout of the room looked like prior, but the bedroom area is quite spacious, too. One bed is closest to the door, and the other is on the other side of the room, slightly higher up to divide the space in half. There's a desk at the end of each bed. Against the platform and next to the stairs is a dresser for whoever has the bed closest to the door. The other dresser is next to the furthest wall from the bed on the platform. I spot Thalia's name on the one closest to the door, so I am on the platform. Off to the right is another door that leads to a singular toilet and sink. At least I won't have to trudge down many stairs just to relieve myself or get ready in the mornings.

I walk over to my bed and read over the itinerary. It's similar to what Aurora said but in excessive detail. I much prefer her cliff-notes version. I toss my duffle onto my bed and begin to unpack. I didn't pick out a whole lot of outfits. I figured I could keep it lighter at first, I can get some more things once we are inevitably allowed into town. If that takes too long, I could always write to Kira and ask her to send some here. My wardrobe right now consists of a lot of short pleated skirts, some pencil skirts, plaid pajamas, and a lot of green sweaters. Mainly pullovers for minimal effort and comfort, but I do have some cardigans to go with some tank tops. I figured with the fall season, my day wardrobe being more light would be okay. Despite the academy being castle-like in nature, it's not very drafty. Whatever magic they have going on is keeping it quite comfortable.

I took a lot longer than I wanted to unpack my things. Mainly because I was trying to decide what I wanted to wear for my first day tomorrow, and I kept bouncing between a few choices. I eventually decided to leave out the oversized sweater and a pleated skirt. I was relieved when we visited the tailor to get stuff for school, and a lot of the clothes between the two realms were similar. It could be partly due to travel being open and adopting some of their styles. There were still a lot of choices I would have imagined existed in a fantasy world.

I so badly want to shower, but given how daylight looks to be nearing its end, signaling food time is near, I should probably head to wherever the great hall is for dinner. "Ready, Tal?" I ask.

She's stretched out on her bed, arms propped behind her head. "I've been ready. I was watching you have a crisis over trying to pick your outfit for tomorrow. Should we get Aurora? I saw the other girl leave already."

"Oh, that's Sebille. She doesn't like me much, and yes, we should."

"Based on her mood when she left, I don't think she likes anyone much. I feel a bit bad for Aurora being so close to her."

Thalia and I retrieve Aurora before beginning the arduous journey of walking down the steps. I swear we left at the perfect time because Meera is ushering everyone out of the tower and pointing toward a direction which must be the great hall.

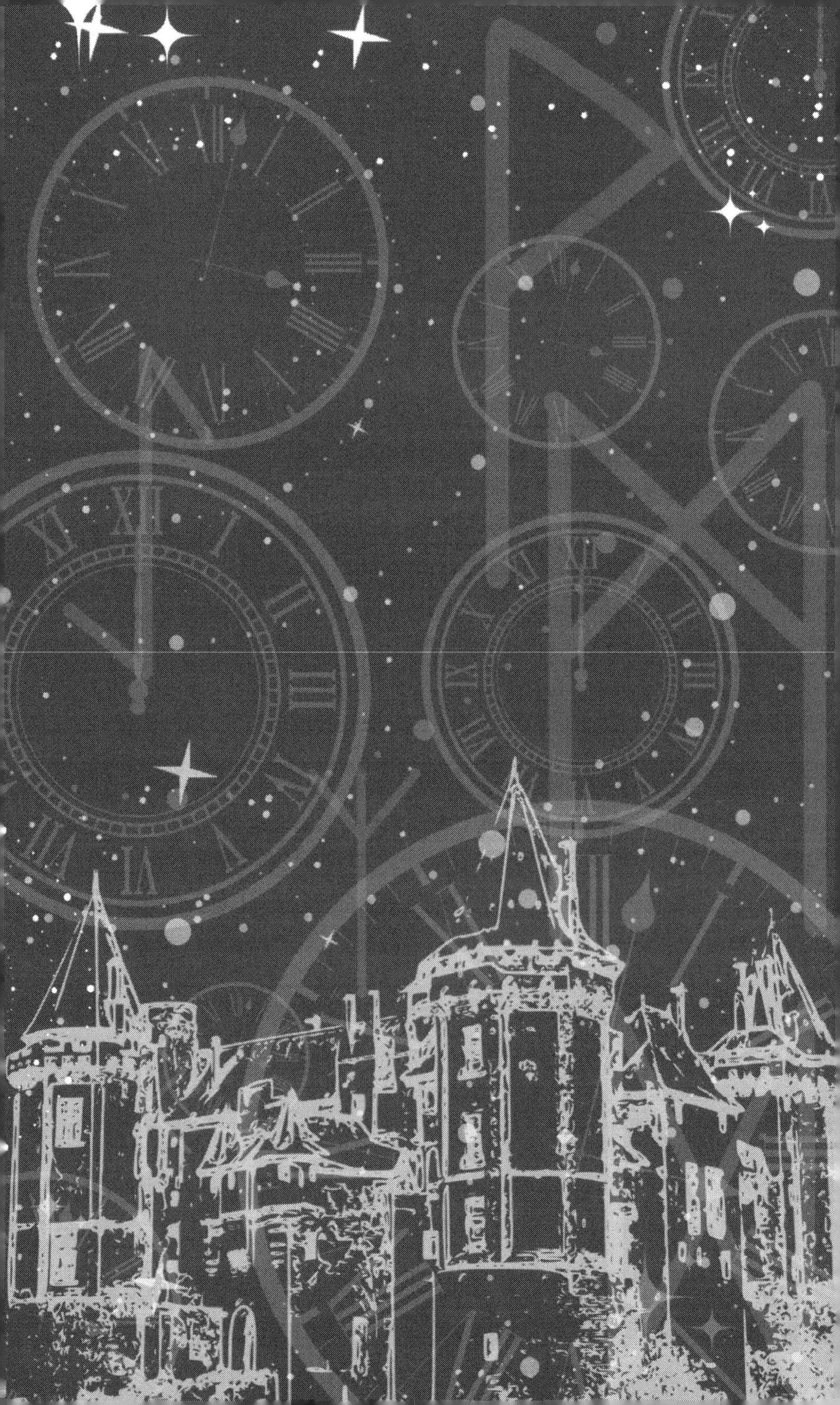

Chapter Thirteen
Sage

The three of us eventually make our way into the great hall together. Tonight is an introduction feast to get acquainted with fellow students and professors before we begin classes tomorrow. When we walk into the grand hall, I first notice the four rows of tables leading up to a staging area, where all the professors are seated. There is spacing in the center of the aisle large enough for a fifth table, but the space remains open. The table furthest to my left has only a few students sitting, and we are being directed to it. I assume it is intended for the first years. I wonder if people in different years have ever ventured to other tables.

My best guess is that seating should accommodate over 200 students, but it's a tight fit at some of the tables. I am a bit surprised at how many students there are. It's a good thing; that means people were able to rebuild during the time I have been gone. Everything I was told about the conditions of the realm when I left made me think I was returning to practically nothing. Was it because I was gone, they were able to? I hope to learn more in my History of the Dark Ascension class.

"That looks like a good spot," Thalia says, pointing further down the table and closer to the staging area.

"Perfect, let's go."

Aurora, Thalia, and I race to the spot before someone else snatches it up. The tables are already piled with foods of all sorts, from stews and soups, roasted meats and vegetables, and pastries galore; there is an unfathomable number of choices. We follow suit with everyone around the room, picking what we want to eat and loading our plates and soup bowls. Some brownies walk around with carts, passing out beverages of choice to each student. We all opt for the ale. I have grown accustomed to it since my time here and find myself pairing it with whatever I eat at dinner time. The alcoholic content in these drinks is so minimal that you would need to drink a lot in a short amount of time to feel any effects.

Clinking sounds from the staging area, and a middle-aged man with long brown hair and a beard to match is tapping a spoon against a flute to get the room's attention. "Greetings, everyone; I am headmaster, Thevin Brawnmire. I have been headmaster for the past 200 hundred years, and I plan to maintain that position for many more to come." The older students cheer. Apparently, he's popular with the crowd. That's a good sign, I suppose. "Part of maintaining my position comes from ensuring the continued safety of Aliria Academy and all who dwell within its walls, as well as ensuring that our students receive the best academic education in both common studies and that of magic. You will notice that on the letters my associates and I have sent out to each and every one of you, depending on what year of education this is for you, match your peers of the same year; these are your nonnegotiable classes. That is not to say that you cannot take more with the time that you have here. There will be a notice with all the extra classes or activities you can participate in posted in the main hallway sometime tomorrow if you so choose to take a look. Remember, this is not a requirement, but everything we can teach you here will be paramount to your success when you graduate. For a long time, this realm has been plagued by war, and by some miracle, we have had peace for 18 years; peace only lasts so long," during the last part, I swear the headmaster is looking directly at me, and I can tell that it is not unnoticed by other students. "Now, I know you all have had a long and tiring journey here, so eat up, chat with your fellow students, and make use of the amenities that are offered to you. We will see you all in the morning for class."

After finishing his speech, the room fills with the sounds of clinking silverware and chatter. I lost a majority of my appetite and mostly poked around my dinner. Thalia nudges me. "Hey girl, even if the peace ends, it's not your fault. Don't let that get to your head. I know that's easier said than done. I'm sure there will be some bitter eggs about your return, but without your return, we stand no chance of reclaiming and restoring the lost parts of Alandria."

"Wait, you're the High King's granddaughter?" Aurora asks.

"Yeah," I mutter.

"Well, I wouldn't have noticed. I've met your grandfather a few times; I'm a part of the noble house, Ailes."

"I haven't met him, but I haven't heard many good things regarding him yet," I say.

"You truly haven't met him yet? That's so surprising because I remember as a kid him always making a big deal about people searching for you. He's nice to nobility but not so much to anyone under that. That being said, I don't like the man. You can't feign respect for people just because they are nobles; all deserve that same respect. I was happy when he stopped allowing the noble families to reside at the main castle."

"When did that start?" I ask.

"Oh, it had to be around what would have been your seventh birthday."

"He needs time to grieve," Thalia mutters.

"That's true. He ended his searches about that time," Aurora responds.

"I wonder why," I say. "Well, I am here now and still expected to fill this prophecy. What if I can't do it or I make the wrong choice? The prophecy is so open-ended that it could go in favor of good or bad. I want to think that I am not a bad person."

"Look, if you fail, I will be right there picking you back up to try again. I will be by your side through it all. I said you and I are going to be the best of friends, and I meant it. Now, please eat; I don't want to hear you complain later when we are in our room about your regrets about not eating."

I shake my head, but I know she's right—not just about the complaints that would come later, but also that failure doesn't necessarily mean the end—at least, I hope it doesn't.

After Thalia's speech, I was able to eat most of my dinner, and we cleared out pretty much right away. I was not really in the mood to mingle with anyone after the speech and wanted to shower before everyone else had the same idea. Thalia wanted to spend some time with Griyf, and Aurora wanted to do some reading, so I went down to the lower levels to shower by myself. The setup was similar to the one on the airship, just on a larger scale. There was also a large tub for bathing; usually, I would question how that was sanitary, but I now exist in a world with magic. There is probably some rune or spell that keeps it purified. There is also a whole area with towels, which I am thankful for. As much as the whole air to get dry thing was cool, there are hundreds of students, and the less exposure to everyone, the better.

I don't see anyone in the shower when I enter the room, so I quickly discard my clothes, walk up, and start rinsing off my hair. Just like the vines on the ship, it extends over to me, offering the gelatinous blob to wash myself with. I just finished rinsing out the last of the soapy residue when a voice sounds from nearby.

"You know that's basically plant cum, right?"

The voice is deep and, dear gods, hot as all hell, but the shriek I let out from the shock is bordering embarrassing. I cover my exposed parts before turning toward the voice, and FUCK. "I-" He's completely and utterly naked, and his body, I swear, was chiseled by the gods themselves. His hair is white and looks so deliciously soft, cut just above his ears. His eyes look like the sea. My eyes wander to his chin dimple before drifting lower and fuck, fuck, fuck.

"Eyes up here, princess," he says, flashing a smile.

"I'm sorry-"

"No, you're not, and that's okay."

"I am sorry. What did you just say?"

He laughs. "You know, princess," he presses closer to where I stand. "If our futures had played out the way they were meant to between you and I; you would have been my betrothed."

"Wait, so you're-"

"Hassian Blackwell. The very same and I know you are Sage Torrin. I must admit, I am disappointed life didn't play out that way."

I scoff, "You don't even know me well enough to know if you would even like me."

"I like what I see; I know that much," his eyes drift down my body, and I realize at some point, I went from covering myself to putting my hands on my hips in a matter-of-factly position. I gasp and move to cover myself again, but he rushes forward enough for the magic of the shower to kick in. "I could have learned to love the rest." His voice is so deep and his breath is hot on my skin with his proximity. I can feel the hardness of his length.

"Yeah?" I ask, biting my lip. I have no idea what's gotten into me.

His hand touches my chin as he angles my head toward his and kisses me, and I, in all my lack of logic, kiss back, pressing against him, wanting more. More that he doesn't give. He pulls away with a devious smile. "If you want more, you will have to earn it, princess, and I am sure you will."

He turns and leaves the room, and it dawns on me that he didn't actually come into this area to shower. He was looking for me. He wanted me to know who he was. I've never felt urges like that with anyone; I've never had sexual desires toward anyone. Right now, the only thing I know is that if I didn't have a roommate, tonight would have been a very long night for me. Although, after receiving the slightest touch from him, I don't think anything but him will ever satiate my desire. I quickly dress and spend the rest of the night trying to shake my thoughts of him.

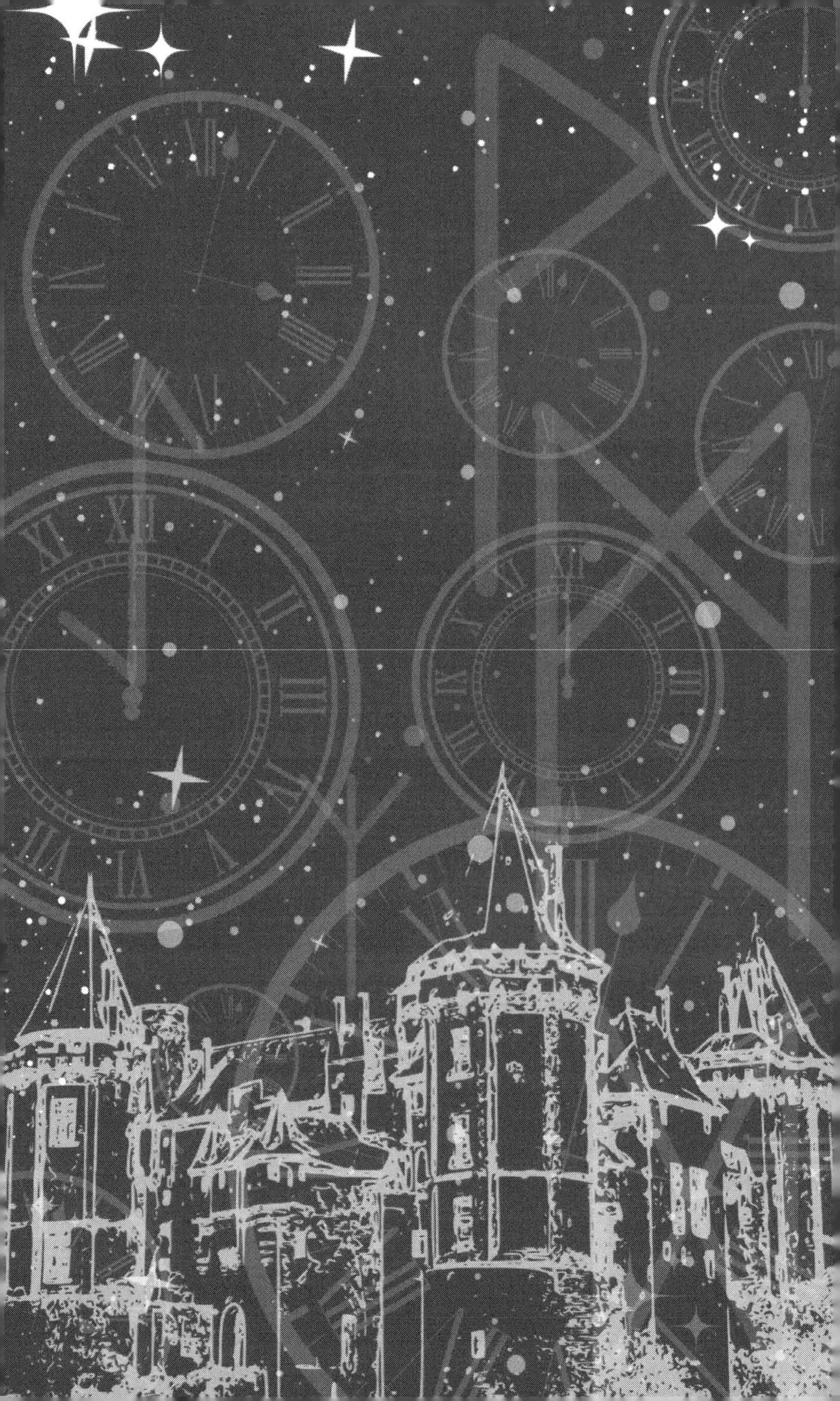

Chapter Fourteen
Sage

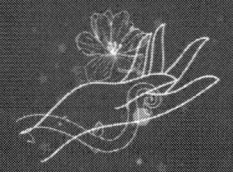

My first class of the day is Herbology. I have this class with Thalia, Aurora, and, unfortunately, Sebille. If there is one thing I can be relieved about, it's that Hassian and I will not be sharing any classes since I'm a first-year, and I've learned he's in this third. Hopefully, there will be no more shower incidents; I wouldn't be upset if there were. No. Stop that. I didn't tell Thalia what happened; I pretended to be asleep when she returned from spending time with Griyf. I feel partly guilty because I was always raised on the idea that friends don't lie to each other.

"Thalia," I whisper, trying not to get anyone else's attention in the room.

"Yes?"

"Something happened last night." She raises her brow toward me as if to say I'm listening. "I met Hassian Blackwell last night, not on purpose. I was alone in the showers, and suddenly he was there and very much naked."

Her eyes widen as she covers her mouth, trying her best not to make loud noises and direct the other student's attention. "Oh, we are so talking about this later."

"Wait, what happened between the two of you?" Aurora heard because, of course, she did. She's sitting next to us. I do like her; I just haven't had time to bond with her since we only met yesterday.

The sound of clapping comes from the front of the room, and we direct our attention to it. It's the same woman who directed us to our living quarters yesterday. "Good morning, everyone. You may call me Professor Auhdaye. You will become quite acquainted with me over the course of the next four years. Herbology is and should always be at the forefront of your mind. The magic and power of nature could very well be what saves your life when your internal power fails you. Now," she snaps her fingers and parchment appears from thin air and floats down in front of everyone. "This is the classroom syllabus. I have outlined only six weeks of lessons; I am not here to coddle you all school year but to show the necessary skills. For the rest of the year, you will focus on the care of your own plants. Some of you may even be asked to take to the field toward the decaying areas of our realm to help with the blight. Now, please open up your books to the first page; we are going over how and why plants are important especially in today's culture."

The irony of being an earth-based affinity fae is that I know damn well that I will be struggling in my Herbology class. I hope I will do much better by the time we reach the hands-on portion of our syllabus. Unfortunately, the only thing I retained during the class period as I listened to her explanation was a massive migraine. Also, that I should chew some peppermint leaves to help with that, which I am currently doing as I walk to my next class. At the end of the period, I separate from my roommates toward my next class. This is one class we won't share due to our different affinities.

A man who looks significantly older than the headmaster stands at the front of the room with his arms crossed, waiting for everyone to get seated and pay attention. He has short salt and pepper-colored hair and a beard that's been trimmed down as thin as it can go without getting rid of the beard. He has a kind look about him, but I might also not be the best judge of character.

"Good morning, fellow earth casters. I am Professor Dublin. I know you all came from Professor Auhdaye's classroom. However, I lack the air magic ability, so you will have to pass along this pile of syllabus until everyone gets one." He hands a stack of parchment to a girl in the front row. She takes one and passes it to the next person, and this continues while he speaks. "You might be wondering why someone with an air affinity is teaching Herbology; well, because she also has strong earth magic. If you take away something from this class, I hope that it is anything possible, including the ability to wield more than one element. Albeit, it is a rare feat, but not an impossible one. You will notice that I have listed all the types of affinities on your parchment, with earth at the top. We will spend the majority of our class together working on that element, but we will also test and see if you are capable of doing more than that. It's important you have a basic understanding if not a good mastery before we dabble into a new element. I expect you all to put in the extra time outside of classes and utilize the advisor system if you are struggling. Today, we are going to dive into casting. This will let me see where each of you are in your understanding of the earth element. The goal for today," he pauses closing his eyes while he raises his hands chest level and vines sprout from a potted plant behind him until the tips of a vine with a closed bud is sitting in front of every single student. "Make that flower bloom."

I look around and notice a few have it done immediately, it's clear their parents fully prepared them for what's to come. Others have a slight struggle, but they eventually get it down. Then there is me with no idea how to tap into my magic and zero experience outside of when my power awoke, and it did the work all on its own. I try closing my eyes, focusing on what I want to happen. Bloom. Bloom. Bloom. I open my eyes, nothing. I look in the direction of the professor, and I can see that he is watching me fail. I close my eyes and try again. Nothing happened during the whole period we had together. I am the only one that's failed.

The bell chimes from the tower, signifying the end of class, and everyone begins leaving. Professor Dublin makes eye contact with me and motions for me to approach. No students take notice, and I appreciate the discretion.

"What do you think went wrong in your casting, Sage," he asks.

"Outside of me not being raised with even knowing about magic and not having any prior training?" He nods. "I don't know. I tried to focus on my intent and what I wanted to do, but I just couldn't do it."

"Intent is good, but reaching into your power is more than that. Your first few times casting, you need to hone in on that. Eventually, it will be just as easy as breathing. When trying to use your innate ability, the key thing is to focus first. It's important to ground your mind into the present moment and think about your bond with the earth. Second, find your inner reservoir of energy. This means you need to dig deep into your center of power to build a connection. You haven't had the chance to do that yet; you cannot expect to cast without establishing a relationship between you and your power. Thirdly, visualize what you want to happen. You can have all the feelings in the world, but sometimes, your magic needs a better understanding of what you wish to make happen. Lastly, release the hold. The earth will respond to your call. I will not lie to you; you will fail repeatedly. It will be frustrating, but keep trying and keep pushing. I might suggest that you find someone to tutor you in the meantime. It doesn't matter what affinity they hold. A list of tutors is posted near the extracurricular notice. I encourage you to also check that out. I don't want to see you fail, Sage; much like the majority of the realm, I believe in the future you can bring. Now hurry along to your next class before you're late."

My next class is intended to teach us how to use our glamour. Seeing as I don't even know how to cast properly, I feel like this is also going to be a flop. Am I just going to be eternally bad at every single class this school has to offer? That's what it feels like with the trajectory the classes are going in. Thankfully, Thalia, Aurora, and I have the remainder of our classes together, so I have something to look forward to.

There is a faint sound of someone clearing their throat to grab attention. I look forward to where a professor stands, but I don't see anyone. The sound of something scraping across the stone fills the room, and I locate the source of the sound. A brownie is moving a platform box toward the center of the room. When it is satisfied with its position, it steps on it. The brownie begins to speak, but I cannot hear what it is saying. This is a fact it becomes quickly aware of.

Reaching up to its chest, it wraps its hands around a clear quartz necklace. "Apologies," it says. Its voice is now amplified throughout the room. "My name is Professor Keevah. Before you ask, yes, I am, in fact, a brownie, and this is not me using glamour to mask myself as such. Glamour is an ability all fae are capable of. The high fae can cast without aid, but the lesser fae like myself need the assistance of something. I prefer a crystal connection. Some races, like the forest fae, can only draw from nature, specifically plants. That race, however, is a dying breed. It's a tragedy, but I am not here to teach you history. I am here to teach you glamour. I hope each of you remembered to bring your crystal with you. I will not be teaching you glamour from your innate ability. First, we will go over the alternatives. You will find that your power may not work in certain situations and puts you in a pickle. This class will teach you how to potentially get out of that pickle. Any questions so far?"

A girl with shorter blonde hair raises her arm. "I have one. What happens if we cast a glamour and don't know how to change ourselves back?"

"Excellent question. As this should be the first time any of you should ever be casting glamour on yourselves because of that reason, I assure you we have ways to get you back to normal. Getting stuck is a very real problem, but it's not a permanent issue. There are potions," the brownie taps on a table that has a crate of vials nearby where it stands, "that can help revert you back. Your Herbology course will teach you how to craft them. As well as someone else can always remove the glamour for you, I recommend you seek out someone with experience, not a fellow student. An untrained eye can potentially make the situation worse. One of the common things that those finally learning glamour will do is use it frequently to alter their appearance by changing the color of their hair or eyes and altering their outfit. I might suggest that you never illusion your clothes. Always make sure you have a garment on before altering it. Some of us have the natural innate ability to see through glamour, and well, we'd prefer not to see you naked." The class erupts in laughter. "You laugh, but I am entirely serious. If you came from the Other Realm or visited the airship docks; you may have noticed whoever checked your ticket asked you to remove your glamour. That is because those with those special abilities are employed to ensure no one is wearing one. Not that we have ever had the problem before, but it is a preventative measure to ensure we are not allowing someone or something that shouldn't be on those ships. Now, let's get started, shall we?"

We spend the rest of the class practicing, trying to cast glamour on ourselves. With the help of the crystal, many of us can do small things, including myself. I turn the tips of my hair blue, and despite struggling to remove it for the rest of the class, I was able to do so. As far as classes go, this might be one of the ones I do better in. The playing field is very equal in regards to none of the first years will have any prior practice.

After the third class of the day, it was lunch in the great hall. It was similar to the same setting as dinner the previous day, but instead of soups and roasted meats, it was an offering of sandwiches and varying fruits. The fruits were similar to what I ate in the Other Realm, but there were some that I had never seen or heard of before. I wasn't quite ready to experiment with those.

"How'd your affinity class go, Sage?" Thalia asks.

"I couldn't cast anything. I don't know what I'm doing wrong. The professor was nice about it, but there's a lot riding on me getting things right."

"Did he recommend a tutor yet?" Aurora asks as she plops a berry into her mouth.

"Yeah, I'm going to look after classes end."

"I think it's a good idea," Thalia says. "Needing help isn't the worst thing. A lot of first-years need help with something. The whole reason the tutoring program even exists is so we can get the help we need and understand our magic better."

"I wish we could help, but we only know how to tap into our abilities. We won't know about others until later in the year when we get to learn if we are capable of more than our main affinity."

"I'm sure I will get it down eventually," I say as I pick apart my sandwich. I lost my appetite sometime during the conversation.

"Shall we go find our seats in our next class?" Thalia asks. Aurora and I both nod.

My fourth class was one I was both dreading and anticipating at the same time—my history of the Dark Ascension class. I dreaded it because I knew I would get pointed stares during the lessons, but I was anticipating it because it was an opportunity to learn more about my family and their actions. Assuming the lore is accurate, it's hard to tell what the biased writings were when you weren't a part of the entire history.

The professor of this class was relatively young and has a very kind-looking face. I know the fae live very long lives, but based on her age, she couldn't be much older than the mother who birthed me. Her hair is a light brown with golden highlights and is pulled back, but two long strands frame her face. She wears glasses, but I remember seeing her in the great hall without them. They might just be used for reading; I also note that fae are not entirely perfect beings. I wonder what other hindrances we can have.

"Hello, class. My name is Professor West. Unlike previous teachers, I will not be providing a syllabus. We are studying history here; there's no need for such things. There will be no end-of-the-year exam covering all that you learned because I know beyond a shadow of a doubt you will remember everything we study in this room. The actions against our people are appalling and unacceptable. Today, you will be provided an overview of what to expect to learn about in this classroom, and for the rest of the year, we will be diving deep into what happened."

I can feel the eyes staring at me by the people sitting behind me. I'm sure if it wouldn't get the attention of the professor and potentially get them in trouble, the rest of the eyes would be on me, too. Thalia reaches under the table and grasps my hand in a show of support. The whole realm knows this is a part of my family's history and I am sure some have made assumptions about my family's role. They also know that my being here means war will return. I will be judged at every turn, every action I make. People will be looking for the slightest excuse that I am not the savior of the realm in an effort to prevent the war and throw me to the feet of Gaiwen.

"Go ahead and open up your texts to the first page. This will cover the first recorded incident. Some like to say that the Dark Ascension began 24 years ago, but his dark deeds began well before that. Your job for this week is to read until you reach the Drifton chapters. We will discuss it next week." Professor West proceeds to sit at her desk and does not acknowledge anyone for the rest of the class.

I'm a little disappointed. I thought there would have been more of an in-depth type of learning regarding this. Instead, we are supposed to read from a text and then discuss the readings. I don't get far in the text before class ends. It was mentally exhausting. I would rather listen to Kira go on about varying types of plants around the world. I did get as far as reading about Gaiwen hiring bandits to hurt people in the surrounding area. It was some ploy to force people to pay him for his healer services.

The final class of the day is Intro to Beasts. This takes place outside, near the back of the academy. There's a slight breeze in the air, which helps with the amount of sweat I have from all this walking. The back courtyard of the castle has a large covered structure with only one back wall, and the rest is open arches. There are some tables, but no chairs. However, the professor is not standing in the structure; she is over near some pens where some small creatures are residing.

This professor is the oldest I have met. Her hair is a deep gray, but her roots are intensely white. Her eyes are such a light shade of blue that, honestly, it looks a little like she doesn't have any irises at all. I think if it weren't for the kind smile, she gives every student as they approach and the smooth sound of her voice, I would be a little creeped out.

"Greetings students. I hope your day of academics has been treating you well. My name is Professor Moore. Welcome to your first-ever beast's class. We will start this course by reviewing the more docile creatures you might have encountered if Alandria was in its full glory. Right now, the only way to find these creatures is through the school or one of the various animal sanctuaries. It's no secret that Alandria has fallen under hard times, and we have not had much success in restoring it. That does not mean we are without hope. I hope that some of you might decide that taking care of these innocent creatures and helping assure them a secure future might be for you. Please come closer to the pen and look at the first beasts you'll be learning to care for, the iguas."

The class moves closer to the pen to see what the creatures look like. They are about the size of a standard house cat with elongated ears and extremely fuzzy bodies. They stand on two hind legs and have long-looking toes. At their rear is a tail similar to a cat, and the upper torso has arms with paws attached. Upon closer inspection, those paws do have thumbs.

"As you can tell, there is a decent amount of iguas in this pen. We have been working diligently to restore their population, and so far, we have been quite successful. We hope for the same success with other creatures and to rehabilitate them into their environments once the blight has been dealt with. Does anyone have any questions so far?"

Anton raises his hand. The professor nods for him to speak. "This class is called Intro to Beasts, so are we only learning about docile creatures, or will we learn defense against them as well? I understand the importance of rebuilding species, but there's still danger out there. The shadow creatures are still a real threat even if we haven't been actively attacked." Students speak in hushed murmurs I cannot make out.

"Calm down, everyone, he said nothing wrong. Yes, we will be covering defense. We will be easing our way into the harsher beasts. We have all year to go over this. Any other questions."

No one else poses a question, so Professor Moore has us bathing and grooming the iguas until the school day ends.

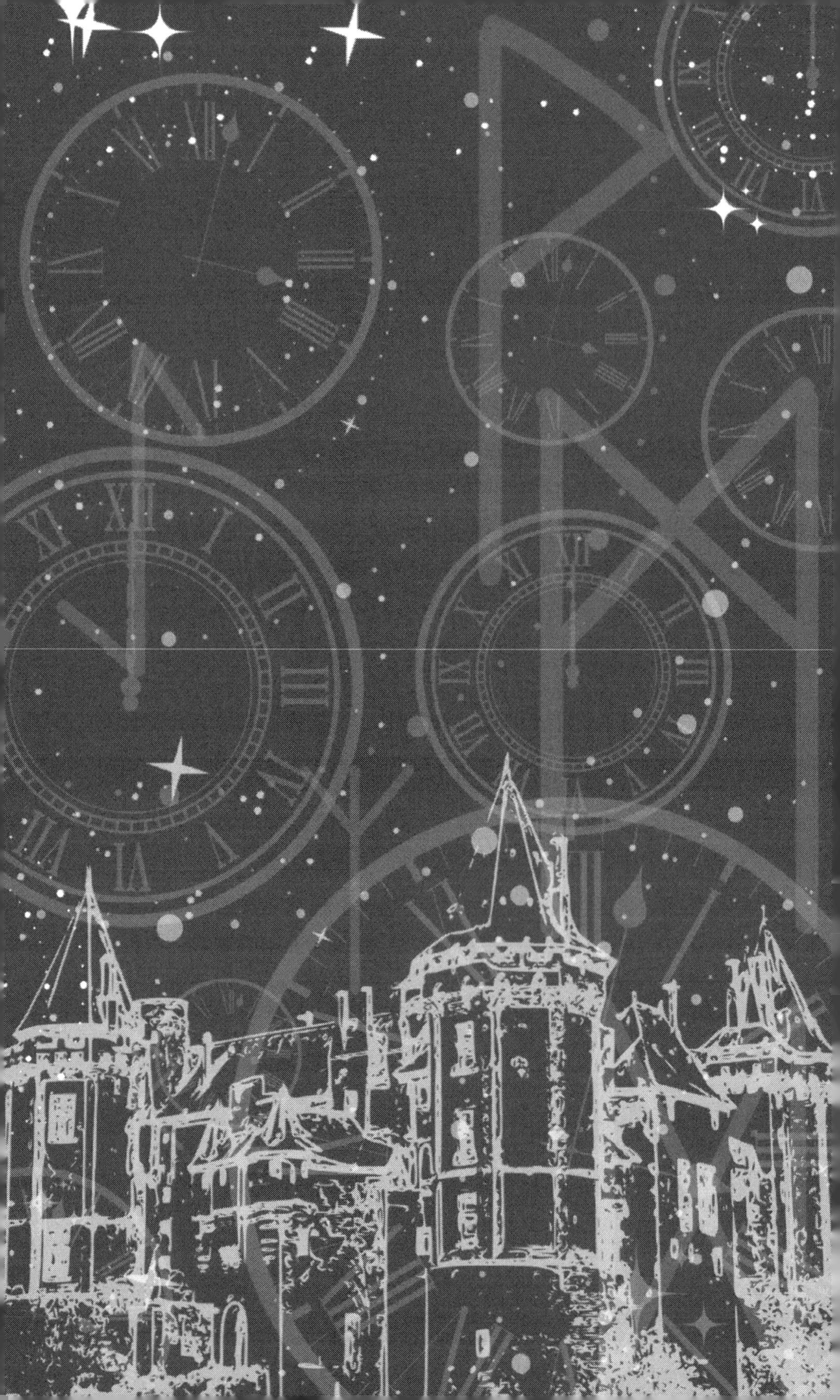

Chapter Fifteen
Sage

After class, students are free to spend the day how they wish, within the academy grounds. Eventually, students will have access to the capital, but we are far from that. As I am only a first year, it won't be happening except on holidays. In year two, we learn better ways to defend ourselves by using more than just our affinity. Not that there isn't extracurriculars to also learn forms of defense. I'm viewing the notice for what is offered outside of the classroom. There are self-defense classes, weapons training, baking, riding lessons, painting, and the list goes on and on, offering a variety of choices. I have no doubt it's to encourage people to take up something, anything, to keep them from being bored. Boredom can lead to people doing reckless things.

"It's safe to go look over the advisors list now," Thalia whispers after everyone else has cleared away to either find something to do or join an activity they found suitable for themselves. "It's okay to need help sometimes, Sage; you don't have to be embarrassed about it."

"I know, Tal, I just-" I let out a deep breath. "Everyone already seems to have certain opinions of me, and I don't know; the idea of showing them they are right about me-"

"First off, they are not right about you, so you stop that way of thinking right now. Second off, we all start somewhere. You might not have grown up the same way the rest of us did, but that doesn't make your challenges any easier. They would do well to remember the help they needed when they were first learning and teach them to humble themselves. I'm going to drop off my stuff in our room before I check out rune-scribing."

"Let me know if you like it. I would eventually like to join in on something, but I think I need to focus on my studies for a while." Thalia nods before walking away.

I look at the list of advisors. The notice crosses out the names when they are fully booked, and every name seems to have a full roster already. I should have checked sooner; I tip my head back and refuse to accept what the notice says, taking one last look. I don't know if it's to my luck or horror, but a new name has appeared: Hassian Blackwell. I know damn well that name wasn't there before. "Absolutely not," I say, backing away from the notice only to bump into something hard, someone hard.

"Hello, princess," the voice of both my dreams and my nightmares says in that deliciously deep husky voice.

I spin around so fast. "I was just leaving."

"No, you weren't. Did you think I didn't see you reading the notice?"

"I know damn well your name wasn't on that list when I first checked. How did your name get on the list so fast?"

"You admit you were looking then?"

"Not for your name."

He laughs, "but you noticed its absence.

I groan. "I'm leaving."

"You need the help; just accept it."

"Not from you."

"Why not?" he raises his brows. "Is it because of last night?"

I can feel my cheeks flush, and I stutter over my response. "N-no. I just don't think you'd be a good fit."

"Is it my size that worries you, princess?" The utter shock of what he said has my jaw dropping. "Judging by your reaction, I think it's just about right."

"That's exactly the problem right there," I let out without taking a single breath. My face is so red, not from anger. Nope, I am thinking about this man in ways my ancestors would be ashamed of.

He laughs. "Judging by my name being crossed off that notice, you've already agreed to this. We will meet in the library after dinner; I have weapons training before then, so it's the only time I'll have to spend with you. Unless, of course, you would like to join me. I'd much like the sight of you on your knees before me."

I practically choke out the words, "See you in the library," before running anywhere but near him. I keep walking until I find myself near the South Tower. I hear screams of frustration coming from one of the doors that's slightly ajar. Curiosity gets the best of me, and I peek into the room. I see Sebille working with a professor I haven't met before.

"Sebille, you need to practice control. Your rage is fueling your element and not in a good way."

"How can I not be angry when she's here?"

"She had nothing to do with what happened to your family, Sebille. She's not her grandfather, and you would do well to remember that." Fire ascends to the ceiling and spreads like wildfire in response to the professor's words. I watch as they throw their arms up, dousing the flames and water drips down to the floor below. "Sebille," the professor scolds.

"Can't I just get a new room?" I realize they are speaking about me, and I retreat. Why does Sebille hate me so much? What did my grandfather do to her family? I know I have made a colossal mistake listening in. I need to make things right with

Sebille somehow, but I don't want to push her. Is she working with a professor instead of a tutor because she can't control her rage?

After dinner, I meet with Hassian in the library. He's not wearing his affinities colors; he's dressed relatively casually. Well, as casual as he will probably ever look. He's wearing black bottoms that leave so little to my imagination and a white tunic top unbuttoned down a decent length of his chest. His fingers are adorned with many rings, some with what look to be rune inscriptions. I don't dare ask what they mean and give him the gloating factor of knowing that I might care what he thinks.

"You're late," he says as I sit down across the table from him.

"I'm literally on time."

"On-time is late; you should be here earlier. I should see you as soon as I enter this room."

"That's ridiculous. I'm not cutting my dinner and conversation with my friends short when it's not necessary."

He runs his hands along the slight stubble that's grazing his chin. "Fine."

"Good."

"Let's get this lesson started."

"Fine by me."

I see a quick smile flash across his features. "What part of casting is hardest for you?"

"I don't know. All of it? I can't do it, at least not of my own free will." I thought I would feel awful after saying those words out loud, but now that it's out there and said and more specifically to him, I feel better.

He leans down, and I watch his muscles flex beneath his shirt as he picks something up off the floor. Oh, no, not something, he brought a plant. "I don't have the same affinity as you since I am an air-based fae. That doesn't mean I cannot walk you through this."

"Okay. How do I do this?" I ask. I know he intends to get me to make it bloom, but I don't know how to get to that point.

"Close your eyes; I need you to close your mind off to everything but that flower, the sound of my voice, and my touch."

"Your touch?"

"Just listen." I release a breath and close my eyes. "Good. Now-" a pause and a warm hand slips over my belly. "Find the core power inside of you. For myself, it's like I'm gliding down a tall cliff side, trusting in the leap."

I search my mind for what I could be looking for. I think of the trees, the grass, flowers, vines, and anything that speaks to me as something in nature until I am transported to a beautiful garden in my mind. I walk toward the center, where I see a pillar of vines. Reaching out, I touch it and watch as the vines move to cover my hand. I imagine the flower blooming and fill it with intent. I open my eyes and release the hold on the vines at the same time. I see the flower in full bloom.

"Good girl," Hassian says, releasing his hand from me. At the same instant, the flower closes its bloom before shriveling up and dying.

"Apparently not," I mumble.

Hassian smiles at me. "It just means we have to work on your focus, and I have a few ideas for that in mind, but I'll save those ideas for later. I want to see what my princess can do." He walks over to me and grips my chin, angling me toward him again, only this time he does not lean in to kiss me. He looks me dead in the eyes and says, "Like I said yesterday, you'll have to earn it, princess." He releases my chin and leaves.

This man will be my undoing.

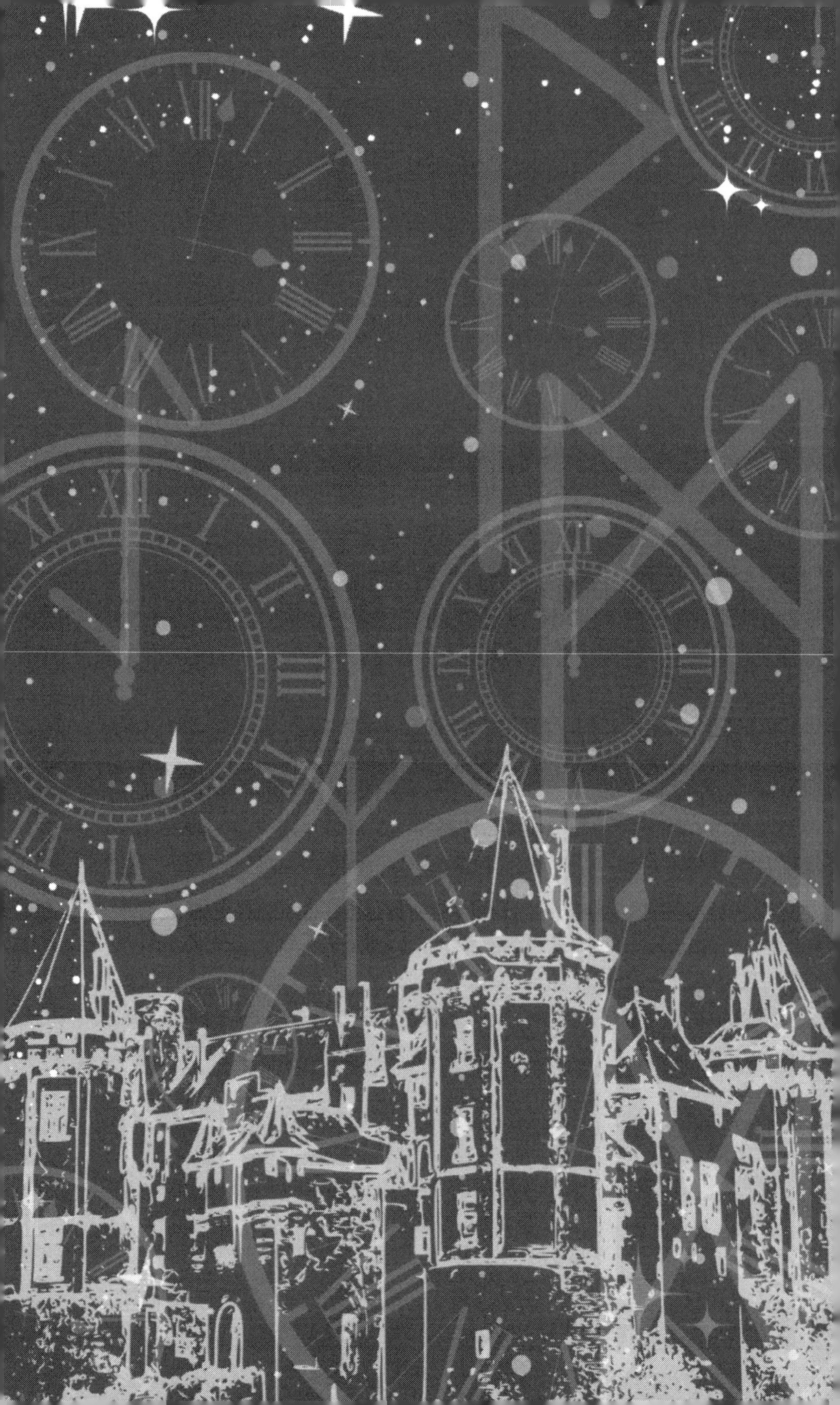

Chapter Sixteen
Sage

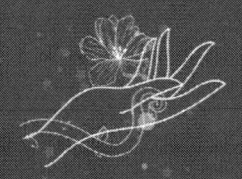

After the library, I practically run my way back to my room. Thalia isn't back home yet, so I grab some sleeping clothes and head to the bathing area to take full advantage of the healing properties of the water. My body is just continuously sore from all this running around. I wonder at what point the muscle soreness ends. I see it's busy when I make it to the shower room tonight. I did hesitate a little this time when I was washing my hair, thinking back to Hassian's comment about it being plant cum. Glancing around, I see everyone using it, so I don't think he was being serious. By the time I am done with my shower and return to the room, Thalia is back.

"Did you go and see Griyf?" I ask.

"Yeah, he is really enjoying himself out there, but having him not as close isn't as easy as I thought it would be. It's so much different having to walk across an entire school ground than just opening my bedroom window and seeing him."

"Does imprinting alter any of those feelings?"

"A little, yeah. I find myself wanting to be near him and can tell if something is stressing him out. Did you find a tutor?"

"Yeah," I say. I can feel my cheeks heating.

"Who is it?"

"Hassian," I practically whisper in reply.

"No fucking way. Speaking of, you still owe me the details of what happened last night."

A knock sounds on our bedroom door. "Come in," I say hoping it'll be someone who'll end this conversation; it's not. It's Aurora.

"Sage's face is all red. What are we discussing?" Aurora asks.

"Hassian," Thalia grins as I glare at her.

"Did I miss the story we were owed from earlier?"

"No, you're just on time."

"You two are unbearable," I groan.

"Come on, Sage, spill."

I proceed to give them a play-by-play of what happened in the showers our first night here. By the time I'm done, my face isn't the only one that's beet red.

"Oh, he is so into you," Aurora says.

"Definitely," Thalia agrees.

I can't help the grin that crosses my face because I am very much into this man. What I desire in him, well, those thoughts are still unclear. Do I like him because he teases me at every turn? Do I like him because he notices things others aren't paying attention to? He didn't have to offer his tutor services to me, but he did.

The girls and I continue talking until we hear Sebille slam the door to our dorm closed. "I guess that's my cue to head to bed. It was lovely chatting with you all. Maybe one day we can get Sebille to be able to stand our company and join us."

Aurora waves to Thalia and I before heading to her room. I decide not to head to bed immediately but to start writing in one of my journals. I had many positive experiences on my first day and want to be able to recall them for my future inevitable breakdowns. I can feel my eyes growing heavy with the exhaustion. It's getting late, but I decide to write a letter to Kira to let her know how my day went before I allow myself some rest. I will send it off to her in the morning.

Once I am done writing my letter, I melt some of my wax stick with a match since the everflames don't produce heat. I let a few drops drip onto the envelope before pressing my ring into it and marking it with my seal. I fall asleep to the thoughts of my old friends and how their first day of school in the Other Realm went. Did they have a good day? Did they make new friends? I like to think that they did.

Morning comes, and I am a bit groggy. I may have stayed up a little too late between talking with the girls and writing. I quickly dress in a pencil skirt and pair it with a cardigan and tank top. I still don't know how to manage my hair, so I put half of it up before making my way to the great hall to grab something quick to eat. I opt for a Brumbleberry Puff, which is probably one of my new favorite treats. I wouldn't say I love it more than cheesecake, but it is a close second. I take my pastry to go as I make my way to the aviary to send off my letter.

The aviary is located in the lower section of the bell tower. The room is mainly lit by natural lighting coming in from the windows, most of which are open. Crows litter the window sills, and the branches of a very massive tree that spreads throughout most of the bell tower. I am noticing a common thing in this realm: you will find a lot of nature inside and out.

"Need to send off a letter?" an older woman asks as she rounds the tree carrying a basket of varying fruit and seeds.

"Yes. How do I do that?"

"You just hand it over to me and tell me where it needs to go."

I hand her over the letter. "This is going to Kira Maye." I proceed to give her Kira's address.

"I will send it off with one of the birds soon."

"Thank you," I say as I leave and make my way to Herbology.

Herbology was more about learning varying types of plants by looking at charts. Professor Auhdaye is doing her best to drill the names and benefits of multiple plants before we set foot in her garden. I get it; I wouldn't want some first-year student damaging my hard work, either.

Professor Dublin's class went a little better. He again wanted to check the progress of our blooms. It wasn't as dramatic as day one. He had individual planters set on the tables. I am pretty sure yesterday was just his way of showing off. If I were in his position, I would have done something similar if I had the capabilities.

I think back on what I could have done wrong in my lesson last night with Hassian, and I just cannot narrow down the issue. I keep tapping into the vines in my mind, repeating the process, being more assertive in my intent, but I get the same result. I am so frustrated I could scream. If I were a better person, I would accept my progress for what it is, but I am not. I feel this almost-aggressive desire to prove myself.

Aggression was not the feeling to feel because I turned my plant from something of beauty to something born of anger. The long bud turns green and elongates into a vine-like tendril with piercing thorns. It's angry, and it wants to hurt something. Unfortunately, I am terrible at magic, have no control, and don't know how to stop it. It shoots its vines toward me, digging its thorns into my flesh, pulling and pulling. I let out a scream, and Professor Dublin yells for the class to clear out as he tries to calm my angry creation.

"What happened, Sage? You were making progress?" he asks as he taps into his magic and calms the vines until they revert back to the flower bud.

"I don't know. I was just feeling angry."

You have to learn to control your emotions when casting magic. What caused you anger?" he asks. His voice isn't condescending or judging, and I can tell when he interacts with his students that he genuinely cares for them.

"I guess I just feel this need to, this desire to get this right, and I am angry with myself for failing to get it right."

"You are not failing. You are learning, and with great stride, might I add. When I was younger it took me weeks to get to the point that you are now."

"Probably because you were a child," I mumble.

"That's the thing I need you to understand. Magic has no continual growth in strength; you are born with all you will have. The only thing you can improve is the amount of time you can wield that power before you need to rest. What I knew as a child when I was first training is far more than you did. Some of your casting is just a little off, and you must work to find your groove. My advice to you is to keep working with your advisor. They seem to be a great resource for you."

"I will."

"As for your next steps, I need you to see the school healer. You are bleeding all over that perfectly good desk. Go on, I'll get this cleaned up. If I have any stragglers outside, tell them to find something to do until their next period." He hands me a cloth from his robes and sends me off.

I walk out the door, and sure as hell, everyone is standing outside waiting to hear what happened. "I'm going to the school healer and am to tell you all to spend the rest of the class doing something productive."

The group breaks up, and I go searching for the healer, but I am completely lost. I'm glad I have the cloth, or I would be making whoever cleans the floor quite angry. I'm checking the plaques on the door, not paying attention to where I am going, and I walk right into someone.

"Let me see," it's an order from none other than Hassian.

"It's nothing. How did you even know about this the periods not even over?"

"Let me see." he enunciates every single word like he's holding back the urge to strangle me if I don't do as he says.

"Alright. Fine, just calm down." I peel back the cloth, hissing as it pulls against the dried blood.

He pulls my wrist closer to him so he can get a better look. "You were reckless. You need to be more careful. Why aren't you with the healer?"

I yank my arm away and cover the cut back up. "I didn't do this on purpose. I didn't even know I could. As to why I am not with a healer, I have no idea where I'm going. In case you couldn't tell by my stumbling into you, I was in a state of shock. Forgive me for not thinking in my moment of panic to ask for directions."

"Come with me." Again, it's not a request but a command. He spins me around back the way I came and past a few doors. He knocks on the door, and there is a plaque that clearly says healer. I don't know if I can get any more embarrassed at this rate.

"Enter!" yells a female voice. Hassian pushes the door open and leads me inside. "Hassian, I know very well you are not a first-year. Why are you walking around with one and not in class?"

"I was just using the restroom, and she was lost looking for you. I'm going back now." That was very obviously a lie, but based on the look on her face, she didn't think so. Apparently the whole fae can't lie is not truth. At least not in Alandria.

"Very well, be off, back to class. I will tend to miss?"

"Sage. Sage Torrin."

"Oh, I understand now. She's safe with me, Hassian. Now go." He looks like he wants to say something else but thinks better of it and leaves. "Now you, tell me what happened."

I recant the story of my pitiful error while she cleans out my gash. It's bigger than I thought, and she informs me it will take stitches. There's no quick healing remedy for wounds, not even in a magical world. She gives me a salve I am to put on in the morning and at bedtime, as well as if I experience any itching throughout the day. It will minimize any potential scarring, which she is almost certain I will have a faint one at the very least.

In class with Professor Keevah, we worked on the same thing as yesterday. Thalia had questions about what happened to me, and I recanted the story to her. She was not nearly as panicked as Hassian. I still don't understand why he reacted the way he did, let alone how he even knew what happened. Based on my experiences with him so far, I doubt I will ever know the answer to that.

I am quickly learning that the meal schedule plays out the same. I decided to just alternate my sandwich options every lunch. Today, I had something that looked similar to ham on my sandwich; ham, it was not. Thalia's response was to just giggle whenever I asked what manner of meat it was. Aurora wasn't at lunch today, so I couldn't ask her what it was. I will find out eventually.

When it comes to Professor West's class, we just spent the few hours with her continuing to read from our textbooks. It would seem she doesn't like to discuss things during class. According to what I read over in my text today, Gaiwen was experimenting on the people coming to him for help. He was caught by the wife of one of his patients, and he murdered both of them. It was said to be the first report of his strange behavior before he fled the town with his wife.

I don't understand why he didn't hide the bodies and claim not to know their whereabouts. It says in the text he left the bodies there and everything in the shop behind. As someone so motivated by money to hire the bandits in the first place, I am just confused. I am also dreading the day I have to face him from the details of the murder alone. How am I supposed to face someone this terrifying when I am literally teetering on the edge of a mental breakdown daily?

    I could not wait for the bell in the tower to toll, signifying it was time for our final period. Professor Moore's class went by with a breeze, both literally and figuratively. We spent more time discussing the care of Iguas. Today's class focused on the grooming aspects of their care and the benefits of saving and recycling their fur. According to her, the fur can be woven into fabric to make cloths for bandages and clothes. She goes on about the topic for the entire duration of the class. The iguas I am brushing out puffs up whenever the professor says the words useful or beneficial.

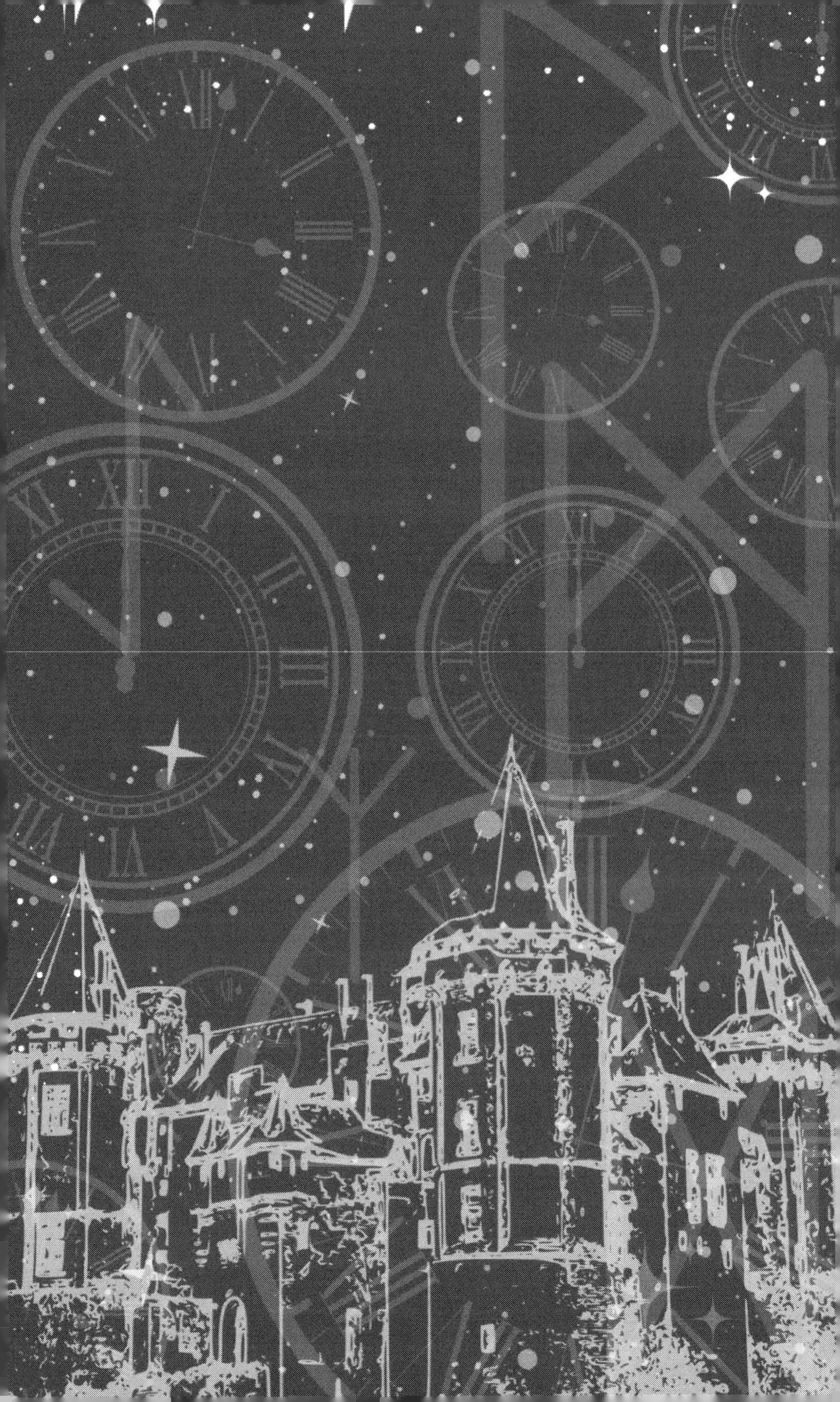

Chapter Seventeen
Sage

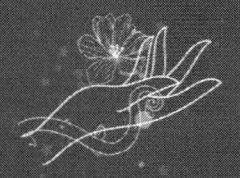

I leave dinner to make my way to the library to wait for Hassian and my lesson to begin. I find him sitting at the table when I make my way through the door. "Don't you dare say that I am late. I made sure to leave early just to beat you here. Do you even eat dinner?"

Hassian laughs. His laugh is so deliciously deep that I want to hear it over and over again. "I eat. Don't worry, princess. I'm glad you are choosing to take these lessons seriously."

I scoff. "Taking them seriously? Okay, I am never coming early again."

"I would hope not; I like to draw it out." FUCK. This man.

"Stop that." He laughs. I need to sit down before I crumble to the floor from my wobbly knees.

"I spoke with your professor to try to figure out what happened with your casting today. You have anger issues, princess?"

"I do not-" Oh, this man is baiting me.

"I can't say I thought you would create a volatile and dangerous plant, but you did cast something that held up more than a few seconds."

"I can't tell if you are trying to insult me or if this is a poor attempt to compliment me."

"A little of both, I suppose," he says with a grin. "You did good, princess, even if it wasn't what was supposed to happen. That was some powerful magic. Professor Dublin practically drained his reservoir to contain it."

"He what?" It was that powerful?

"That's why he had you send the students away instead of back into the classroom; there was no way he could contain another incident if there were one. Truly impressive."

"I didn't mean to burden him that way." I wipe my palms on my skirt; I can feel them getting sweaty as my anxiety starts to kick in.

"Don't feel bad about that princess. He isn't upset over it. If anything, it gave him more hope of what you can accomplish when you are able to control it."

"Great, can we start our lesson now?" I ask.

"No, you were injured today, and until you are healed, we will not be casting. I do have something else planned, but first, let me see your hand." I offer my hand to him. He traces his fingers along the stitching. "This looks irritated. Where's the salve she gave you?" I dig through my bag until I find it. His hand is extended toward me, waiting for me to give it to him.

"I can apply it myself," I say. I uncap the lid and try to pull my hand away, but his grip remains firm. He reaches over and grabs the salve, dipping two fingers into the container. They come out with a decent amount of the salve, and he strokes my stitching. When he's done, he reaches into his jacket and pulls out a cloth, wrapping it around my wound.

"Now grab your things, princess; we have plans tonight."

Hassian's plan lead us outside. I guess walking around the school all day isn't enough walking. I groan.

"What's wrong, princess? Am I boring you?"

"No, I just don't understand why we must walk around. Don't your muscles ache?"

"I wanted to show you something. How long have your muscles been bothering you?"

"Since coming here, I don't know. I haven't had to do this much walking before."

"You've been using the water in the school for some time; you shouldn't be this sore."

"It's fine. I'm just adapting, but seriously, I could use a break."

He stops walking. I think we are about to sit on the perfectly nice bench nearby, but I am so very wrong. Hassian scoops me up into his arms and carries me down the pathway.

"Put me down," I demand.

"I will when we get there." I try to fight and break out of his grip, but this man is strong. I can tell he trains a lot. Eventually I give up fighting and relax into him. It's not much longer when we come to a stop, and he sets me down. We are somewhere in the courtyard where there isn't as much foliage and a blanket lying across the lawn. "Have a seat, princess." He points to the blanket. I don't fight it and sit down.

"Why are we here?" I ask.

Hassian lays down beside me and motions for me to do the same, offering his arm for my head to rest. "It's the Solaris event tonight. They happen every few months, and I figured since I can't train you, you can learn more about our realm."

I accept his offer to lie beside him. I go to readjust myself from sitting up to laying down and despite thinking I am a decent distance away still; I am not. Instead of being at least a few inches from that ridiculously perfect body of his, I am instead pressed right up against him. I don't bother readjusting, and he doesn't make any complaints. "How soon until it starts?"

"A few more minutes," his voice vibrates through my body from our proximity.

I wait, practically holding my breath until I see it. The sky turns a brilliant blue-green, and stars shoot across the night sky. It's truly incredible and I begin to wonder if it's appropriate that I am here with my tutor. I push the thoughts to the back recesses of my mind and lay there watching the stars dance across the sky. The heat of his body against mine is soothing, and at this moment, I feel completely relaxed and at ease. I fight against my eyelids as they wage a war with me for sleep. This is a battle I eventually lose.

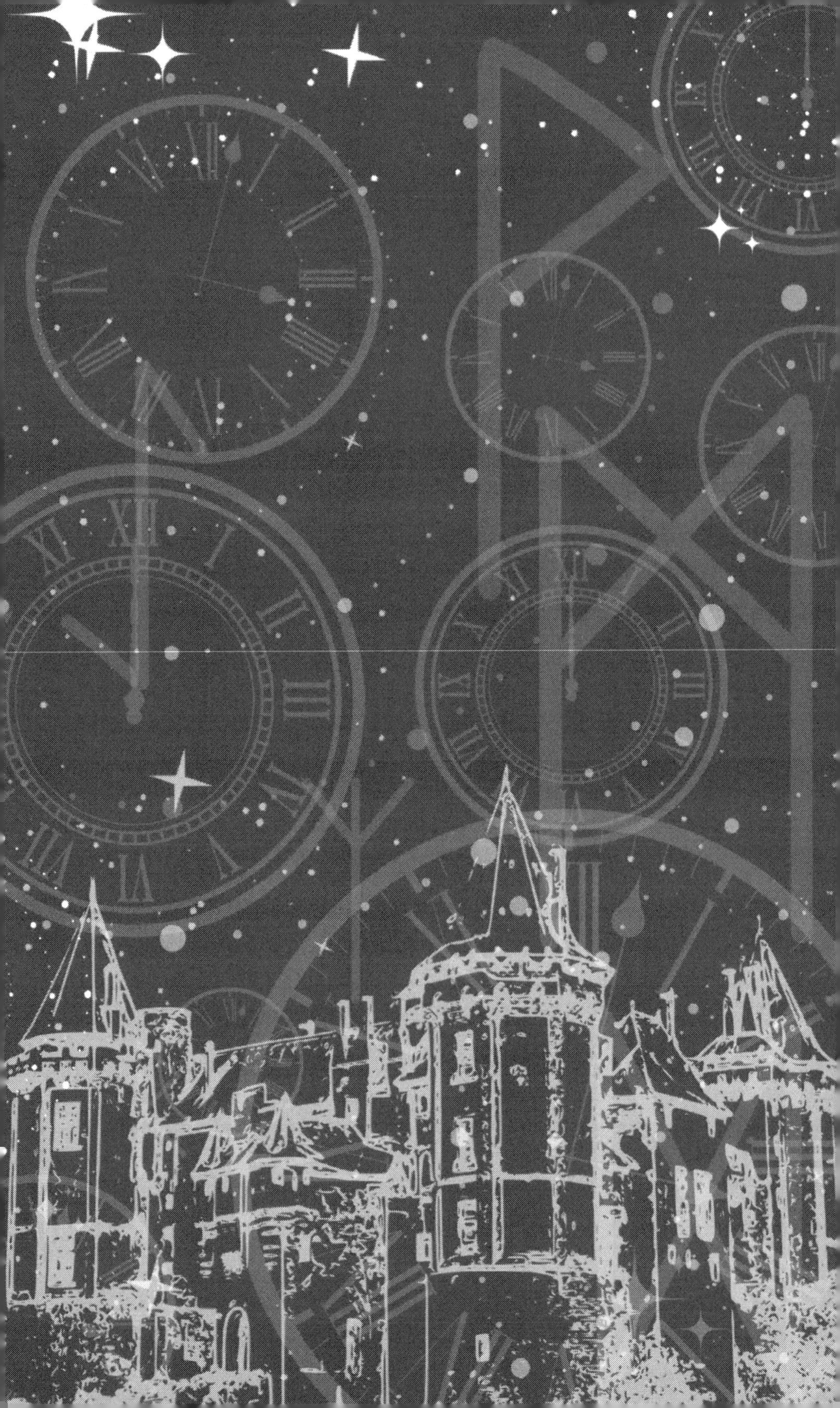

Chapter Eighteen
Sage

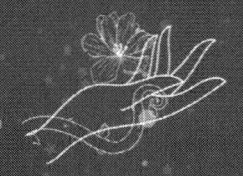

The fall season passes by in a blur and is nearing its end. I am getting better at magic, and I can keep hold of my bloom much longer now despite them always dying. I feel bad that I am destroying so much of nature. I am still not sure where I am messing up with my casting, but if I am being honest, I enjoy the time I get to spend with Hassian. His charm is undeniable, and every time he touches me, it's electric. It was not my intention to come to this school to develop feelings of any kind for anyone, but I think I may not have a choice when it comes to him. Aurora, Thalia, and I have become inseparable throughout the fall season. Sebille and I are still a work in progress. Every time I try to speak with her, she makes herself scarce.

"Quiet everyone, please," Headmaster Brawnmire addresses everyone in the great hall. I am sure some of you have heard by now that the winter Solstice ball is right around the corner." Excited chattering continues. "Please, just let me get through this announcement." The room goes quiet again, and he continues. "It is customary that there are no academic studies the week before the ball. This allows each and every one of you to go into the city to find the proper dress and allows the many tailors time to make suitable adjustments if need be. That being said, you are still expected to return to the academy by nightfall each night. If you would like to participate in decorating for the ball, sign-ups are on the notice board. Okay, you may resume your excitement."

The noise in the room instantly grows loud as everyone chatters about what they will wear and who they will go with. I hear a few people mention Hassian's name, and I can feel the rage and jealousy settling in. What if he goes with someone else? I know he's just my tutor, but I want to believe it's more than that. Every interaction I have with him feels like there is more meaning to it. He cared enough to return me to my room when I fell asleep watching the stars with him. I doubt tutors go out of their way like that.

"Are you thinking about Hassian?" Thalia asks.

"Only every minute of every day, it feels like. What is wrong with me? I had never desired anyone in the Other Realm."

"Maybe the mention of the arranged marriage you would have had put the idea into your head?"

"No, I don't think that's it. I desire his touch constantly. I go weak in the knees from a finger graze."

"Maybe you are fated?"

"Wait, that's legitimately a real thing?"

"Yeah. It's kind of like the imprinting, in a way. The connection could be there, and it's trying to get the both of you to accept it. Who knows. You two did have an interesting first meeting."

"I could totally see that being the case," Aurora says.

"We are always talking about Hassian. What about you guys? Do you have your eyes set on anyone?"

"Well, there is someone. You've met her already, actually," Thalia says. I wonder if she's finally going to open up about Meera. I've had my inklings about her since the first day.

"Her? Wait who? Tell me right now. Wait, how long has this been going on?" Aurora asks.

"Spill. Now. Please," I demand, taking a bite of my dessert.

"It's Meera. We have been kind of seeing each other for about a month."

"A whole month, and you didn't tell me, Thalia! I'm hurt," Aurora feigns sadness.

"I knew it," I say. "I just didn't know you made it official yet. I called it from day one."

"I'm sorry, but I just didn't want to say anything until I knew for sure it was serious. Anton knew from the beginning, and apparently Sage."

"I will forgive you because he is your twin, but I can't believe you held out on me this long. Wait, serious? Like you already know?" Aurora has stopped eating, fully invested in this new found information.

"Well, I hope it's serious. We talk about the future a lot, and Griyf gets along well with her, and she's so good with him. She's been helpful with getting him comfortable in his flying. Because of her, he will be ready for saddle flying soon."

"I am so happy for you, Tal," I say.

"Speaking of, I am going to go formally ask her to the dance. You should go run along to your training with Hassian. Maybe he will ask you, or you might have to do the asking yourself." She winks and gives me a shove off the bench.

Hassian is waiting for me in the library before I arrive. "I'm surprised you were able to make it out of the great hall unscathed," I say to him as I plop down in my usual chair.

"Why's that?" he says with his mischievous grin. He knows damn well, and he wants me to play along.

"Oh, you know, from the multitude of women declaring that they will be your date to this ball."

"What if I say yes to one of them?"

I stiffen. "Do what you want." My mood turns sour. This is not how I wanted this conversation to go.

"Well, if it doesn't bother you, princess, then I will go secure my date right now."

"Fine. I'll be here when you are ready to start our lesson. Try not to take too long."

"Very well." Hassian gets up and leaves the library.

The ache in my heart hits me like a ton of bricks. This wasn't how it was supposed to go. Eventually, I get tired of the wait, of waiting for him to come back and break my heart when he gives me his stupid grin on how they said yes. I push my chair back away from the table and walk toward the rows of books. I hear the sound of the library door opening not long after.

"Sage?" Hassian's deep voice booms around the nearly empty library.

I wipe away the tears that slip out before I respond, "Over here!" I don't turn to look at him while I pretend to read a book on, I look at the title page, birds.

"Turn around, Sage," He demands.

"Hang on, this book just got to a good part." My hands grip the book painfully as he steps closer.

"I said," he pauses moving my hair away from my neck, "turn," he runs a finger down my exposed skin, "around."

I slam the book closed with more force than I intended before I shelve it and spin around. I was ready to yell at him for continuing to play this little game with me after he had just asked some poor, unsuspecting girl to the ball. What I turn around and see is nothing that I was expecting. Hassian changed into the same outfit from our very first night together in this room, and he's holding fresh-cut flowers. He no doubt offered something he deemed precious to him to convince the brownies to let him have them.

"Were you crying, princess?" he asks.

"No."

"Please don't lie to me." I feel a tear slide down my cheek, not from sadness this time but more from embarrassment. I thought he was going to ask someone else, but clearly, he was doing, well, this. He wipes away the tear that slid down my face. "Please don't cry over me, princess. Have I not made it obvious that you are mine from the day we met?"

"I distinctly remember a lot of teasing, not an admittance of possible feelings."

"Sage, I have spent every evening with you and you alone for months. I feel like I have made my intentions very, very clear," he whispers the last part into my ear, and I almost crumble. Are knees supposed to feel this weak?

"I think I am going to need some form of proof." He waves his hand, and I hear a chair slide across the floor to what sounds like the library door, blocking anyone from entering. Not that anyone ever comes up here in the evenings. "What are you-"

I'm cut off by his lips crashing into mine as he picks me up and slams my back into the bookshelf, causing books to fall around us. My legs wrap around his waist as I kiss him back, craving him. Wanting him. Needing him. It is a clashing of tongues and teeth as we let out everything we have been holding in for months. We are saying everything we so desperately wanted to speak to each other since the day we met. He unhooks my legs from around his waist, and I think he's about to set me on the ground when suddenly he's lifting me onto his shoulders.

I brace onto the bookshelf for dear life, knocking down more books in my haste as he slides my skirt up my thighs, exposing the lace of my underwear. He lets out a moan as his eyes lock onto the final piece, obstructing his path from where he truly wishes to go. "Hold on, princess," he says in a husky voice as he releases hold of one of my thighs to pull the lace out of the way. I let out a yelp, not from what is about to come, but because I am terrified this bookshelf is going to fall over on us.

In an instant, all fear is forgotten as my head slams back onto the now-barren shelf, as his tongue slides over the most sensitive part of me. For months, I have thought about what he would feel like. For months, I have painstakingly ignored my body's desires because I knew nothing would be able to satiate it more than him. I wrap my legs tighter around his head, urging him to get closer. I want more of him. I need more of him. One hand moves off my hip to wrap around to the other side as he frees up his other hand.

It's as if he's reading my mind as he plunges two of his fingers inside me, curling them as he increases his pace. I moan as pleasure hits my body in wave after wave. He continues the motion with his tongue and fingers, riding out the orgasm until my body stops quaking. He releases his fingers from inside me and slides me to the ground. He holds up his cum soaked fingers and looks at me. "Open," and so I do. He slowly sets his fingers in my mouth, avoiding putting his rings inside. "Lick it clean." I don't know what takes over me, but I do, staring into his eyes as I do it. When he is sure I have licked every remaining drop off his fingers, he pulls them out.

"Your rings," I say, realizing they are coated in, well, me.

"They're fine, princess," he says, not taking his eyes off me. He waves his hands again, and the books replace themselves on the shelves, and the fallen bouquet is back in his hands. "Now, before things got away from me, I was in the middle of trying to ask my princess if she would like to go to the winter solstice ball with me."

I take the bundle of flowers from his hands, "I would love that very much."

He takes my chin in his hands once again and kisses me deeply. "Good. You are a mine princess. I want you to remember that and not just because of some arrangement our parents made before you were born. You are mine because from the moment I saw you, I saw my heart, my soul, my future." He kisses me on the lips again. "I think it's getting late, princess. You better head to bed. After all, I hear you have to go dress shopping tomorrow."

I don't want to leave his arms, but he's right. It is late, and Aurora and Thalia are probably holed up waiting to see if he's going to be my date.

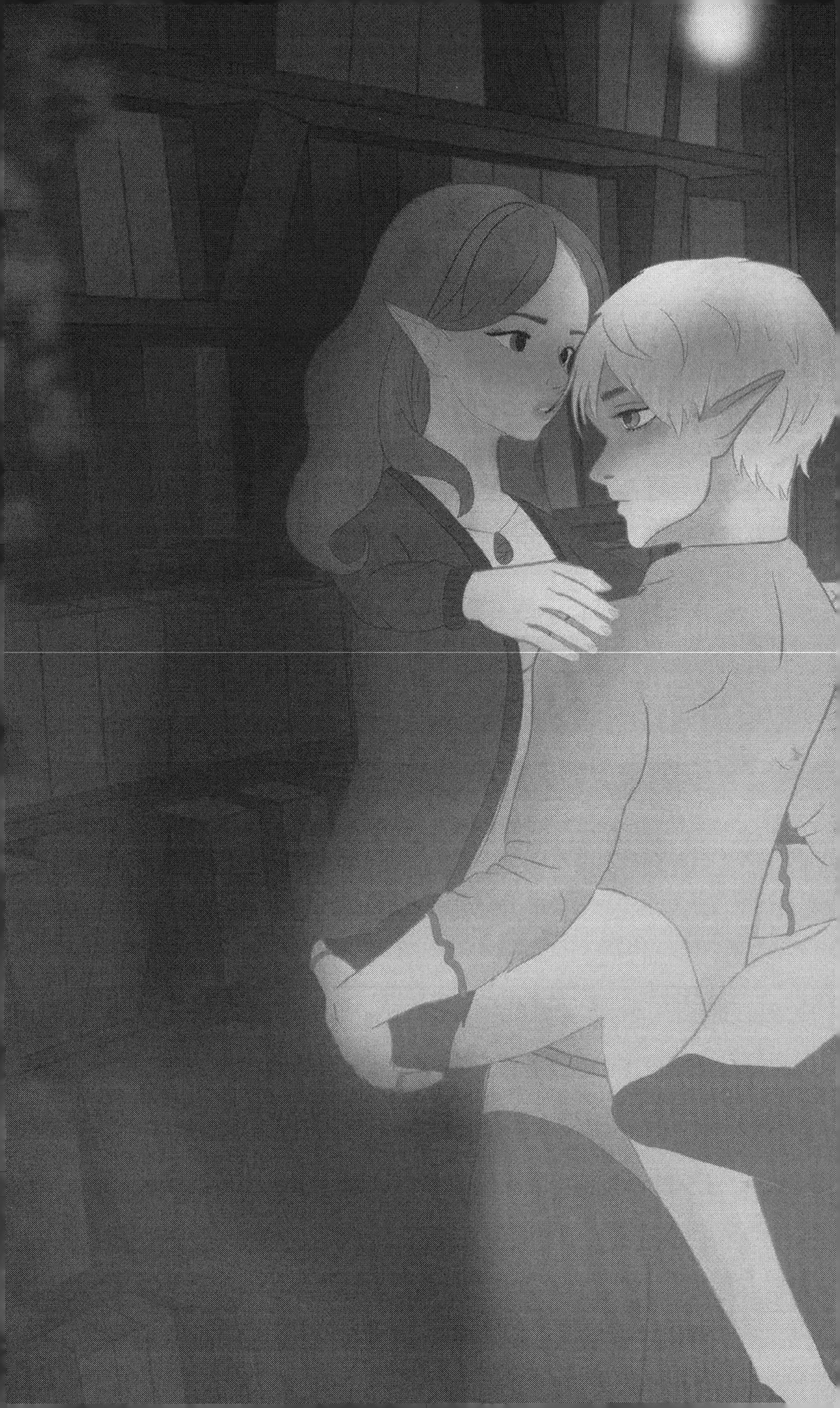

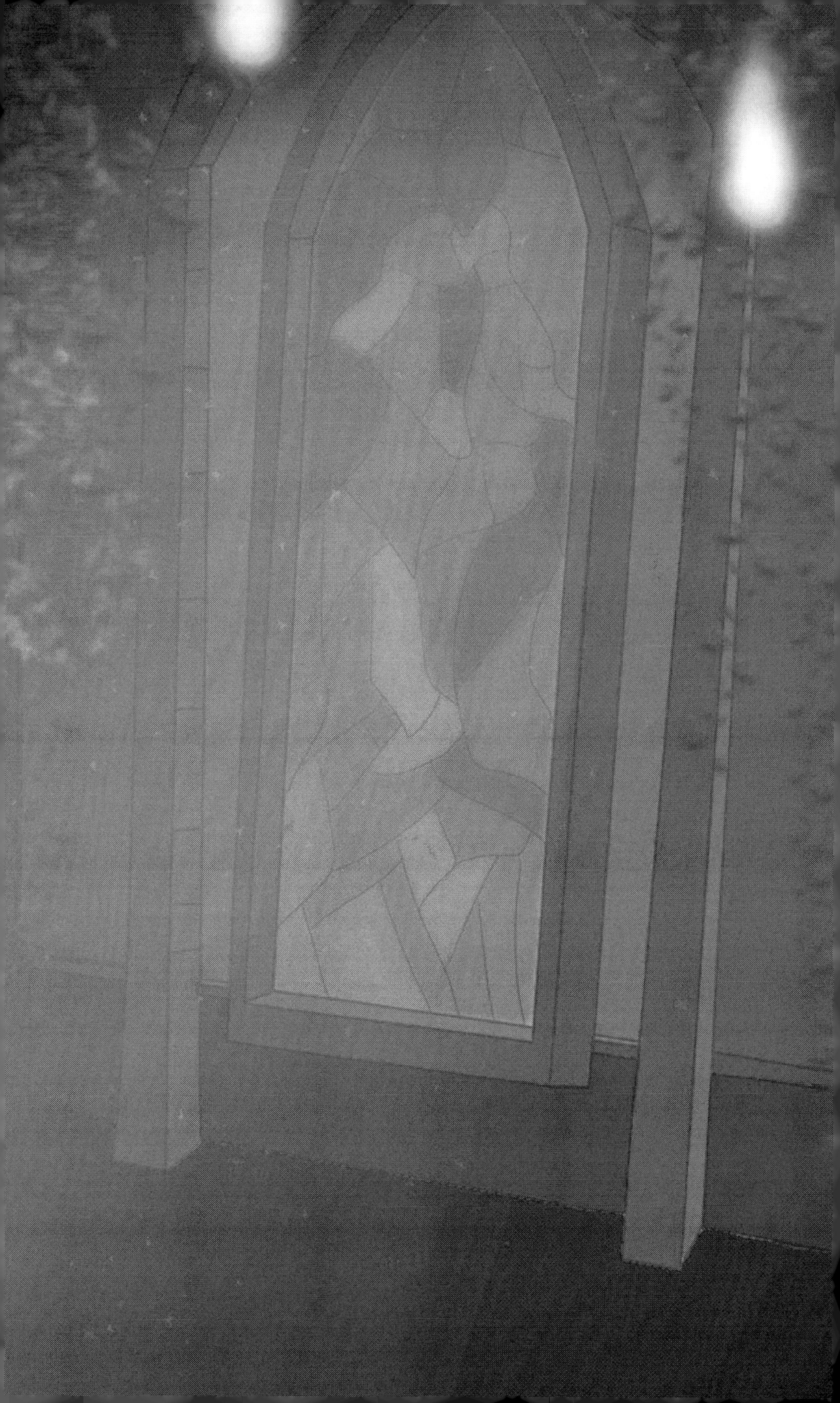

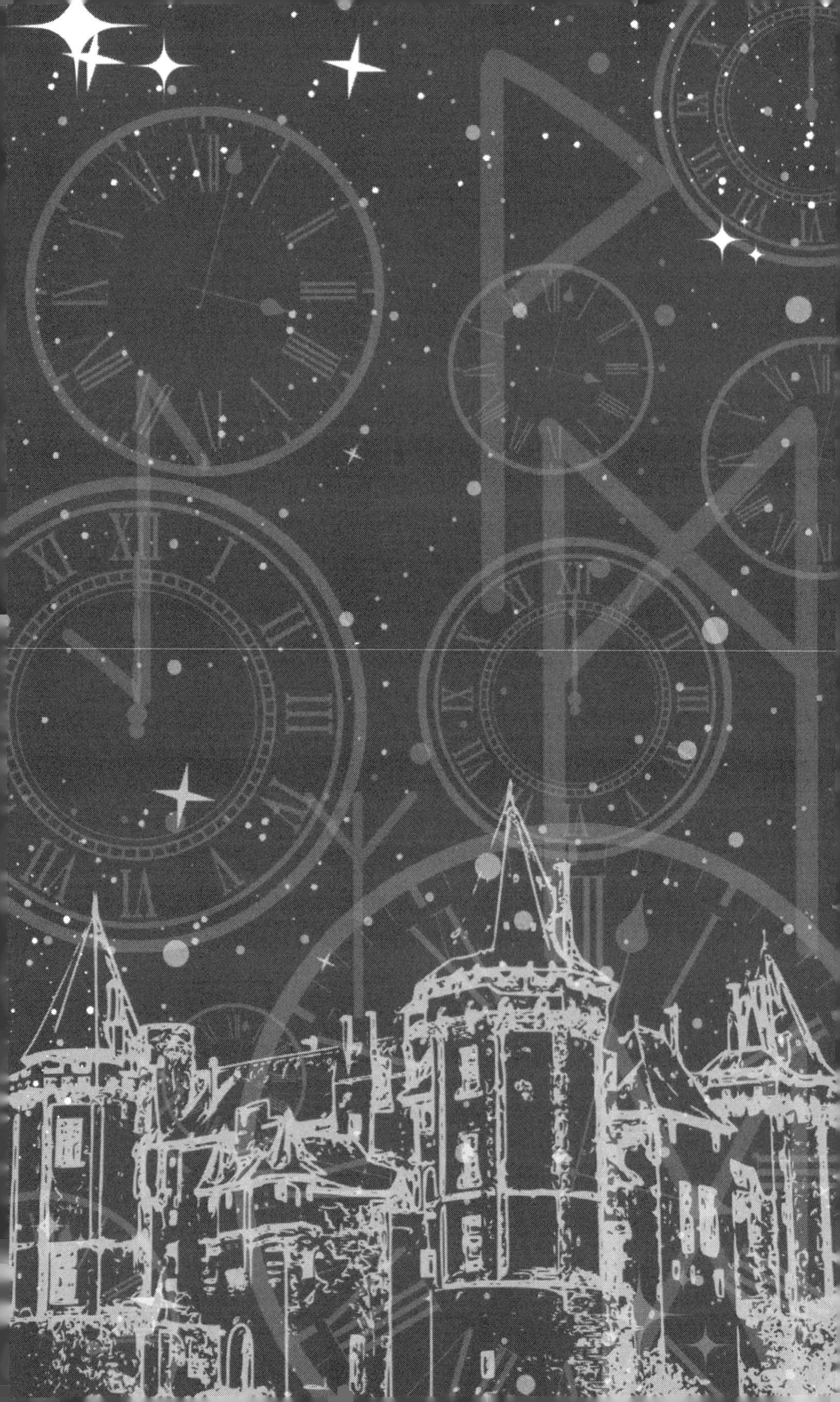

Chapter Nineteen
Sage

Kira met Thalia and me at the tailors near the Day's residence. Aurora couldn't join us as her family expected her to do this with them. Kira was over the moon when I told her I was seeing Hassian. She said the only reason Hassian and I were matched that early was because my mother foresaw it in one of her visions that we would be happy together. I like to believe that's true, but I also know that you can't know the whole story from just a glance at a moment in time. Hassian feels right to me, and I hope that he truly is.

"Do you have an idea of the color dress you are looking for?" Modey, the shop's owner, asks.

"I had thought green due to my element, but come to think of it, I wouldn't mind blue," I reply.

"Oh good, then I can wear green," Thalia says.

"I'll take both of your measurements and see if I have anything in your sizes." After she takes our sizes, she quickly heads into the back.

"Care to let me in on why you chose those colors," Kira asks with a raised eyebrow.

Thalia and I look at each other, knowing the reason is the same for both of us. "It's their eye color," I say.

"I should have known." Kira shakes her head before taking a seat by the window.

"What have you been up to while I've been away?" I ask Kira.

"Tending to the Day's garden and my own. They really are such a pleasant bunch."

"Alright, girls, I don't have too many options that are close in size in stock right now, but I do still have a few. I'll put them on the rack and let you choose if you wish to try them on. I will give you some space so you don't feel pressured. If you do desire to try them on, there's a divider over there you can undress."

Thalia and I look through the dresses. I know there aren't a lot of choices, but I see one that is similar to what I had in mind, and judging by Tal's face, she has the same feeling. We both look at each other before barreling over to try on the dresses. We are a fit of laughter, oohs, and ahhs as we help each other into our potential gowns. When we have them on and tied them as best as we can, we walk out to look in the mirror and show Kira.

The gown I chose to try on is almost the perfect color to Hassian's eyes. A dress as vibrant in color as the ocean itself. The petticoat is adding decent volume to the skirt of the dress. It falls a little bit too much to the floor so that it will require some hemming, but I am in love with the way it shimmers when I move. As well as the embroidered design the goes part way into the skirts. The bodice is a corset top, and I like the way it looks. I might have Kira put in a request for some corsets after the ball. I don't want to overwhelm Modey this week. The corset is decked out in a floral pattern in the front and plain in the back. The sleeves hang below my shoulders, extending about the length of my elbow, and are made of a sparkling sheer fabric. In the back, there is also a sheer attachment similar to a cape; to say I am in love with this dress is an understatement.

Thalia's dress is stunning, too. It's deep forest green with a sparkly bodice and short off-the-shoulder sleeves, maybe an inch in length. The skirt isn't as poofy as mine, but it has a slight layered effect with a simple green fabric. She's a sight to behold.

We do a quick spin to give Kira a good look. "Well, what do you girls think?" she asks.

"I love it. I would like to add a cape similar to Sage's gown if that would be possible." Thalia replies.

"I can do that," Modey says, coming around the corner. "The fit looks good on you. I will need to tighten around your waist more, but I can have that done in time for the ball." She walks over to me and inspects the dress. "How are you feeling about this one?"

"Honestly, it's perfect," I say. "You wouldn't, by chance, have a tie to match it, do you?"

"Hmm, I can check. Let me pin where your alterations will be needed first so you can change while I check my stock." I nod. She pins Thalia's dress first since fewer alterations are involved and makes a note to add a cape. After which, she comes over to me and pins up the length of the dress that's too long and brings in the waist and bust. I am not exactly well-endowed in the bosom department. "Alright, I will be right back. You are free to change. Be careful undressing so you don't pull out any of my pins."

After I undress and get back into my clothes, we take off the heels we wore for our fitting and slip back into more comfortable footwear. "Is there a particular person you wish me to send this to?" Modey asks.

"Yes, can you send it over to Hassian Blackwell? Sign it from Sage, please." Modey nods. "You can also charge all of this to the Torrin accounts." Another thing I have since learned after our stop at my family's vaults, is that I can say things like that. I have this fancy ring with my family's crest on it now. It's basically to say hey, I am me. I can press my seal into things.

"Sage, you don't have to," Thalia starts.

"I am doing this for you because you are my friend, and your family has already done so much for me. Just accept the gift, Tal."

"Okay, I'll just have you add your seal to this slip for the account, and you'll be good to go. I'll try to have the dresses delivered to both of you the day before the ball. They will arrive the morning of the ball at the latest." I press my ring into the melted wax, it feels oddly satisfying.

"You girls are going to look so beautiful. I will send the cobbler over a request to have some dancing shoes made that will match your dresses. Do you want a different crown, or are you okay with the one you picked?" Kira asks.

"It's fine; I will be wearing the stone anyway. It won't be a perfect match, but it will mean more to me wearing my mother's first crown than one that goes seamlessly," I say.

"It looks like afternoon light has passed; we best get going, Sage," Thalia says.

"You're right. I missed you so much, Kira. Thank you for joining us for the fitting. It wouldn't have been the same without you." I hug Kira before Thalia and head out to our assigned carriage to head back to the academy.

Despite there being no academics this week in preparation for the ball, Hassian and I still meet up in the library. I was fully prepared to practice trying to maintain a bloom like we usually do, but to my surprise, that's not what I walk in on. The tables and window sills are covered in a multitude of candles, and Hassian waits by the window for me.

"It's come to my realization that you have had no formal dance training, seeing as you didn't grow up in this realm. I want the ball to be perfect for you, so I have taken the liberty of dedicating what would be our training sessions together to teach you how to dance."

"It's awfully bold of you to assume that I cannot dance," I retort.

"Am I wrong?"

"No."

He laughs, and I swear my heart just melted into a puddle on the floor. Everything about this man is so blissfully wonderful. He pulls me close and places his hand on the small of my back while the other takes my hand. "Place your hand on my shoulder," he says. He begins to move at a slow pace at first, and I follow his movements. "There you go, good girl. You're doing great. Now let's try picking up the pace a little bit."

I don't know how I should feel at this moment, but I feel like I am floating as we dance in the candlelight, swaying to nothing but the sound of our beating hearts. I could stay like this for the rest of the evening. His arms feel like home. I am just starting to get a feel for the rhythm of the dance when one of the windows opens snuffing out the candles, and sending a chill through the air—Hassian moves to close it.

"The latch appears to be broken; these are fairly old. I'll let one of the professors know before I go to bed so it can get repaired. As much as I would love to dance with my princess all night, I don't want you to catch a cold from the chill. We will have to cut this short. You look divine today, Sage." He bends down and kisses me deeply, like relinquishing the kiss might end him. The window swings open, and a thud sounds from across the room. I get a cold shiver down my spine. "I have to let one of the professors know about this before it causes some damage."

"You know I plan on bathing tonight if you want to join me."

He groans. "I would want nothing more than to see all of you, but I have to find a professor and let them know. I'll do my best to meet you there if it doesn't take too long. I promise." He kisses me again, and we both exit the library.

I've only used the showers since starting at the academy, but something about sitting in the bath after a romantic dance with the man of my dreams feels right. I haven't been here long when a hand moves the hair from off my neck. A cold finger slides down the length of my exposed skin, just as Hassian did all those days ago. "You found the professor awfully fast," I say, and as I speak, I can see my breath. I turn to face Hassian, but he's not there. No one is. A shiver goes down my spine, much like how it felt in the library. I have seen far too many horror movies to be comfortable with this.

I quickly make my way out of the tub, not bothering to dry myself off. I snatch my pajamas off the ground and run into the hallway. I begin hightailing it toward the dorms. I am aware I am completely naked, but something just happened in there, and I am terrified. Hassian comes out of Professor Auhdaye's room as I am about to pass by.

"Sage!" he shouts as he runs to catch up with me, sweeping me into his arms. "What's wrong? What's going on? Why are you naked? Did someone try to touch you?" His nostrils flare in anger.

I am trying to relay what happened but am a stuttering mess. Hassian looks around to ensure no one is about to walk by and helps me slip into my clothes. I need to calm down, and I think he is aware of that.

"Sage, listen to me. Professor Auhdaye is still awake and in her classroom. It's right over there. We are going to go in there, and you can tell her what happened. Can you do that for me?" he asks. I nod. He's calling me by my given name and not princess, so I know how serious he is right now. He helps me to my feet, and we walk slowly to Auhdaye's classroom.

She takes one look at me before her eyes widen. "What happened?" I'm still too worked up. "I'll make her some lavender tea to help calm the nerves."

When she goes to her back room to make some tea, there are hurried knocks at the door. Hassian moves to see who it could possibly be, but before he can, Thalia and Aurora come barreling through the door.

"We're so sorry to burst in like this. We thought we hallucinated a naked Sage running down the hall. We were heading to the showers. We saw Sage's clothes, which she had been wearing earlier, still in the bathroom. What the hells happened?" Thalia asks.

"That's what we are trying to find out. She was running through the hallway terrified when I found her."

"You weren't with her?"

He shakes his head. "I had to find a professor; the latch to one of the library windows broke. "I felt how scared she was and went to go look for her."

I think my brain might be going into overdrive, and I misheard what Hassian said, so I let out a laugh. All three of them stare at me.

"By The Nines, I think she's broke," Auhdaye says as she comes out with a cup of lavender tea for me. She hands me the cup. "Are you ready to talk?"

I take a sip. "I'm sorry. I think my brain is all scrambled right now, and I misheard Hassian. I could've sworn he said he felt how scared I was."

"I did. That's what I said."

"How?" I ask.

"We can talk about that another day. What happened?"

I begin to recant what happened in the bathroom and compared it to the chill of the library.

"You don't think something got through the protection boundary, do you?" Hassian asks.

"It shouldn't be possible, but I will alert the headmaster immediately. Given the circumstances, I will allow Hassian to stay in your dorms with you. He is your calm in a storm, and what we don't need is a worked-up elemental on our hands. Besides, he is one of our best fighters, even if he is a student. He's been training for The Order since day one."

"You aren't afraid I will try anything inappropriate?" Hassian jokes.

"Blackwell, I do not care. You are an adult, and what you choose to do with your chosen, within consent, is up to you."

"Then why even have separate dormitories?" Thalia asks.

"That's an old and archaic rule that I never understood. We have a shared bathing area, but sharing a sleeping quarter falls under unreasonable. It makes about as much sense to me as it does to you. Now go on, you four, off to bed. I will speak with the headmaster about the situation."

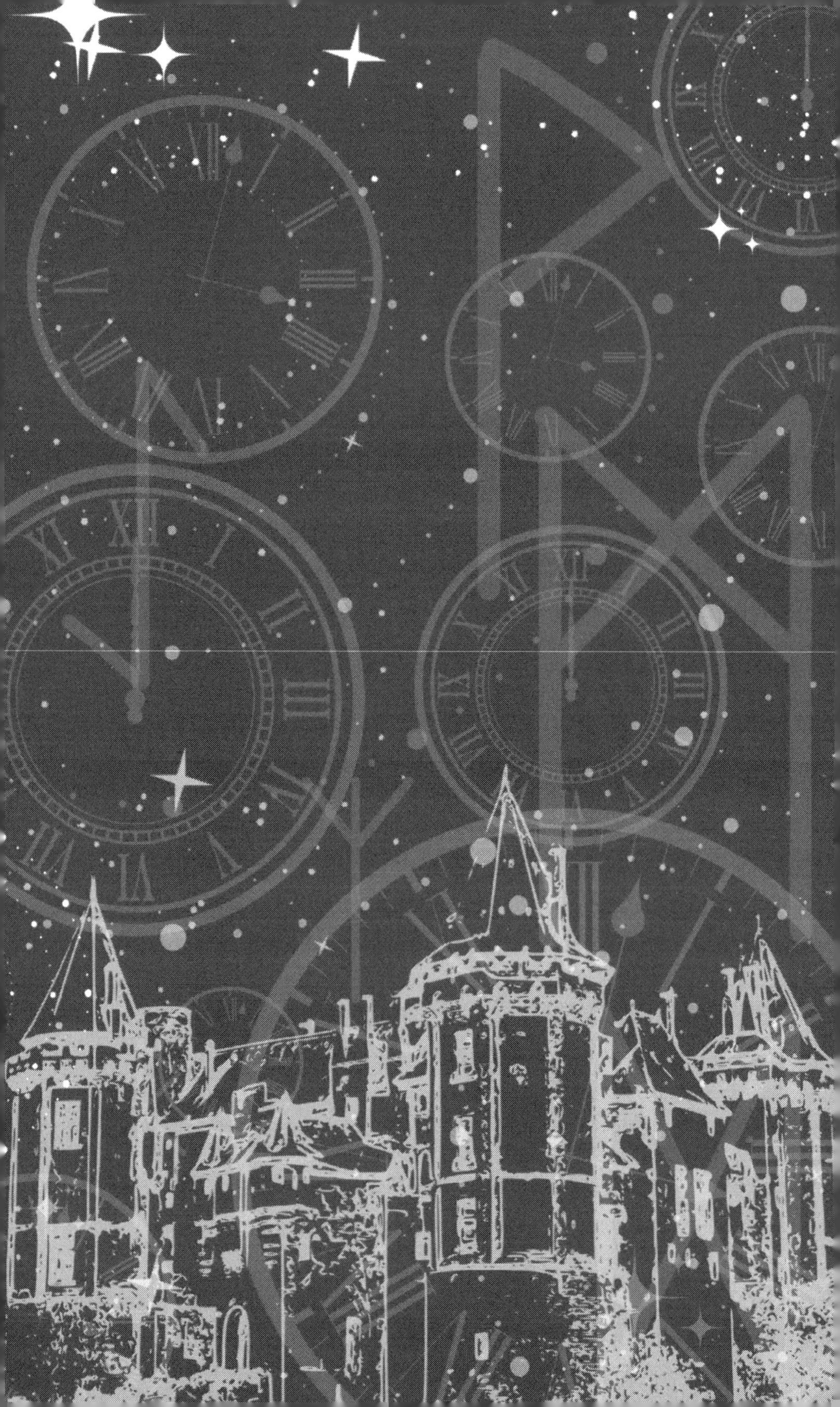

Chapter Twenty
Sage

Everyone is gathered in the great hall, waiting for the headmaster to speak on the incident; for once, it is complete silence. "Last night, it came to our attention that we had a breach in the wards. I can assure you the threat has been dealt with, and the wards reinforced. The brownies have returned to the gardens this morning. The winter solstice ball will continue as planned. We believe last night to have been an isolated incident, but we encourage you to report anything that seems unusual to you. That is all." The headmaster doesn't even stay to eat a meal; he just walks down the length of the great hall and leaves. Murmurs break out among the students, a cacophony of excitement that the ball is still ongoing and shock that something has broken through wards that have never been broken through before.

Hassian has remained by my side, refusing to even sit with the rest of the third years. Despite him putting on this strong mask right now, that's how I know he is bothered by the situation.

"I hope you know that break-in or not, we are still going to the library today," I tell Hassian.

"I don't like the idea of you being in the very room the ward was broke before. For thousands of years, this school has stood, and the wards have never failed; suddenly, you're here, and it's happened. The brownies left. Do you not understand the seriousness of that?"

"Yeah, Sage, brownies leave when an evil presence is near. They come to the academy for peace. I don't like the idea of you going back up there," Aurora says.

"I just don't think the situation is so black and white. Look, I am freaked out as much as everyone else, but whatever it was, it did something only Hassian has ever done to me. It didn't just arrive last night; I have a feeling it's been watching us up there for quite some time."

"And you want to go back up there?" Thalia almost yells the question at me.

"I do. I think it was up there the whole time; there is something to find. I didn't want to bring this up, but the way Professor West teaches about Gaiwen-"

"The man that wants to kill you?" Hassian stiffens.

I ignore his statement and continue, "The way she teaches about Gaiwen just doesn't sit right with me. She is adamant about teaching word for word from the book. It's like she's studied it multiple times. That, to me, is screaming something isn't right with what we are being told. The library could have those answers."

"I can't say I have dealt with Professor West's teaching. She was only recently implemented this year by your grandfather when he was alerted you would be attending this year. She doesn't teach any other grade," Hassian says.

"I did not know that," Thalia says when I give her a look.

"That's just all the confirmation I need to know there's something not right about her."

"You don't trust your grandfather?" Hassian asks.

"No. I find it funny that he would implement some textbook professor for his granddaughter's class but never once try to meet her."

"Hassian, I know you are concerned about me, but if you keep hovering right next to me and not helping me look, we will be up here longer," I say.

He turns to face the bookshelves behind me and starts looking at books. "You know, I was thinking you should join me during my combat classes. It would be good for you to learn some basic self-defense. Magic isn't going to get you out of every situation, and let's be honest, princess, you are still struggling with it."

"I still don't know why I'm failing time and time again. We've been at it for months. As for your combat training, I distinctively remember you making an innuendo; however, would any training get done?" I joke.

"I was serious about what I said then, but not serious about it happening during that. The only one who gets to see you on your knees is me. As to your magic, we will figure it out. You are doing it correctly; it's just not holding onto the connection."

"If I take up combat training, will you go back to just being the man who presses me against a bookshelf while doing unspeakable acts and dances with me in the library?"

I hear the sound of him dropping a book to the floor as he presses up behind me. "Oh, so you like it when I make you become undone in the library?" he whispers in my ear.

I bite my lip, "I very much enjoy that."

He kisses my shoulder before saying, "Well, I'm sorry to disappoint, but my princess was very adamant about searching the books in the library today."

"What if she changed her mind?"

"Oh no, I am not falling for that, princess. You'll try to bring us in here later because you'd be upset that I distracted you."

I groan from the aches caused by the absence of his body to mine. I flip through books faster. I have skimmed through two rows of shelves; I am beginning to feel like this is useless. I examine the books we've been browsing and I realize something. "Look at these books and tell me what they all have in common," I say.

"They're all history texts?" Hassian replies.

"They are all new. I know we aren't looking for something extremely old, but at the bare minimum, an accurate text would be nearly two decades old. I've seen some of those books kept in the herbology class. We need to be looking at slightly more worn books."

"I will admit my fault there. I've been here three years, and I forgot about the library getting new books last year. The older books will be more toward the east wall."

"Great, let's look there."

Hassian and I begin scouring the history section of the older books. Based on the state of some of these, they should be in a museum; they are so old. I bypass the more ancient-looking ones. I'm not looking for an ancient text, just something that might be a little more worn. I make my way to the next shelf, and I practically trip over something on the floor. Was this there the whole time? Something did fall last night; maybe it was this. I pick the book off the ground and examine it. The exterior is made of leather and is very faded and worn. It's almost like it has been picked up and used multiple times. I unwind the leather straps that are keeping it bound and take a look. My eyes widen when I realize what I am looking at: Gaiwen's journal.

"Hassian, I found something."

"Is that?" I nod.

We leave the library; I know what I am doing for the rest of the day.

Part Two

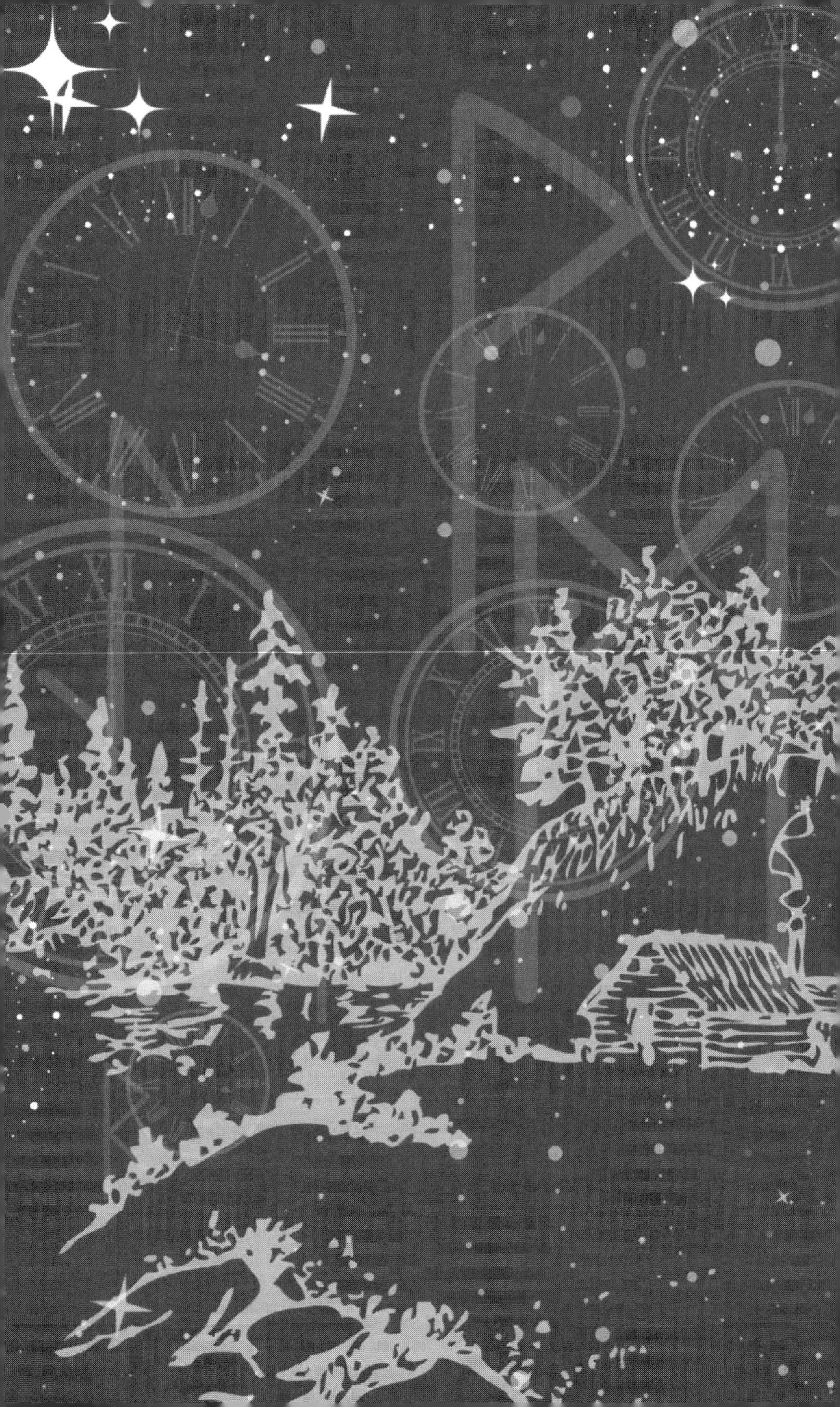

Chapter Twenty-one
Gaiwen

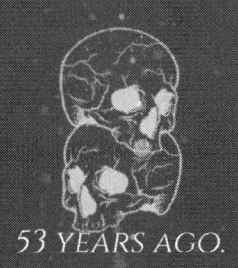

53 years ago.

"Can I get you another one, Gaiwen?" asks Min, the owner of the tavern.

"This will be it for me, thanks," I reply with a nod. It's not every day that I nurse a drink, but I've just been offered a job that I'm not sure I am prepared to take. I'm not sure this is the type of man I can say no to either.

This morning, I was tending to an infection of a woman who got into some trouble with bandits when she tried to withhold her coin from them. It's always easier to just give them what they want; they'll let you leave with minimal injuries. According to her, it was the second time in a month. She knew she wouldn't win, but she fought back anyway.

That's the problem with this realm today: bandits are an issue, but the High King doesn't care because it's not affecting his precious royal court. It's not a problem until it becomes an issue for him or one of his favored. I've never met the man, but somehow, I am constantly entangled in his crap.

Whether it's dealing with his lack of protecting the realm or being requested to perform magic for someone in the royal courts, Forbidden magic is not a price I'm willing to pay, but I don't think I have a choice. There's an absolute fuck ton that can go wrong, maybe not so much for them, but for me. There is a natural order to magic, and when you break it, well, things tend to go wrong.

I hear the tavern door clanging open and the scampering and scuffing as patrons quickly file out. "Time's up, Gaiwen. You had your time. Now give us your answer."

They act like I have a choice. Well, I guess I do. Say yes, and I will get rewarded in some way, assuming I survive the process or say no, and they break my kneecaps and force me to do it anyway. "Fine, let's go."

"Good answer," says the heavy one. He has a ring on his finger, so he's obviously married; I wonder if he feeds his wife or just gives her crumbs. He yanks me by the shoulder and shoves me out the tavern door. I hear the clang of coins as one of the men throws it at Min for his troubles.

There's a carriage waiting outside. It's not like the ones around the poorer sections of Alandria, like where I currently am. The framework is made of some kind of metal as are the wheels. There are no horses either. They shove me through the carriage door. "Sit down," the bald one says.

A man in fancy white garb and a matching thin cloak is waiting in the carriage. Looks like Order trash. They say they are all for the people, but at the end of the day, what have they done to keep us safe? "Palm," he orders. I know I have no choice, so I extend my hand to him. He slices deep and holds my hand over a bowl, releasing it when he's gotten enough blood.

"Is this really necessary?"

"Yes," the reply is short as he slices his palm and adds to the mixture. I'm used to the strong scent of iron. In my line of work, I get a lot of very wounded patients coming through my door. Being the only fae that can cure an infection with my magic alone, I am a bit of a big deal. He starts chanting the words to perform a vow of silence, sworn in blood. This is probably one of the most disgusting and barbaric dealings I have encountered. When he is done reciting the words, he pours the blood into a goblet, and here comes the appalling part. "Do you vow to keep what information you are about to be told to only yourself until the day your light fades?" He's not very good at his job because I have already seen a million loopholes in his wording.

"Yes."

He tilts the disgusting mixture of his and my blood to my lips, pinching my nose as he pours half of it into my mouth to keep me from spewing it out. He takes the goblet and downs it, licking his lips like its casual wine at a dinner party. I can feel my gut twisting from the ritual. Pain laces my forearm as the outline of the blood oath tattoo sears its way onto my skin.

We travel for hours; there are no windows on this cart, so I cannot see what way we are going. Based on the number of turns, I cannot tell where we are heading, either. They are doing their best to disorientate me from figuring it out, but the extra steps they are taking scream to me that this is at the top of the nobility chain. No doubt, the High King himself. I don't know what I could offer him that, literally, anyone else couldn't. I specialize in deep infections. There's no active war, there shouldn't be wounds and the only threats in this realm right now are bandits. Bandits don't fuck with the nobles.

I can hear the scraping sound of a gate rising when the carriage comes to an abrupt stop before we jerk forward again. The asshole in front of me gives me a quick grin before sliding a hood over my head and binding my hands. Apparently, saying I'll do what they ask and taking a blood oath isn't enough for them. The carriage comes to a stop again, and I hear the sound of its door being opened before a rough hand grips me and yanks me out.

I'm being pushed and shoved for not walking fast enough when all I am trying to do is focus on not tripping since I can't see anything. We take many turns until, eventually, we are descending some stairs. I trip a few times, scraping up my knees in the process. A door opens, and I am shoved through, and the hood is ripped off my head. Before me is an atrocity; a child no more than the age of one lay dead. Its face contorted in a look of pain as if it froze to death.

My hands are unbound, and a book is placed in them. I look over the words of the book. It's written in an ancient language that would take me years to decipher. "I can't read this," I tell them.

"The spell you need is already deciphered. Just do the job, and you can go."

I flip through the pages until I find the parchment with the translated spell. Before setting the book down, I double-check that they etched the runes correctly around the circle. I look over the spell. "Are you telling me you wish me to revive this child? How did she die?"

"That's none of your concern. Just perform the spell."

"Why me? We are in a realm full of magical users; why use someone who is the last of their kind?"

"Just do it."

I look at the spell again. It calls for blood because, of course, it does. "Can I borrow someone's blade for the spell?"

"No, but I'll give you a hand," says the bald man from earlier. He's dragging in the frail body of someone who barely looks alive. "They went over the spell to us. It ain't got to be your blood, and we can't risk you dying." He cuts the man's hand, holding him by the arm as he drips the blood onto the child. "Go on, get going with the ritual."

I start chanting the words, and the light of my element begins to glow over the corpse. The man whose blood they used begins to scream as the color of the child's body begins to return to normal. The man stops screaming, and the child's eyes fly open. The hood immediately goes back over my head, and I am shoved out of the room and back into the carriage. I can feel something is wrong; something is missing. I feel cold inside.

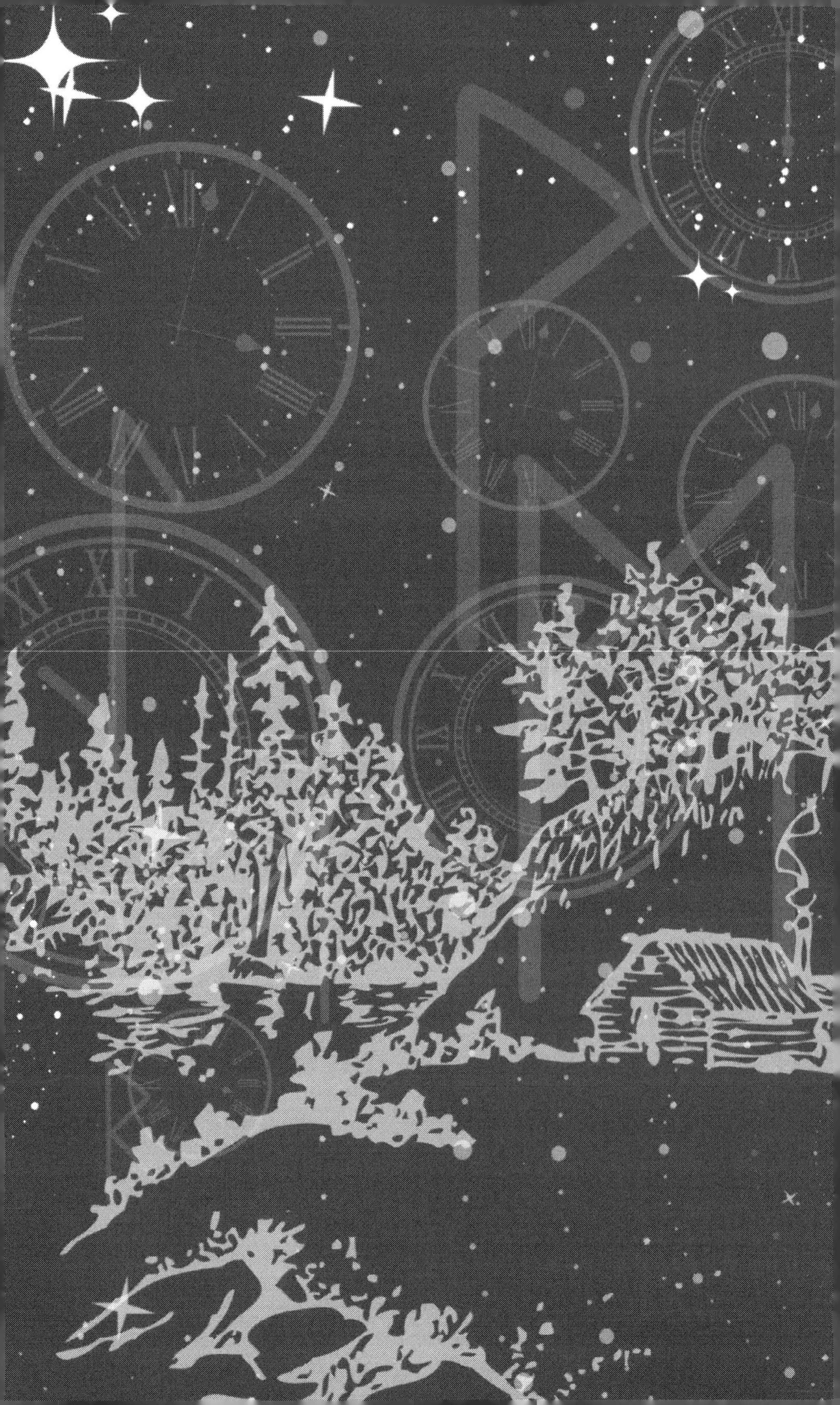

Chapter Twenty-Two
Gaiwen

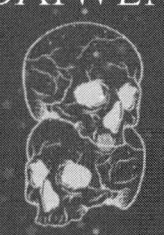

It's been one day since I have been returned to my home. I tried to use my light when I got home. It was dark, and I was trying to see my way to bed. Nothing came. I had to stumble my way there. I feel drained, like every ounce of energy has been sucked from my body. I need sleep. Everything will feel better in the morning.

Morning comes, and I do, in fact, feel better. I am still struggling to conjure light, but it could very well mean I just have some magic drain from the previous day's events. I hope that is the extent of it. I get dressed for the day and head downstairs to open my shop. I am arranging and checking the dates on my salves and balms when the jingle of my shop bell goes off.

A woman with long blonde hair and green eyes walks through. She gives a small smile. Everything about her is in too good of a condition to be injured, and she doesn't have the look of trauma to be from around these parts. I'm pretty sure I know everyone who resides locally at this point. Based on her health, she looks to be noble-born or close to it. I'm not the biggest fan of nobility.

"How can I help you?" I ask. I'm not using my friendliest tone, and she looks startled by me.

She reaches into her cloak and pulls out a roll of parchment. "My name is Adelin. I am to give this to you." Her hands are shaking as she extends it over to me.

I unravel it and look it over. "Tell them I reject," I say, returning it to her.

"You can't, it's already finalized."

"I'm not looking for a wife."

"Well, I wasn't looking for a husband. At least not the likes of you."

"This is what they meant by I'll be rewarded handsomely? This isn't a reward. This is a financial burden I cannot take on."

She looks hurt, and I will admit my responses have been harsh, but realistically, I can't. I am barely able to buy supplies because I refuse to raise my prices for those in need to keep up with the rising costs. "Well, I come with a house too. Near the woods and enough coin for you to retire. You don't need to work here." She makes a face, and I can tell she just got wind of an unsightly smell.

"This is my home."

"In two weeks, it won't be. They are seizing the property. They want you out of town."

"Why?"

"I don't know. I'm only passing along what I've been told."

"What did you do to be married off to a lowborn?" I ask.

"I got caught with a man."

"Well, that's no sin, nor is it something to be punished for."

"It is if he's married."

"Who was it?"

"That's none of your concern. It's over now."

"Do you want kids?"

"Eventually."

"I don't."

She guffaws, "then why did you ask?"

"Just trying to get a feel for you is all. You will be lonely if you stay."

"I don't have a choice."

"What if I let you sleep with whoever you want?"

"Why would you do that?"

"Well, I'm not going to do it."

"What if I end up pregnant?"

"Don't."

"How?"

Is this woman daft? "Take precautions. I'm sterile; you could never have a child by me."

"Why would you get sterilized when it's already hard to conceive in this realm?"

"It wasn't by choice. It's a light fae thing. Males are born sterile. It's why I am the last of my kind. My mother didn't have a daughter and died during birth."

"I'm sorry."

The bell chimes again as a woman brings in a man whose leg is nearly torn off. "What happened?" I ask as I help her carry the man to my medical cot.

"He was running from the bandits and got too close to a direwolf. The bandits let him go when they saw the direwolf trying to rip off his leg. He shot a flame at the wolf, and it ran off, but not before it did some damage. Can you treat the infection and patch him up?"

"I'll do the best I can." I place my hands over his wound and feel for the magic inside me. The familiar tendril of power comes to my hands, and I make my way to weave it into his flesh, but there's something wrong. The color is all wrong. It should be white. I try to break the connection, but I can't stop it as the black tendrils burrow into his leg. The man screams in agony as black veins spread from his wounded leg throughout his body.

"What are you doing to him?" the woman screams.

Adelin backs up against my medicine cabinet, and I hear things fall and break.

"I'm not doing this on purpose. Something is wrong."

The man's eyes blink open, and they are nothing but blackness. They are so very wrong. He bolts upright and bites into the tender flesh of the woman who brought him in. She screams as he tears out her throat. He stands up in search of something else to kill. His black eyes dart around until he lays eyes on Adelin. He lets out a scream that shatters my windows and makes a move to go after her.

"STOP!" I yell, and he freezes in his tracks. The screaming stops, and he makes no motion, indicating he is about to move. I motion for Adelin to go upstairs while I grab a blade from under the counter. He's still not moving. I decide to test a theory before killing him. "On your knees." He blinks for a second and moves to his knees. "Close your eyes." He does, without hesitation. Well fuck, I think I can control it. I want no part in this. I swing my blade and cut off his head.

I lock the door to my shop and flip the sign to closed.

"Adelin, it's safe now!" I yell up to her.

She comes down the stairs. "What in The Nines did you do to that man?"

"I don't know. We should leave for that house sooner than the two weeks."

She nods. "That's probably for the best. We should burn the bodies."

"Agreed."

We wrap the corpses in cotton sheets, and when nightfall hits, we bring them to the woods and burn them. This was just the beginning for Adelin and I.

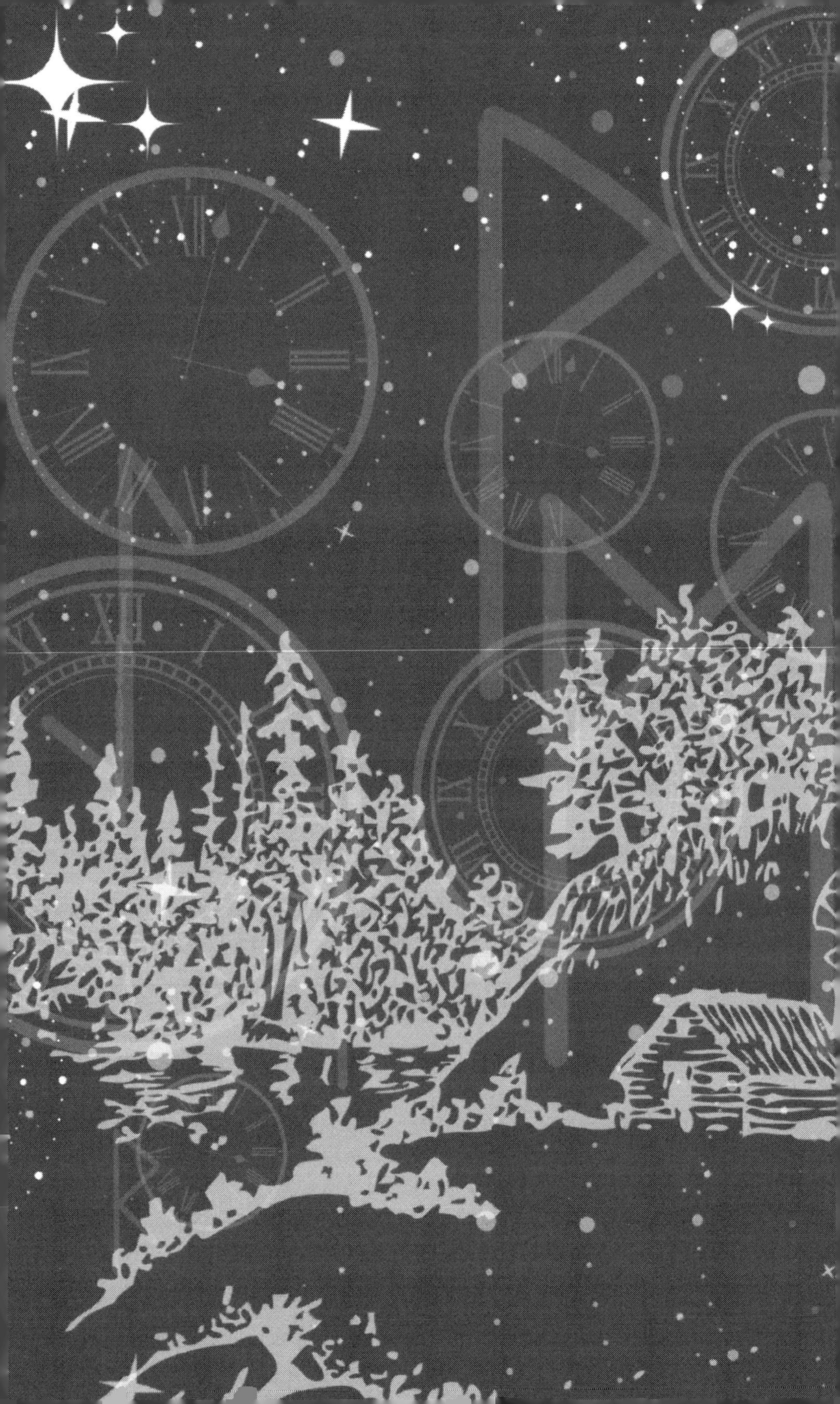

Chapter Twenty-Three
Gaiwen

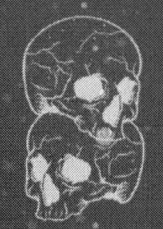

26 years ago.

Twenty-seven years have passed since I last was able to access my light magic. With that same thought, it's been many years since the voices also began. Adelin hasn't tried to leave. She's been a friend and a comfort during these past years. She did take me up on the offer of sleeping with other men to get what she needed, allowing me to go to the forest and make my sacrifices of small animals. It satisfies the voices enough to give me some rest, and with her being away while I do it, she can pretend she is unaware to save herself.

"How do I look?" Adelin asks as she looks over to me. She's glamoured her hair a different color with some runes someone sold in town. One of the things I have learned about Adelin over the years is she was born without magic. In part, I feel that's why her family so easily tossed her aside as they did. They never sent a single letter or even attempted to see her. It's their loss.

"Marvelous. How long do you plan on being out?" I ask.

"Past dark. We are going to check out the bard event going on in town since I can glamour myself now. I'm excited to finally be able to do something in public. Thank you, by the way, for letting me get them. It means a lot."

"You've been a good friend to me. If this can give you happiness in the situation we have been forced to live in, then it's worth it. Why don't you stay in town today? It's already getting late, and I don't enjoy the idea of you traveling in the dark alone. I'm sure your suitor in town would enjoy a full night with you."

"Are you sure? I don't like the idea of you being alone for too long."

"Of course, I am sure. I'll be hunting anyway." Hunting is the term we agreed to use for my less-than-kosher habits. "I fixed that wheel; by the way, the wagon shouldn't wobble anymore. I hope it doesn't break any more than it has; with the upgrades to the metal wagons, I won't be able to replace it if it does. Horses are reliable, I don't understand why all this change."

"Change is inevitable." She makes her way to the closet to get her cloak.

"Wear the thicker one, please, it's chilly out." She nods in agreement, humming as she sweeps it over her shoulders.

She leans over and gives me a kiss on the cheek. "Take care, my friend. I will see you in the morning."

When she leaves, I pull the bookshelf away from the wall and reach into my hidden compartment. The book I had to use that day was sitting on the counter when we moved in. Honestly, that's when the voices got the worst. Since then, I have been studying the book and have translated almost everything inside. This also means I now know what the spells can do and their capability. I like to think I have reasonable control and grasp of reality, but I don't. What part of me that is human and good goes away when she leaves. She is a conduit for anything good in me, which also means when she's gone; I am at my worst.

I've been journaling a lot, keeping track of what I did back then and what I am doing now. I can't talk about what I did to anyone, so I keep a record. Well, I could just in how the oath was phrased, but I am not in a position to want to risk that.

Losing my life isn't worth that possibility to me no matter how much I struggle being cut off from my light. I hide the journal from Adelin when she's home, not because it breaks my oath for her to read it, but because I just don't want her to know how bad it's gotten.

After I finish updating my journal, I head out to the woods to see if the direwolves left behind anything for me to use today. I walk past about thirty trees or so when I spot my gift. A dead fawn lies in a mound of leaves with nothing but its stomach torn out. This is perfect; the heart and brain should be intact.

I draw my circle around the fawn, etching in the symbols for the spell I have had the most success with, using a small twig I found nearby. I grab the dagger I keep on my belt and hold it to my palm before making one slow, thick cut. I squeeze my hand over the fawn and watch as the blood trickles from my palm to the body of the lifeless form before me. I recite the words I have come to know so fondly over the course of time.

I am rewarded with the fawn taking on a new life form. Its legs straighten and snap until they are sharp as blades. They grip the earth as the fawn stands upright. Its fur begins to darken into charcoal as my magic works its way through. Tendrils break flesh as it continues to contort into my beautiful creation. Saliva drips from its mouth onto the leaves and smoke billows as the acidity singes and eats away at them. It blinks and looks at me with its beautiful black eyes.

"Come here, my little fawn," I say, trying not to sound too excited. Every time I do this, it is an absolute thrill. I can feel something inside me shift as the spell finishes creating my creature. It feels good. The fawn listens to my command and walks to me. I rub my hand over its cold fur. Its acid singes my clothes but does no harm to me.

"Good," I remember another spell mentioning the benefits of using a sacrifice, and I wonder if the offering can be made after the fact. I spot another deer in the distance, a doe. It's alive and the perfect opportunity to test my theory. "Kill it," I order.

The fawn runs to the deer at an incredible speed, ripping it to the ground with its tendrils. The doe calls out a cry as the acid saliva breaks open her flesh. The fawn raises its legs up and down repeatedly, cutting through the doe. Blood splatters against the trees and leaves, and the fawn lets out a triumphant screech. When the doe takes its last breath, my precious little fawn comes running back to me.

"Good, my little creature of the dark." The fawn looks stronger now. I've never killed another creature before that I didn't intend to raise. I wonder if I am supposed to do the sacrifice beforehand so the creature doesn't deteriorate at all. I wonder how that will work. Does the soul remain in my reserve if I kill while I recite? I will have to test this out soon. I watch as my precious creature prances around. I don't think it is going to disappear this time, so I need to find it a spot to hide when I am not around.

There's an old cave deeper into the woods, and I decide to bring my creature there. I cast an orb of shadow in my hand that emits a faint purple glow as the night grows dimmer, and I walk my creature off toward the cave.

"Stay here, little one," Do not move from here until I return. Kill anything that spots you that is not me." The fawn vibrates in excitement.

I make my way back toward the house. My wagon has returned home, and my horses are still on their reins. Something is wrong.

My front door is wide open, and there is a bloodied handprint on the door. I walk inside, and there is a blood trail leading to my sitting chair. Adelin is there, holding a hand to her stomach, the blood wetting her hands; in her other hand is the journal I left out.

"There was an accident on the road—the bandits," she's gasping for breath. "I came straight to you for help. Why didn't you tell me-" her lips begin to get a film of blood, "that you were getting worse? That they made you do that, to desecrate a child against your will." She drops the journal, and I can see the life slipping from her. My light magic is gone. I cannot help her.

"Adelin, stay with me. Please don't leave me. You are all the humanity I have left," I try to staunch the bleeding.

"Gaiwen, I'm so sorry. I was selfish to go into town and not be here for you."

"Don't say that, Adelin. You are my best friend and you deserved those moments of happiness, to experience love."

"I don't want to die," a tear falls down her face, and she takes her last breath.

The voices get stronger. *Bring her back. You don't want to be alone, do you?*

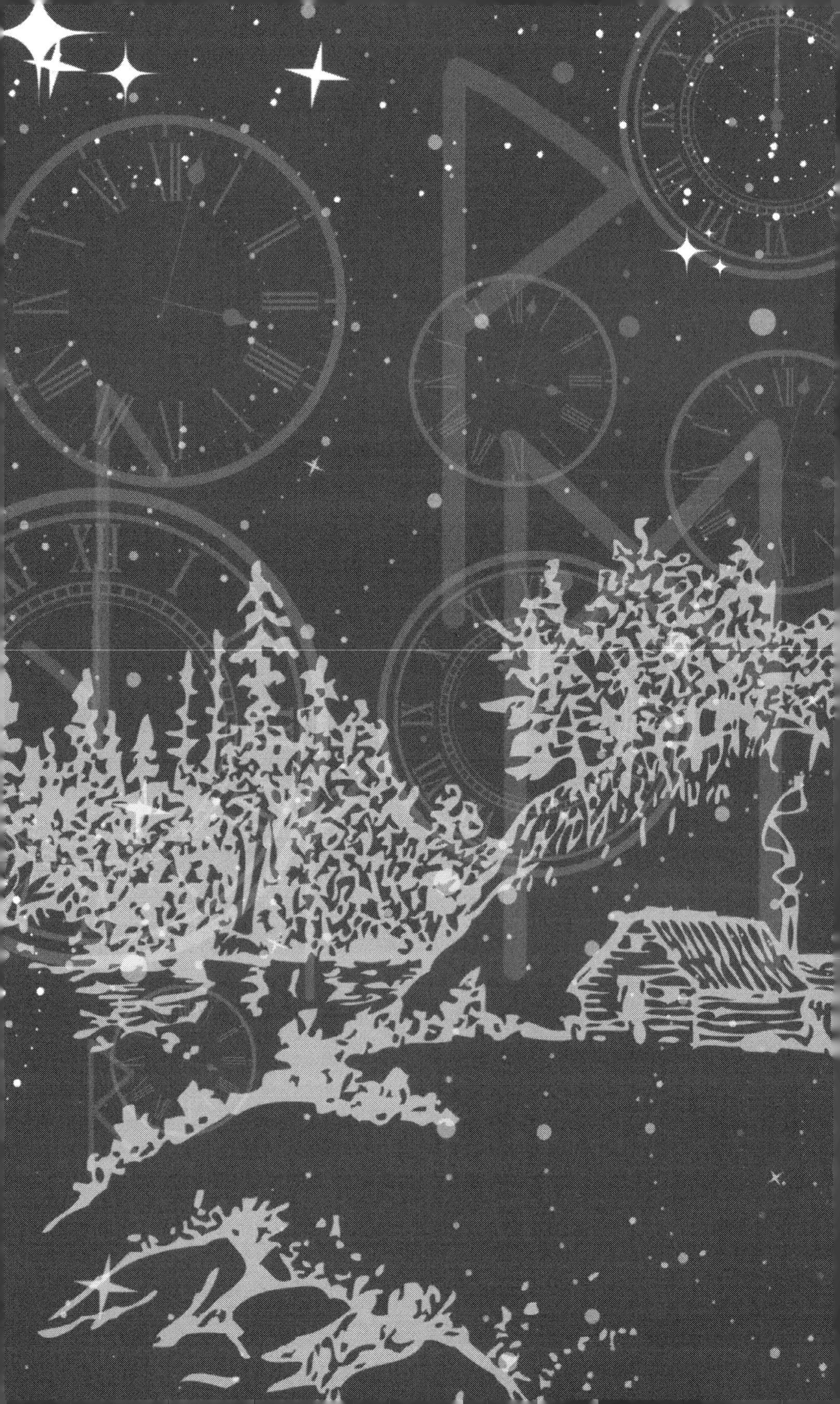

Chapter Twenty-Four
Gaiwen

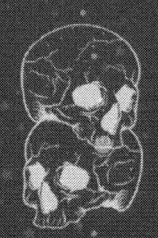

I spend all of Frostfall deciphering the rest of the spell and making excuses for my wife's sudden disappearance when her friends stop by to see her. They only wrote part of what they deciphered in the book, keeping half of the spell's knowledge to themselves. I didn't dabble with it again because I knew what it was intended to raise. I never planned to take another fae's life in that way ever again. I have her body sitting in a bin of salts to try to preserve her while I work on bringing her back to me. We may not be in love, but she has become my dear friend during our time together.

The inscription from the latest part of the book I deciphered says it can be offered before or after, as long as I am reciting the rights for my wife to return to her original form using this spell; the price to be paid is a human soul. The reason I was able to bring the child back to life was because the screaming coming from that man was the sound of him dying. He was paying the cost for the child to live.

I begin thinking about how to bring my Adelin back. I recall who frequents my woods; I know just who to use. A woman comes into my woods to wash clothes in the creek. She is always alone, always there every seven days, season to season. It's currently the second day of Skyfall, which means she will be there tonight.

I remove the items scattered amongst the table and begin etching my ruins in. It will be enough to fit two bodies on. I place the required ingredients down onto the center of the table, adding the two black candles, one for each body. I bring Adelin's body up from the salt preservation. She still looks so beautiful; her skin is a little dried out, but the spell should fix all of it.

After placing her body on the table, I head out to wait in a good hiding spot by the creek. It doesn't take long for her to show up. She is very predictable. I hit the side of her head with the butt end of my dagger and bind her legs and hands before carrying her back to my house.

I lay the offering on the table and begin chanting the words of the spell. As I say the final word, I plunge my dagger into the stranger's heart; her eyes flutter open right before I make an impact. It almost stirs something inside of me as life leaves her body. One of the candles lights itself before the flame dances in the air and moves to the other unlit candle. Adelin's eyes snap open, and her skin restores to its beautiful youth.

"Gaiwen, I thought I died."

"You did; I couldn't bear to go on without my friend."

"What have you done? Gaiwen, you paid a great cost the first time. What will it take from you now?" The worry in her eyes almost breaks me. "Can you reverse it? Will it restore whatever it took?"

"Why would I want that?" *tell me why I wanted to bring this annoying woman back?*

"Gaiwen your eyes," Adelin backs away from me.

I stalk closer, wrapping my hand around her throat as I lift her from the ground.

"I-can't-breathe."

I squeeze her neck, holding her there until her face turns blue before I drop her to the ground. She gasps for air, and I can see the imprint of my hand on her throat.

"This isn't you. Gaiwen, it's taking your humanity from you. You need to shut out the voices."

"Stop talking already," I say. She doesn't utter a word, but the tears on her face, now I can see those clear as day.

"You do not fear me. You trust me. You are not sad. You will follow me without question." The look on her face changes to one I have grown accustomed to all those years ago. *It's not enough. Break her completely.* I should feel bad about this next part, but I don't feel bad about anything anymore. "You love me, only me. We are going to make this world burn together."

Her eyes change to black, much like the man in my shop all those years ago. I do something I never desired to do before as shadows billow around me, and I stalk toward her. Grabbing her by the throat again, I kiss her with a passion I never had before. I kiss her until she is blue in the face, and I am forced to release her throat again before I throw her onto our bed and test the limits of how far I can take her pain.

Part Three

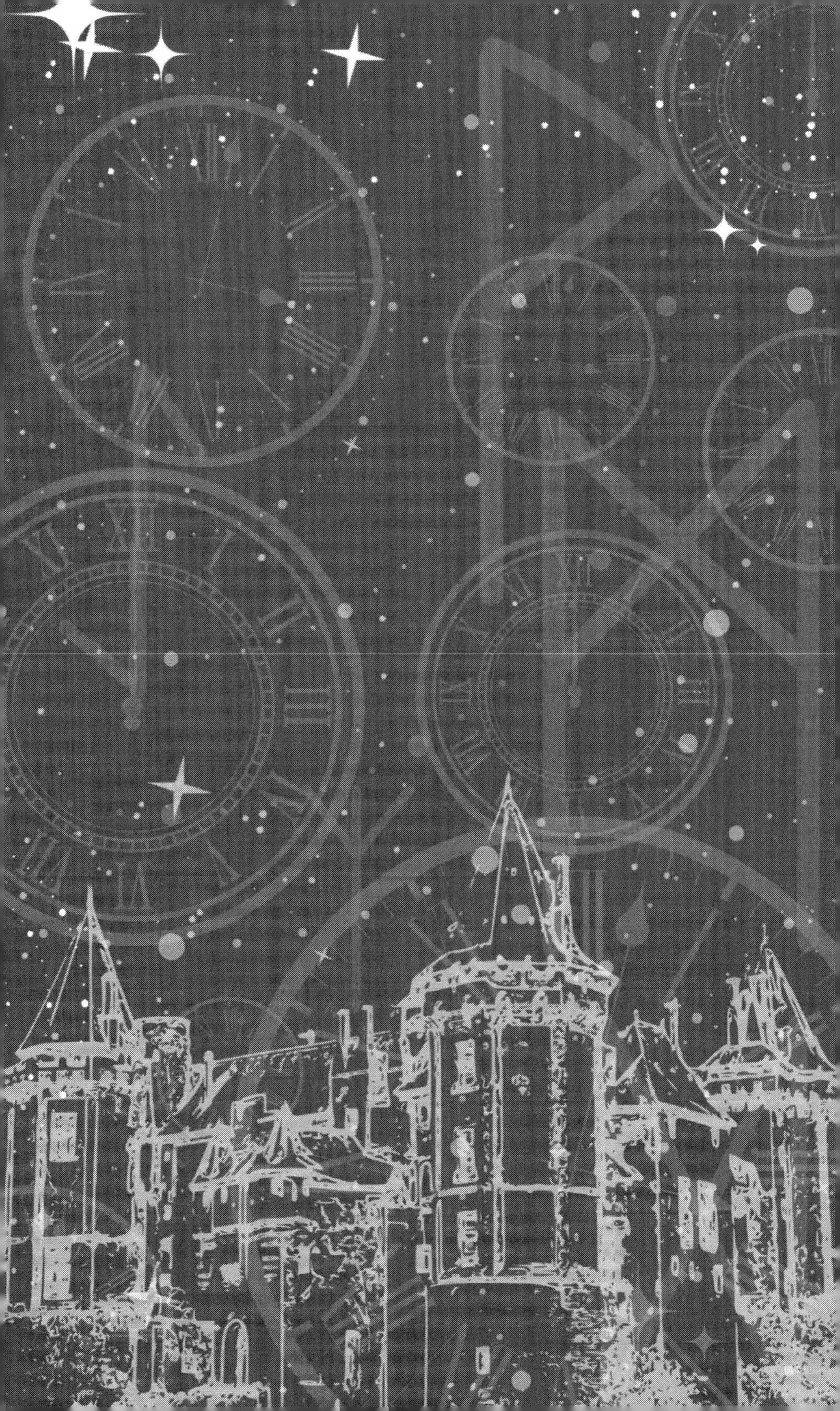

Chapter Twenty-Five
Sage

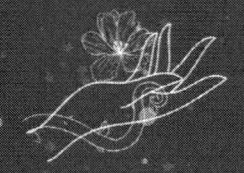

Hassian and I scour every inch of the journal over the course of the next few days. We got a clear grasp of what happened that changed him, but the events after he resurrected Adelin are unclear. The text becomes a mix of symbols and drawings we can't make out. We will have to see if we can find anything in the library during the evenings or see if Kira or, potentially, Thalia's parents know how to read them. We would try The Order, but I don't think they can be trusted from what we read.

There are a lot of questions I need to find the answers to; what noble was responsible for this, and how did the child die? Gaiwen thought it could be my grandfather, and I am inclined to believe it to be true. Everything I have heard of has not been good things. Can Gaiwen be saved, or is he too far gone? I know I shouldn't feel pity for Gaiwen, but I do. Someone forced his hand and made him the monster he is. I haven't met all the fae nobility attending the academy outside of Hassian and Aurora. I still haven't reached out to Sebille; I need to. I make a mental note to speak with her during or after the ball.

As promised, I do go with Hassian to train, learning to protect myself where magic might fail. I'm not the greatest at this either, but I'm a lot better than I am at casting magic. I suppose that isn't saying much, as all I manage to do is kill plants repeatedly.

"Sage, pay attention. Remember, mind off the journals when you are in the training room with me. I need you to pick up on this," Hassian scolds. I know it's scolding because he's not calling me princess. It's a sure sign he is getting frustrated with me. A valid feeling, considering I promised him in this room I wouldn't think about the journals. I can't let them consume me and hinder my progress.

"Sorry," I mumble, throwing a punch at the bag he's bracing.

"Good girl, that was much better. Just remember to keep your elbow in."

"Got it" I cock my head to the side to relieve tension before lifting my arms back up to continue. My fists connect with the bag over and over again. I can feel my muscles straining from the exhaustion of this continued routine and the sweat rolling down my back. I keep going, pushing through the ache and the pain.

Time feels like it's at a stop, and I continue to rail into it, releasing all the frustrations of the future ahead. Training with Hassian has been very therapeutic in a way, admittedly; I should have joined him a lot sooner. I throw one last punch that leaves the knuckles of my scarred hand bleeding from the impact. Hassian drops the bag and grabs my hand.

"Alright, we can end training for the day. You did great, princess. The ending was a little overkill, but that's okay." He motions me to sit on one of the benches while he collects the bandages and salve from the table. "It doesn't look too bad. The water should have this healed up by tomorrow. I'm still going to clean it up in the meantime.

"My hero," I tease. He lets out a grin as he dabs away the blood.

"Before we run off to dinner, I have something for you," he says as he discards the soiled cloth and walks over to his bag. He digs through it until he pulls out a small blade in a leather strap. "I'm not convinced the wards are entirely safe anymore, so I commissioned this for you. It's meant to attach to your thigh. I know you like to wear a lot of skirts and dresses. I figured that would be more practical. Please make sure you wear it every day, even during the ball. I hope that you won't ever need to use it."

He hands it over to me, and I unsheathe the blade. "This is very uh-" I pause, "sharp."

Hassian laughs. "No kidding, it is a blade, princess, forged from Alandrian steel. That can do some real damage, so be careful."

I stick it back into the sheath and examine the handle. It's not overly decorative. There is an orange stone to match my necklace, but it's not the same. I am not sure if there is another stone like my necklace. I still haven't figured out what's special about it. I hand it back over to Hassian and slowly raise my skirt.

"Well, we have to make sure it fits okay, don't we?" I ask.

"Princess," he groans as I lift my thigh off the bench so he can access it. His warm hands graze my skin as he wraps the leather strap and secures it in place. His hands reach up further than they need to before he tugs on the strap to make sure it's stable.

"Perfect fit," I say. It just got unbelievably hot in here. "Want to get out of here?" I whisper into his ear.

He grabs our bags and practically drags me out of the room in his haste. Hassian leads me down the corridor toward the East tower and into an alcove. Students are either in their extracurriculars or getting ready to head to dinner, so the chances of us being caught here are pretty slim.

Hassian presses me into the wall as he kisses my neck. I fumble for the button on his pants, and he lets a groan out when I graze his cock through the fabric of his pants. We've only had moments of stolen kisses and falling asleep in each other's arms since that night in the library. Both of us need more. My hands finally make contact with the button of his pants, and I begin undoing them. I only stop when I feel his cock spring to life as it thumps against my belly.

Hassian trails kisses further down my body as he makes his way to remove my panties. A grin spreads across his face when he realizes how wet I am. It's a mix of the euphoria of training with him and this moment. I watch as he shoves my panties into his pocket before coming back up to kiss my lips. He grabs me by my ass and lifts me higher as he aligns himself with me. He looks at me for confirmation this is what I want.

I pause briefly, wondering if it will hurt. Can I handle this? Is this how I want it to happen? I realize I don't really care. I need this with him more than I need the air that I breathe. I nod. He searches my eyes. He is gentle at first, teasing my entrance before entering a little at a time. I feel the stretch and tug as he goes deeper and deeper. I bite my lip to silence the moans from the pleasure that is way more overwhelming than the pain of my first time.

I try to stifle the moans as he decides that my body has been prepared enough and thrusts completely inside me. My head rolls back against the wall. "Eyes on me, princess." He says and I raise my head to look at him once again. The pleasure increases when I lock eyes with him watching as the dimples form on his cheeks as he smiles at me. "Good girl."

He takes one of his fingers and begins to rub circles on my clit, matching the speed of his thrusts, and I come undone. Biting my lip isn't proving to be effective as the waves keep hitting with each thrust, and I let it all out. I'm sure everyone in the academy can hear my cries of pleasure as he keeps going. He presses his lips to mine to try and muffle my moans. I let out a whimper as the orgasms begin to let up, and he releases himself into me. He stays there for a moment, looking into my eyes and assessing that I am okay with what just happened.

I am aware I probably look like a complete disaster; I can feel the sweat coating my forehead and the hair clinging to my face. "I'm sorry, I just got caught up in the moment."

"It's okay. I've been taking herbs since the library. I've been really hoping this would happen soon." That was apparently the very right thing to say because I feel him go hard inside me. I kiss him in response, and we become undone again.

We were a little late for dinner, and my friends definitely noticed our absence. We probably smell like sex, so that isn't helping our case either. Showering first would have been a good idea, but I needed food.

"You two totally did it," Thalia says as soon as we sit down. I'm glad I didn't have any food in my mouth yet, or I would have spit it out.

"Keep it down, Tal," I whisper.

"Oh, you so did," she laughs. Aurora blushes and tries to distract herself with some food. Hassian's hand moves onto my thigh, traveling to very dangerous territory. He still has my panties in his pocket because, of course, this man does.

"Thalia," I groan.

"I bet you did a lot of that, too," Aurora jokes, and we all turn to look at her at the same time. This is our innocent Aurora cracking a sex joke. "What?" She continues to eat her food.

"Where did you even go? It's so hard to find any place private around here?" Thalia asks.

"An alcove," I automatically respond. I can feel my face turning beat red as I just admitted what I did.

"A public area; that makes sense, considering how you two first met."

"You told them?" Hassian says as his fingers trail up higher. I clench my thighs together.

"It's what girl friends do; we tell each other our secrets and gossip about boys."

He laughs as he removes his hand from my thigh and begins to eat dinner. I thought I wasn't going to be able to eat anything after Thalia told my entire friend group of my deeds, but it turns out I get quite the appetite after sex. I eat more than I ever have since being in Alandria. Hassian almost looks proud over me stuffing my face.

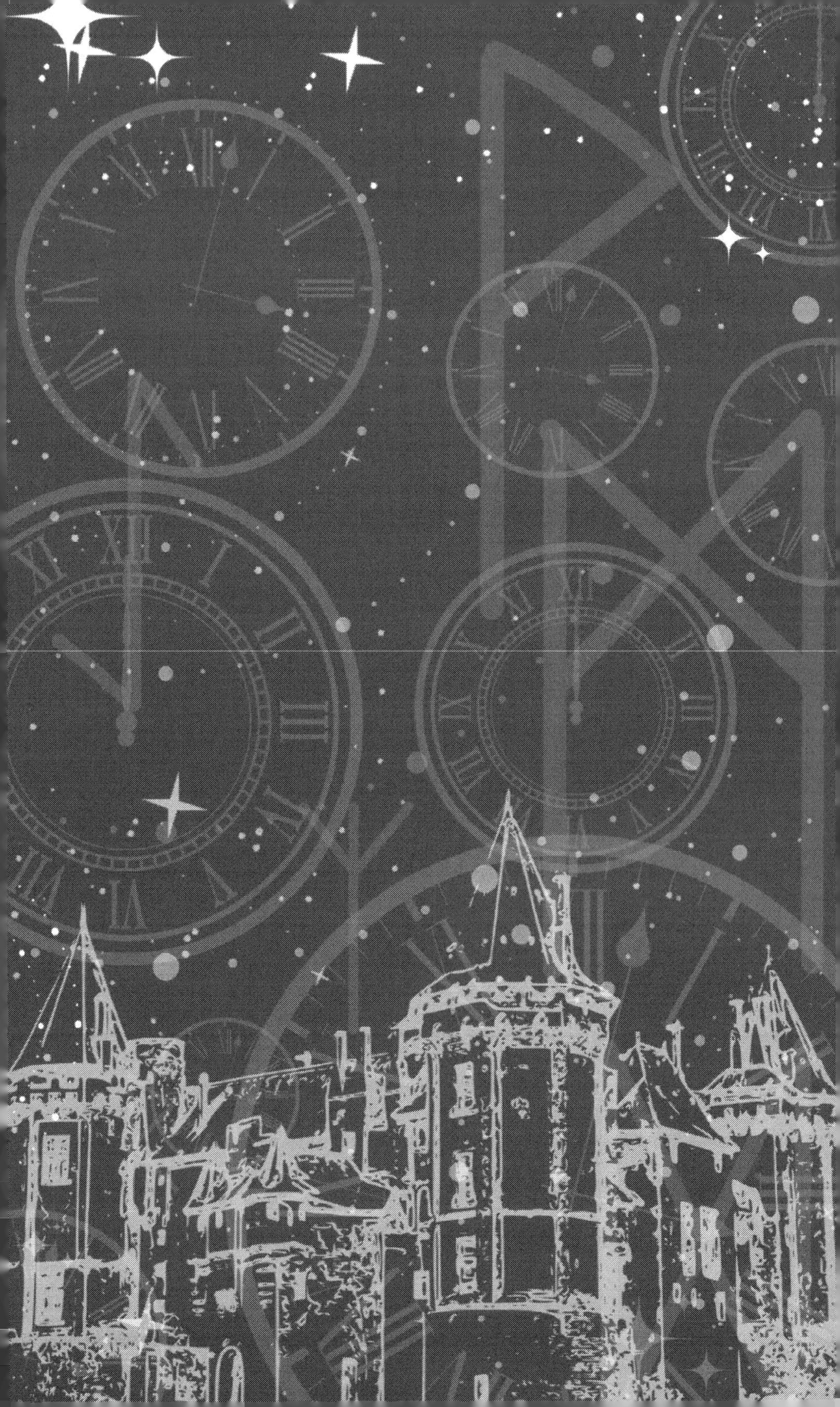

Chapter Twenty-Six
Sage

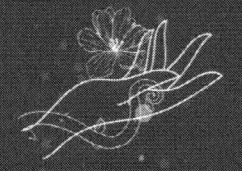

The tower chimes, signaling the start of the day, and Thalia and I practically burst from our beds. It's the day of the ball, and our dresses have yet to arrive, but Modey sent word that they would arrive sometime after breakfast. We take one glance at each other, and we know the same thought has crossed our mind, and we go barreling toward Aurora's room to retrieve her. Aurora is still sleeping through the first tower chime, so we bound onto her bed, and she jolts awake.

"For fuck's sake!" Sebille yells as she storms out of the dorm.

"Shit, I forgot. She's so absent all the time. I was going to try to talk with her during or sometime after the ball. I hope I didn't upset her too much."

"You don't owe her anything, Sage. She's never tried to be nice to you," Thalia says.

"She has her reasons."

"Oh, and you know this how?" asks Aurora.

I tell the girls about how I overheard her during one of her private lessons. "There's a lot your grandfather could have done. In any case, her behavior toward you is unwarranted. You are not your grandfather," Aurora says.

"Sebille isn't of the noble houses; he could have done any number of things. I think you should have us with you when you speak with her. She's a fire elemental; things could get dangerous.

"I suppose you're right."

A knock on our door sounds, and I walk to answer it. I open the door to see someone carrying four long bags, and they waltz in, placing them on the couch before quickly departing. "Dresses are here!" I call to the girls. No sooner do I yell for the girls than there's another knock on the door. Thalia answers it this time, and someone hands her a pile of shoe boxes.

"Oh, goody! Everything is here," Thalia sets the boxes on the table. "I'm going to fetch us some breakfast. Do you have any requests?"

"Anything pastry," Aurora says.

"Agreed."

"Great, be back soon!" Thalia bolts out the door.

I check the tags on the gown and the labels on the shoe boxes and separate them. I set Sebille's items on her bed, refusing the desire in me to peek and see what gown she picked. We sit on the couch, waiting for Thalia to return. Not much time passes before we hear a tap tap tap at the door. I make my way to open the door, and Thalia comes waltzing in. She came fully armed with goblets tucked under her arm, a pitcher of juice in one hand, and I am pretty sure she just took one of the plates they use to serve some of the pastries.

Aurora grabs the plate, and I relieve her of the pitcher so she can set the goblets down.

Aurora walks to her bedroom and retrieves a very large box before setting it beside the couch. "Who is getting their hair done first?"

"You don't want to just glamour everything?" Thalia asks.

"Absolutely not. I want to remember this, and I'm not risking something going wrong today."

"Good point."

"Agreed, considering I suck at magic."

"You'll figure it out soon, Sage," Aurora says.

"I vote Sage gets her hair done first," Thalia says.

I didn't even have a chance to respond before Aurora starts working on my hair. I would say I miss the convenience of a curling rod from the Other Realm, but there's just something special about this.

"Is Meera going to come and get ready with us, too? I ask as Aurora begins to roll up another section of hair.

"Yeah, she will be here around lunchtime. She is helping with the finishing touches for the ball and is going to bring us up some food so we don't have to go back downstairs."

"What about Anton? Is he going to join us?" I ask.

"No, he hasn't wanted to hang out much this year. I think he's over the whole twin thing. I don't even know if he's coming tonight. That's how little we talk."

"That's a shame," Aurora says as she locks the final roller into my hair. "Alright, Thalia, you're next."

Thalia and I swap seats as Aurora pulls out product for Thalia's hair. "I agree with Aurora that it is a shame. He was literally a part of our summer trio. Come to think of it, I never really see him outside of class."

"How could you? You are always staring at Hassian," Thalia teases. It's only mildly accurate. I do stare at Hassian often, but most of my time is spent training.

The door to our room opens, and Sebille walks in. "Come get ready with us," I say before I have time to process who I'm asking.

"Why?" asks Sebille.

"Well, we are roommates, and you've been avoiding us since the year started. I think that should change." I should learn to hold my tongue.

"Fine," she says as she plops on the couch beside Thalia. HOLY SHIT. "Why don't you just glamour this part?"

"We are creating memories to look back on Sebille," Aurora replies.

"Why don't you like me?" I ask. I am making real, winning decisions right now.

Sebille pulls the sleeves of her sweater down and picks at a loose thread. "Is that why you invited me, to interrogate me?"

"No," I quickly reply. "I've been meaning to ask for a long time; I just never found the moment." I'm really fumbling the ball here.

"It's not you. It's your grandfather. Okay, it's a little you, but only because it's hard to separate the two of you in my head."

"I've never met my grandfather, and I already don't like him. None of us do."

"You've never met him? I thought-" Sebille begins but changes her mind.

"No, I haven't, and I hope I don't for a very long time."

"I saw him here when everyone was moving in. I thought he was visiting you. You were so cheery, I thought maybe you liked him."

"He never came to see her. He may have been visiting Professor West. He's the one who got her hired here," Thalia says.

"She's literally the worst professor, so I guess that makes sense on how she got the job," Sebille mumbles, and we all laugh.

"She really is," Aurora says.

I see Sebille genuinely smile for the first time. "I'm sorry for how I've been behaving. I've always struggled with my emotions. The curse of being a fire elemental, I suppose. I don't like your grandfather because he's the reason my parents are dead."

"What did he do? If you don't mind me asking. You don't have to answer if you don't want," I say.

"Bandits. I was only a child, and my family couldn't afford to move to Halaris. My village kept asking for aid, but the High King refused. The only reason I am here now is because I had an aunt in the city. She couldn't afford to pay for my whole family to get to Halaris, but she could afford to get me. Trust me, she tried her hardest. She sold anything she had of value, but it just wasn't enough. Back then, the fare was a lot higher."

"I don't understand. Wouldn't it have been more logical to get the people up to the capital? Just because Gaiwen wasn't attacking, the blight is still a threat," I ask.

Sebille shakes her head. "A lot of the poorer villages didn't make it out. The High King didn't even try. I think he was trying to eliminate as many people in the realm that were beneath him as possible. The poor villages were also home to a lot of lesser fae. If you take anything from this realm, it is that many races are dying or have died out."

"The goddesses don't try to stop it? They created this realm. How can they just watch?"

"You could always try and ask Kamira?" Thalia says.

"You can speak with Kamira?" Sebille asks.

"I don't know how; she's only ever reached out to me when my powers came back," I reply.

"The goddesses can't. It's the limit to their power. They can intervene when it comes to you because you are of the same blood," Aurora says as she crosses over to Sebille to start her hair. Sebille tries to object, but Aurora swats her hand away.

"How do you know all this?" I ask.

"I volunteer at the temple during the summers. You should go there sometime. You could probably learn a lot about yourself."

We continue to chat as we get ready, and the time really flies. Sebille isn't a bad person at all, and I wish I had approached her sooner. She's spent a whole season despising her roommates and being uncomfortable in the situation she was forced into. I'm sure we will spend the next long while trying to make that up to her. After hearing her story, I understand her anger toward me.

Since I hadn't volunteered to help prepare for the ball, being so caught up in Gaiwen's journal and combat training with Hassian, I wasn't aware of where the preparations were being done. Let alone what room could be big enough to accommodate the hundreds of students, especially those in large ball gowns. As it turns out, the academy has an actual ballroom that used to host extravagant parties centuries ago when the public was allowed to join in. Now, the events are students only.

When I get to the door to the ballroom Aurora pulls me away before I can enter. Thalia, Meera, and Sebille don't look surprised and continue to enter. The green, blue, and red colors of their gowns flashing away. I'm so glad I didn't peek when it came to Sebille's dress because it transformed when she put it on. Not in the sense that magic caused it to change, but it flatters her so well. She chose this stunning red laced gown that has a white garment underneath. The lace is coated in silver accents that sparkle as she moves. Meera is wearing a light blue gown with bell sleeves. There are no real designs or adornments other than a small bow tied around her waist.

Aurora's dress also looks incredible. It fits everything about her. She is wearing a burgundy velvet floor length gown with puffy sleeves. No doubt the red was chosen due to her betrothed being a fire elemental.

"We have to be announced," Aurora whispers. "You enter last with Hassian. I've taken the liberty of telling them how to announce you when the time comes."

"Why didn't you warn me beforehand? Is there something special I have to do?" I speak so fast. I really don't do well with surprises.

"I meant to this morning, but we were all so caught up getting ready. When you are announced you and Hassian will enter the center of the ballroom and hold your right hand a breath apart. The rest of the nobles will join you in a line and we will perform the first dance. It's okay. Just follow Hassian's lead."

"Okay."

Aurora and the man escorting her are called in very early on. I assume that was her betrothed, but Aurora hasn't been very forthcoming about who he is outside of he's a fourth year and a fire elemental. I'm still unclear if that's her personal choice or something her family requires of her. Thankfully, Hassian appears shortly after.

I had no prior knowledge of what Hassian was going to wear tonight, but I am glad he did put on the tie I had sent over. The blue from the tie is about as much color as his wardrobe has, but I would expect nothing less from him. He was always eager to get out of the schools required uniform and into his darker clothing. Tonight is no different. He is wearing an all-black suit with off-white accents around the edges. It makes me think of how the elementals on the airship that brought me here dressed. The very sight of him is making my knees weak.

"How are we being announced?" Hassian asks.

I shake off my nerves to try and reply as steady as possible. "I have no idea. Aurora took care of it."

"I have a feeling we will be presented as a couple then. Is that what you want?"

I deflect the question back to him, "Is that what you want?"

He laughs. "I already said I am yours and you are mine. Whatever you are comfortable with."

"Well, I guess I'll let it remain a surprise then."

The last pair of nobility are announced into the ballroom which means we're next. My heart is beating so unbelievably fast. There are a few things I am terrible with and that's change and crowds and my new reality seems to have both.

"The High Princess, Sage Torrin, and her suitor Hassian Blackwell."

Heads turn toward us as we make our way toward the center of the room. This is my first time wearing a crown and stating my status as the High King's granddaughter. This is also the first public outing between Hassian and me, and it's a big step for both of us. The realm knew of our parent's arrangement of wedding us together, and with the announcement Aurora chose, it's equivalent to us stating that we will be. We are most definitely not engaged, but I do see a chance of a future between the two of us, maybe with time.

Once we reach the center floor and raise our right hand as the rest of the nobles make their way toward us. When all the nobles are in position music begins to play. The dance starts off simple with our hands raised and we walk around each other for about half a turn before switching hands. Eventually this stops and Hassian breaks form by leaning down and kissing my hand. We begin to dance together, just as we did that night in the library. Dancing with him, it's like we are the only two people in the world. I can easily drown out the noise of the people around us, getting lost in his blue eyes. I have never seen him this dressed up before. He dresses well regularly, with slacks and a dress shirt, but today, he looks like a king.

I don't know how many songs have played as we sway on the ballroom floor, talking about our lives before the academy and what we like to do for fun. After I found out he had never traveled outside of Alandria, I explained what a cell phone is. As it would turn out, nobles don't get to travel to the Other Realm. A common fear among households is that the portal suddenly does not work and that they will lose an heir to the Other Realm. I suppose that it is a valid fear to have.

I tell him about the Other Realm and how different it is from here. "I couldn't imagine living in a world where magic isn't a common practice."

"It's not so bad. I will say I love it here and don't miss much of the stuff back home. There are some things I do miss, though."

"Such as?" he spins me outward before twirling me back into his arms.

"Television. I miss sitting for hours watching shows about vampires, magic, and even a good zombie show. Now all we have is just the DVDs we brought with us."

"Well, now you're living in it," he says.

"Wait, vampires are a thing? Hold up, zombies?"

"Yes, to the vampires. I am not sure of their number, but The Order employs them. Come to think about it, that journal, he might have been one. There's not a lot, but maybe we can visit their headquarters when summer comes or sooner and see if we can speak to him."

"If they made him keep the secret through a blood oath, what makes you think they will tell me."

"There are only two reasons they wouldn't answer your questions. Neither is good. The first being that it was corruption within The Order, and someone paid them off to do it. The other being it was the High King, himself that did it."

"You think my grandfather could be capable of something like that?"

"I think that out of all the time you have been here, he hasn't come to see you, and that, to me, speaks volumes."

"Already you don't like my grandfather?" I joke.

"I like-" he pauses. "I-" Is this man nervous right now? "My heart is yours forever, Sage. That's enough for me. You tease me relentlessly, but I know you do not care for him. I know with every fiber of my being you will never be him. Where he is unkind and cruel, you are caring and selfless. You walked into this realm with a burden no one deserves to shoulder, but know this, you will never be alone, not as long as I breathe."

I remember we are in a room full of people, and I must remember to focus on the dancing. If I randomly stop, there will be stares, and my heart is already racing. Is it hot in here? Should I go outside to get air? I am very much nervous because I have been thinking about just how we would say I love you to each other for the very first time. I knew I held a flame for him from the moment we met in the showers. I knew I wanted him to be mine when he found me in the hallway in a panic because I was hurt. I knew I loved him when he danced with me in the library among the candle flames. Love that it is what I, too, feel for him.

"I love you too, Hassian." I breathe out, and his lips crash into mine. We forget all decorum at that moment as we kiss each other long and hard until we are gasping for air. I don't know where my friends are and I should probably seek them out, but all I want to be is right here
in his arms.

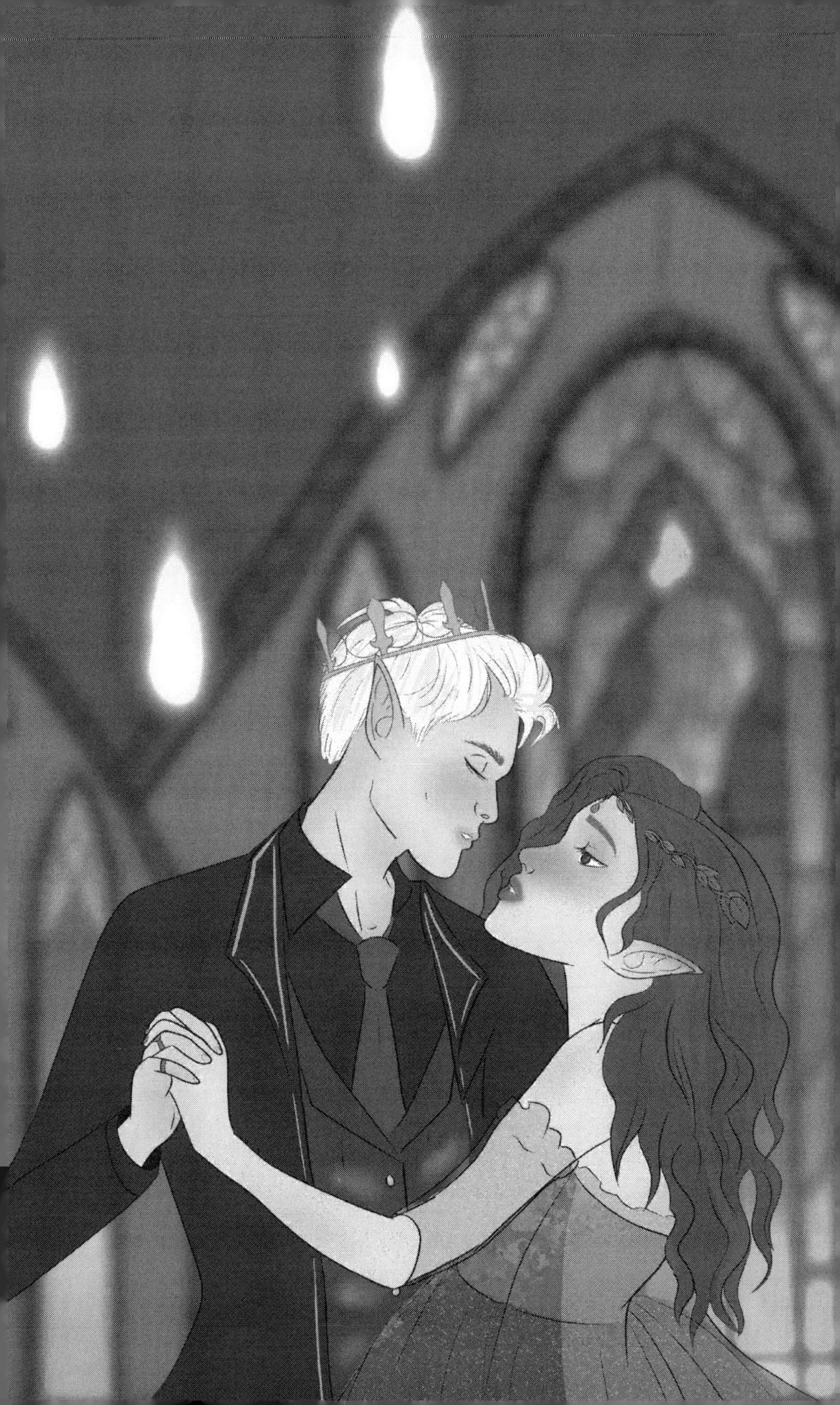

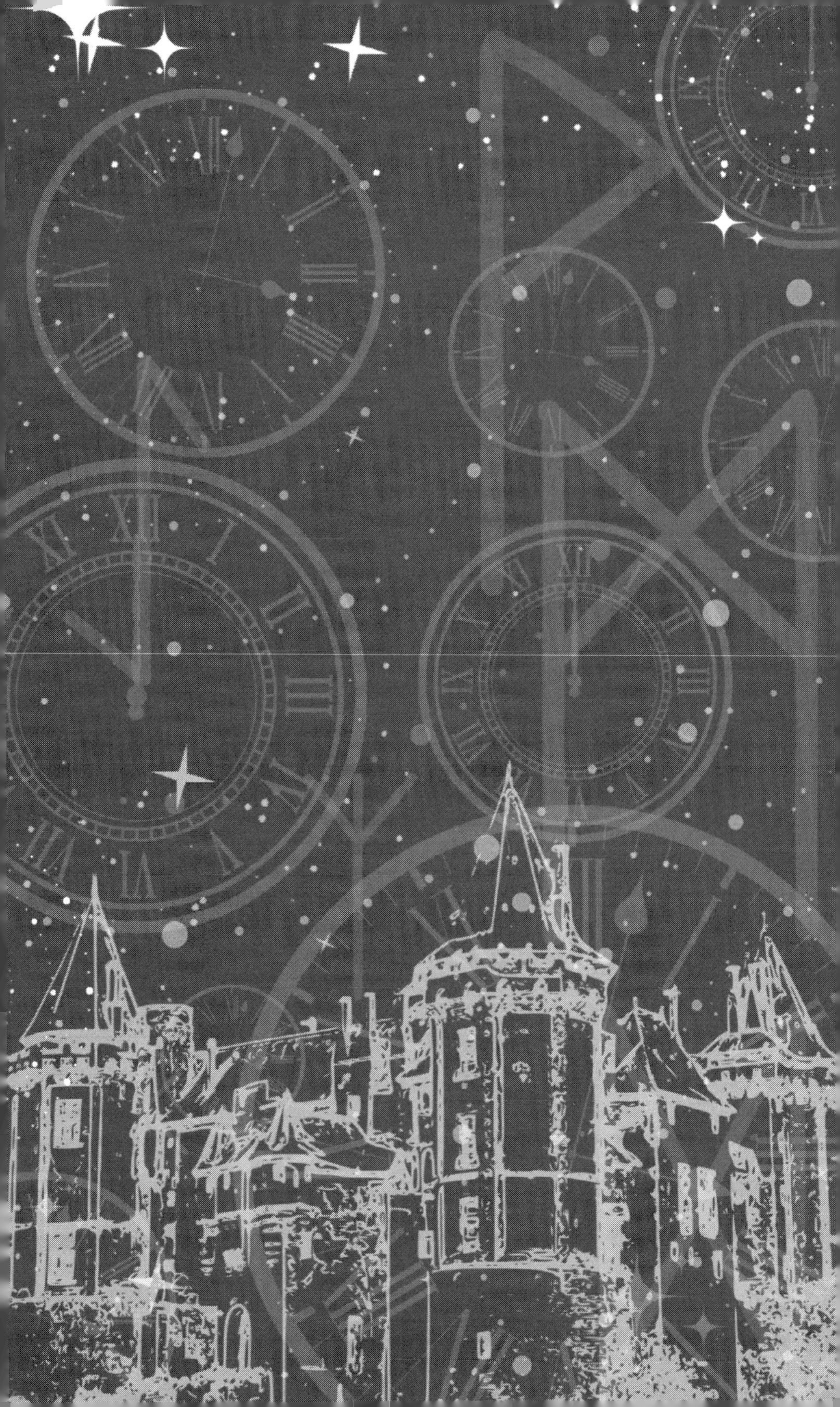

Chapter Twenty-Seven
Sage

Classes are back in full swing once again with the ball ending. Even though Hassian and I have been seeing each other on a very intimate level since the night in the library, tradition dictates that you have to announce your status as a couple at a formal event. Which the night of the ball we did thanks to Aurora. Hassian insists on walking me to my morning class and informs me he will continue doing so.

In Professor Dublin's class students are now continuing to learn based on their handle of magic which means a lot of the class has moved to advanced casting. As an earth elemental we have the power to cast protective wards and forge stones and metals. I'm still stuck at the basics and it is highly embarrassing.

"Sage, I want to try something different with you today. I know you have been committing really hard to your studies outside of class, but something is stuck and we need to address it."

"What do you have in mind?"

"I spoke with Kira and she told me about what happened when your power came out. About the nosebleed from being in the sun all day. I think your magic might work more on the sacrificial side. It's very rare for someone to need to pay some sort of cost."

"Sacrificial? I don't follow."

"Well, your nose bled during your awakening and when you turned your bud into a raging vine, it sought out blood. It didn't shrivel back into its bud state until I forced it back down. I think the key to accessing your magic and making it last is blood. I suppose sacrificial was a bit of a morbid term to use. I just mean your magic takes a cost. It might only take a drop; it might take more. I want to focus on figuring that out."

"You want me to cut myself? That doesn't exactly sound appealing professor."

"Right now, I am not talking dagger to palm. Although, that may be a requirement if you need to cast a large-scale spell. I'm saying let's try a needle prick. A singular drop on the bud then cast your intentions. Let's see what happens and go from there."

I nod. He reaches into his pocket and pulls out a kit of needles and hands me one. "Is this thing sterile?" I joke.

"It's safe, Sage. Go ahead and give it a try."

I prick the tip of my finger and squeeze it enough that a single drop of blood touches the flower bud. I close my eyes and look into myself traveling to the garden inside my mind, to the pillar of vines. I reach out, letting them wrap around my hand. Bloom. Bloom. Bloom. I think about what I want to happen. Chanting the words over and over again inside my head. I open my eyes and release. My hands are glowing with a green aura and the bud is in full bloom. I count. One. Two. Three. It made it past where it always reverts. I look to the professor to see if it stays if I break my focus. I look back. I fucking did it.

"It's just as I thought. Blood is the key to accessing your power," Professor Dublin grins at me. "Congratulations, Sage, you finally beat the first casting and you've discovered how to access your power."

"I feel sorry for my fingers," I joke.

"I recommend taking advantage of your Herbology lessons and keeping salves on hand, especially once you are out of the academy. They will help with the ache and speed up the healing process. In the meantime, take advantage of the water in the school."

"What should I do next?"

He pauses thinking about my next steps. "Actually, since you are a bloodletter, I would like to try something else. Bloodletting is a lot more powerful form of magic than just a basic elemental. That's why they are so rare. I will be right back."

He leaves the classroom and is gone for quite some time before returning with a very dead plant. "What do you expect me to do with that thing?" I ask.

"I want to see if your element is powerful enough to restore life. Keep in mind that this is a plant, not a human. If this works, do not go trying to resurrect things with souls. That crosses into forbidden magic and that always has a price." He sets the plant in front of me. "This is going to take a few more drops of blood so try to get more on it this time, okay?"

"Sure thing." I lift the needle to my finger again and poke. Bringing my finger above the plant I squeeze out a few more drops of my blood. My finger is starting to ache from the slight torment of the needle. I close my eyes to focus thinking about what I wish to happen. Live. Again, I am pushing all my intentions into making it happen. When I open my eyes, it's not just my hands glowing but my whole body. I look at the plant, still focusing on what I need to happen. The droplets of my blood absorb into the leaves and the plant's coloring begins to return before it rises into a lively state.

"By The Nines. I wasn't sure if it was possible."

"You asked me to do it with no idea if it would work?"

"Yeah. There's not much on bloodletters as I said."

"If I can heal this, does that mean I can potentially heal the dead land?"

"With lots of practice, I think it is very much possible. I don't know how much blood it would take. You'd experience so much drain. You might be able to heal a little at a time, I think if you were to try the entire area in one go it might kill you."

"Do you think The Order will try and make me do it anyway?"

"It's possible. I will not be telling them and I hope the rest of the student body sticks to the same honor system as I do. It's your body, your magic, and you decide how far you are willing to go."

I suppose testing this out in a room full of students wasn't our best idea, but judging from the people around us, they were so focused on their own casting that they weren't even paying me any mind. At least, I hope that is the case. I already have one big thing to face, I'd rather not be beaten down before then.

"Settle down everyone; this is just an illusion made with some runes," Professor Moore says. Apparently, we are learning defense against more dangerous beasts today. There's a very disturbing-looking direwolf standing in the open lawn of the back courtyard. It looks extremely realistic, and if I didn't know what I did from Gaiwen's journal, I would be inclined to believe it was. There is drool coming from its mouth, but it's not singing the grass. Hells, it's not even adding any weight to the grass.

"What exactly are we learning today, Professor? I was much enjoying the small animal studies," asks some boy whose name I can't remember. I really need to get better at that. If I am to rule over these people one day, it would be best if I learn their names at the very least.

"I am going to show you the best way to kill a shadow creature or creature of the dark, as some refer to it. Beasts class isn't all about rescuing and repopulating dying beasts. It's also about learning to protect yourself from threats."

I stand up straighter, rolling my shoulders back. I know this will be important for me to retain. Shadow creatures equal Gaiwen, and he's the first threat I must deal with.

"In order to successfully resurrect, the creature must have a brain or a heart that is intact. Please, don't resurrect anything that has a soul, that comes with a cost. The realm is already paying enough of those consequences. Not that you should be trying to resurrect anything. Now, where was I? Oh, right." Professor Moore walks up closer to the illusion with a small stick in hand. "A creature must have a brain or heart intact in order to be resurrected, which also means that is the creature's weakness. The host cannot survive without either. Goddess forbid, if you are ever in a situation where you need to fight one, always go for the head. You could try for the heart, but it might not be in the typical place."

"The shadow creatures have acidic saliva. Is that correct?" I ask. I know I read it in Gaiwen's journal, but I'd rather confirm with a source I trust.

"Yes, they do!" Professor Moore practically yells with excitement. "You've been studying the beast's books, have you?"

"Something like that," I respond.

"Most excellent. Now, as Sage has brought up these beasts do have very dangerous saliva, often spitting it at their victim. It's best to try and keep your distance."

"I heard you can't use magic. Is that correct?" asks Melony. She's one of the quieter students in my year.

"That it is. You won't be able to use magic. I do believe runes work, but I haven't personally encountered one of these beasts in person to verify. I just read the public records."

Professor Moore continues going on about the different ways to defend yourself and avoid getting hit. It's a really interesting lesson. I do miss the cute little creatures we have been working with, but this is something that could potentially help me when the time comes.

I meet up with Hassian and recant what happened in my affinity class today. "Bloodletter? I am not familiar with that term. I knew you were doing everything right, princess."

"I'm just not sure casting is going to be a great experience having to do that every time. Honestly, that kind of sucks from a danger standpoint, too. Others can just cast on demand and I have this extra step. It's not like if I am in danger I will have time to poke myself with a needle or slice my palm. Even then, I'm probably going to hesitate, danger or not."

"Hmmm. I have an idea for that. I want to keep it a surprise so I am not going to tell you just yet. I will draft up my idea and send it by raven later. Now it's time for your fighting lessons. Which I think you are doing really good with basic hand to hand and I would like to move on to slightly more painful methods."

"Painful?"

"Spear fighting."

"You really want to give me a stick with a point at the end?"

"Well, not quite yet, but I do have some practice staves. They'll hurt if you get hit, but you shouldn't kill me or anyone else in the process of practicing with them."

We walk toward a barrel of staves on the other side of the room. He takes two out and hands one to me.

"I am going to show you some spear-fighting basics. We are going to start with a short thrust. Watch me first, then try on your own."

He places his right foot forward, moving his right hand to about the middle of the shaft, bringing his left hand down to the end of the stave, and holding it in an upward position. He jabs the stave forward and pulls back in quick succession, repeating this so I can try to understand the movement. "You can also wave the spear when you hold it forward to deflect any possible movement coming to your face. Give it a try."

I face the same position he is standing in and try to repeat his movement, but it is like my thought process just stops working as soon I get into the upward position. "Can you show me again?"

"Of course, princess" He moves quickly but slows down right to where I got stuck. "This is where you jab it forward and pull back. Try to do it quickly when you get to that part. Try it again."

I give it another go. I am a little slow on the delivery, but I keep repeating the movements until it becomes fluid. "I did it!" I know it's lame, but there's something about getting things right when he's teaching me that just feels so damn good.

"Good girl, now let's try the long-range thrust." He places his hands and feet in the same position as before making the same beginning movement, except this time he brings his left hand up to his armpit and then back down to the original position. "Now you try."

I give it a go. This time remembering what he showed all the way through. Much like the previous move, I repeat time and time again, just trying to remember the steps until it's fluid. Hassian goes on to teach me more ways to fight with a stave and by the end of the lesson I am drenched in sweat and sprawled on my back in pure exhaustion.

"You are lucky the school has water with really nice healing properties or I would be very upset with today's lesson," I joke.

"You did good, princess. I'm glad you are taking this seriously. I never want you to feel defenseless in a situation or be reliant on someone to save you."

"I appreciate that you care so much to continue to go out of your way to teach me."

"I would do anything for you princess. If you asked me to burn the world to the ground. I would do it. I might question why we are going dark side, but if it was what you wanted or needed. I'd be there. My dashing good looks and all."

"Rest assured; I don't ever intend on trying to burn the world to the ground. The only thing I want to do is make this realm feel safe for everyone in it. A lot of damage has been done and those responsible will pay."

"Are you thinking about the nobleman again?"

I nod. "They obviously knew there was a cost, but didn't care. Whose life or what secret could be so important, that you destroy an already dying power? Do you think he will ever be able to get access to his light again?"

"I don't know. I would like to believe anyone can be redeemed, but that journal. It got dark at the end."

"I know. Can I tell you a secret?"

"You can tell me anything, princess."

"I'm terrified."

"I know." He pulls me onto his lap and runs his fingers through my hair. We just sit there in silence, watching as the sun begins to set in the sky through the windows of the training room before we head in to see what food is left in the great hall.

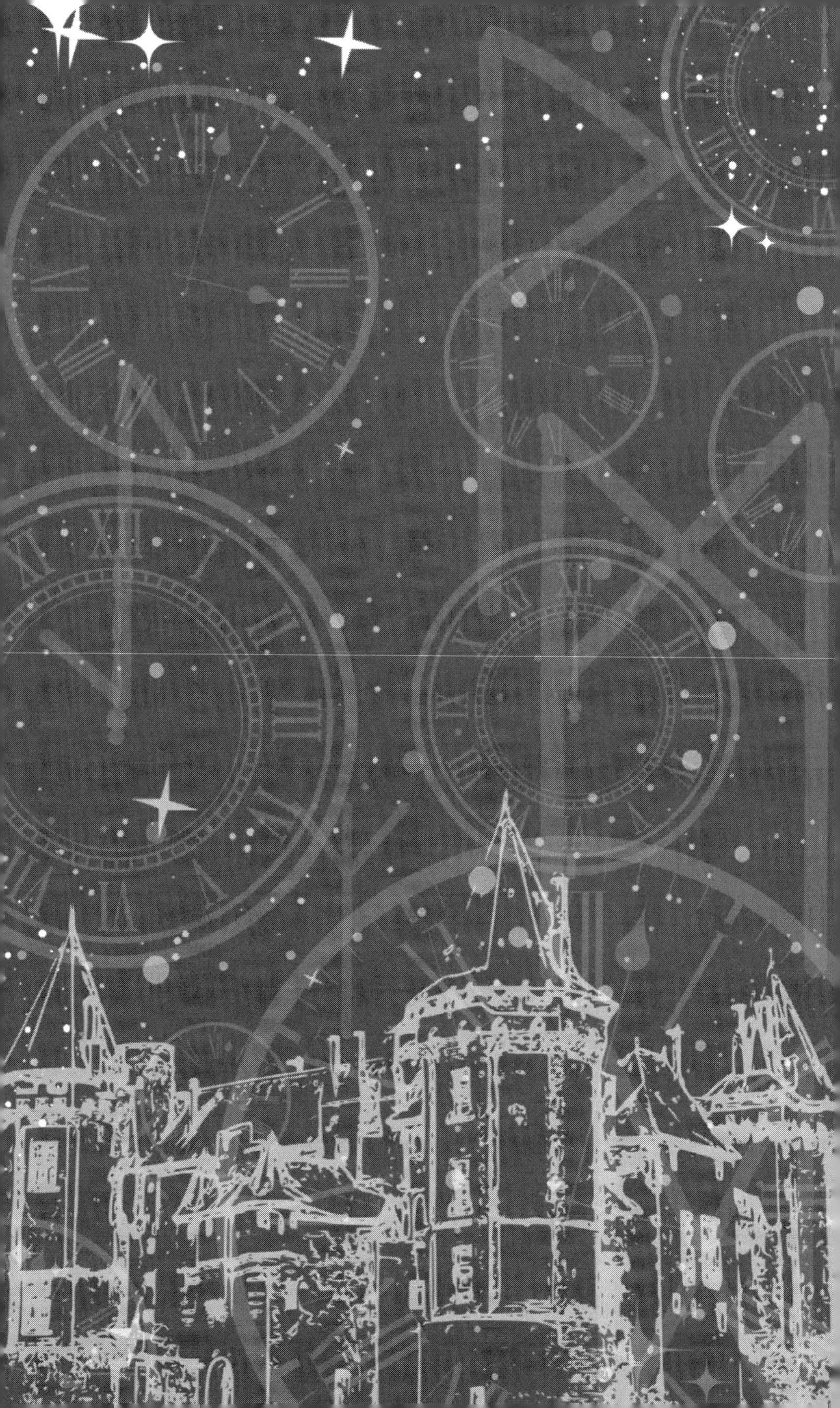

Chapter Twenty-Eight
Sage

Hassian has been relentless in his weapons training. He is adamant that I learn it all. I was feeling very confident about what I was learning up until the point when he said I was ready to spar. My arms are quivering from the constant impact of his stave against mine as I try to push him back and away.

"Come on, princess, don't let me win."

"I'm not letting you do anything. We are not exactly equals in this."

"No? What makes me different?"

"Well, look at you. You're so big." My face flames when I see the mischievous grin on his face, realizing I just walked into that one. I think making me blush is one of his favorite pastimes.

"You just have to keep practicing. Size doesn't matter, but the delivery does."

"Yeah, well, my delivery sucks." I groan.

"Do you want me to bring back out the training posts?"

I nod. "Please. I just need to get my arms more attuned to the impact. That's the hardest part for me. I get so distracted by the sudden pain in my bicep or forearm that I start to falter."

"If you think it will help," he jogs over to the supply closet. I regret not joining sooner, and only because I could have watched his muscles flex as he hauled all the bulky equipment.

I have to admit; I am a little jealous of all the women who were already training and saw him like that.

He returns with the wooden training dummy I was practicing on when I first joined him. I stretch my head from side to side while I focus on how I want to approach this. I grip my stave just as he showed me, thinking back on the moves he taught me in the beginning. I do strike after strike. I keep going until my arms and everything else is so sore, they shake from the blows, and I cannot grip the stave any longer. I debate not even using the healing properties of the water to stay with this pain for a night. I end up thinking better of it. It's not like the water erases our progress, and I smell revolting right now from the layers of grime and sweat.

Hassian picks the stave I was using up off the ground and returns it to the bin. "Come on, princess, let's get you off to the showers."

I wince as I try to pick up my bag holding my books for the day. "I might have overdone it just a bit."

Hassian takes the bag from me, "We all have to learn our limits. Just thank The Nines, that you did it while at the academy, princess."

I haven't tried the bath since the night I had my panic attack, but I want nothing more than to lean back in the water while it does its work. Hassian helped me into the water, leaving as soon as he made sure I was comfortable to get us some clean clothes.

The water's healing properties are not instant in effect, but they work quickly. After a few minutes, I am able to raise my arms again, so I take the gelatinous glob from the vine and begin washing my hair. Every time I use it, I cannot help the smile that crosses my face as I think about the first night Hassian and I met.

"What's so funny?" he asks as he slips into the water beside me.

"I was thinking about the joke you made on the day we met. It was a joke, wasn't it?"

"Yes, it was a joke. It's no different than someone extracting what's required from the plants and making it themselves. I just wanted to get a reaction out of you. I like to watch the way your face changes color when you blush." As if in response to him, my face reacts. He kisses my forehead. "Just like that, princess."

"I have a question," I say as I trace invisible circles on his skin.

"I have an answer."

"When did you know you loved me?" I've been curious about this for quite some time.

"From the day I met you."

I push him playfully. "No, be serious, Hassian." I laugh, waiting.

"I am."

"There's no way you knew that early on."

"I did."

"How?"

"I've never been in the Other Realm, so I don't know their teachings or how things work there, but have you heard of the term fated mates?"

"Wait, that's a real thing?"

"So, you have heard of it."

"In fictional stories, yes."

"Well, it's not fictional here. What do your fictional stories say about it?"

"Men can tend to get a little aggressive over their mate."

"Well, I'm not sure I am aggressive towards anyone speaking to you. I experience jealousy."

"I get jealous, too," I admit.

"What would make you jealous? I've only ever given you, my time."

"It's not even anything you do or are around. It's when I overhear conversations, and someone is talking about you. Like, for instance, the winter solstice ball, when girls were saying who they were going to ask."

"I would have said no."

"I didn't know that then. I was so hurt when I thought you were going to ask someone else."

"I will spend the rest of my life apologizing for ever allowing me to be the cause of your tears." He kisses my neck. "I'm sorry for teasing you that day. I will be more mindful of how I choose to elicit a reaction from you."

"That's all a girl can ask for," I joke, splashing him with water. "Will you stay with me again tonight?"

He splashes me back. "You don't even have to ask. Until you kick me from your room, I will be there."

"Thank you."

"What for, princess?"

"For making me feel safe."

"It's an honor to do so."

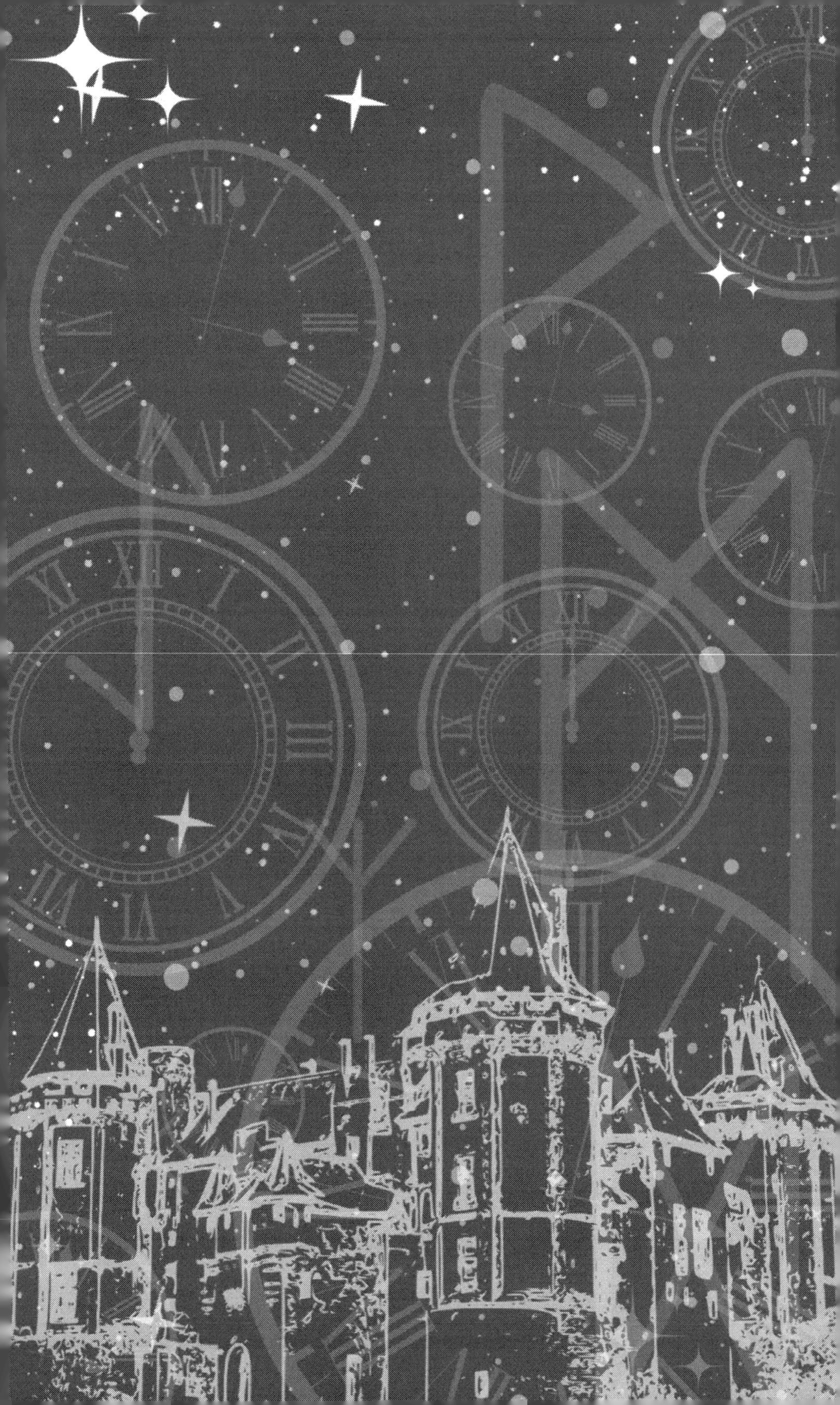

Chapter Twenty-Nine
Sage

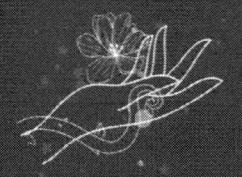

Winter goes, and spring arrives. The flowers are back in bloom, and the brownies are back to spending the majority of their time outside. Today marks a holiday week in Alandria, so we are once again allowed to leave the academy and head into town. Thalia is with her parents while Hassian and I are heading to the blacksmith in the city.

"This is a long time to wait for a commission," I joke.

"Well, I wanted it to be perfect and made from only the best metal."

"Do I get a hint as to what it is?"

"No," he says, pulling me closer to him as another man walks bumping into townspeople.

"Hey, watch it," someone shouts as they get shoved hard.

"I wonder what his problem is," I say, glancing back at the man.

"Who knows, but I'd rather you not be made collateral to whatever it is." We walk faster until we eventually reach the blacksmith shop and head inside.

"Lord Blackwell," says the blacksmith.

"We've talked about this; just call me Hassian."

"Of course, apologies. The commission you ordered turned out beautifully if I do say so myself. Let me get it from the safe. I'll be right back."

"He put your commission in the safe?" I ask.

"It was rather expensive."

"Ah, right, here it is. Go on inspect it and make sure everything is correct. I followed your sketches and notes to the exact."

Hassian takes the small box and turns away from me as he inspects the piece. "You did a great job, Hinley."

"Of course, it was not a problem. You already sorted your accounts, so you are good to go."

Hassian nods, taking my hand, and we exit the shop. "Where are we going now?" I ask.

"Somewhere with less people."

We walk a few more blocks before eventually rounding a corner and making our way through a tall metal arch into a blooming garden near the city's heart. We continue walking the path until we find a bench and sit. He pulls the box from his pocket again and holds it to me while removing the lid.

"This is not a proposal, princess, but a weapon."

"I was just going to ask; a handsome man taking me to a secluded area filled with flowers and holding out a ring feels awfully proposal-ish to me." I joke.

"On the day I ask you, princess, your ring will look much better than this. I can assure you of that."

I let out a nervous laugh as I reach for the box and look at the jewelry. It's a ring with a long triangle-shaped metal bit. I slip it onto my middle finger, and a red glow quickly appears, showing some kind of rune and then vanishes. I curl my hand, and the triangle becomes a sharp curved point, similar to a talon. As I straighten my hand, it reverts back. "That's very sharp," I say, looking at him.

He laughs. "I am beginning to notice a pattern when I give you gifts, but yes, it is. Sharp enough to pierce your skin for casting. You can easily poke a finger on your opposite hand or make a deeper cut for more difficult magic. The rune disappears, so it appears to be a normal object at first glance. If you take the ring off and put it back on. It will flash again."

"I love it, thank you."

"You're very welcome, princess. I'd recommend not sleeping with it if that can be helped. You do have a tendency of gripping in your sleep, and I would appreciate not being sliced to bits."

"I'll do my best to remember to take it off. It's very beautiful and thoughtful. I will very much enjoy ditching the needles."

"It's also more discreet, so you can have less anxiety when you are casting in class."

I kiss him on the cheek and admire the ring some more. "You really put some thought into this. It was worth the wait."

"I'm glad you think so."

"Shall I give it a test run?"

"Go ahead, princess. Show me what you got," he gives me a wink.

I walk over to some shrubbery that doesn't have any flowers. I focus on what I want to happen. Transform. Bloom. The two words I repeat in my head over and over again while I access the pillar of vines in my mind. While focusing on my intent, I prick my finger. It's painless this time and undoubtedly infused with more runes than he let on. I release my power into the hedge and watch as hundreds of flowers burst into full bloom. I surprise even myself. I wasn't sure I could force something to grow when it wasn't part of its original makeup, but I figured with the angry vines from class that it just might.

"Absolutely incredible princess."

"Hey, while we are in town. Do you want to come with me and see what we can find out at The Order's headquarters?"

"That sounds like a great idea."

"I don't know what to tell the two of you. We don't deal in sacrilegious acts like blood oaths anymore. The last time has been centuries ago."

"I have it on good authority that a vampire from The Order over thirty years ago did one."

"Who or what is the source of this supposed accusation?" he asks.

Hassian interjects before I say anything. "You would do well to remember your place when speaking to a member of the high family."

"My apologies to the High Princess, but there is nothing I can tell you. Even if such a thing exists, that's confidential information."

"Thank you for your time," I say before grabbing Hassian's hand and exiting the building.

"You caught onto that too?"

"I sure did. It's as you said, the only reason I wouldn't be able to be told the information was if The Order was corrupted or my grandfather initiated it."

"What are you thinking?"

"I'm thinking, my grandfather hasn't visited me once, but yet brought someone to try and ensure I believe a false history. I also think we need to discuss this somewhere more privately."

"To Tal's?"

I nod.

Thalia's family is full of many secrets, including a hidden door behind their pantry, which leads down some stairs to a hidden room in their house. The room isn't too big, but it's well stocked with preserved food and some resting places set up. It's about the size of the main room of their house. Everyone gathers into the room, including Anton, who has been MIA for most of our time at school. If I am being honest, his lack of being around makes me not want to divulge the information in his presence, but Tal assures me he can be trusted, so I relent.

"Hassian and I were at The Order's headquarters today discussing blood oaths with one of the vampires that work there."

"Blood oaths have not been a practice for centuries. Why were you talking about that?" Thalia's father asks.

"It's come to my knowledge that someone in The Order still does or did it about 34 years ago."

"Where did you come across this?" Kira asks.

"A journal," Thalia says.

"Whose?" her dad asks.

"Gaiwen's," Hassian says.

The room is a murmur of hushed inquiries of how we found the journal and what was in it. I pull it from my bag and set it on the table. "I was hoping either the two of you or Kira might be able to understand the final pages of the journal," I say, speaking to Thalia's parents.

"You're the High King's granddaughter. Did they say who it was that asked for the blood oath?"

"No. In fact, he said he couldn't tell me even if the information existed," I say.

"Well, that's not right. There are only two reasons that-"

"Oh, I know," I say.

Kira looks pale as she hears this information. "You said this started thirty-four years ago?"

"Yes, why?"

"That's about the age of your mother, and if they refused to say then-"

"My mother was the baby," I nod. "That's what my theory is."

"I don't understand; how did she die in the first place?" Thalia's mom asks.

"That I don't know. There's another thing. The magic doesn't just revive them. It makes them a thrall to Gaiwen. I don't think he is the one who murdered my mother. He could have just ordered her to tell the truth."

"You think someone else is responsible?" Kira asks.

"Yes, I do. Gaiwen has a lot to be blamed for, but my mother's death isn't one of them. I also find it curious that my grandfather has never sought me out since my return."

"That doesn't make any sense. He was distraught over your disappearance. He didn't think you were in the Other Realm, given the state of your mother and the distance to the portal," Thalia's father says.

"My mom made a portal and sent Kira and I through."

"That's impossible, though; no one can make portals."

"She had help from the goddesses," Kira says. "Sage was in danger, and her mother never had a chance to say by who. I always assumed it was Gaiwen."

"Oh, she's still in danger from him. He's resurfaced, there have been reports of him being spotted, and the rot has grown." This is the first thing Anton has said the whole meeting.

"How do you know this?" Thalia asks her brother.

"I've been keeping my ear to the ground all school year. The noble's kids talk a lot. They're always privy to information we lessers don't get." He nods to Gaiwen and me. "Sorry, not meaning any offense. I know you two have been out of the loop. One of you by choice."

I look to Hassian, and he gives me a look as if to say that he will explain it to me later. "There's another thing. I'm going to need something specific for this. Kira, are there any dead plants?"

"Only one didn't make it. I will go fetch it."

She returns moments later and I motion for her to place the plant on the table. Using the ring Hassian crafted for me, I prick my finger and let a few droplets fall on the leaves. Eyes widen around me for my use of blood for casting. I do just as I did in Professor Dublin's class and resurrect the plant.

"That's impossible," Thalia's father says.

"Professor Dublin says I am something called a bloodletter. That my magic takes a cost. When I had the nosebleed and, my powers showed for the first time since they were silenced. I had paid the cost required. I was thinking about the prophecy after I came to the conclusion about my mother. A child born of life and death; I don't think the meaning is my mother dying giving birth to me. I think it means my mother was undead; my father was alive. I shouldn't exist."

"So, you are both dead and alive?" Anton asks.

"Something like that. I think my powers might be capable of giving life and taking it. I also think that my mother and my connection with Kamira might have something to do with us being not entirely alive. I'm not one hundred percent on that yet, but it's a current theory."

"Wait, so does that mean Hassian has been courting a dead fae?" Anton jokes. At least, I hope he is.

"She's not dead. She's just born different," Hassian says.

"That's not helping. Can we not make that the focus here, please?" I ask.

"What are we supposed to do about the High King? He controls everything, and if you look around the room, we don't exactly have the numbers to face up against him."

"No, you are right, Anton, we don't have the numbers. We also have Gaiwen to worry about. As far as I am aware, my grandfather isn't threatening the realm itself; he's just guilty of creating that threat. You said you've been keeping your ear to the ground?"

"Yeah, what about it?"

"Maybe you can also find people who would be willing to stand against my grandfather when the time comes?"

"I can do that."

"Good. In the meantime, I will keep training, and we hope that for the realm's sake, I can do what needs to be done."

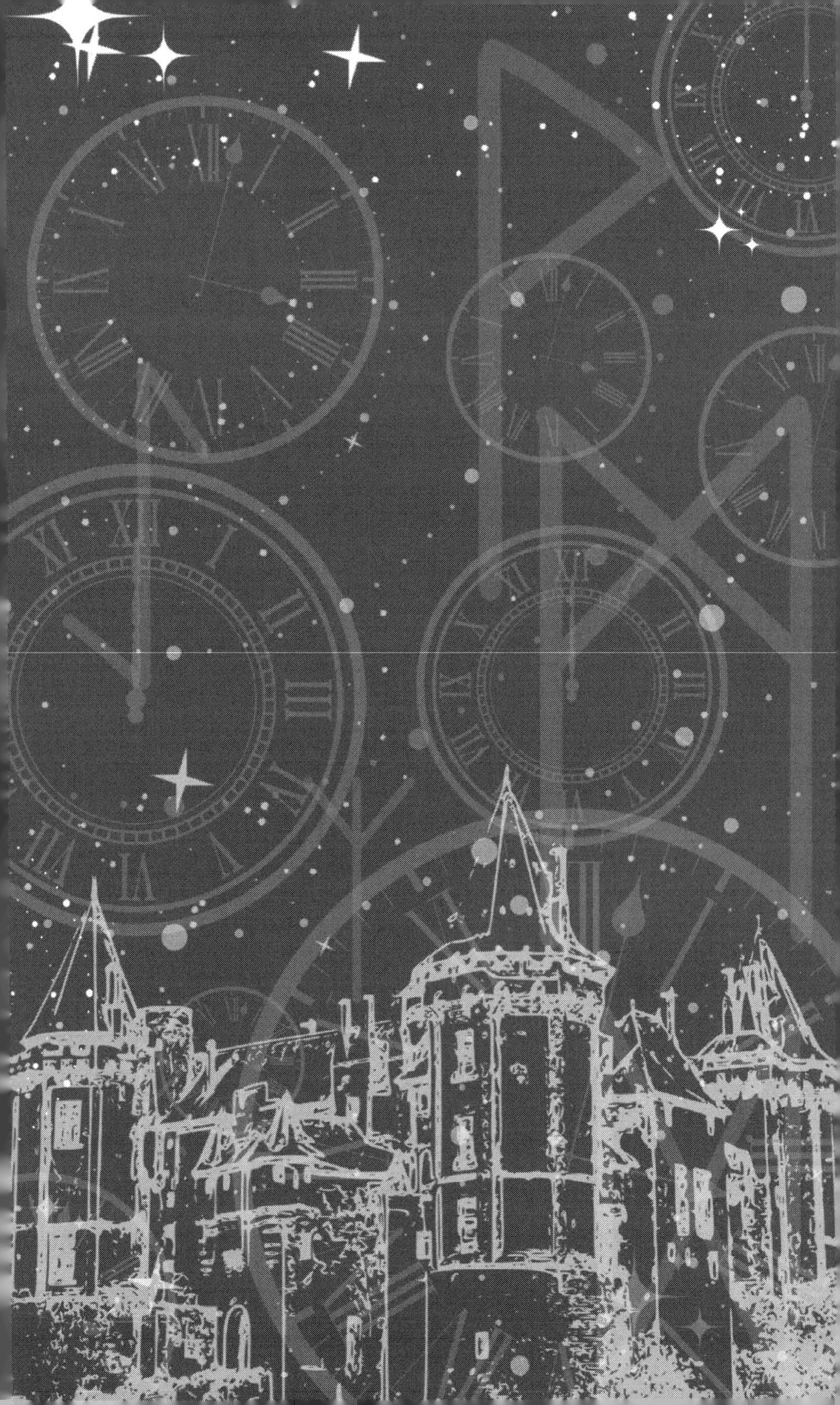

Chapter Thirty
Sage

Hassian and I decide to head back to the academy early so we can get some more training in and allow Thalia and Anton time with their family. Hassian is helping me into my seat on the carriage when we catch sight of the white-colored uniform that is the staple of The Order members.

"I'm afraid you won't be going back to the academy anytime soon, bloodletter." The Order member lifts the hood of his robes, revealing his face to us. It's the same vampire who refused to tell us any information. It's Ivan, the asshole.

"I don't know what you're talking about. Now, if you'll excuse us, we'd like to return to school before curfew."

Hassian makes a move to load up in the carriage beside me, but Ivan cuts him off, "I'm a vampire; you really thought I wouldn't be able to smell the blood on you?"

"I slipped and cut myself. Why are you making such a big deal out of this? Let us go."

"I would, but the thing is, magic powered by blood has a distinct smell. I was going to overlook this at first, but then one of your schoolmates came to us and was more than happy to tell us all about your lessons. They didn't even want a reward for doing so."

Hassian glares into Ivan's eyes. "Do you understand who you're accosting?"

Ivan flashes his fangs. "Oh, I am very much aware, as you so kindly stated back in my office earlier. I come with full permission from the High King. It would seem he is not so concerned about her well-being."

"I'm not going with you," I state, ready to hold my ground.

"Oh relax, Princess," the name that has been endearing coming from Hassian feels fowl and disgusting from him. "Unlike your grandfather, we do care if you live. We won't let too much harm come to you, but we cannot continue to ignore the threat of the blight. If it spreads any further, it will start cutting into our water supply. You don't want to be the reason more fae die, do you?"

"She was not to blame for it. How dare you try to make her feel guilt for something she was not responsible for, not when you know who was," Hassian interjects.

"Something we have been trying to make right." Something akin to guilt flashes in Ivan's eyes, and I think that as much as he might have had a role in this, he might not have had a choice. Whether he was for the idea initially or reluctant, he wouldn't have been afforded the option to say no.

"Fine, but Hassian comes with me. I also want you to tell me the truth of what went down. I have my suspicions, but I deserve answers."

Ivan looks as if he is contemplating his next steps, and there is a long moment of pause before he responds, "Deal, but only once we are aboard the ship."

The ship is more packed than I thought it would be. Just how dangerous is this blight? I see at least three dozen Order members loading crates onto the ship. Ivan walks Hassian and me toward the captain's quarters so we have somewhere private to speak.

"What's in those crates?" I ask as soon as he closes the door behind us.

"You have a lot of questions," he states, slipping into his chair.

"Well?" I ask, and Hassian chuckles, slipping into one of the seats opposite Ivan's desk. I sit in the chair beside him.

"Well, I guess you were going to find out soon enough. One of the main reasons we need this blight situation dealt with is because it's cutting off access to most forms of magic. This will make it very difficult to protect ourselves, you, or anyone else for that matter. This is something we have been preparing for. The advancements in Halaris haven't been the only thing we've been working on."

Ivan opens one of the drawers to his desk and pulls out a metal-looking cylinder. "What's that?" I ask.

"Patience, Princess. I'm getting to that. Don't stand too close." He scoots his chair away from his desk before getting up and moving to a more open space. He flicks his wrist, and the cylinder expands. He slams it on the ground when it reaches its full length, and blades come out from both sides. He whirls the spear over his head, and ripples of lightning begin to swarm around the length of the weapon. He moves his finger over a button on the length of the pole, causing the lightning to stop, the blades to retract, and the pole to compress back down to a cylinder.

"Wait, I don't understand; how does the lightning not hurt you?"

He points to a necklace he's wearing. Each one of these," he holds up the cylinder, "has a matching one. It forms a unique connection between the wielder and the weapon protecting them from the current."

"What if the necklace is pulled off of you?"

"That's kind of a safety feature. If the necklace is broken or removed in any way, the current stops. However, it doesn't make it completely useless. We can still attack with the blades."

"Why have the lightning at all, then?" I ask.

"It helps with the dark creatures. They are different," Ivan says.

"So, I've read," I say.

"Ah, yes, the History of the Dark Ascension studies, correct?" Ivan asks.

"More like Gaiwen's journal."

"So, the accusations from earlier were because you read his journals?"

"Yep."

"I suppose I owe you those answers now."

"I suppose you do. Starting by telling us who the baby was is a start. We have our assumptions."

"Your mother."

"What happened to her?"

"She froze to death."

"How?"

"I don't know." Ivan pauses. "We have theories but never dared accuse the High King outright. I may be a vampire, but that doesn't mean I am wholly immortal."

"What are your theories?"

"This stays between us, right?" Ivan asks, looking between Hassian and me. Hassian looks over at me, allowing me to make the choice for myself.

"I cannot promise that."

Ivan and I just stare at each other. He didn't exactly make me feel like he was someone we could trust based upon our first interaction, but we were also standing in the very headquarters of The Order. The very place my grandfather controls. Ivan is taking a huge risk just by telling me anything. It's like we are at a point where we want to be truthful but questioning if it could result in someone's death. I want to bring up the rebellion I am forming, but I don't know if he can be trusted not to run back to my grandfather, and he has more of the story to tell.

He looks hesitant but continues the conversation. "Look, I will be the first to admit that I wasn't kind in my interactions with you. I have spent a very long time at the beck and call of your grandfather, and I didn't have much time with your mother or father to see if they acted the same way. We weren't allowed at court; after the incident, we were to focus our attention on Halaris. If a threat needed to be dealt with, we would be called for. One of our biggest leading theories as to why your grandfather went through all this trouble was to hide an affair he was having."

"Is it not common for those in power to have mistresses?" Hassian looks at me like I have just spoken complete lunacy. "I'm not saying you or I would ever."

"No, we don't practice that in this realm. It gives too many weaknesses to those in power. If someone were to find out that there was a mistress, well, they aren't as protected as a member of the court, and they could be used to sway dealings or start wars. Those of non-nobility can take on multiple lovers, though."

"I see. Then why do you suspect an affair?"

"Your mother passed away in her nursery. The latch was broken from the inside, which resulted in her freezing to death. When he told us where she was found, we asked to question the wet nurse on duty that evening. He refused us and said that she was traumatized enough by the death. The death of a royal is a serious matter, and no one should have been excused, let alone for that reason. When your grandfather sent The Order members out of the court, well, some of us began to speculate."

"You said theories, not theory, as in more than one?" Hassian says.

"Yes, I did. Our other theory is an add-on to the first one. This is more as to why we were removed from court. After all, we had just been let in on one of possibly the biggest secrets in all of Alandria's time. A first-born royal child died and was then brought to life using forbidden magic. Wouldn't you want them close to keep an eye out?"

"Well, yeah," I reply.

"Well, those of us that were there that night got to thinking as to why someone who had clearly trusted us enough in desperation would push us away, and we think it boils down to the wet nurse. That he made her with child and knew we would suspect something of it. Obviously, it's not uncommon for wet nurses to bear children, given their duty; it's just that in this case, we would have suspected and seen the similarities."

"So, you think I have an aunt or uncle out there that he has been keeping secret?"

Ivan nods. "I truly do."

"Are they a threat to Sage's crown?" Hassian asks.

"No, their claims would be illegitimate. You are the last living being with god's blood. The succession must pass onto you. Unless, of course," realization hits Ivan. "Unless, of course, the only living heirs die. With Gaiwen having murdered your mother-"

"I don't believe he did," I interrupt.

"No?"

"I've read his journal front to back more than once. Based on the magic he performs; he would have had control over my mother. She would have been a thrall if he had asked her to do something, like giving me up to him. She would have. He resurrected her, and when he did, he became master, and she the puppet. I don't believe that was something my grandfather knew. I think that my mother may have found out the truth, that of which I don't know. Was it the circumstances of her being reborn? Was it seeing a child with a likeness to her father?"

"Either way, whatever it was, it had to be a secret he couldn't let get out. If your theory about him having a child with the wet nurse is true, then Sage's life could be in danger from more than just Gaiwen," Hassian says.

"I'm inclined to agree, but I would like to believe she is at least safe until the prophecy is fulfilled. However, from what I gathered from this conversation, the High King can be irrational. We must not let on that we know before Gaiwen is dealt with in case he tries to take matters into his own hands. I would also be leery that if he waits until Gaiwen is dealt with, he might remove you from the equation soon after, especially if he favors this other child," Ivan says.

"Well, I don't have a lot of hope that my grandfather cares for me. He's never made any attempts to see me since my return to Alandria. I've been gone for 18 years and nothing. The only thing he's done is implement a professor in the academy to tell inaccurate dealings of Gaiwen's history.

"What's this professor's name?"

"I don't know her first name, but she goes by Professor West."

"I can't say we have anyone in The Order with that surname, but I will look into it and see if anyone's on mission. The file should have passed my desk if they were. There hasn't been a new professor at the academy in a long time, and even then, they have to pass through The Order first for clearance. It's unusual that I haven't heard the name. We don't care if they don't like us, but we do care about their intentions. Aliria Academy is the future of our realm, and security cannot be risked."

"About that," I start.

"Did something happen? We received no reports."

"There was an incident the week of the winter solstice ball." I go on to explain what happened the night Hassian was dancing with me in the library.

"That is rather peculiar that Thevin didn't report the incident. As headmaster I am sure he thinks he is making the best decisions for the school. I should like to be informed if anything ever happens again."

"I can do that. How long until we reach the blight?" Hassian asks.

"A few hours. It's moved toward Scourge Lake."

"That's really close to the main waterway," Hassian replies.

"We know. I do apologize for my approach, Sage. I know it doesn't mean much, but I am partly to blame for this blight in my hand of performing the blood oath and participating in apprehending him for the crown. This is a mistake I am long overdue to fix. I don't know if it will make up for any of the things I have done."

"The best you can do is try," I say.

He nods. "Please go get yourselves one of the weapons from the crates out there. We have some people practicing on deck if you feel inclined to learn how to wield it. I don't know if Sage's magic will work on the blight, but it might. Being a bloodletter is both a curse and an extraordinary gift."

Hassian and I thank Ivan for his honesty and make our way out of the captain's quarters.

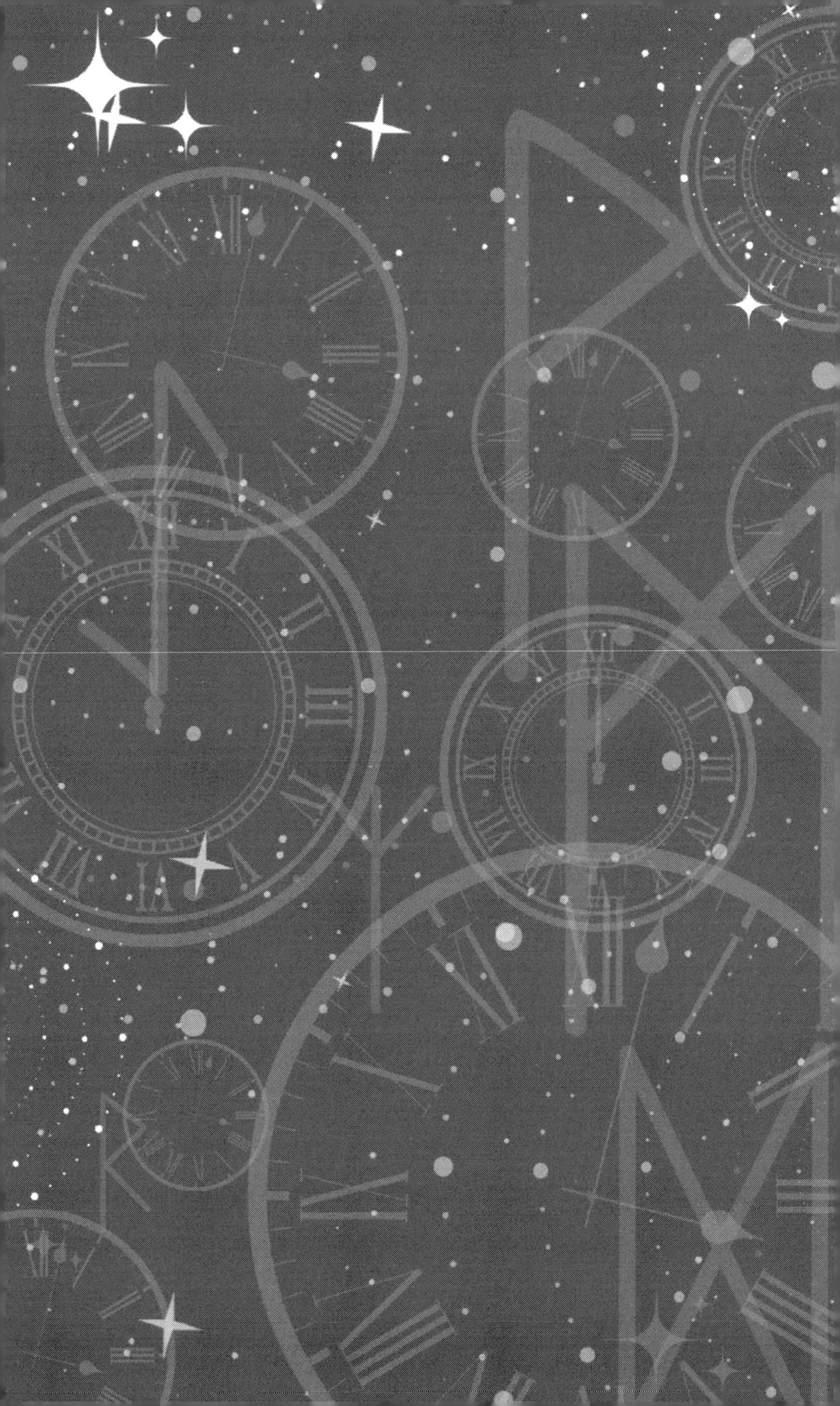

Chapter Thirty-One
Sage

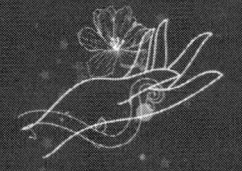

After helping me put the holster on for my spear, The Order member asks, "Would you like to go over the spear basics real quick? It can be tricky to figure it out at first."

"Sure."

"So, we like to use these spears because it allows us to keep some distance from ourselves and the enemy. This is especially vital since the enemy in question here has an acidic bite. The metals we forge the spear with have a higher resistance but not complete resistance. In the event your spear does break, try to grab a spare spear or take cover below deck. The enchanted lighting down there will protect you for a time."

"How can enchanted lighting protect me?"

"Well, it can't protect you in a sense it will stop the beast, but you won't be stuck in the creature's darkness cloud. It will be blinded if it tries to follow you down, and you should, with careful and quiet movements, be able to avoid getting hurt."

"Why not use the wood all over the ship?"

"There's too much open space. If the creature were to use its darkness cloud, the only thing it would do is make the creature go back a little further, putting it out of our reach while keeping us within its."

"I guess that makes sense."

"Now, let's have a test run, shall we? First, we are going to try to call your spear. You are going to make a wrist motion like this. Go on, give it a try." I make an attempt, and nothing happens. "Try starting horizontally and ending at a 90-degree angle. Make it one fluid and fast movement."

I try again. The cylinder expands into a whole spear. "Oh, fuck yeah," I breathe out.

"It gets better; let's get the blades out. This is the top of the spear," she points to the thinner portion of the weapon. "If you try and slam it down, nothing will happen because, on the bottom, there's a little mechanism that calls the blades out. If you slam too lightly, nothing will happen; you want it to be stronger than the force of its just dropping. Keep your hands on the grooves of the spear; that way, you don't get hurt. If you look, you can see the slits where the blades come out at. Give it a try."

I slam the spear down, jumping a little bit as they snap out of the spear. It's like trying to mentally prepare yourself as you open up canned biscuits. You cannot stop the shock value. I glance over at Hassian, who is with another member. He's already got his retracted and sheathed because, of course, he does.

"Great job, Sage; let's move on to how to call your lightning. It's going to be important to get through this step as fast as possible, or you may not have time. What you are going to do is lift the spear above your head and whirl it. Don't worry about getting shocked; the runes in your necklace protect you."

I do just as she instructs, and the bolts of lightning begin to ripple across the spear's arm and over where my hands rest on the weapon. "What happens if the runes don't work on the blight either?"

"In that case, you just have a spear with some blades on it. Everything in that spear, up to the lightning aspect, is mechanical. The runes are the only magic-based part of the weapon. Now, go ahead and disengage your weapon. There's a button just a little way away from where you are holding it. Use a little force; it's not meant to be easy in case your hand slips during battle."

I raise my thumb higher and push the button. The spear retracts into a cylinder, and I put it into my new holster. "Well, I have to admit, this is cool as fuck."

The Order member laughs. "I love everything about the design. Although, I wish they had a cover mechanism for the button to eliminate the need to push so hard. In training, we had to practice this repeatedly, and my thumb did not appreciate it one bit."

"Hey, thanks for being so nice to me," I say.

"Look, we don't want anything to happen to you. I know Ivan came off harsh in his approach, but he holds a lot of guilt for his part in the blight. I wasn't there when it happened, but I've seen the aftermath of how it affects him. All of us on this ship right now are his most trusted members. I know you probably won't take the word of someone you just met, but I hope we can prove ourselves to you."

The ship can't fully land on the ground, so part of the crew stays on board to tend to the steam system, keeping it floating. Chains with hooks at the ends are anchored into the ground to keep it from rising too high. The rest of the crew climbs down a rope ladder, and we make our way toward the site of the blight.

"Let me step onto the blight alone," I turn and say to everyone.

"Sage, please let me at least come with you," Hassian argues.

"No. Just please let me do this alone. If you think I am in danger and you see no other option than to step onto the blight, then you can. I cannot focus with the idea that this could be hurting any of you. Now," I turn to face Ivan, "how do I approach this?"

"Well, the blight is basically death itself, so approach it similarly to how you did with Professor Dublin when you resurrected the dead plant. I'm unsure where resurrecting things in a blight versus a dead plant stands on the forbidden magic level. You should be fine. The blight doesn't contain a soul to our knowledge."

"Do you know what causes the blight to spread?"

"We assume it's like a fungal disease that spreads through spores carried by the wind, water, insects, and animals. We believe you to be immune because of the conditions of your birth."

"What if you are wrong about all of this?" Hassian asks.

"Then I have just damned the future of an entire realm with this mistake, but I do not think myself wrong in this case."

"Very well." I nod at Ivan and turn around to face the blight. Stepping onto the blight feels like descending into a murky abyss; the shadows around me grow almost immediately, and the air thickens with a palpable sense of decay. There is a sickly crunch similar to bones snapping and a mushy sound with each step I take. These are just the vines that have extended from the source, but I wouldn't be surprised if the land itself caved in from the corruption.

I walk deeper and deeper until I am near some of the trees. At a close enough distance that they can still see me but deep enough that if I am successful, it will heal a decent-sized area. I look at the area around me. The trees stand gnarled and withered, with no life left in their coloring, just a dull gray. A flicker of self-doubt passes my mind. I am only in my first year of learning magic. I have only just discovered how to access my magic, and now I am about to attempt something no one has ever done before. The lack of light filtering through what feels like a permanent overcast over the blight seems to add to this feeling of failure before I have even begun. I wonder if it's an effect the blight has.

I drop down to my knees, taking the ring Hassian commissioned for me; I cut a deeper wound into my palm. I am thankful for the rune's ability to dull the pain. I let a decent amount of my blood fall onto the withered vines before I plunge my hands further, gripping onto what I can. I close my eyes and enter that space in my mind where I connect with my magic. As I approach my pillar of vines and see the overcast of what's happening in the real-world taking hold of my magic. Normally, a bright and vibrant garden in my mind is slowly decaying around me. I don't turn back; I push onward to the pillar. I will do what needs to be done. I follow the steps of casting, fill it with my intentions, and release it into the world.

When I open my eyes, the land remains as lifeless as ever; The blight is clinging to it like a shroud of darkness. I persist and try again. Nothing. I repeat over and over again. I slice my hands some more. I keep going until I feel like I am about to pass out from the loss of my blood, from the drain of my magic. I don't know if there is enough in me, and I am bordering on dangerous territory, but I refuse to give up if I cannot push this blight back; hundreds, if not thousands, of souls will pay the price.

I push one last time, exerting the last of my magical essence until my body is drained and I need to recharge. I collapse the rest of the way out of pure exhaustion. I can hear my name being called, but I focus on what needs to happen. Life. Return to life. Tiny shoots of green push their way through the soil, their delicate leaves unfurling around me. The overcast above begins to open up as dots of light crash through its barrier. The blight screeches as the light touches down on it. It tries to recede into a more shadowy area, but the shadows become less and less as the sky opens up and new life sprouts throughout the decay.

I see nothing but green around me as my eyelids droop from the energy drain. "Stay with me, princess." I hear the deep tone of Hassian's voice as he scoops me into his arms. "Can you open your eyes for me?"

Slowly, I lift my lids and wait for my vision to clear. "How did I do?" I ask.

"Well, the blight has cleared out in this area, at least as far as we can see. We won't know if it's completely gone or just reduced down." I nod. "Princess, I am going to need you to be strong for me and climb the ladder when we get back to the ship. We don't have any gear to assist you. Can you do that for me?"

"I'll try."

"I'm going to need you to do more than try. It's a long drop, princess."

I shake my body to try and wake myself out of the drain some more. "I can do it."

"Good girl."

We reach the boat, and Hassian helps me get onto the rope ladder, not releasing me until he knows I have a firm enough grip. When I have made it a decent way, he starts climbing up as well. My whole body is shaking, and I can tell he feels it as he climbs, but I need to do this one last thing. Then we can see how much blight is left, and I can get some rest at the academy to be safe in the academy walls again.

"Take her below deck and set her up in one of the rooms. She deserves some rest. We are going to fly more toward the origin source of the blight and see what remains. It'll give us an estimate of how much time we have. Judging from what we can see, she's bought us a few years. If it spreads at the same speed."

They begin to wind in the chains, pulling open the lever that releases the clamps into the ground, and the ship starts to rise. Hassian heads toward the stairs with me in his arms. He takes three steps down, and the vessel jerks forward, causing him to tumble forward. I feel my head slam against the wall, and warm liquid follows near where I made an impact. Hassian is lying motionless on top of me, and I hear the buzzing of the lightning spears sounding from above, followed by a screech that sends chills down my spine.

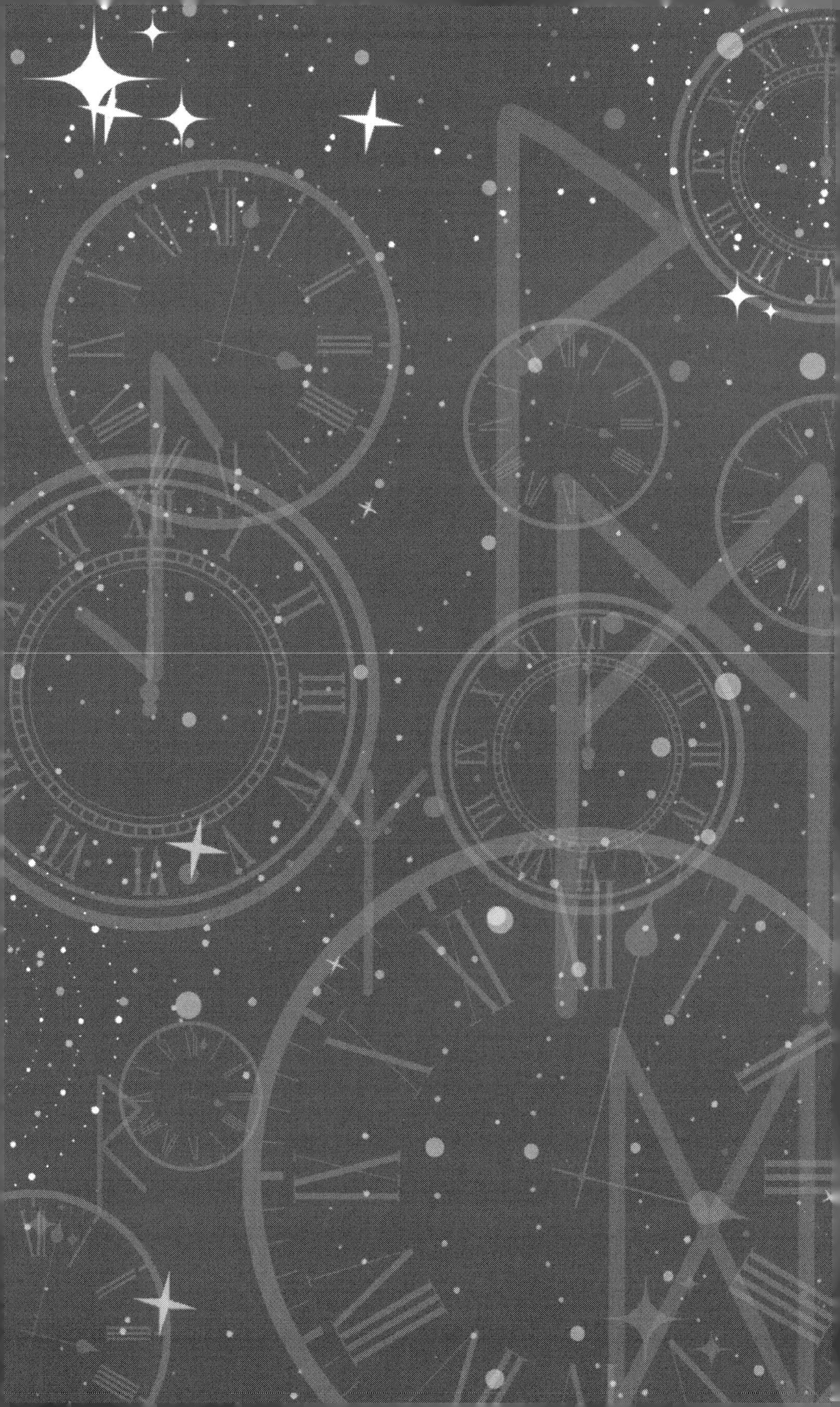

Chapter Thirty-Two
Sage

"Hassian, wake up, please." I shake his body as best as I can, trying to get him to wake up. The way he landed on top of me makes it difficult to move, and I'm woozy from the magic drain and whatever head injury I just sustained. I keep shaking him, watching as the ship's deck gets darker. He's not budging; for a second, I think he's dead from the fall. I don't know if he landed on something. I feel his body for any sign of movement, and I am relieved to find he is still breathing.

We are not in an area for protection, stuck between the opening of the stairs and surrounded by storage barrels. I grab onto my mother's necklace and let out a soft prayer for help to The Nines. That familiar feeling of falling through the floor and entering Kamira's realm is almost immediate.

"My child, sit with me," Kamira motions me to my usual seat beside her waterfall.

I listen and take a seat beside her. "I need help, Kamira. Everyone on the ship- We're being attacked. Hassian won't wake up. I can't move."

Kamira stares off as if looking into the universe for what she may do. I wonder if she can offer me aid or just send me back. I'm not worried about how long she takes to respond; time does not move in their realm as it does in the others. Kamira will return me to the time I arrived in.

"This is not the battle you are destined to make the choice. I will give you a blessing to help aid your companions and wake your beloved so you may face the threat together. Be careful, Sage. Do not over-exert yourself; your fate comes sooner than you think." She conjures a goblet and scoops up some of the liquid from the fountain. "Drink this; it will give you some strength to stand with your friends; this will heal your physical injuries but not your magic drain. There is nothing I can offer to restore that."

I sip the liquid from the cup, and although I am not currently with my body, I can feel relief from the pressure on my head and the exhaustion of my body lift. I hand Kamira the cup back, about to say thanks when I am shifted back to my body.

Hassian stirs awake. "I'm so sorry, Sage. Are you hurt?" He tries to check me for injuries.

"I'm fine. I was, but I'm okay now. Kamira helped me. We are under attack, and they need our help."

"I will help. You stay here, princess."

"No! Hassian, we did not just spend all that time together training. Kamira did not just restore my strength so I could sit idly by when I could have helped. I love you, but I do not need you to be my protector but an equal."

He looks me over as if searching for a lie and that I am not really okay. "You will be the death of me, princess." I know he doesn't mean it in a way that my poor fighting skills will get him shanked, but the fear of me getting hurt will break him.

"We will survive this. We have a bigger battle to face. Let's consider this a warm-up, shall we?" I tease.

He guffaws before pulling me in and kissing me. "Let's go."

We unsheathe our spears and ready them before charging up to the deck. We make it up the stairs when we see a member of The Order being pulled across the deck by a shadowy tendril, a crimson path following in their wake. The man being pulled cries out, trying to reach toward the tendril to pull himself free, but one hand is twisted at an odd angle, and the other doesn't have enough strength to free himself.

The creatures are horrifying in person. They are so different from what we read in Gaiwen's journals. These are bat-like, with razor-like claws at the tips of their wings; their feet are sharp like blades, acidic saliva flying from their short snouts, and shadow-like tendrils coming from various areas of their bodies. It's fucking terrifying. I didn't grow up on this shit and the selfish thought that I should just run below deck and leave them to deal with this crosses my mind. I need to get these thoughts from my head. I am in no way a perfect person, I am so fucking flawed, but I refuse to be like my grandfather. I refuse to not care.

I squeeze my mother's necklace in my hand for luck, and the stone feels warm. Like the women in my family are telling me, I can do this. I charge at the beast that's trying to carry the man away, stabbing my spear directly in its eye. It screams and lets out a blood-curdling hiss before it bursts into nothing but ash. I help the man up.

"I can't fight. I can't do it. My hand is broken," the man cries.

"It's okay. You did your best. Please get below deck. It's safer there."

He looks at me as if to ask if, I am sure. I nod. "May The Nines bless you," he whispers before running down the stairs into the safety of below.

The woman who showed me how to use the spear earlier is being circled by three of the bat creatures. I run up beside her to help. "Three against one didn't seem too fair," I jest.

"Yeah, I like these odds better," she says.

I spin my spear to try and gain a bit of momentum before lunging toward another creature. I miss. It swipes at me, and I jump backward, stumbling a bit. I think back to lessons with

Hassian to determine my next steps. I don't have a whole lot of time to think, so I have to be quick. I thrust my spear upwards toward one of the creatures. I miss as it anticipates my attack and swerves. I'm going to have to make it think I'm attacking one way, but we haven't gone over any diversion tactics in our training. This is going to hurt. I whirl the spear to gain momentum, faking that I am about to strike from the left but quickly forcing the spear in the other direction.

I feel the strain of my muscles from the abrasiveness of the move, but it strikes the creature. It's not a mortal blow, but the lightning jolts through it, causing it to fall to the ground. I pull my spear back out and aim for the head. I'd go for the heart, but I cannot say for sure where it is. I don't know if it's been altered in any way. My spear connects with the skull, but it doesn't pierce. Instead, the head lobs loudly against the deck, and the creature falls unconscious. I should move on to the next creature, as this one is unconscious, but I refuse to take the risk of it waking before we get back to it. The beast is on its belly, so I can't go for the eye socket again. I have to build momentum and hope my strength is enough. I whirl my spear faster and faster, trying to time the moment one of the ends lines up with the skull just right. It's now or never. I grip onto the handle as quickly as I can and smash it into the beast's skull.

Honestly, I don't know if whirling my spear faster does anything other than provide me with a confidence boost, but I like to think it does. I want to believe that it increases the impact; whether it's useless or not, I don't think anyone is going to tell me. I watch as the second creature I have now killed bursts into ashes.

I whirl around to see what's left of the other two on her when I get knocked back. I can see Hassian, with his spear, pointed at the creature as he charges toward it, as shadows envelop my vision. I hear a wet squelching sound before something, no, someone lands on top of me. A moment of panic hits me. Not just someone, Hassian. I can't see if he's alive. I hear a blood-curdling scream and the sound of hissing as acidic spit rains down around me. Hassian finally speaks when the scream stops, and it's breathy. "Get below deck, princess. Please." His voice cracks on the word please and I know that I shouldn't argue with him.

I scramble to get myself upright and almost slip on something slick; visibility is a bitch. It's like walking around in nearly complete darkness. The lighting of the spears is the only thing providing any type of visibility. Even that is barely bright enough. I try to remember what way I was facing from the stairs. I'm worried I won't be able to make my way down, but then I see the faint glow of the wood. I run as fast as I can in that direction. The difference between what I can see above the deck and what I see below is astonishing. I have nearly clear visibility down here. I make my way into the first room I can find. Why are my clothes so fucking wet? I look down, and my green blouse is wet with dark splotches. I raise my shirt to inspect, a big mistake. The sheer amount of pain as my shirt pulls away from the dried blood makes me scream in agony. I was wounded. I look around for a mirror or something reflective of any kind, knocking things down in my urgency. I can't bend over; the pain is too much, so I keep searching. There's nothing in here, and I am going to need bandages. This is a military-based ship; they have to have medical supplies somewhere.

I exit the room, leaving behind blood-smeared hand prints on the doors and walls as I go in search of the medical room. It's only a few more doors down from where I was. There is a handheld mirror on the counter, and I make my way toward it. I lift the shirt back up, biting back more screams as I lower the mirror and take a look. There is a large wound in my abdomen, and my veins are darkening around it. It must have knocked me back with its legs; it happened so fast. The Adrenaline must have prevented me from feeling it at the moment. I need to sit; Hassian will find me of that, I am sure. I make my way toward one of the chairs in the room, but the Adrenaline is wearing off. The room is spinning, and I fall. I'm dizzy. I try to get myself to move, to get back up, make it to that chair. My body doesn't listen. My eyes feel heavy. I think I'll rest awhile.

I don't know how long it's been, but I can feel my torso being raised off the floor and my shirt being removed. I can't open my eyes. I can't move anything. I hear the muffling of voices. I can feel a damp feeling as something touches my wound. It stings, but I can't back away in reaction; I can't scream out in pain. I am trapped inside my own body. Sharp. I feel sharp going in and out. Have they found me here in the medical room? No, that can't be; there was talking. Can they talk? Cool. I feel something cool being smeared onto my skin, followed by soft. The soft keeps going around and around, over and over. They must be patching up my wound. My torso is raised again, and I feel a soft, dry fabric being placed over my body.

My body is being lifted off the ground, and I can feel the warmth of bare skin against my cheek. I feel every thud of movement with each step as I am carried away. There are more voices; I can feel the rumble of whoever is carrying me as they speak with another voice. I am being lowered. The feeling is soft on my back. The pain in my abdomen increases when the contact is lost with whoever is carrying me. Every nerve in my body is on fire. I want to scream, but I cannot move.

My lid is lifted open, and a light shines on my pupil. It's too bright; turn it off, please. The light sways back and forth before my lid is released, and my other one comes up. I hear the mumble of voices again, but it's all inaudible. The murmuring continues before I feel a sharp jab in my left arm, followed by a cool liquid. The sounds around me are silent, the pain goes away, and the world goes dark.

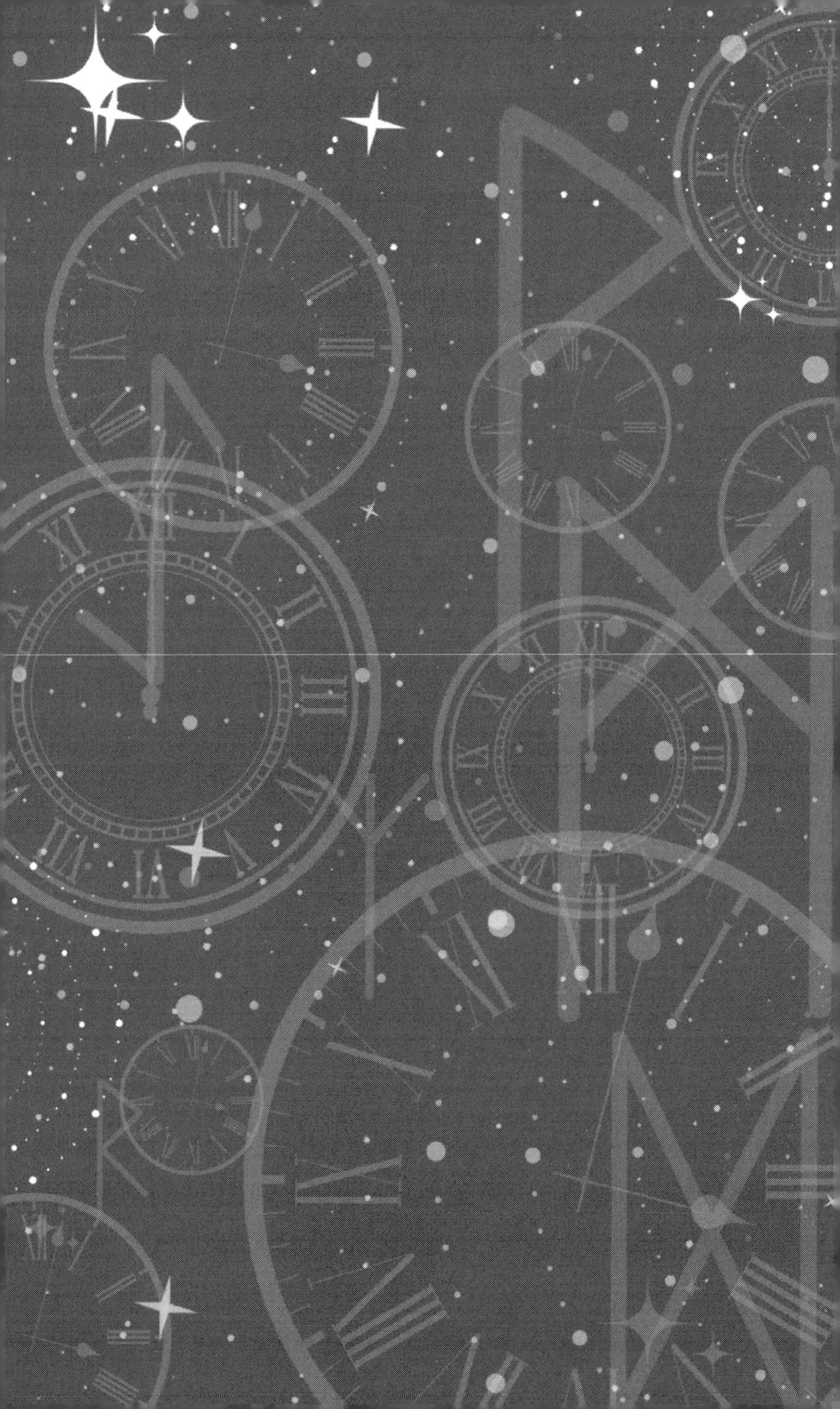

Chapter Thirty-Three
Sage

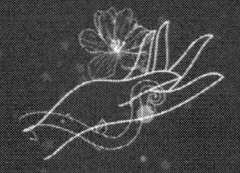

I awake in my bed—no, not my bed. My head turns to a man with long white hair lying beside me. When he turns to face me, he is not Hassian. Who is he? Where am I? I make to move my body to leave, but it doesn't listen.

"Are you watching me as I sleep again, wife?"

What the actual fuck? I try to respond, but it's not my voice that comes out, nor with what I was trying to say. "Me? I would never." I feel myself laughing. My back is uncomfortable, and why the hells does my belly ache? Did I eat something weird? I look down as the man rolls over and kisses my belly. Holy fuck, I'm pregnant.

"Well, good morning to you, too, little one. I cannot wait until the day you are born so I can teach you how to wield a sword and be a great warrior, just like your father."

"Love, we've talked about this; you can't teach a baby how to sword fight. She needs to grow a few seasons first," the sound comes from me, but again, it's not my words or my voice. What in the hells is going on? I need to get back to Hassian, to the ship. How did I get here? Last, I remember, I was trying to deal with the blight. No? The ship. I was on the ship.

Oh gods, I'm going to be sick; we're falling through the floor. I am familiar with this place. This is Kamira's realm. "Sage, what are you doing here?" Kamira asks me. It's not coming from her mouth. Her mouth is saying something else. I try to speak, but nothing comes yet again. "Speak with your mind, child."

"I don't know. I was on the ship. I think I was hurt. I woke up here."

"Inside your mother's mind?" she asks with a question that is bordering surprise.

"My mother? So that man I saw was my father?"

"Yes. I don't know how you are here now, but you must return to your time. This is the day your parents die. The day of your birth."

"How do I get back?"

"I am unsure. Perhaps your mother is trying to tell you why she died. Maybe pay attention to the conversation, and you'll go back."

"What if I don't go back after she shows me what she needs to?"

"Then the realm is doomed."

Kamira pulls from me until we are no longer touching, and the scene around me changes back to that of my mother's room, and time resumes once again. "Well, dear husband, it looks like we will be planning for our little one's future today.

My mother is walking down a hallway, making her way toward the kitchen area to find Kira and let her know about their plan. Being trapped in my mother's head for nearly a day while they discuss my future is weird.

"Is Kira in here?" my mother asks an elderly-looking woman stirring a pot that smells incredibly delicious.

"She's out in the garden, milady. Would you like me to fetch her for you?"

My mother glances at the already busy woman. "No, that's fine. The walk would do me and the baby some good."

"You take care not to overdo it, milady. We want that babe to be nice and healthy when she's born and born on time at that. Don't need you forcing yourself into an early labor."

"I promise I'll be fine. I just got out of bed a short while ago. I will go rest my feet soon." My mother was lying, of course. She had gotten out of bed hours ago and had been performing loads of magic in preparation for what was to come. I'm not sure I am ready to face what will happen to her today.

My mother exits the kitchen and begins walking toward the garden when she hears the sound of a man's voice. He's not alone, and I feel my mother's heart pounding in her chest before she ducks into an alcove. She and my father had agreed earlier in the day that no one but Kira could know what they were about to do. The man begins to argue in harsh whispers to a woman.

"We are not discussing this right now. You need to go before someone sees you."

"Father, that's not fair. You promised that I could join you at court. You promised me. You promised moth-"

"I know what I promised, girl. Idril and Gildor are with child thanks to the many tonics I have had put into their drinks. You can be with me in my court soon, but I need you to be patient with me."

"Why not just let them both die? I will bear you a child. I can fulfill the prophecy for you, Father."

"No, you cannot. It's impossible. My sweet girl, you know how I favor you so. I adore seeing your face in my court; you remind me so much of my beloved, your mother, but you cannot fulfill the prophecy. A child who is born of both life and death. That's the only way to fix my mistakes."

"Idril's child threatens my place on the throne beside you, too, Father. Will you take care of the child after it fulfills the prophecy?"

"Quiet, if anyone were to hear you say that, it's treason. My protection can only go so far, my darling daughter. In time, we will take care of the child if it proves to be a problem. I will raise her in Idril's stead."

"Where will Idril be?"

"Dead. I have a plan in motion to take care of her soon enough. With the child being born, she is bringing forth an heir, and my position as High King will be given to her. I will not lose my crown, to that girl. I bred with her mother out of obligation to gain my crown. Your mother knew my heart belonged to only her. If I control the girl, I can control the stone. You need to go; I will see you soon. Wait a few weeks after Idril's passing before you return; I cannot have anyone suspecting you."

"Yes, father."

The sound of heels clicking against the stone floor begins to grow distant, and the man continues walking in the other direction.

"Pardon me, High King."

"Watch where you are going, cook."

"My apologies. I was hoping to catch Idril and give her favorite pastry to her. She's been loving them during the pregnancy. Is she still out there?"

"Out where?"

"The hall? She was just in here, left to head to the gardens but a moment ago." I can feel my mother's heart racing faster and faster.

"I must have missed her. Don't give her any more of those things," he orders.

"My lord, these have been a comfort to her."

"Are you disobeying a direct order from your High King? If you are, then I might be inclined to inform you I can have you deposed and hanged."

"No, my lord."

"Very well. Back to the kitchens with you."

The scurrying of feet followed by the closing of the kitchen door shortly follows. The High King's footsteps sound closer and closer toward where my mother is hiding. Just a few more paces and my mother will be discovered. "High King, you are needed in the throne room. It's urgent," says a very breathy voice.

"What's so important that you felt inclined to tell me what to do?"

"It's Gaiwen, sir. One of the scouts just returned. He's marching this way with his creatures. Be a day or two more."

"Very well, let's go." We wait in the alcove until the sound of feet cannot be heard in the distance. My mother peaks out and ensures no one else is there before running to the garden to Kira.

"Kira, you must come with me quickly."

"What is it, my Idril?"

"I cannot say out here in the open, come with me to my chambers. Gildor is waiting for us."

"Of course, whatever you need." Kira sets down her gardening tools and follows my mother to her room. They didn't rush straight there like I thought. My mother was very elusive as she made her way toward her chambers. If she heard footsteps, she would pull Kira into an alcove.

My mother closes the door to her chambers behind her, sliding the lock into place. "Gildor, can you move some of the furniture to the front of the door? Just in case."

"My lady, what's going on?"

"Kira, I need you to trust me and listen to whatever I tell you to do from this point forward. Can you do that?" Kira nods. "Good. Follow me."

They all head to a picture frame near my mother's changing screen, and my father pulls it open, gesturing for the two to get inside. He casts a small ball of everflame and closes the door behind them. They don't say a word as they descend deeper and deeper down sets of stairs. I can feel the ache in my mother's feet and the pain in her belly. I can tell that I am warning her it's nearing time. My mother doesn't say anything as her water breaks, holding her skirts to try and muffle the sound as they keep going. Eventually, they come across three different archways leading in different directions. They turn down the left one and continue walking until they are in an open room with an altar table and another random archway—this time with no walls or anything surrounding it.

"Kira, come speak with me while I prepare, will you?"

"Of course, milady."

"Have you much experience raising children, Kira?"

"Not so much. I wasn't exactly a favorite to my people back home. They weren't a fan of elemental magic users; I was. We didn't get along much. It's why I left for the academy where I met you."

"If you were to raise a child, how would you raise them?"

"I don't know, milady. I cannot have children of my own, so I never thought about it. What's with these questions, and what are you trying to cast?"

My mother ignores Kira's questions. "I think you would raise a child with honesty and kindness. Yes, that much sounds like you." My mother pauses her speaking as I grow restless in her womb. The feel of warm liquid runs down her legs. I recall Kira saying how I was born and that it was done due to complications. We must be getting closer now.

Kira looks around. "This is the portal room? Are you trying to open a portal? You aren't strong enough, even if you weren't pregnant."

"I'm gods blessed right now, Kira."

"I don't understand."

"I'm going to die soon."

"What? How?"

"There are a few different ways it can happen. All of which are soon. My child's life is in danger, my Sage. I need you to promise me that in the event I cannot make it through that portal, you will take my child and raise her as if she were your own."

"Milady?"

"Promise me, Kira."

"I promise."

"Good. Now I need you to promise you will bring her back to Alandria when her magic awakens."

"Awakens? Milady, we are born with magic already awoken. What's going on?"

"Gildor and I suppressed her magic this morning. Magic is like a beacon, Kira. Where I need you and this baby to go, I cannot have them follow. You are not equipped to train my child, but you are who I trust most in this world outside of my husband. Her magic will awaken sometime after her 18th birthday when she can attend the academy. She should be safe there while she learns to wield."

"Should be? There are wards in place; evil magic cannot get in. They've been up for a thousand years."

"She is in danger because she is the next High Queen of the realm. There are some that are plotting against her as we speak. Plotting against an unborn child. Tell me, Kira, what is your idea of the perfect home." Kira begins to describe the home I was raised in, in vivid detail as my mother's hands glow, forging the omni-vessel. "Take this," she hands Kira the necklace containing our house. "Tap it three times when you have picked a spot you wish to live. Raise my child there; when it is time for her to return, tap three times once more, and take the home with you. You can use this however many times you like. This is my gift to you, a home."

"You talk like you won't be coming with us."

"I can't." My mother finishes the portal spell, and it opens up in the archway.

"The portals right there, milady. There's time."

"I can't, Kira. The baby has been in distress. I need you to take her from me."

Kira's eyes widen with panic. "No. No. I won't do it."

"I need you to."

"Why can't you just come through the portal? Live with us. Please, you are my dearest friend."

"And you are mine, but Kamira has shared with me what must be done. I need to make this sacrifice so she can be born blessed. There's no other way." My mother moves her hand to her mouth to muffle the pain I am causing her. "I need you to take her from me. It won't hurt; the Goddesses ensure this will be as easy as possible for me." My mother hands Kira a dagger and lays in between my father's legs. His face is stricken with tears. He hasn't said a word this whole time, and I think it's because he said all he wanted to my mother this morning. From the moments I saw this morning, he wouldn't leave her in death, even if it wasn't part of his destiny to die alongside her. He would go wherever she went. They were true mates.

Kira's hand is shaking as my mother raises the skirts of her dress to expose her belly. "I cannot do this. This isn't right." Kira's face is stricken with tears as my mother guides the hand with the dagger to her belly.

"It's okay, Kira. You are the only one I trust to do this for me, to raise my child. Your heart is pure and kind, and I do not doubt you will raise her to be a phenomenal young woman."

I brace myself for the pain I expect to feel as my mother pushes Kira's hand down, forcing it to cut into the tender flesh of her belly, but there is no pain. It's disgusting. I want to gag watching this, but the pain is not there. Kira finally realizes she needs to finish what my mother started. If she doesn't, she risks me dying too. Kira's blade slides down my mother's belly with precision, and I think that perhaps this isn't Kira's first time performing a cesarean. She widens my mother's belly enough to pull me from her, wiping off some of the blood from my face before handing me to my mother and tending to my umbilical cord.

"Oh, my sweet Sage. I love you so much, my little flower. Aunty Kira is going to raise you with all the love and laughter, and one day, you will come back here. You will come back here, and you will save us all. Know that I am proud of you, and I will be watching you from the stars every night." She kisses my forehead and hands me back to Kira. "Take this. She will need it in the upcoming battles." My mother slips off the stone necklace Kira gave to me all those months ago and hands it over to her. "Don't tell her what it can do. She will learn in time. It's best not to rush it. It will also help you gain access to the vaults when you return. Now go." I can hear the sounds of footsteps approaching as my mother watches Kira take me through the portal to the Other Realm. The portal vanishes immediately. "Take care, my little flower."

My father leans over and kisses the back of my mother's head as a thump sound is heard. My mother looks down at her chest, an arrow protruding through Gildor's heart into hers. An older-looking man steps in her line of sight, crossbow in hand. "I knew you were listening, daughter." He spits at the ground near her feet. "It's a shame I have to get my hands dirty, but with Gaiwen being spotted nearby, I can easily blame this mess on him. Where did you send the child?"

It's hard to breathe as blood is filling my lungs. He kicks my mother. I still feel no pain; the Goddesses don't plan on abandoning my mother, even in her last moments.

"I will find her; if I don't, well, she is bound to seek me out. After all, I am all she truly has now." He sneers and walks away. I know that's everything my mother wanted me to see as she releases me from her body. I float away back toward my time, but not before I watch my parents take their last breath.

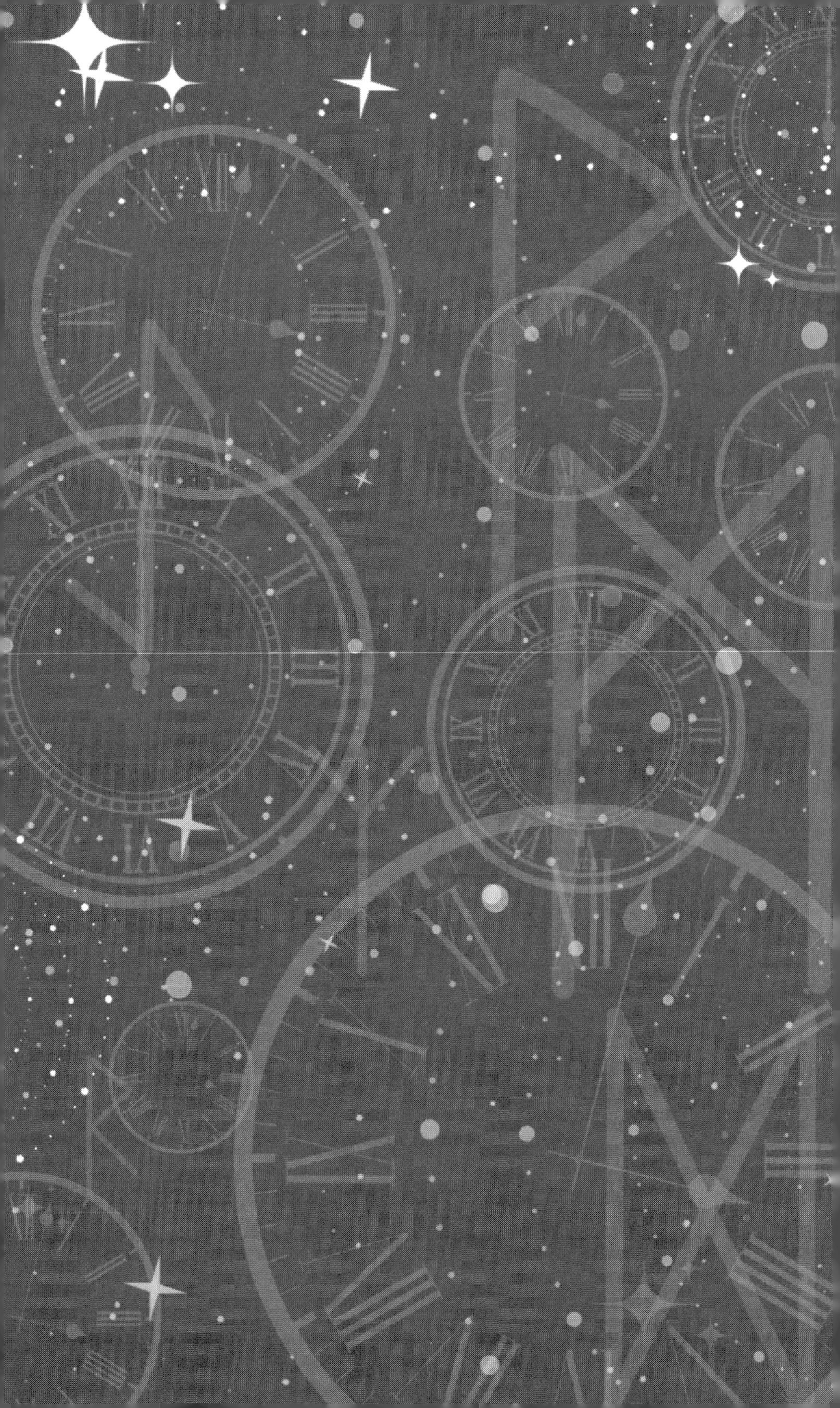

Chapter Thirty-Four
Sage

I am back on the airship, lying on the bed in medical. A healer stands over me, no doubt monitoring me and ensuring I remain stable. Hassian lies asleep, his head lying on the side of my bed, and his shirt is missing. I glance down and realize it's because he gave me his. I pull back the covers and see the shirt is slightly stained pink. I must have bled through some of the gauze.

"You're awake," the healer says. "I'll let the captain know." She leaves the room.

Hassian opens his eyes and moves toward me before he notices I am awake. "Princess, can you hear me?" he whispers. I nod, trying to speak, but my throat is too dry. He walks over to where some stored water is and unscrews the top before handing it to me. "Here," I take a sip.

"How long was I out for?" I ask.

"Just a few hours. I felt you through our connection; I knew you were seriously hurt. I saw the blood on the deck and knew I had been too late in keeping you safe." The look in his eyes tells me that he blames himself for my getting injured. "We aren't used to flying creatures. It's one of the main reasons we sought sanctuary in Halaris. We thought the threat was primarily land walkers."

"Oh," I say, touching my abdomen; it's tender. "Sorry, I didn't mean to respond with oh, my brain is foggy right now, and I think I just came back from the past."

"I don't follow. What do you mean?"

"Well, it was like I was inside my mother's head on the day she was born. I saw everything, from her overhearing about how my grandfather was planning on having her murdered, finding out he has a secret daughter, being shot with an arrow to the heart, her conversations with Kira, literally all of it."

"So, your grandfather really was the reason your mother died?"

"You believe me?"

"Of course I do, Princess."

"To answer your question, yes. He was plotting to have her killed long before she died. I think he sped up the timeline of her murder because he knew she overheard his conversation."

"Did you get a look at who the secret daughter was?"

"No, but I did hear the voice. It sounded familiar, but I don't remember from were. I have definitely met her before."

"Did he say why he wanted your mother dead?"

"It seemed like he wanted his secret daughter to take her place, and he didn't want to give up his title as High King to my mother."

"Was he planning on killing you too then because you are next in line?"

"Yes and no. He was going to raise me in his image and have me murdered if I became too much of a problem. Hassian, he's a terrible man. I heard how he interacted with some of the people in his employ. How is someone so cruel in a position to govern over all of Alandria?"

"Your family rules because of what runs in your blood. Your family's bloodline is mixed with God's blood. The very first family that was created for Alandria. You are special in so many ways to The Nines. That's not to say every single person in your line has the blood in them. If they were married into it, they don't. For instance, your grandfather married into the line. It's why your mother was set to take the throne after you were born. All she had to do was produce an heir."

"Why is the crown passed on after an heir is produced?"

"Bearing a child in this realm is extremely difficult. We are not a very fertile people. The reason there are so many people attending the college this year is because The Nines blessed us. Our numbers were dwindling to near extinction."

"So, if my grandfather weren't married into his role but born into it, then he wouldn't lose his throne if a child was born?"

"Correct. The throne is intended for those of God's blood to rule. He would hold the throne until he passed or became unable to handle his duties. Since he isn't of the bloodline, he must pass it down and having a child, in the eyes of the fae, proves you are ready for a role of that magnitude. Typically, it doesn't happen so soon, but I think The Nines might have also had a hand in that."

"He spoke about my mother with such hatred; I just don't understand how a man can hate his child so much. I don't think he even gave her a real chance. From the sounds of it, he was in love with the woman he had a secret daughter with. I would bet a lot of money that it was the wet nurse. I don't think my grandfather was romping around with anyone he could. I think he hired her so they could seek time with each other."

"Maybe he reminded her of what he had to do to get that position. It was a reminder of how he hurt someone he was in love with. I'm not saying he was right; he was far from it. I'm just trying to get into his head and figure it out."

"Well, now we know that there is, in fact, a secret daughter, and my grandfather will probably try to manipulate me to get what he wants. He won't be afraid to have someone remove me from the picture, either. At least I know what her voice sounds like and who to avoid. She's also probably around the same age as my mother given her mother was potentially a wet nurse."

Hassian kisses my forehead. "You're so smart, princess."

I smile at his praise before doubling over in pain, yelling profanities probably not fit for a princess.

"Lay down; the healer should be back soon. You are under the effects of some kind of poison. That's what those dark veins are. This ship isn't equipped with many herbs or salves, mainly weapons. Although this poison has not been seen before, it might take some time until we find a cure."

The healer arrives shortly after, informing us that we reached the blight and that I had managed to push it back to the forest it started in. This means Alandria has a few more years until they have to worry about it. I hope to finish the job before then, but not in my current state. The healer works some magic on my belly to alleviate some of the pain, and Hassian holds my hand as I drift off back to sleep.

Hassian enters the medical room, where I'm still lying in bed with a cloak in hand. "This is new? You couldn't find ours?"

He shakes his head. "Either someone took them, or they were sitting on the carriage whenever it returned to the school. No one except Thalia and Anton would have noticed our disappearance, and those carriages don't stay out after curfew."

Hassian helps me out of bed, and I feel a little breeze graze my back—the holes from the acid. My vision was a blur over the last day. "Turn around," I order.

"It's nothing, Sage."

"Hassian, please."

"It doesn't hurt, I promise." He turns around, and I don't know why I didn't see it before. His back is riddled with painful-looking burns from when he protected me from the spit. They look clean, but outside of that, there appears to be no treatment of any kind.

"Why aren't they treated?"

He gives me a look, and I know. There wasn't enough to ease both my pain and his. He told them to use everything on me. "Oh, Hassian," a tear escapes my eyes.

"Princess, I'm alright. I promise. I've had worse. Now, let's get to the apothecary and see what she can do about that poison."

"Only if you promise to get yourself treated too."

"For you, princess, anything." I don't understand why I cannot feel when he is hurt, but he can sense when I am. He has been there every time I get hurt since the beginning of the school year. It's not that I don't love him because I do, but I don't understand how his connection is stronger than mine. I should have remembered he was hurt. I should have sensed he was in pain like he did for me. Why didn't I feel anything?

It wasn't far to walk from the airship to Agene's Apothecary, and I am thankful for that. I feel so weak. "What happened to you two?" Agene, the shopkeeper, helps Hassian settle me into a chair.

"We were dealing with the blight on one of the military ships. We were attacked."

"The blight? Why in The Nines were you out there? You two are still enrolled in the academy. That was dangerous! Who sanctioned such a thing?"

"The Order, but for a good reason," Hassian replies quickly. "Can you take a look at her stomach? She's been poisoned by one of the dark creatures. Please tell me you are able to help."

She approaches me, "May I?" She motions to my shirt, asking permission before she examines it. I nod. She carefully raises the shirt from my wound. "This is bad, Hassian, really bad. I can try to extract some of the venom and formulate a cure for it, but it could take weeks, maybe longer. It won't be a painless process." She looks at me, "You might pass out."

"Please, do whatever you must, but if I do, please see to Hassian's back as well. He was hurt protecting me."

She glances at Hassian, raising her brow as if they are having an unspoken conversation. Oh, he definitely has a secret he is keeping from me. "I will, but first, you are the priority here. Lean back in the chair. I will go fetch a syringe and some salve to relieve some of that pain afterward, and I'll be sure to send Hassian with some extra to ease the pain while I try to make a cure."

"Thank you, Agene." She nods before heading to a back room to retrieve what she needs.

I turn my head to face Hassian. "What aren't you telling me?" I ask.

"You caught onto that, huh?"

"Hassian, you can't answer a question with a question."

He sighs. "It's nothing."

"Tell me."

He shifts. "I was going to tell you, eventually. At a young age, I learned my father was, well, he was an unkind man."

"Did he hurt you?" He nods. "Oh, Has-"

"It's okay, I couldn't feel it."

"That's never okay. What do you mean you couldn't feel it?"

"I can't feel pain," he admits.

"Like any pain?"

He shakes his head. "My father was, well, creative with his punishments after I didn't react. I didn't realize I was supposed to, so I eventually just started to pretend it hurt."

"The scar on your chest is from-"

"From my father," he nods.

"I'm so sorry, Hassian."

"It didn't hurt. I'm okay," he tries to reassure me.

"It doesn't matter if it didn't hurt my love; that's traumatizing. Emotional pain is still pain. Is this why I can't sense when you are hurt through our bond?"

He nods. "I can feel when you're hurt, and it's like I just know where you are to see if you are alright. You would be able to sense my emotional distress."

"Would?"

"I'm good at masking that, too."

"Well, I need you to get not good at that. If you are in trouble of any kind. I need to know because I need to be able to find you. This partnership works both ways."

"I promise, if I am ever in any real danger, I will send it through the bond, princess." He bends over and kisses my forehead before taking my hand in his as Agene returns.

Agene pulls up a chair beside me. "I truly apologize for the pain you are about to feel. Are you ready?"

"No, but it needs to be done." I can feel my heart racing as the fear settles in. Hassian's thumb moves in soothing circles on the back of my hand.

"Alright then. Here we go."

I immediately feel a sharp burning sensation when the needle passes through my skin. It starts at the surface of my skin before exploding and spreading throughout my body in a hot inferno. My nerve endings are on fire, and the pain only increases as the needle plunges deeper into my blackening veins. My discomfort levels rise as she pulls back on the syringe to extract some of the toxin, my vision dotting as the pain becomes too much to handle. I am so close to losing consciousness when I feel the needle slide out of me and clang against a metal tray.

"I'm surprised you didn't pass out on me," Agene says.

"Yeah," I say. I would say more, but the idea of exerting more energy to form words sounds like it would take too much.

"Here, drink this," she tilts a cup with liquid near my mouth, and I take small sips. I'm not entirely sure what's in that cup, but whatever it is cooling the raging fire of pain inside me. "I'm going to apply some salve to this. Hassian, take over holding this cup for her, please." He takes the cup from her. I watch her as she removes the lid from a jar, scooping a decent-sized glob onto her hand. I expect pain when she applies the salve to my belly, but I don't feel a thing. I wish I had whatever was in this drink before the toxin, but I guess it was to prevent this from tainting the potential cure. "All done. Alright, Hassian, let's tend to you now." Hassian lets the cape fall from his back and turns to expose the damage. Agene tsks. "This is really infected boy."

"Is it? I wish I could feel pain sometimes so that I could know if something is wrong."

"I'd say, in this case, you should be grateful." She dips a cloth in some liquid and presses it to Hassian's back. I can see foam bubbling up on each of the fissures on his back. It must be some kind of peroxide eating away the bacteria. Agene then takes a long pair of tweezers and pulls away infected tissue. I was either nose blind before, or whatever layer was covering the wound before she cleaned it up was masking the scent really well because, gods, the smell is awful.

"Fuck, that smells bad," Hassian groans.

"Yeah, well, the infection is deep." I watch her pull a giant string of rotted tissue from his back. I try to mask the horror from my face.

"I appreciate the attempt, princess, but I can feel your emotions, remember?"

"I'm so sorry. It's just, love, that's really bad."

"So, I've gathered," this man laughs. Not exactly the response I would expect in this situation.

Agene blots his back again, pulling out a seeing glass to inspect the wound. "It looks like I got everything. I'll put some salve on you too, boy; make sure to reapply each night and be sure to shower. Those waters at the academy will help, but given the degree of the damage, there will be scars. It will still heal slowly, even with the water's aid. Princess, you are going to have to help him with the salve." I nod. "Now, please go, visit the tailor, and get some decent clothes that do not have blood or rips on them before you spook the rest of the city."

She takes a pouch from underneath her counter and fills it with jars of salve. "Thank you," I say.

"Be more careful next time. I will personally deliver this cure to you when it's ready. In the event I can't, I will send my assistant with it and a letter carrying my seal." She shows me her ring. "Do not accept anything from anyone, not even if it's me, if you do not verify my seal first. There are many things in this world gunning after you, princess, and you would do well to remember that. Now, off you go!" She ushers us out of her shop and bolts the door behind us. The closed sign on her shop remains.

I don't feel right returning to the academy just yet without seeing Kira. There was so much about the past she kept from me. The weight of everything she's carried. I just need to let her know she's not alone in it anymore.

"Sage what are you doing here? You should be at the academy. It's getting late." She gives me a glance over. "You look pale? Are you sick little flower?"

I motion for her to take a seat on the couch. "After our meeting, and Hassian and I left to go back to the academy we were intercepted."

"By who?" I can see the panic in her face.

"The Order obtained information that I was a bloodletter. In part, that was my fault for testing the gift from Hassian prior to my meeting with them."

"What did they do to you? It's been days. I thought you were at the school." Hassian sits beside her and holds her shaking hand so I can continue speaking.

"They used me to push back the blight," I start to say.

"You are too untrained for that. You could have died!"

"I know, Kira It had spread dangerously close. If I didn't do something and soon people could have gotten hurt. It was nearly touching the water supply."

"That's impossible. The spread wasn't that far out when we crossed over it. That's years' worth of movement." Her eyes dart back and forth as she processes the information.

"They said I pushed it back enough to gives us years," I say.

"I don't think we are operating on the same time clock anymore. You shouldn't have had to deal with the blight until well after your academy days. I don't understand."

"Wait, where was it when you crossed over?" Hassian asks.

"Just a little way past my people's forest. Something or someone has to be amplifying the spread, but why?"

As if in response I get an intense pain in my wound and hunch over. "Sage!" Hassian yells as he runs over to check me over.

"What's wrong with her?" Kira asks.

"I got hurt by one of those dark creatures." I raise my top up just enough to show her my wound. Kira practically breaks. Her eyes welling with tears.

"My sweet darling girl."

"It's okay Agene is working on a cure. It was our first stop when we made it back to Halaris. I wanted to see you before I went to the academy." I pause trying to think on how to approach this topic. "I was unconscious after the attack. While

I was, I was transported to the past by my mother. She showed me what happened the day I was born."

Kira's eyes go wide at the admittance of what this means. "I never wanted you to know those details, to see what I had to do."

"It's okay Kira. You were so brave. You have been so brave and strong all these years."

Her eyes portray so many emotions. "I've been doing my best to be strong for you. You are all I have left in this world. I didn't want to make that experience miserable for you."

"You would never be a miserable experience for me, Kira."

"I'm sad all the time, Sage. I couldn't bring that burden to you. I carry around so much guilt with me every single day. Living in a world being the last of my kind and losing my most dear friend. They are hard things to carry around. There is no instance in this universe where I would want you to experience anything but the happiness you deserve."

I push past the pain and hold Kira while her body wracks with sobs as she admits her feelings. I know she's not sad that she had to raise me, but she is rightfully upset pertaining to how it happened.

"Kira, write to me when you need someone to talk to. I don't care if I receive twenty ravens a day. Don't carry the burden of your heart alone anymore."

I wipe away the tears from her face with my thumbs and she nods in reply.

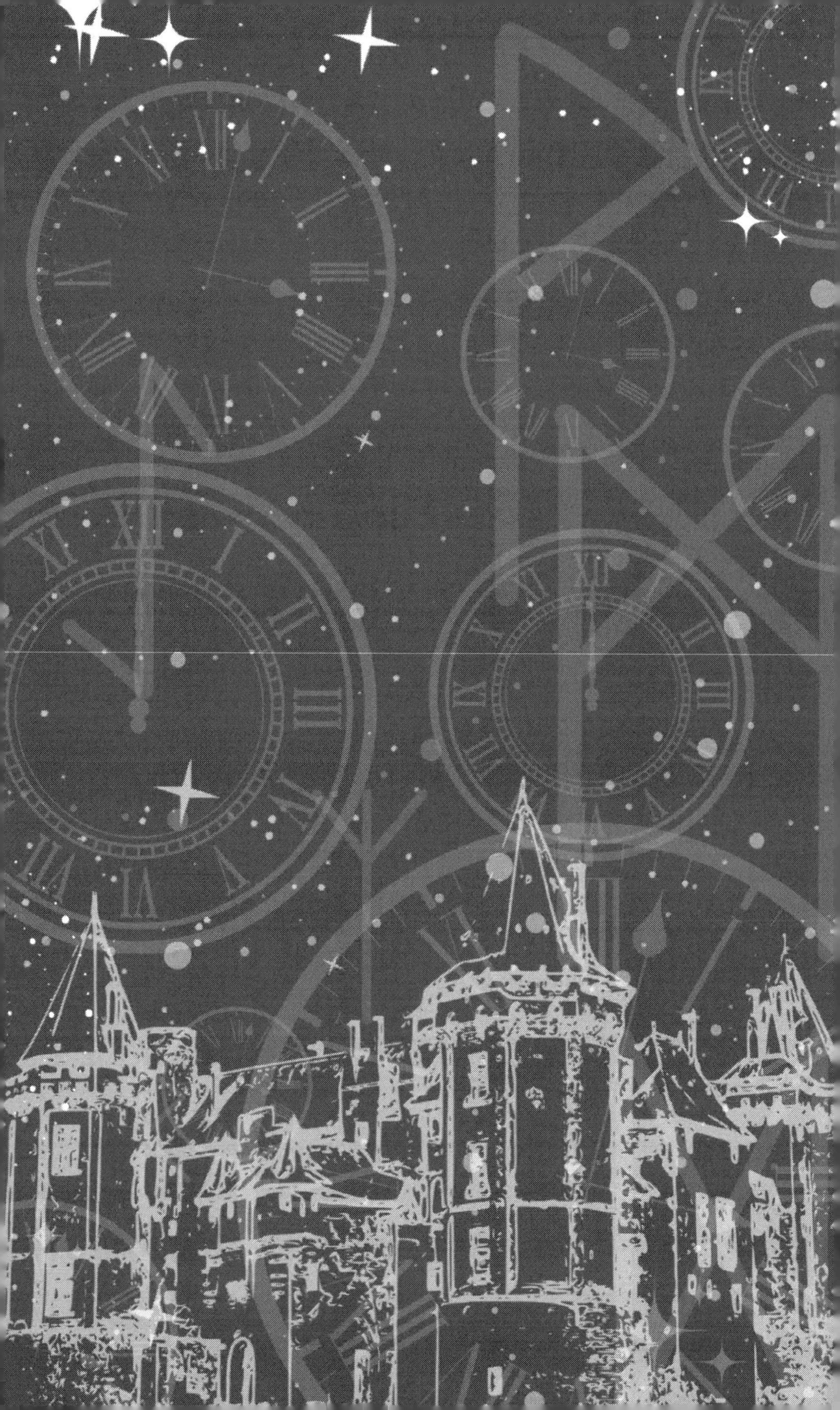

Chapter Thirty-Five
Sage

The girls practically tackle me to the ground when they see me enter our dorm. "Careful, careful," I hiss out between bouts of pain.

"What happened to you? Where were you? You disappeared after that meeting, we thought the worst," Thalia says.

"Well, we were trying to get back here, but then we were intercepted."

"Intercepted by who?"

"The Order."

"I'm going to kill all of them," Thalia's face contorts with rage.

"They're on our side. Well, at least the ones I was with. Sit down; this is a bit of a long story."

The girls sit with me in our living area, and I go over all the events of what happened during my absence, including the fact that I was poisoned and my grandfather's secret child.

"So, the voice sounded familiar?" Aurora asks.

"Yeah, like more than I heard it passing the street type of familiar. I've heard it a lot. It's someone I know, and if I wasn't in such a fog from this poison, I might have been able to pinpoint who."

"I wonder if it's someone in this school, or maybe they were someone you spoke to in the Other Realm?" Thalia says.

"It's hard to say for certain. I'll know if I hear their voice again. When I do, I can't let on that I know. I don't think my grandfather will hurt me before I fulfill the prophecy, but who is to say he won't hurt anyone else that I care about? I'm also not about to ignore the prophecy to ensure he won't harm me."

"Enough about me now. How are you doing? How is Griyf? I've been gone a whole-"

"Three days," Sebille says.

"Three?" She nods. I recall Kira saying it's been days when I saw her earlier. I don't know why it didn't register with me. I'm well aware of all the things that happened during that time. "Okay, well, it's been three days; catch me up on what's been going on.

"Other than nonstop worrying about you, things have been going great on my end. Anton is finally being communicative about what he's been doing. He's found some people for our cause and even scouted a place where everyone can meet up. Griyf is great! He's taking to the saddle well, and I got to fly with him," Thalia says.

"No fucking way!" I shout.

She nods, grinning ear to ear. "It was amazing, Sage—the amount of progress he's made. You'll have to visit him once you're better, though. I don't want you anywhere near him while you're injured. He may be doing so well in his training, but he's still a hyper griffin with no concept of boundaries."

"I can't wait. I'm so glad he's making progress. What about you two? How are the two of you doing?"

"Outside of worrying about your disappearance, not bad. You should have invited us to the meeting, though," Aurora says. "I am only joking; I was stuck visiting with my parents."

"Right," Sebille scoffs.

"Excuse me?" Aurora glares. I am very confused right now.

"I saw you talking to that Nick guy. You weren't with your family. Why are you lying?" Sebille bites.

"Why are you being so hostile right now?" Aurora responds.

"What's going on?" I ask. "What's wrong with her seeing someone?"

"Nothing if she was just seeing someone; Nick is an earth elemental like you."

"We can date outside of our element. What's the big issue?" Aurora says.

"Well, considering, you're betrothed to one of the fourth years, and there was zero chemistry toward him on your end. I doubt that."

"Of course, we invite you into the friend group, and you try to start a fight," Aurora rolls her eyes. Something is off with her. Aurora doesn't have a mean bone in her body.

I nearly jump when a crystal falls to the floor, and I see a glimpse of a moving shadow. Sebille and Aurora continue to verbally rip into each other's throats, and I bend down to set the crystal back on the table when I remember you can use crystals to enhance glamour. Crystals don't require concentration to hold glamour like casting innately requires. I glance back at Aurora and see there's one attached to a bracelet wrapped around her wrist. We haven't learned how to reverse glamour yet, so I am not exactly sure what to do in this situation.

I make eye contact with Thalia to see if she's thinking the same thing as I do, and she gives me a subtle nod. Fuck. I slide my hand through the slit of my skirt, slowly unsheathing my dagger and hide it behind my back. With my intention set, I squeeze the crystal in my other hand and try to remove the glamour. A glimpse of brown hair shows, but this crystal isn't strong enough. I'm not strong enough; this poison caps my reserve. I don't have one of the reversing elixirs; those always stay in the classroom. Thalia shakes her head at me; she failed, too. Sebille glances at me, noticing we see something is off.

Sebille sees it, too, and continues to distract the fake Aurora by arguing with her.

I don't know what I should do. I grip my necklace, trying to innately ask the goddesses for some help when I feel a soft hum between my hands. I again focus on what I need as I curl my hand enough that the ring nicks my skin. The version of Aurora we see flickers away, and I see the same man who was pushing people around in the city. I immediately move my dagger to his throat, adding slight force, just enough for blood to trickle down his neck.

"Who are you, and what did you do to our friend?"

"Your friend is fine," he rolls his eyes. I get angry and push further. "Okay, we don't need to do that." He says, eyes darting between my face and the dagger.

"Tell me where she is," I demand.

"It's as I said. She's fine."

"Where is she?"

He gasps as the blade pushes in further, and the blood flow increases. I might end up murdering this man before I get my answers. "She's with her family. Ask the Headmaster if you don't believe me."

"That can't be true. Everyone is supposed to return to the academy before nightfall. Did you do something to her? Did someone send you? Was it my grandfather?"

"A gentleman never tells," he grabs my arm and pushes my blade further into his neck before yanking my arm. Blood sprays all over me as he uses my hand to sever his carotid artery. He falls to the floor dead.

I am aware of Thalia trying to speak to me, but all I hear is the faint hum. I just killed a man. I know he used me to kill himself, but it was my hand on the blade. I'm a murderer. I've killed someone. This wasn't some kind of monster brought back from the dead. This was a man with his own thoughts and choices to make. I watch as Sebille moves to the man on the floor, checking to see if he's dead. I see the shadow move again as if it was leaning against the wall, watching the whole thing. My eyes follow it as it walks through the door and out of our dorm.

"Sage, please." Thalia is trying to remove the dagger from my hand.

"Sorry," I say as I release my grip on it.

"It's not your fault, Sage. He forced you to do it."

Hassian and Meera come barreling through the door. He sees the sight of me covered in blood, and his eyes dart to the dead man on our floor. "What happened?" He runs over to me, holding me in his arms. I crumple into him. "I'm so sorry. I felt your panic. I tried to get here sooner, but Meera wouldn't let me enter the dorms."

"Why not? You have permission to stay with us," Thalia asks.

"Professor West revoked his rights at the beginning of the holiday week. I assumed he was aware, and that's why he hasn't been coming around," Meera says.

"That wasn't her right to revoke," Hassian hisses as he checks me over for more damage.

"I thought it was weird. I should have asked Auhdaye. I'm so sorry. I'll get the headmaster. He's going to need to know about this," Meera says, exiting the room in a hurry.

"What happened?" Hassian asks.

Thalia and Sebille give him the rundown of how he was glamoured to look like Aurora. Hassian stares at me. "How the hell did you unshift someone?"

"I don't understand. It was just a glamour removal spell."

"Princess, that wasn't glamour. That was a shifter. Glamour can do many things, but it can't make you become someone else. Sure, it can make you look human and change the color of your skin, but it can't make you become someone else. Not everyone is capable of shifting, and even then, it's animals. There's shifting, and then there's shapeshifters. If a shapeshifter is to take on someone else's form, they need to be in close proximity, literally touching the person as they shift. Aurora could very much be in danger or, worse, dead."

"How do you know all this?"

"I'm a third year, remember?"

A single knock sounds on the door before it opens, and Headmaster Brawnmire walks through the door, followed closely by Meera. He takes sight of the scene before him. "Meera, please go fetch Professor Auhdaye, will you?" Meera nods and leaves again. "Would someone care to explain to me why there is a dead man in this dorm?"

We are a cacophony of voices as we all try to explain what happened. Sebille and Thalia make multiple hand gestures as they speak while I sit on the couch, holding my wound from the ship. They explain to him about my disappearance and my injury to discovering that Aurora wasn't Aurora. When they mention the man forcing me to kill him, he doesn't bat an eye.

"I see," Headmaster Brawnmire says, rubbing his chin in thought.

"How long have the wards been failing?" I ask.

"They're not-"

"Don't lie to us like we are children, Headmaster."

A look of defeat crosses his face. "It's not that they're failing. We have cracks."

"Cracks?" Hassian asks.

"The wards on this school are ancient, as is the academy. It's natural for things to weaken over time. We have been monitoring the breeches," the headmaster says.

"Clearly not enough if a shapeshifter was able to get in," Sebille bites.

"I'm afraid it's more serious than that. Someone in the school helped them get in. They had intimate knowledge of your friendships and habits. I don't believe his intention was to hurt you but seek information."

"If that's the case, why did he use Sage's blade and kill himself? We are just students learning; he could have gotten away," Sebille says.

The headmaster glances at my necklace. "I don't believe he could. No doubt he was under oath to eliminate himself if caught." Auhdaye enters the dorm with a gasp as she looks upon the dead body. "Professor, perfect timing. Can you check him for an oath mark?"

'Of course, Headmaster," she pulls back the sleeve on his left arm. In the upper area of his forearm is a marking. The marking looks like two letter Vs with one upside down stacked on each other. The bottom portion has two small dots. "It appears to be a blood oath, sir."

"I am going to ask that the three of you head to the great hall for dinner. Tell no one of this. Do your best to remain normal. We need to handle this situation delicately. I still believe the academy is the safest place for you to be. Professor, will you add some extra warding to this dorm?"

"I'm going to need some hair from each of you. I can cut it, or you can pluck me a few of your hairs. Anyone who is to enter this room needs to give me some. Aurora is not present, so I will collect it from her brush." Auhdaye heads into Aurora's living space while we pull a few strands of our hair from our head, including the Headmaster, Meera, and Hassian. "This ward will prevent anyone from entering your dorm. It will take me a few hours, so try to stay away in the meantime."

"Neither of you seem concerned that Aurora is gone," Thalia says. "Do you know where she is?"

Headmaster Brawnmire flushes. "My apologies. I thought I mentioned it earlier. She is with her parents and will be away for a little while. Her grandmother fell ill. I assure you she is safe. I received word when she arrived."

I feel a sense of relief, but I am still confused. "When a shapeshifter changes into someone, they have to be touching the person they are taking on, correct?"

"Only for the first initial switch. When a shapeshifter takes someone's form, it also absorbs their recent memories. Those fade over time, just like their ability to shift," the headmaster says.

"Is there a way to prevent a shifter from taking your form?" Hassian asks.

"Hmm, I believe so. I will look into it."

"Sage should probably shower first. We all should," Thalia says. The headmaster looks us up and down and now realizes the blood splatter all over my face.

"Right. You should do that."

I'm not sure if I will be able to handle anything too heavy right between the trauma I just experienced and the poison coursing through my system. I opt for something that looks like it might be a broth and has some vegetables in it. It smells good, so it's not the worst option in the world. We are all still on break for a few more days, so students are filtering in, in small waves, as they make it back to the academy, trying to beat curfew. Even some of the professors are still making their way inside.

Professor West and Professor Dublin walk in at the same time, entirely engrossed in conversation, and that's when I hear it—the familiar voice. I try not to drop my spoon from shock as I finish taking my bite and turn my head toward Hassian to whisper in his ear. "She's here. It's Professor West."

Hassian tilts my chin and comes in close as if to kiss me. "Are you sure?" I nod. He kisses me before moving over to whisper in my ear. "I think it's time we go take a bath and get ready for bed, don't you think, princess?"

"A bath sounds lovely." I'm aware we just came back from the showers, but it's so loud in there we won't be overheard.

Thalia gives us a questioning look, and all I say is, "I'll talk to you both later." They get the hint and wave me off. They know I will tell them back in the dorm.

Hassian and I strip down and move to the furthest side of the bathing pool, toward where the fountain shoots out a steady stream of water. "It's her; the voice is unmistakable," I whisper.

"It makes sense that it would be. He installed her as a teacher the same year you started and to teach the history of something he caused no less. I wonder what her aim is in being here, though."

"Maybe my grandfather thinks my mother saw them, not just overheard them and told Kira about it?"

"There are so many questions I have as to why she's here. Especially after you told me about the conversation between those two, he needs you alive to fulfill the prophecy. If they kill you before the prophecy, I have no doubt certain members of The Order will out him. He would have secured the fate of the realm."

"I am curious, though, if he does plan to kill me sometime after I succeed, what will the gods do? Based on my history, I am the last standing member of my family with god's blood."

"That could potentially change the whole hierarchy of the realm. I cannot even imagine the implications."

"I'm worried."

"About your grandfather?"

I shake my head. "Well, yes and no. He is obviously a threat, but I'm mainly worried Agene won't make the antidote in time.

Whether it's from Gaiwen making a major move or this poison finishing the job."

Hassian tucks a loose strand of hair behind my ear and looks into my eyes. "The cure will come before it's too late, and if Gaiwen comes for you before then, well, he will have to go through me first."

"I don't know if I can stay at the academy."

"Why?"

"If Gaiwen tries to attack me here, many students will get hurt. We know he has flyers now; what if he uses them? What if he attacks the city?"

"Shit, there was a ward breach. He was testing the security of the school. Do you think he was a part of the second attack?"

"No, I don't. I saw something in the dorm."

"What did you see?"

"A shadow. It was like it was warning me about the shifter."

"A shadow sounds like it has something to do with Gaiwen."

"I know he needs something from me. From my understanding, the shapeshifter wasn't there to hurt us, though, just to get information."

"The information he would have passed along if it was going to your grandfather could have, though."

"Professor West could be responsible for letting him in."

He nods. I don't know what comes over me, but in that moment, I am just so overwhelmed, and I start to cry. I cry because I am scared, tired, and hurting. Hassian pulls me into his arms and runs his hands up and down my back.

"We will be ready, princess. Don't you worry. Everything will be okay."

"How can you be sure?"

"Because you have an army of people that already care about you. Your selflessness on that ship put The Order on your side. Your kindness to everyone around you is leading to a rebellion in your name. Anton has been busting his butt to ensure you are not alone when the time comes."

"Thank you," I whisper.

"For what, princess?"

"For always looking out for me."

"I would go to the ends of any realm for you, princess. My love for you knows no bounds. You are quite literally the person that makes me feel whole and alive. No one else in this entire realm can make me feel. I am yours, now and for all eternity. There is no me without you."

I cannot help the giggles that come forth as he casually slides in the fact that he can only feel pain because of me when I hurt, as someone who grew up in a world full of humans in some shitty backwater town in America reading fantasy novels. This is everything I could have dreamed of. He is everything.

I don't know if it's because I hate myself or I just love him clearly beyond reason, but I ignore the pain and move myself onto his lap. "Princess, are you sure?" he asks. The question is asking about more than one thing, but my answer is yes to all of it. Yes, to him. Yes, to this. Yes, to forgetting about the pain and the horror of what's to come. I need him. I nod.

That was all he needed before his lips are on mine and his hands are moving, touching every inch of me as if he is not sure where to start. He trails tender kisses down my neck, the top of my breasts, and back up to my lips, communicating our deepest desires without uttering a single word. My fingers weave through his tangled and wet hair as we inch more and more under the fountain of water in our desperation to be close. Hassian lifts me by the waist, adjusting himself before sliding me back down. He pulls out before going all the way, teasing me. I need all of him. My body is filled with so much desire that it's like electricity is coursing through my veins.

A soft whimper escapes my throat as the teasing becomes unbearable. He grins as he kisses me deeply before finally giving me what I want by plunging into me. The sound of water splashing becomes a rhythmic beat as we lose ourselves to our desires. At this moment, there is no past where we didn't know each other, no future full of terror, only the here and now. The raw intensity of our connection builds up like a storm. Tonight, I become undone by him. By the man I love. My mate.

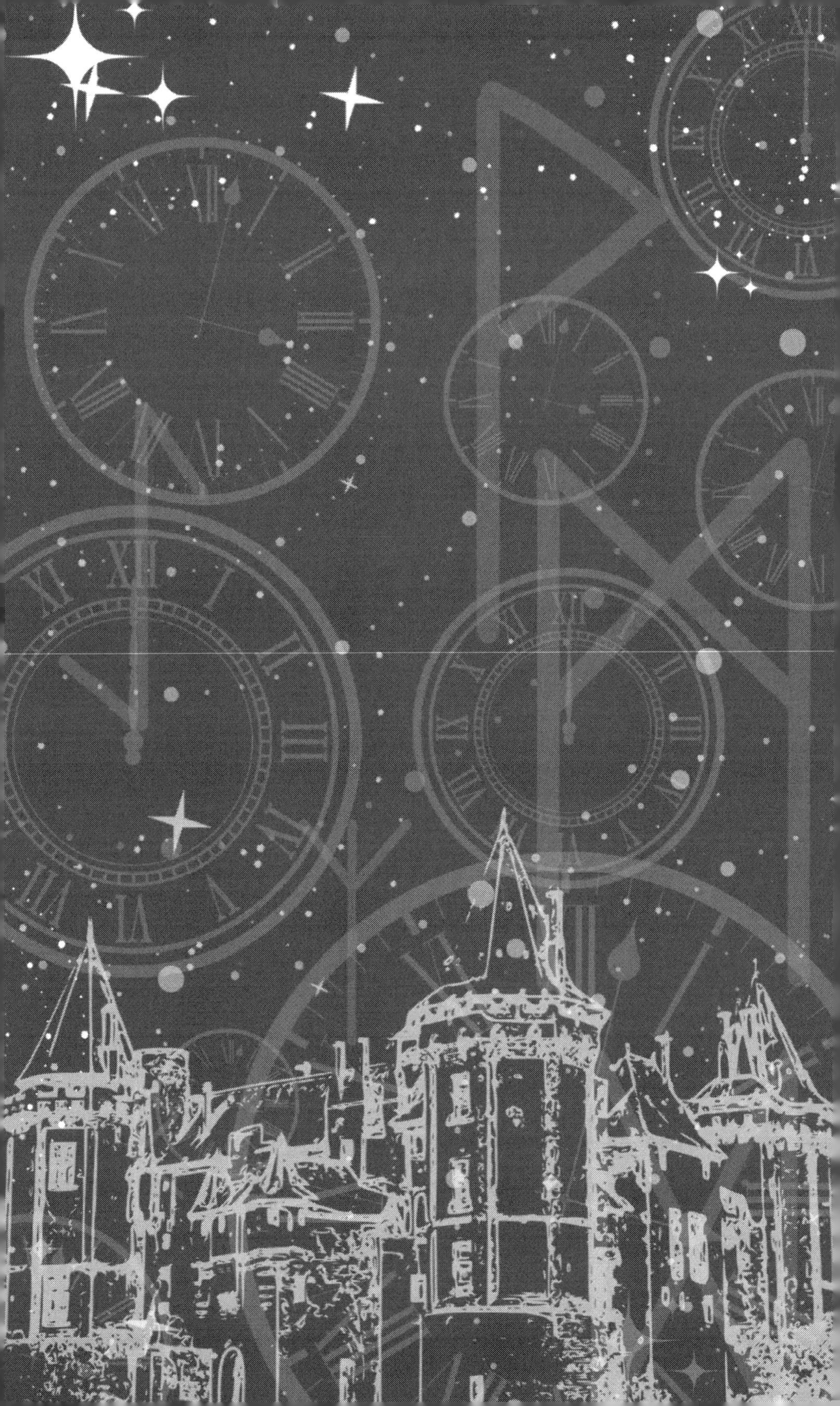

Chapter Thirty-Six
Sage

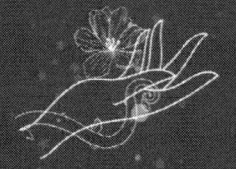

It's been weeks since we were at the apothecary, and still no word on an antidote. The veins continue to spread, extending to the lower parts of my breasts. It doesn't seem to be doing any damage to my heart, but my muscles and bones ache. I don't know how to describe it, but it's like a constant throbbing from within. Hassian can't feel it, and for that, I am grateful. I am grateful that one of us functions to the best of our bodies' capabilities.

Hassian has been permanently staying in my dorm. I don't understand why they even bothered to separate the men and women; the rooms don't stay that way as the year progresses. It's not like they ever do checks. I mean, why would they? We are all consenting adults just learning how to hone our magic.

Last week, I started experiencing a lot of discomfort when I am trying to sleep. My ribs have this constant dull ache in them, and no matter what way I lay, it's nearly impossible to feel relief. I haven't tried any tonics to alleviate the pain, just the salves we were given. I'm too afraid to consume anything and worsen the poison.

Professor Dublin is aware of my condition and allows me to just study text instead of casting. My reserves are too low to be able to cast anything of use. I can make a flower bloom, but it leaves me exhausted for hours. I still observe my classmates in between chapters of my text, watching them as they cast stronger spells like shaping metal into something useful. I take notes of what I may potentially do one day, to practice once I am better.

"Sage, are you sure you won't try this tonic, just to help you for now?"

"No, Professor. We don't know how it will affect the poison. Until I get the antidote, I can't risk it."

"It will be here if you change your mind." He walks back to his desk. This is a question he asks every single day during class and if he happens to catch me in the halls. Of all my professors, I believe Dublin cares about me the most. He has become somewhat of a father figure to me over the course of the year.

I continue to read the chapter I was working on about techniques you can use to ground your element. This specific section discusses the use of stones to amplify your power. This leads me to think about what the stone I carry can do as I think back on what my mother showed me when I was first poisoned. She didn't want Kira to tell me, so it has to be important that I figure it out on my own. Seeing as only females with the god's blood in them are the only ones that can wear it, it must have some kind of connection with that, right?

I go to the front of the room where Professor Dublin stores all his texts related to our element to see if he has anything on gemstones. He does, so I bring it back to my desk and flip through it. Comparing what pictures are in the text to the stone I am wearing, when that doesn't yield any results, I read the descriptions. I don't get far in the book before the tower chimes and class ends. I write in my notebook what page I ended on and go to return it to his shelf.

"Sage, if you want to continue studying this particular text, there is a copy in the library. I'd loan this one, but it's the only copy I currently have for inside the classroom."

"I think I will do just that, professor. Do you recall where exactly it is in the library?"

"It was closer to the back of the room, on one of the end shelves last I saw it."

"Thank you." He smiles at me and I make my way to my next class.

The rest of my classes go by fairly quickly. It was hard being in Professor West's class knowing who she is, but Headmaster Brawnmire was adamant that we act like we don't know anything, even after we told him about her being my grandfather's secret child. He wants to ensure that she is the only threat before he acts.

Since being poisoned, I haven't been able to train, so Hassian has grown accustomed to me focusing on studying my texts. He still trains to keep his body in shape, and I wouldn't dare ask him to give that up just to watch me study, anyway.

When I get into the library, a few students have already settled at some of the tables, so I pick a spot and set my stuff down before I go in search of the book. It's not often that I am in here before dinner time, but the times I have been, that's when I notice other students occupying it. I was beginning to think no one ever visited the library, as it was always dead when Hassian and I spent our evenings in here.

I make it to the back of the library and try to search in the general area that Professor Dublin told me he last saw it. It doesn't take me long to find it. I guess students don't have much interest in stones. I pull the book off the shelf and blow off the layer of dust forming on the top of the pages before settling into my seat. I open up to the page I left off in Dublin's classroom and begin to read.

I make it a decent of the way through the book before my stomach protests, and I realize that the students that were here had since cleared out. The library doesn't have a checkout system; we are just allowed to take things as we need them. If the books get misplaced once they leave the library, it's not the end of the world. They always find their way back home.

Personally, I think the brownies are responsible for their safe return. They are always so tentative to things that belong to the academy.

I store the book and my notes in my bag and make my way to the great hall. It's not as packed as a lot of the students have already cleared out, but Hassian and Thalia are waiting at the table.

"I was about to send out a search patrol if you didn't show up soon. Hassian would have already left to find you, but I told him to wait and be patient," Thalia says as I slide in between the two of them.

"Sorry, I was in the library studying."

Hassian feigns hurt. "How dare you go to our special place without me." He lets out a laugh. It's one of my favorite sounds; I wish he did it more often. I have heard it less and less since I was poisoned. "What were you studying?"

"Rocks, stones, crystals."

"Any particular reason?"

"Yeah, I'm trying to figure out what's special about this stone that's been passed down through my family. When my mother was showing me a vision of the past, Kira was told not to tell me what it could do. That I needed to figure it out on my own."

"And you think you can find the answer in one of the books there?" Thalia asks.

I reach for what I think is roasted bird meat that has been baked into a fluffy bread slathered in butter and seasoning before answering, "I don't know, but I will continue to research. I have the book in my bag right now if you want to take a look. I decided to borrow it even though I will be back up there. I didn't want anyone else to have the same idea, not that I think they will. There was a literal layer of dust on it when I grabbed it."

Thalia reaches into my bag and continues reading where I have it bookmarked. I bite into the flakey bread. Hassian pours me a stein of ale, calling the fact I will need to wash this food down after a few bites. It's delicious, but it leaves you feeling very parched. "Thanks, love," I say after taking a gulp.

"You know you could have come and gotten me from the training yard, and I would have joined you in the library," he says.

"I know, love, but you would have scoured over books on poisons again. You deserve to be able to let off some steam in training. I miss joining you out there. I miss the physical contact of it all."

"I miss the physical contact too," Hassian growls in a way that sends heat flooding through me.

"Guys, please keep the sex levels down; I'm still here," Thalia scolds.

It's not like we have had any sex at all since our night in the bath. I wish we were because Gods was that the most incredible feeling I have ever experienced. It's just the following day, the darkening grew, and we realized physical exertion speeds up the process. Now, there's guilt tied to sex. When this antidote eventually comes, and I fully believe it will, I will get him alone, and I will tackle him like a wild animal in heat. Fuck, I need to stop thinking about this, this is not helping.

"Your necklace sounds close to the carnelian stone in here, but I don't think that's what it is. Honestly, I don't think your stone is going to be found in any of these books. It's unique to your family. We would have better luck going to the High King's castle and seeing if there are any journals left behind, and that's risky."

"It was worth a shot, I guess. Thanks for the help, Tal," I say as I take the book back from her.

"I'm sorry I couldn't be of any help. Look, I hate to bail, but I am meeting Meera in the courtyard. We're giving Griyf off for the night and plan on going for a walk under the stars. I'll see you in the dorm later." Thalia blows us a kiss and practically races out of the great hall.

"I think I am going to have to play nice with my grandfather to work my way into his castle."

"That could put you in a very dangerous position, princess."

"I know. Whatever this stone is meant to help me with, I don't think it's for the battle to come with Gaiwen. I don't see how it could be; I haven't even figured out what it can do."

"We will figure it out." He kisses my temple. "What do you want to do tonight?"

"Hmm, well, I need to return this book to the library since I guess I don't need it. Then a bath sounds lovely." Hassian groans, and I can tell the lack of physical intimacy is wreaking havoc on him as well. "Sorry, my love. I just meant the water always feels nice for all the aches. You don't have to join me if it will be too much torture."

"Oh, I'm coming. Fuck." He groans again.

"You know I have an idea for something we can possibly do in place of sex. Hmm, but the risk of someone walking in on us might be too great."

"Oh no, you just got me going. I will take any risk right now."

"I do have one question."

"Yeah?"

"How is the water clean? Like all those bodies. The things we did can't be very sanitary."

"I'm not sure how the process works exactly, but the water is constantly being purified. The whole tub is lined with runes."

"Oh good, because I was about to feel really bad for whoever takes a bath after us."

I think I pushed Hassian a little too far because he lifts me from my seat at the table and marches me straight to the bathing room.

"Tell me, princess, what did you have in mind?" he asks as he begins to unlace the strings of my corset. I can feel my body surging with desire as his fingers graze against the thin layer of fabric covering my back each time, he reaches for a new lace to loosen.

"Well, physical exertion speeds up the process, so I was thinking," I pause to build suspense.

"Go on, princess," I can feel his length harden as he presses into me, issuing his demand.

"I could watch you, and you could watch me." I bite my lip as I work up the courage to speak these words to him.

"Watch what exactly?"

"Touch ourselves, watch how just being in the same room as each other can make us come undone." He pulls hard at my laces, and my corset falls to the ground. He stalks around to the front of me and rips the dress shirt I wear alongside my corset because forget buttons right now.

He groans as he stares at my exposed breasts. I slide my skirt and panties to the ground, exposing the rest of myself to him. "Get in the water, right fucking now." He orders. I do as he says. I watch him from the depths of the bathing pool as he hastily tries to unclothe himself. His cock practically bursts from the confines of his pants the moment the zipper is down.

Hassian steps into the water, following me to the furthest end of the pool. I set myself onto one of the ledges that wrap around the length of the pool. My entire body is bare and open to his viewing. "Sit over there," I point to a spot just a little bit away from where I am currently sitting. It's close enough to watch him, but far enough we won't be touching.

"What now, princess?"

"I want you to stroke your cock for me." I want to say I am surprised about my actions right now, but I'm not. My desire for him has been doing nothing but getting built up since the last time we had sex. I watch him as he grips his cock and slowly moves his hand up and down his shaft. "Good."

"Now, now, princess, I can't be the only one. Be a good girl, and show me what those fingers can do." It's now that I truly realize how fucked I actually am.

I bring my fingers and start circling my clit. I have been desiring release for so long, just this touch alone, in the presence of him, is about to make me reach my breaking point. "Fuck," I whimper.

"Good girl, now imagine that hand is mine." My body elicits a reaction from the sound of those words, how quickly he has taken control from me. It's so fucking hot. I let out a whimper as I increase the pace. "Not yet, Princess. It's too soon." He picks up the speed that he's stroking himself with to be in tune with mine.

I can feel my nipples hardening to utter agony as my desire for him rises. I circle faster and faster and throw my head back. I want to be a good girl and hold out for him, but I don't think I can do it. I want release. I need release. I let out a cry of relief as my eyes roll back and my body quakes. Warm liquid shoots across my face and the top of my breasts, and I know he's reached his peak of pleasure, too. I open my eyes, wiping a little bit of his cum that's blocking my vision. Quite frankly, I'm impressed by his aim.

"I'm sorry. I meant that to last longer."

He grins as he stares at the mess he made. "That was, well, that was an experience, princess. We should get you washed off, though." He scoops me up, walks me to where the water comes out of the wall, and helps me rinse everything out of my hair and off my body.

I'm glad to know that the water is sterilized because this is now the second time, he and I have done this in here. After he is satisfied that I am clean, we lay there in the water. Just holding each other for now this will be enough. The antidote will come, and we will be okay.

Hassian and I return to my dorm rather late to find the headmaster waiting on the couch with Professor Auhdaye. Sebille, Thalia, and Aurora are sitting across from them. Aurora is back. I wonder when she returned.

"Glad you could finally grace us with your presence, you two," Professor Auhdaye says. "I suppose this means we can begin." Auhdaye gets on her knees to get closer to the table resting between the couches. There's a mortar and pestle sitting alongside a bundle of herbs and a carafe filled with what I think is water. She begins plucking ingredients and grinding them down.

"What's going on?" I ask.

"I've discovered how to prevent a shifter from taking your form. Unfortunately, it means we will have to mark your skin with a special rune. This is non-negotiable," the headmaster says.

"You will receive no fight from me," I say. Glancing at the table, I watch as Auhdaye continues to grind the herbs until they are all a fine powder before adding a piece of charcoal. Once everything is ground down and mixed well, she adds a little of whatever liquid is in the carafe until it has an inky texture.

"Who is first?" she asks as she unravels a kit out onto the table. I can see an assortment of needles and a small hammer.

"I guess I will," I say. She motions for me to sit on the couch and lay my arm on the side of the chair. She intends to place it on my forearm.

I've always imagined what a tattoo would feel like. I watch Auhdaye pour some of the mixture into a separate jar before pulling a needle from the kit. She inserts the needle into a little block and dips the tip slightly into the mixture. Afterward, she brings it over to my arm, aligns it where she wants it to go and begins tapping out the rune. It hurts like a bitch.

"Hold still, Sage or your lines will be bumpy," Auhdaye warns.

"I'm trying; this doesn't feel the greatest."

"It's really not that bad. I think it's just the poison in your body making you extra susceptible to pain. This will be over quickly. Just hang on." Hassian bends down in front of the couch and holds my hand as Auhdaye continues to tap out the shape of the rune.

"I think we should all take that rune class like Thalia does," I joke.

"Yeah, about that. I actually only took the one lesson. I have just been using that time for Meera and me," Thalia shrugs.

"Where is Meera? Shouldn't she be getting one of these too?" I ask.

"She'll be here a little later. She's doing dorm checks first."

"I didn't know that was something she had to do," I say.

"It wasn't until the shifter. Auhdaye gave her some silver to test the students with in case there's another. You haven't needed to be checked because you can cross into the dorm."

"Will the rest of the student body be getting these tattoos then?" I ask.

"No," Headmaster Brawnmire replies. "We still have the investigation going and to require this of every student would bring too much attention."

"I never asked, but how did the Nick questioning go or can you not say?" I ask.

"He was just a boy smitten with Aurora. The shifter, while disguised as her, asked him to watch you during Professor

Dublin's class. He no doubt thought he was doing the right thing, thinking you could help with the blight."

"For the record, I have stayed loyal to my betrothed. I don't need to be banished from my household," Aurora mumbles.

"All done," Professor Auhdaye says. Thank the goddesses. "You can put some of the salve you use to temper down your infection site. You might be more prone to ink rejection with the poison in your system. Come to me if you notice anything wrong with the rune. I mean it, Sage."

"I will."

Auhdaye continues to work on everyone's arms. After she finishes with three of us, Meera makes her appearance.

"Everyone was clear in this tower," she says as she makes her way into an open chair.

"Thank you for continuing to do the checks Meera," the headmaster says.

"It's no trouble. I'd rather walk the thousands of steps every night than see another dead body in one of these dorms again, or anywhere else for that matter.

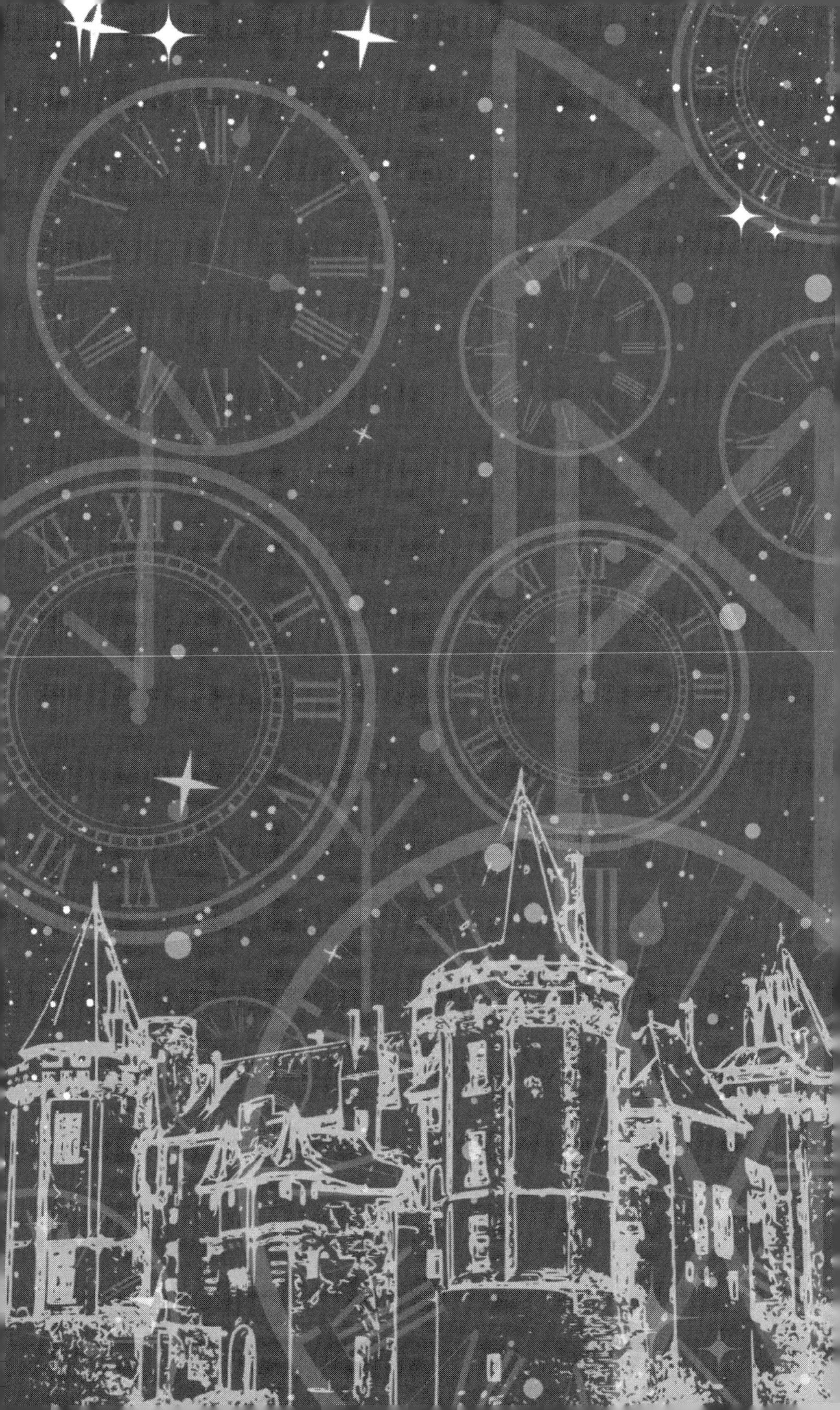

Chapter Thirty-Seven
Sage

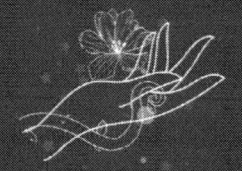

The days turn into weeks, and the weeks turn into a month, and we are nearing the end of the school year, and still, we have yet to hear word of my antidote. It's been getting harder to function. I'm exhausted all the time, inattentive in lessons, and I'm losing sleep because no matter how I lay, my whole being aches. The black veins have extended beyond my torso, and I have resorted to wearing long sleeves, even as summer is quickly approaching. Hassian's touch used to alleviate the pain, but nowadays, it just hurts to fucking breathe. The poison doesn't seem to be killing me, but it does feel like it's weakening my body somehow. I am grateful for one thing, though and it's that whatever is going on in my body doesn't seem to be hurting Hassian through the bond.

I wonder if the bond only allows us to feel things as they are happening and not as they are progressing. I wish my mother were still alive to help explain it to me. Since returning, I have done some research into it, and based on the history records, finding your fated mate isn't as common these days.

It's so fucking hard to pretend that everything is normal when war is coming, and I am possibly going to die from poisoning. I tried to reach out to Kamira, to seek her guidance to see if the path is unchanged, but she didn't answer. There's no word from Agene yet on the cure, and I have to pretend like my history teacher hasn't been wishing me dead since before I was born.

"I think you should visit Griyf tonight. I know I have been relentless in saying to wait until you get better, but I think seeing him again might help cheer you up. Anton would also love for you to check out the progress he's made with the rebellion."

"I'm sorry I haven't come by sooner. I've been meaning to; I'm just exhausted all the time. I'll come visit you and Griyf tonight, but I'm not ready to see the rebellion yet. I don't want them to see me like this." I point to my pallid and sweat stricken face.

"I know. I'm your roommate, remember? It'll be worth pushing past the exhaustion today, I promise."

"Okay."

"Great, we can go there after dinner tonight then," she winks. "Griyf will be so excited to see you. I'll make sure he doesn't jump on you or anything. Agene will create the cure soon. I just know it."

"Am I interrupting something important, girls?" Professor Auhdaye narrows her brows at us. "Anything you are willing to share with the class?"

"Only if they are willing to fight for the greater good," Thalia says it like a jest, but I don't miss the way her eyes dart around the room to see reactions.

"Well, if you don't mind, I would like to get into explaining how to make this elixir."

"Not at all. Carry on, professor," Thalia says.

Auhdaye rolls her eyes and resumes talking to the class. "You need to be careful when you pluck the petals from this particular flower. If you cause the petal to tear, try again, reach for the base, and try to remove it in one swift motion. You can use a damaged leaf in a pinch, but you won't get the same effect had you done it correctly."

"What elixir are we working on?" I ask Thalia. Neither of us have been paying attention; that was evident when she shrugs at my question.

The boy on the other side of me bends over to whisper, "Serenity's Embrace. It's supposed to help with calming the nerves. It will be great around exam time."

"Thank you," I say to him, and he goes back to taking notes.

"Once you've done that you need to crush the shard into a nice fine powder before adding to your cauldron. Remember to stir in a clockwise motion."

The rest of my classes pass by in a blur and before I know it my third class of the day is over. I head to the great hall to locate some lunch. I'm not sure where Hassian is, nor my roommates, for that matter. I realize I'm sitting at the wrong table, but I don't care. It took so much of my energy to get here. I'm not particularly hungry today, either, but I have to eat something. I look at the food options, grab a sandwich, and begin munching away. I was halfway through my lunch when a woman approaches me.

Tapping on my shoulder, she asks, "Are you Sage?"

I nod. "Who's asking?"

"Madame Agene sent me. She said to give you this letter first."

She hands me over the letter and I check the seal. It's a match. I open up the letter to find the words: *Were you expecting some kind of literary genius in here? Drink the damn potion, girl.*

The girl hands me a vial of liquid and leaves. I swirl the vial to ensure all the ingredients are mixed before uncorking the lid and swallowing it down. In retrospect, I probably should have gone to an isolated area before doing this because being surrounded by a lot of people when the room is spinning and spinning doesn't make for the most pleasant of experiences. I don't know why I thought a potion in a magical realm was going to be slow-acting. There is this fuzzy tickling in my abdomen as it works its way through my body.

I stand up to try and sneak my way out of the great hall unnoticed. I am certainly not unnoticed because someone swoops in beside me and helps me out of the room. They walk with me until I am resting on a bench in the hallway. "Thank you," I say, finally looking at my helper. "I've seen your face before. Who are you?"

"The name is Nick. I saw you drink the potion. You looked like you were going to be sick, and quite frankly, I wanted to apologize to you."

"Apologize for what?"

"I was the one that ratted you out to The Order."

"Oh." How could I forget?

He scratches the back of his head before continuing, "I didn't mean it in a malicious way. It's just I was at one of the taverns for lunch and I overheard one of the members talking about how the blight was spreading. I remembered seeing you in class healing that plant after Aurora asked me to keep an eye on you. I told her, and she said I should let The Order know straight away. I just thought you could help. I thought I was doing the right thing. I didn't think you'd get hurt."

I want to be angry at this random stranger for betraying my trust, but I can't. This wasn't something that was ill-willed. He was just concerned about our people, and as the next future ruler, I should have stepped up myself. "It's alright. It's not the blight that hurt me."

"What did then?"

I look around. I'm not sure if I can trust him. I mean, also, taking into consideration what he just told me, the chances are slim. "I should go."

"Wait!" He slides out an embroidered emblem of a baby wrapped in vines. "I'm a part of the group Anton's putting together. We all have these to show we are on your side. You can trust me. I wanted you to know the truth because you deserved to."

"Is that—"

"It's meant to be you as a baby, to symbolize the day your fate was set. The vines are symbolic of when you learned you were a bloodletter."

"Anton's really out here telling you all everything, huh?" I joke.

"We want to know the truth because we are here to stand with you." He whispers, grow quieter, "I've seen what your grandfather does to people he doesn't care for, and I've seen how you treat people. The realm needs you."

I decide to trust him. If I'm wrong then I'll pay the price, if I'm not, well then hopefully I am building a stronger relationship with my allies. "I got hurt from one of Gaiwen's creatures when we were on our way to see how far back, I pushed the blight. Ivan called it a chirocra, a bat-like creature. Some of their limbs are made from blades, and, I guess, coated in poison. I got slashed because I got distracted for a moment. The vial you saw me drinking was the antidote."

His eyes widen. "The time is really drawing closer?" I nod. "Thank you for telling me," he says before he walks away, the emblem he showed me gripped tightly in his fist. I look around to ensure I am alone before raising my shirt to inspect how much damage remains. All the black lines are gone now, there's just a thick inflamed scar left behind. The lines may be gone, but the ache is still persisting. It's not nearly as bad as it was. Maybe the antidote needs more time, even in a realm filled with magic, to work its course. I pray to The Nines that this antidote will fix everything.

It didn't take me long to locate Hassian as he was in the first place I went to look. The place that has become sort of our spot over the course of the year.

"Well, hi, handsome," I say, pulling up a chair beside him. I look to see what he's reading. *Various Poisons and the Common Cure*. "Love," I wave my hand in front of his eyes to break his concentration.

"Sorry, princess. I was just doing some research."

"On poisons?" I raise my brow at him.

"You caught on to that, huh?"

"Yes. I'll have you know Agene had the antidote delivered today." I lift my shirt to show him the darkened veins are gone.

"Thank The Nines. Sage, I have been losing sleep over this nearly every night since we got back."

"I can tell, you look awful," I tease.

"Princess, are you making fun of me?"

"Why yes, I am. What are you going to do about it?"

"This." Hassian tackles me to the ground and kisses me. "As much as I would love to take you here right now, people actually use the library during these hours." A nod in the direction of a very mortified woman holding a stack of books. "Case in point."

"Awe, just when I was hoping we could get a replay from the isle over there," I point to the row of books where he made me come undone all those months ago.

"You are a cruel and wicked woman, princess."

I stand up and smooth out my skirts, offering a hand to Hassian. He accepts it and we sit back down at the table. "Thalia and I are going to go visit with Griyf after dinner. I was thinking that since I have the elixir maybe I can finally go see what Anton's done with the rebellion. I would love for you to meet us there," I say.

"I would not miss your reaction for the world. Anton has been working his butt off. Honestly, he could have a career as a general in The Order if he wanted. I don't want to spoil it, but I have a feeling you will be thoroughly impressed with everything he's done."

"I am very much looking forward to it. During my time with Thalia over the summer, he gave off the vibe of being very charismatic when he wanted to be." I look over at the book Hassian was reading earlier. "You can shelve that book again; I feel fine, love. If it comes back, which I don't think it will, Agene knows what she's doing."

"What if Agene isn't around the next time it happens?"

"Well, I met her apprentice today, and she gave off the vibe of knowing what she's doing. We will get through it. The answer won't be in that book anyway. Besides that, there is an amazing Herbology teacher who works at this school that is very capable with elixirs, as well as a healer who probably has decent knowledge. Don't let your fear of me getting hurt consume you."

"Tell me, princess, do you still ache? Do you still feel the lingering pain that came with that toxin because I can't tell. I can't feel your pain through the bond even if I try, and it destroys me not knowing what kind of pain you are in."

I look him in the eyes, and I know that I cannot keep the truth from him. He deserves the transparency. "Yes." He throws his hands up in frustration. "It's not as bad as when my veins were blackened. It's manageable for now. We can look into tonics to ease my daily pain if it doesn't go away."

"You would be dependent on tonics just to get a good night's sleep; that's not the life you deserve, princess."

"It's what we are dealing with right now in this moment, my love. There's a chance the antidote just takes time. Please don't let this consume you because I need you here in the present with me. Let the healers and all the people trained in this look into it. I need my mate present with me."

"You're right, I'm sorry. It's just-you cry in your sleep, princess, and it breaks my heart. My touch used to give you some relief and now it doesn't. It doesn't hurt you, but it doesn't help either. I feel helpless on how to help you."

"I will be okay, Hassian. I can face anything as long as you are by my side."

"I will always be by your side. I am yours, and you are mine, whatever may come." I watch him as he places the book back on its shelf. I know how hard it was for him to take that step, but it needed to be done.

"Excuse me," an air elemental approaches us as we were getting ready to head to our next class. "I was told to deliver this letter to you, Hassian. It's from the Headmaster."

Hassian takes the note from the them and reads it as the student rushes out of the library. "I might be a little late meeting up with you and Thalia tonight. The headmaster wishes to discuss something with me. It doesn't say what, so it could be pertaining to everything that's going on. I promise I will be there tonight. Just be on the lookout for the most attractive man in the room."

"Professor Dublin?" I joke.

Hassian practically stumbles down the stairs at my jest. "I'm going to pretend I never heard that come from your mouth. Should I be worried?"

"Gods no!" I give him a shove and he grins at me.

"I'm not above squaring down with a professor to win the hand of a beautiful woman."

"Stop," I groan. He laughter doesn't stop until we depart to our separate classes. How I missed that beautiful sound.

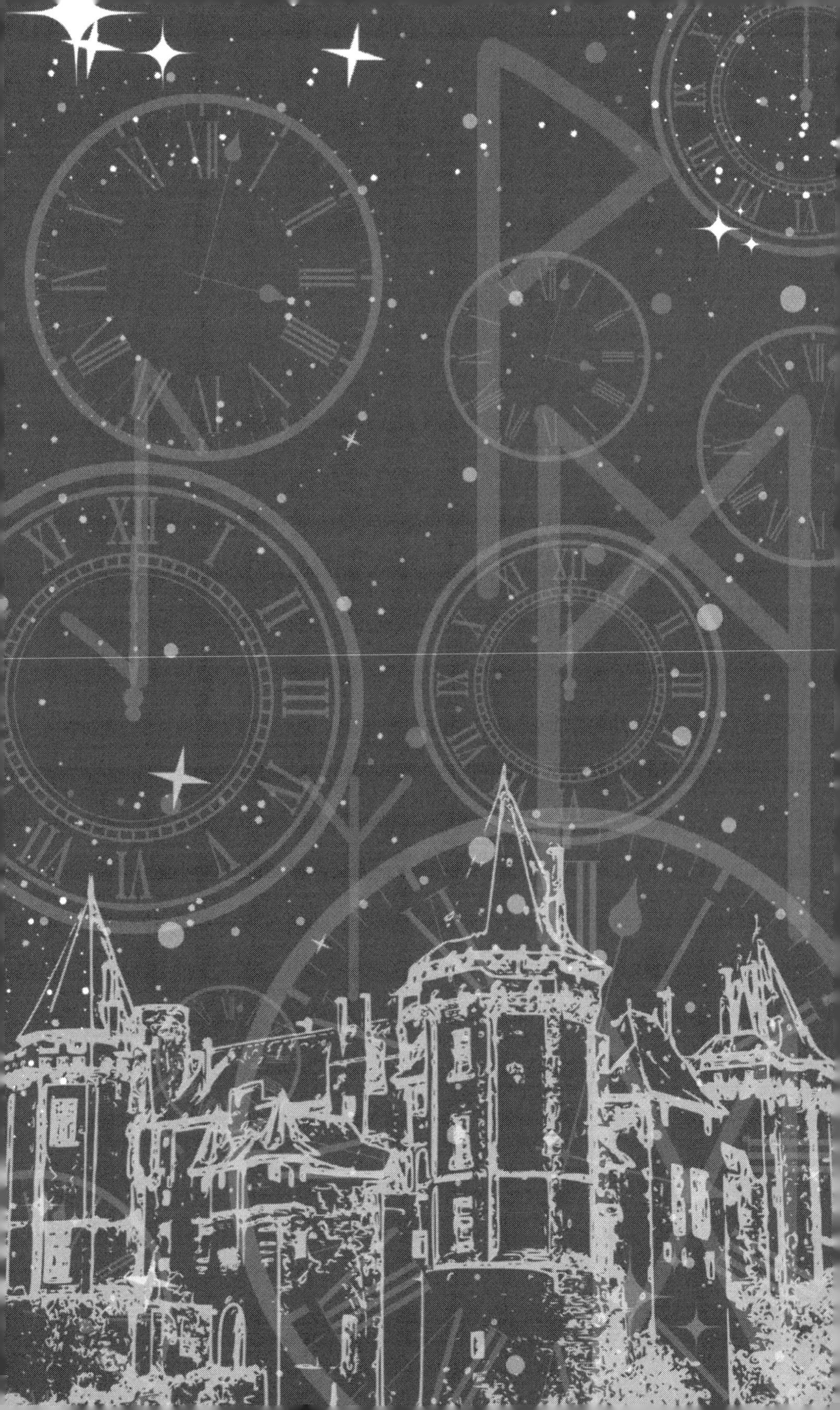

Chapter Thirty-Eight
Sage

"How are you feeling, Sage?" Aurora asks as we sit in the great hall for dinner.

"I feel a lot better. Breathing doesn't hurt. There's still a lingering ache in my joints, but nowhere near as severe as it was. I don't expect this to be an instant fix. I know even potions take time."

"I'm glad to hear. Are the lines gone?"

"Yeah. It was one of the first things I checked. I am so thankful for Agene. Thalia, I wanted to let you know I am up for seeing Anton's progress if that's still on the table."

"Of course it is," she says as she covers her mouth with a cloth while she finishes chewing. She sets the cloth back down and her face is all smiles. "I really cannot wait for you to see everything, everyone."

"I'm looking forward to it. Will you girls meet us there, too?" I ask pointing toward Aurora and Sebille.

"Absolutely we will. I personally haven't been to a lot of the meetings, but from what I saw I am quite impressed." Sebille says, her cheeks flushing.

I raise my brows at her. She darts her eyes down to her plate and proceeds to plop food into her mouth to put a halt to what was about to be my questioning. Someone definitely has Sebille's attention. Aurora gives her a knowing look as if this is a topic they have discussed prior. Interesting.

"Where's Hassian? Why isn't he joining us for dinner?" Aurora asks.

"He got a letter from the headmaster so maybe he took his dinner to go?" I look up and see the headmaster sitting in his usual spot. Weird. I look around and I don't see Hassian anywhere. "The headmasters still here. I don't see why he's not joining us for dinner."

"Maybe he's sneaking back into the library to continue reading those books on poisons," Sebille suggests.

"You're probably right. I suppose I can't break that habit out of him immediately," I say.

"He's spent a long time with this routine. I don't think he will be satisfied until he knows every single poison and their antidote that the library has to offer."

I groan. "If we were talking about anyone other than Hassian I wouldn't believe you, but you're right. He's a worrier. I don't sense anything wrong in our bond, so he must be doing just that." I angrily stab the meat on my plate. I just wish he wouldn't obsess over things out of his control. He could be spending the time he is getting lost in those books with me, living in the moment. It will just be a conversation we will need to have soon.

"Who's excited for the summer solstice dance?" Aurora asks.

"There's another dance?" I ask.

Aurora nods. "We get a winter and a summer dance."

"There's no autumn or spring dance?"

Sebille shakes her head. "Those are festivals. Actually, the last break we had was when the spring festival took place, but with curfew we miss those. The older classes get to go out past curfew though, since they are better at defensive spells and more well trained."

"If I'm being honest when I didn't see you at the academy when I returned, I thought you had snuck off to the festival with Hassian," Thalia admits.

"I wouldn't do something like that and not tell you Tal. What happens to students that break the rules like that though?" I ask.

"Not sure. As far as I know no one's broken the rules before. If they have then they have never been caught."

"Honestly, with how the headmaster is handling other things. He probably just made them keep it to themselves," Sebille grumbles.

We all laugh. We know how much the students like the headmaster, but his way of handling things hasn't exactly been done in the best way.

"Stop right there Griyf. I know you are excited to see Sage again, but she just got her antidote. She's still healing." Thalia raises her hand in a halting gesture as she speaks with Griyf. Griyf chitters back as if he's complaining. "None of that backtalk. She's here to see what you've been learning all year."

Apparently, that was the very right thing to say to him as his look of irritation switches to that of excitement. He rushes over to the stable where he's been staying and comes back with a saddle in his beak. A two-person saddle.

"Thalia, I don't think I can-" I start to say.

"I promise you will be fine, Sage. Riding on a griffin, at least this particular one," she says as she pats his head before beginning to strap on his saddle, "is smooth. I thought riding him for the first time was going to be bumpy, but it wasn't. The only problem area was his landing and he's been doing great with that. He's been working really hard to build up the strength to carry two people at once."

Griyf chitters in response as if to emphasize the working really hard. "Okay, fine I believe you," I say.

"Good." Thalia hops onto Griyf's back and motions for me to sit on the seat behind her. I am grateful for my long legs that make mounting him fairly easy. "Good, now wrap your arms around me. This isn't a necessary step, but seeing as you only just got your antidote at lunchtime; I am taking no risks."

I wrap my arms around her waist and she pats Griyf's neck twice and he starts charging down the path. It's a little bumpy as he builds the speed he needs to before leaping toward the sky. The speed that he ascends is incredible. He flies up to the very top of the clock tower and holds himself there for a moment while I take in the view. I can see the tiny outline of Halaris. The sun is only beginning to lose its brightness, but I can still see the faint glow of the everflame. It's breathtaking.

"I need me a griffin," I whisper to Thalia. She smiles and Griyf lets out a loud screech.

"Shall we do a lap or two around the school before we head back?" Thalia asks.

"Yes, please."

"Alright, boy, you heard her. Show her how it's done."

Griyf chitters with delight as he picks up speed zooming around the towers of the academy. I do my best to take in every single detail. It's not every day you get to soar on the back of a griffin. We are flying past where Professor Moore keeps the beasts we work with during her class. There is actually quite a bit. I wonder how she tends to all of them.

It doesn't take Griyf long before we are soaring past the north tower. There's not much here outside of mountain side and some forest. Halaris is on the southern side of the school. I look around at the vastness of the trees and mountains. I see an odd glow coming from the trees.

"Hey Tal, what kind of creatures live in that forest?" I ask.

"I'm not sure. As far as I know none, but I have also never ventured out of the academy dome barrier. Why do you ask?"

"There's a glow coming from it. I was just curious," I say.

"Perhaps we can ask Professor Moore tomorrow? She does have knowledge of all thing's creatures."

"Yeah. I think I will."

We soar around the castle one more time before Griyf lands back by his stable area. "One moment I have to go get Griyf's nightly snack. Mervin always leaves him one."

"Who's Mervin?"

"Just a brownie that's taken a liking to Griyf. He's always leaving him snacks." Thalia and I dismount and she heads into a shack near the stables. She's out in a matter of seconds, empty handed. "Sorry bud, looks like Mervin forgot tonight or was too busy." Griyf makes a sad chittering noise. "It's okay bud, I'll bring you back something in the morning before class." He perks right back up at that and nuzzles Thalia. "Alright enough of that. Go on to your stable."

Griyf walks back into his stable and curls up on his makeshift bed and Thalia and I head to where the rebellion has been meeting up at.

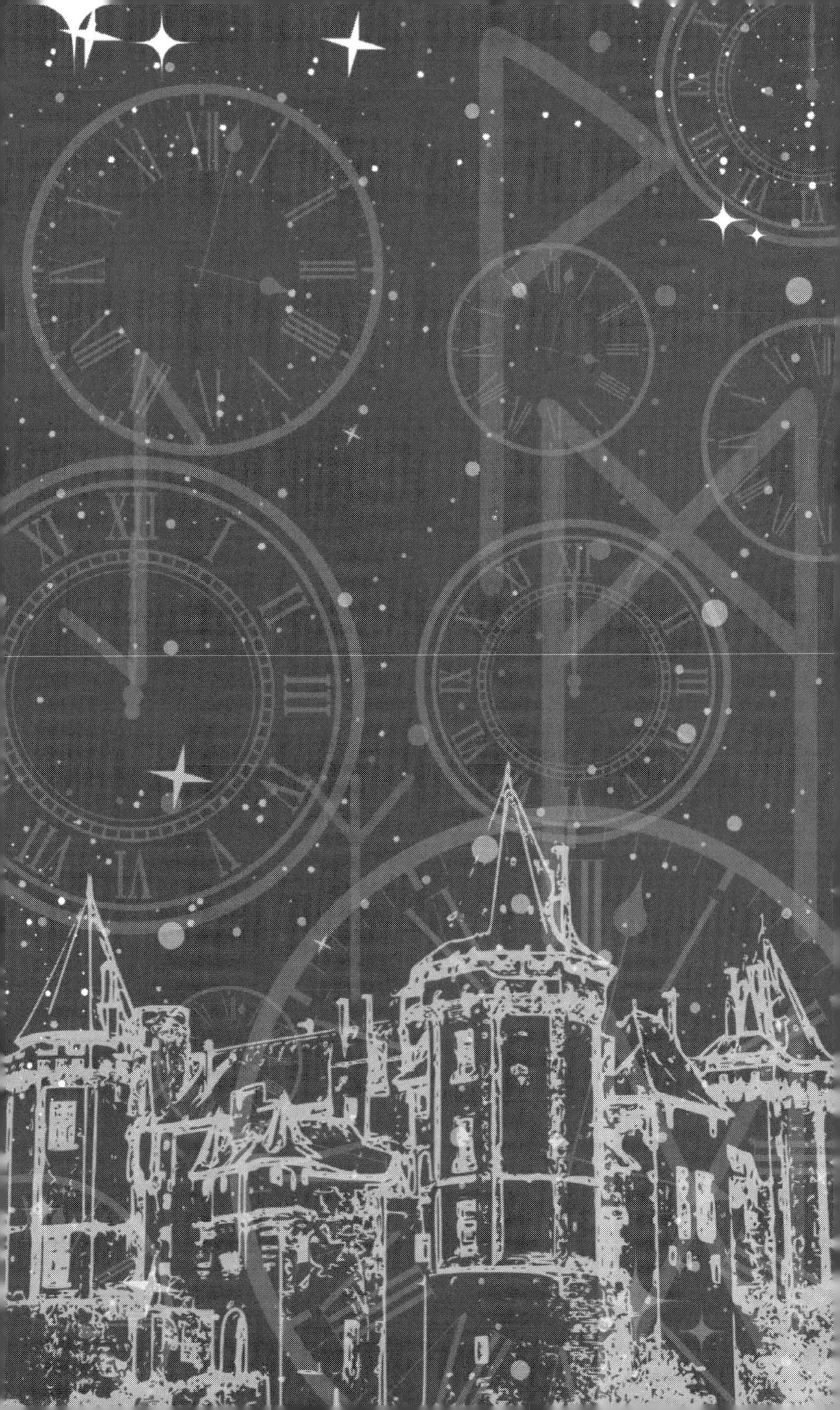

Chapter Thirty-Nine
Sage

Thalia is leading me down the hallway toward the room Anton has set up as the official meeting place for the rebellion. Aurora and Sebille are already inside. Hassian might be a little late with whatever the headmaster requested him for.

"Shoot I forgot to take the saddle off Griyf. I can't believe he let me walk away without removing it. It's fine I can do it after this meeting. Maybe I can see if one of the brownies in the kitchen will sneak me a snack for him." Thalia closes her eyes and lets out a deep breath, "Okay, before you go in, I just want to say that I am proud of you and all the hard work you have been putting in since the beginning of the year. You had a prophecy thrown onto you, and you really took it like a true queen. People have been paying attention to that."

"Tal, come on, the suspense is killing me." Thalia grins at me as she slides a key into the lock and pushes open the door.

As I step into the room, the first feeling that hits me is shock. I was expecting, at most, maybe a dozen people to grace our cause. Anton has rallied hundreds and more than just the students in the school, there are some people from the capital here too. These faces are familiar to me, but not.

I lock eyes with each person, feeling a surge of some unknown feeling coursing through me. The fact that this many people believe in me, and not because they got to know me over the years. They believe in me because they think I can make a difference. How long have these people struggled under the hands of my grandfather and his actions?

These individuals have placed their trust in me, and I will not let them down. I refuse to. I try to think of something to say, but I come up with nothing. What do you say that's going to be appropriate to a group of people willing to die to see you rise?

Anton comes up to me, clasping a hand on my shoulder. "Meet your rebellion. I have personally vetted every single one of these individuals. Some have made mistakes in the past but are willing to do what they can to right those wrongs. They don't just believe in the prophecy; they believe in you."

"I am overwhelmed," I let out a breathy laugh. "Not because of anxiety, Gods no. I'm overwhelmed with joy, with pride, with whatever positive emotion I cannot seem to think of in this moment. Thank you, all of you, for coming together. To be willing to risk everything is no simple feat. In the Other Realm, there are so many stories written about people like you and I feel so blessed in this moment to be standing among you all."

"I heard Nick apologize to you today," says Anton.

"He didn't have to. He was just looking out for our people."

"He knows. He told me the same day he sought me out to join. He said he needed to apologize to you so you would know you can trust him. I told him to give you time, and the proper moment would present itself."

Anton shows me around the room at all the different training stations. This is more decked out than the training I've been going through with Hassian. Now that I am thinking about Hassian, I don't see him here yet.

"I noticed Thalia had a key to get in here; how did you obtain keys? I thought this was a secret operation."

"It is, but also the headmaster is aware of it as he is a part of the rebellion as well. He made keys for certain members to hold. Only what we are calling our officers have keys, everyone else is told the next meeting date. At the end of each session, everyone is shown a paper with the following meeting password, date, and time. After everyone has seen it, we burn the paper. It's worked out okay for the most part. We have had a few people forget the passwords, but we check to see if anyone is a shifter regardless. We have plenty of silver on hand."

"What about the sigils? What are those used for?"

"Honestly, I just wanted everyone to have something to make them feel connected to the rebellion outside of this room. It's also a great way to let others know who you are, in terms of recruiting new members or to pass along a message to another member."

"Do you have a name for the group yet other than the rebellion?"

"Not yet. It's still a work in progress. Everyone has different ideas of what to call us, but none of them fit just right, so for now, we are just sticking with the rebellion."

"So, what do you all teach in here? I'm seeing a lot of different things, but I'm not familiar with some of it."

"Well, initially, I was just teaching pole arms and sword fighting since that's what I spent the year working on in between my other hobbies. Now we teach that and archery, advanced elemental work, runes, you name it, we are probably teaching it."

"Advanced elemental work and runes?"

"Yeah, we have a bunch of the older student body helping teach, and after what you did for The Order, Ivan sent over some guys. They taught us a few things and even gave us some supplies. Did you tell them about us?"

"No, I didn't."

"Well, they certainly knew and wanted to help. They're a pretty cool group. I will be the first to admit I was nervous after you told us what happened when you went to ask about your grandfather, and then they showed up. They had nothing but good things to say about you. They told us how you took down two chirocras on your own before you got hit."

"I got distracted at the end. I should have just moved onto the next, but I wanted to make sure it was dead."

"Don't doubt yourself, Sage. What you did was probably a really smart move. You didn't risk the creature getting back up and taking everyone by surprise. You saw a potential future threat, and you dealt with it. I'd say that's very brave and smart."

"Thanks."

"Let me introduce you to some of the other fae in here. Come on." He walks me over to a face I could never forget, one of the first people in the city who showed me kindness, Elwin.

"Evening, Miss Sage, or should I say princess?" he winks. "I knew I did right picking you to have my wee wagon. You did right by me, lotsa people came to my shop and got them one. I won't soon forget that. Not to mention the amount of business this rebellion brought in. The Order came by and requested a lot of stuff for the lot of ya from both my brother, Hinley, and me-self. Go mingle with everyone; don't stand here all day listening to me ramble." Elwin waves us off.

Anton continues to introduce me to both people I met in the city and faces I have never seen before. Before I know it, hours have passed by, and the moon is already shining. I look around; there's no Hassian. What the fuck? He said he would be here. He doesn't agree to anything he won't commit to. Let me see if I can find him with the bond. I've never tried this before, so I don't know how it works, but this isn't like him.

Closing my eyes, I focus on one person: Hassian. I am brought to the garden in my mind and I continue down the path that leads to the pillar of vines. I know my bond isn't there, but I expect it to not be too far from it. I look around, trying to find something that feels like it's related to him and me and the connection we share. It also needs to relate to the garden somehow. I think back on the memories of us. He said he knew from the moment we met. We met in the showers—underwater. I need to find a water source. Sure enough, as I make the connection with water, a fountain materializes near the pillar.

I walk up to it, wondering how I should approach it. Well, I was under a showerhead when I met him, so maybe the answer is to dunk my head. Can I drown here? One way to find out. I hold my breath and dunk my head into the fountain, and it pulls me further in until I am completely submersed and popping out the other side. The feeling is similar to entering Kamira's realm.

I look around. I am in the great hall. The tables are knocked over, and plates are scattered across the floor. That's not right. The brownies would have cleared the dishes after dinner. Why are they still here? The lights in the room are dull as if masked by fog. I look around at the stained-glass windows, and some are shattered. Something isn't right here. Something is wrong. I pull myself out of my mind.

"I'm sorry to interrupt everyone's night, but I think we might have a big problem."

The room falls silent. "What is it?" Anton asks.

"I went into my mind to look for Hassian. He was supposed to be here, and he isn't, and it took me to the great hall. The tables were thrown around, plates scattered on the floor, and the windows smashed. I think the academy is under attack, and Hassian is in the heart of it."

I expected gasps of fear and cries of outbursts, but everyone in the room starts grabbing weapons and handing them out.

They are arming themselves. They are ready to go to battle without confirmation, but because I felt something was wrong.

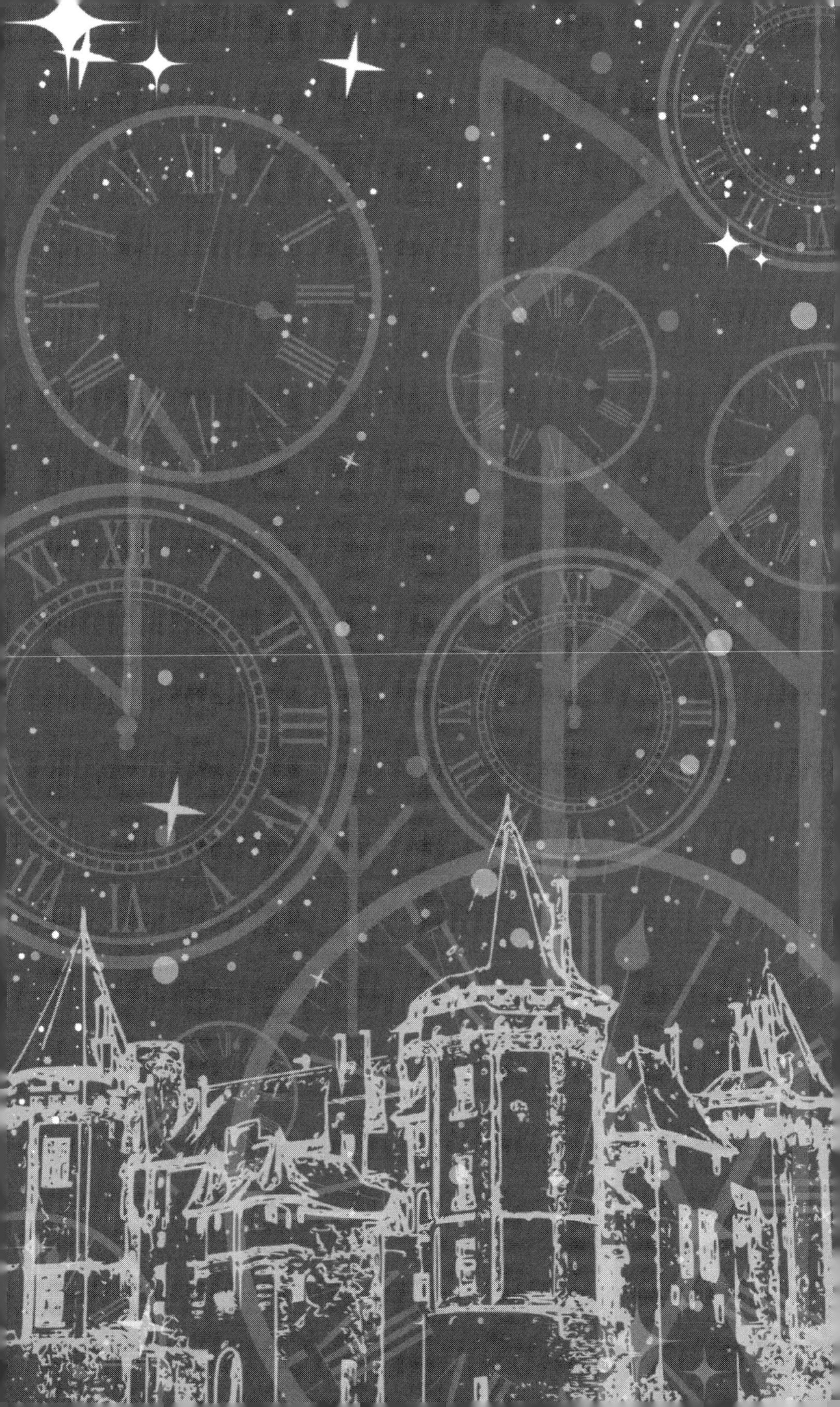

Chapter Forty
Sage

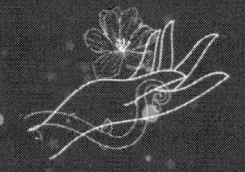

We exit into the hallway of the academy, not separating too far from each other but spreading out enough to check each turn for potential danger. The academy is quiet, an unsettling quiet. Even on a normal night, there are still students in the halls chattering, practicing their spell work; there's nothing. We continue to walk down the hall, ready to defend. We reach Professor Dublin's classroom door and it's not locked. We push it in to check and see if anyone is there.

A vine whips in our direction, but instead of hitting us, it redirects toward the ceiling. "By The Nines! I almost hurt you. You should all be hiding right now. We are under attack."

"We know. I was looking for Hassian in our bond, and it felt wrong. We are headed to the great hall."

"You can't! He was walking that way." I know just who Professor Dublin is referring to.

"Professor Dublin, with all due respect, I am saving Hassian."

He nods. "In that case, it's my duty as a professor to help their students succeed." Professor Dublin makes his way near the front of our group. The halls remain eerily silent. I expected screams of fear because we are under attack. I recall back to when I was being told about the creature's strengths and weaknesses and I remember being told that some of them are blind, those were mainly the flyers. Which are probably what are here now, there's no other way up the mountain to the academy unless he stole a ship, which I doubt. He wouldn't have the crew to man it.

As we get closer to the great hall, I can see smears of blood across the floor. I try not to follow where the smears lead, but I can't stop myself. The trails lead to several bodies of dead students. No doubt they were just on their way to bed after finishing their studies and were taken unaware. I can't help but feel guilt that if they had been a part of the rebellion then maybe they would still be alive.

One of the members of the rebellion must recognize one of the dead students because they let a sob filled with what can only be grief wrack through them. I feel for them, but also, at the same time, I'm frustrated because I know we are absolutely fucked now. The windows running down the length of the hallway burst into shards as chirocra come bounding through them. They let out a loud screech, no doubt signaling to more of their friends.

Balls of fire, ice, and lightning all burst through the air as members of the rebellion do their best to fight the oncoming attack. I hear screams as some of the chirocra grab onto some of the rebellion members, tearing into their skin. I don't dare use my magic yet; I need to conserve as much strength as I can for my fight with Gaiwen. I ignore the ache of my body as I thrust my spear toward the creatures.

Aurora uses her air elemental magic and throws a shield of magic over us just as one of them lets out a blood curdling scream, protecting us from the acidic saliva. "Avoid getting scratched or cut." I yell out. "It's coated in poison."

I duck down as one lunges for my head. The ache of my body exhausting me. The antidote hasn't had enough time. I'm barely working at my full capacity. I'm stronger than what I was, but if I do too much now, I might not have enough to use against Gaiwen. Aurora continues casting shields to block the acid whenever one of the chirocra try to spew saliva at us. Thalia shoots streams of water to try and push them back out the window. Sebille throws flames up in the window after Thalia has pushed enough out to try and prevent more from coming in.

"You need to go to the great hall, Sage. This isn't your fight. Some of the rebellion will follow you, but you have to go now," Anton shouts to me.

I nod and start racing toward the great hall, slipping on a puddle of blood. I feel the impact of the stone against my hip, but I push through the pain and keep running. Hassian needs me. The thought is the main thing that is fueling me as I race down the hall.

I nearly barrel past the broken doors of the great hall as I struggle to slow down my Adrenaline-fueled body. I'm breathing heavily as I approach the archway and make my way inside. A man with short blonde and a more prominent, gauntly shaped face stands in the staging area of the great hall where the professors usually eat. A crumbled Hassian lay on the floor beside his feet. I have a feeling the note wasn't from the headmaster.

"So glad you could make it, Sage. I was beginning to think you wouldn't show up to my party. You are the guest of honor; after all, that would have been awfully rude. Come, come." He waves me over. "Don't be shy. I just want to have a chat. A little heart-to-heart."

I don't make a move. "I think I'm fine right here,' I say.

He grips Hassian by a scruff of hair. "Now, now you don't want me to do anything rash. Do you?"

"Please don't," I beg. "I'm coming; just hold on." I make my way toward him, the Adrenaline having worn off now, and the soreness of my body returns. "What do you want from me?"

"I want your help, Sage. Your grandfather was naughty, naughty. Yes, he was. He snuffed my light, and I want it back."

"You did forbidden magic; I don't know how I can help with that."

He whips his head at me, and I swear his eyes flash black for just a second. "Oh, but you can and you will. I have waited a long time for you, girl. A long time indeed. Have you read my story? Of course, you have. I made sure it got to you. Safe and sound."

"You gave me your journal?" I ask.

"Who else would have given it to you? It's my journal, after all. You read what your grandfather did, didn't you? You learned of his crimes, yes?" Gaiwen lets out a laugh.

"I shouldn't pay for the sins of my grandfather. I am not him. I will never be like him."

"No, no. You shouldn't pay the price for his shortcomings. That's not what I am asking you to do. I do, however, need you to come with me. I cannot think in this place. It's not safe for you here."

I hear the sounds of feet approaching as members of the rebellion enter the great hall. They shout at me to ignore him and his lies. Gaiwen waves his hand and the room goes silent. I look expecting the worst, but he's just put a dome around us.

"Look, I don't want to hurt you or your mate to get you to listen, but I will if I must."

"Why now? After all these years. You could have come for me in the Other Realm."

His face falls. "No, I couldn't have. The dead cannot pass through portals to other realms unless accompanied by a god. Last I checked, I didn't have one of those. It's why your mother was forced to stay behind. You are both life and death, you see. You were able to pass through because you are special. Yes, yes."

"You are dead?" I ask.

"In a sense yes, yes. I died when your grandfather made me do his bidding. My light gone. My light is my essence, my very being. I am my own person. Yes, yes, but I am changed. I grow weary of these voices. I want my light back."

"My mother shared a vision with me of her last day. You were mentioned, that you were coming toward the castle. You would have hurt my mother."

"LIES!" he yells. "She was innocent. I need you, only you to help me. Yes. That's what I needed. It was never to hurt. I have done bad things in the past, I know. It's the voices. They don't shut up." He smacks his hand against his head over and over. I can't help thinking of the students and staff that just died. Is he that far gone that he isn't associating that with doing a bad thing? "Enough of this chatter. Let us go."

"I-" Just as I am about to try and stall some more, Hassian begins to stir. He's waking up, and it's probably not the best time to do it either.

"Princess, I am running out of patience. It's time to go NOW!"

"Don't do it, Sage," Hassian croaks. Gaiwen kicks him hard in the ribs. I know Hassian cannot feel it, but it doesn't mean he hasn't taken a significant amount of damage. I watch as he coughs up blood.

"I can't do that, Gaiwen. I don't know how to help you. I barely know how to use my magic."

"You can help me, girl!" His responses are becoming more venomous as his patience begins to wane. I glance behind me and see that he is not without his limitations either, as the dome begins to flicker and wane.

"How do you think I can help you?" I ask, just trying to stall for my opening.

"Your magic can restore death."

"At a cost. I wasn't the reason you became what you are. Why should I be forced to pay that price?" I ask.

He glares at me. "I didn't deserve to pay that price either. You can do what needs to be done if you just COME WITH ME!" he screams so loud, and I see my opening as he loses his concentration.

I use my ring and poke my finger just enough for a droplet. I reach into myself and call forth vines to hold onto him. Vines break through the stone of the floor and grab onto his arms. He fights back. He is strong and I don't think they will hold for much longer. I need to think. What can I do?

I grip my necklace and close my eyes. I don't know what to focus on, what to try to cast in this moment to save me, so I leave it up to my magic itself. I hope it's enough as I release my power. Vines burst through the stained-glass windows, their thorns latching on Gaiwen, latching on me. I forgot to cut my hand to offer a form of payment, and I just asked for magic on a scale I have never used. The droplet allowed me to cast the first time, but this second casting required payment. I look to Hassian as the realization of what's about to happen crosses his features.

His scream practically breaks my heart as he can feel everything that is happening to me right now. The thorns winding around Gaiwen and me, crushing our bodies, breaking every bone as it takes what it is owed. Flowers bloom across the floor of the great hall as if in tribute to my sacrifice, to my death. I don't know what is supposed to happen when you are dying, but what I hear is the sound of my blood as it drips onto the floor. It echoes in my mind with each drop. It's a song I do not wish to hear. Drip. Drop. Drip. Drop.

Am I making the right choice? I think back to the shadow that appeared. It was helping me, and if it was sent by Gaiwen then maybe there is some humanity left in him. I glance toward Gaiwen's body. It's limp. I wonder if there was truly another way. If I could have saved him and undone the horrors of my grandfather, but I guess now I will never know. I will never get to live. I feel as though my life was only starting, but a price must be paid. I knew the cost of using my power. I knew the risk. The vines squeezing Gaiwen emit a sickening crunch as they tighten more and more before letting up and tossing him into the shadowed area of the room.

In truth, I did see myself growing old alongside Hassian. If I could undo this choice, I would like to spend the rest of my life with him. I think he would have made a great ruler. My hope is he can stand alongside my friends and end the tyranny that is my grandfather. I believe in him. I believe in them. I let out a silent prayer to the goddesses to look after my friends and my people.

The vines must be laced with something because my entire being is on fire. My very veins are surging with heat. I scream, and an inferno of heat ripples off of me. The vines loosen their grip as they make a pained sound before they toss me in the direction where Gaiwen was thrown. In that moment, time feels as if it's frozen, and I watch as my entire body erupts into flame, and my vines turn to nothing but ashes around me. The last thing I see is a large burst of white light before the world goes dark.

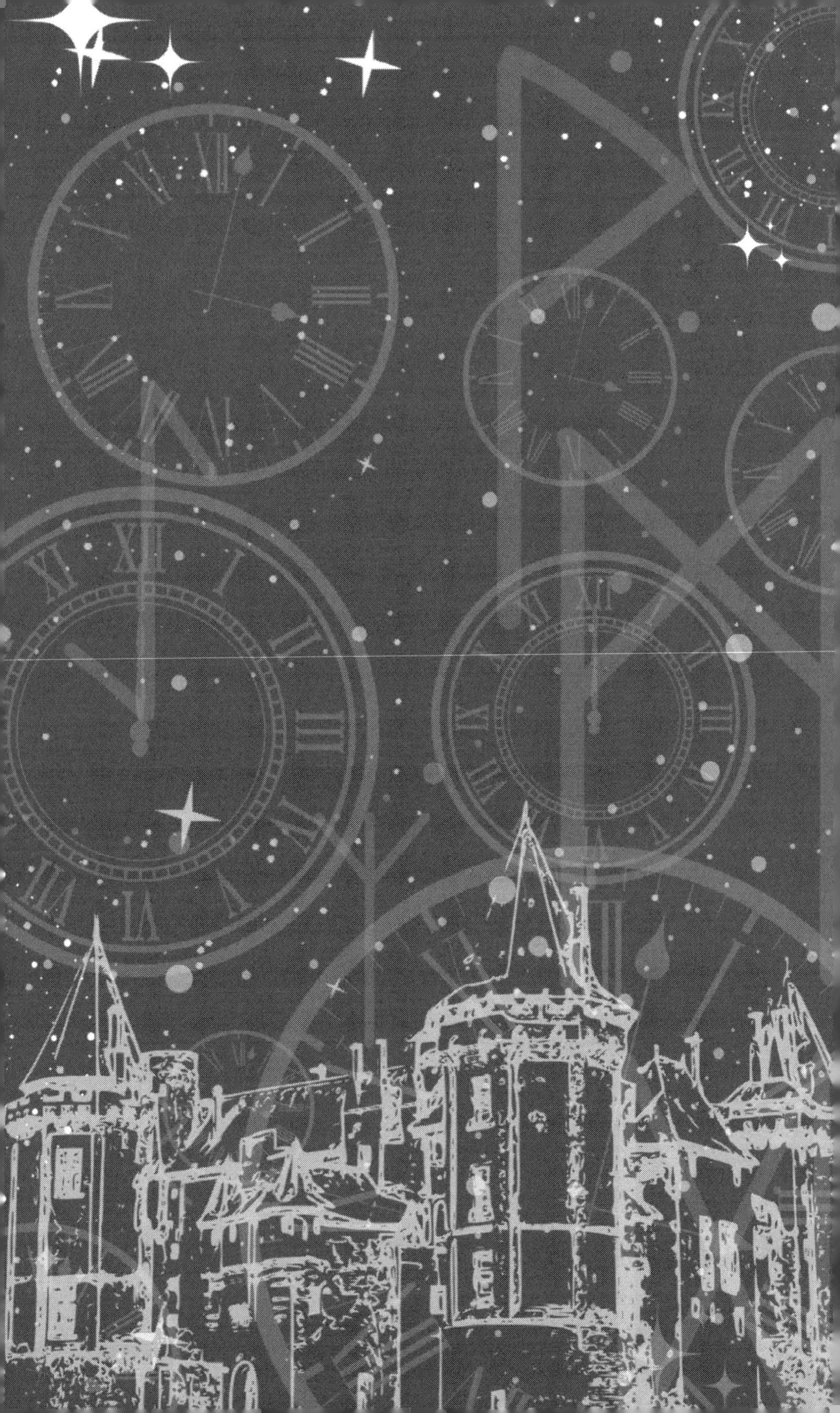

Chapter Forty-One

Hassian

"Sage," I croak out between the haze of the smoke. I watch as the chirocras come barreling into the room cutting through the shadows and back out the windows. Trails of blood follow their stead. The blood of the students and staff that died here tonight. The shadows dissipate as they clear out of the academy. I see pile of ashes where she once stood. I watched my princess as her body burst into flames, as the color of her eyes left her as they burned white hot. I saw the pile of ashes that fell from where she once was. I knew the moment she died. The moment I felt her pain no more. Her death was not painless. It was agonizing and it felt as though it lasted a lifetime.

I crawled to where I saw her remains fall to the floor. Her body disintegrated into dust. I scoop up the ashes, pulling them into me. I just want to feel her again; this wasn't how it was supposed to go. We should have been able to survive this.

I scream into the air until my voice cracks. I scream her name over and over, holding onto the ashes, willing her to come back to me. This is too soon. We were meant to have our whole life together. I continue to scream until a hand touches my shoulder to comfort me. I look up, and Thalia is there. Her face streaked with tears. I wasn't the only one who lost her. I look around. Aurora collapses into Sebille, sobbing at the loss of her friend. The great hall is littered with the bodies of dead students and professors. There has been so much loss here tonight.

I look around at those who remain alive; each face is filled with grief. She wasn't just the love of my life; she was meant to be the savior of this realm. In a way, she was. She sacrificed herself to stop a man riddled with insanity. As I survey the crowd of faces, I see something is off.

The High King is here standing with Professor West, and they are smiling. They are basking in the reality that Sage is gone, the threat to their plan removed. I don't know where I get the strength, but I stand up. The warm liquid rolling down my body from the wound Gaiwen gave me prior to knocking me unconscious is a reminder I need to take it easy, but I don't care. I just lost everything that has ever mattered to me.

I grind my teeth as I make my way toward the High King. The man so selfish he created all of this. He is the reason my Sage is dead. I pick up a fallen blade from a dead body off the floor and continue my path toward him. I don't say anything, but he turns his head to face me and smiles. He knew my intentions, but he let me get close anyway. I make a move to slash him with the sword, but I feel my body rocking, and I lose my grip on the handle. My eyes dart to my side where a spear with an electric current is protruding.

The High King continues to smile at me. He has the same eyes as Sage, but instead of seeing the world in his like I do hers, all I see is cruelty. "Didn't you know it's treason to threaten the life of your High King?"

"You are not my High King," the words slip out between gasps. My body must be faltering from all the damage it's taken.

"Pretending you have a choice in the matter, cute." He points to the men surrounding me. "Take him to my castle. I'll decide what to do with him later. As for everyone else, search them. If they are carrying one of these," he raises an emblem with a baby wrapped in vines, "take them too or kill them. I don't really care." I watch as the room breaks out into chaos; students are fighting men in red-colored military gear. Some are fleeing, realizing they are wholly unprepared for this.

I watch as some of the students are thrown into a heap on the floor, adding to the already dwindling numbers of our kind. The rest are being subdued just as I was. I didn't expect the first battle to go smoothly, so I would be delusional to pretend that I did, but I didn't think it would turn into this. I didn't think the High King would show up. Sage was going to die today, that I now know for certain. My only question is, how did he know to be here on the same day as Gaiwen? What don't we know?

I see Aurora, Sebille, and Thalia fighting back with their elements as they try to get away. Griyf comes barreling through the broken window. His eyes alight with rage as he makes his way toward Thalia. I watch as he makes all three girls get on his back. I know he's never carried that much weight before, but for Thalia, he will do it. He will see her to safety. He narrowly avoids an oncoming spear as he begins to lift off the ground and into the sky. As he flies out of the window another spear goes hurling toward him.

I struggle with turning my head, so I don't see if they got away when they leave my line of sight. I look at the men in the red-colored clothing. They aren't a part of The Order. Most of The Order hates this man. Who are they?

My thoughts drift to the memories of how my princess looked when she smiled at me. It's the only thing I can do at this moment: think of her. My vision begins to blur, and I know my body's limit has been reached. I continue to think of my princess and what could have been as my head slumps and my eyes close.

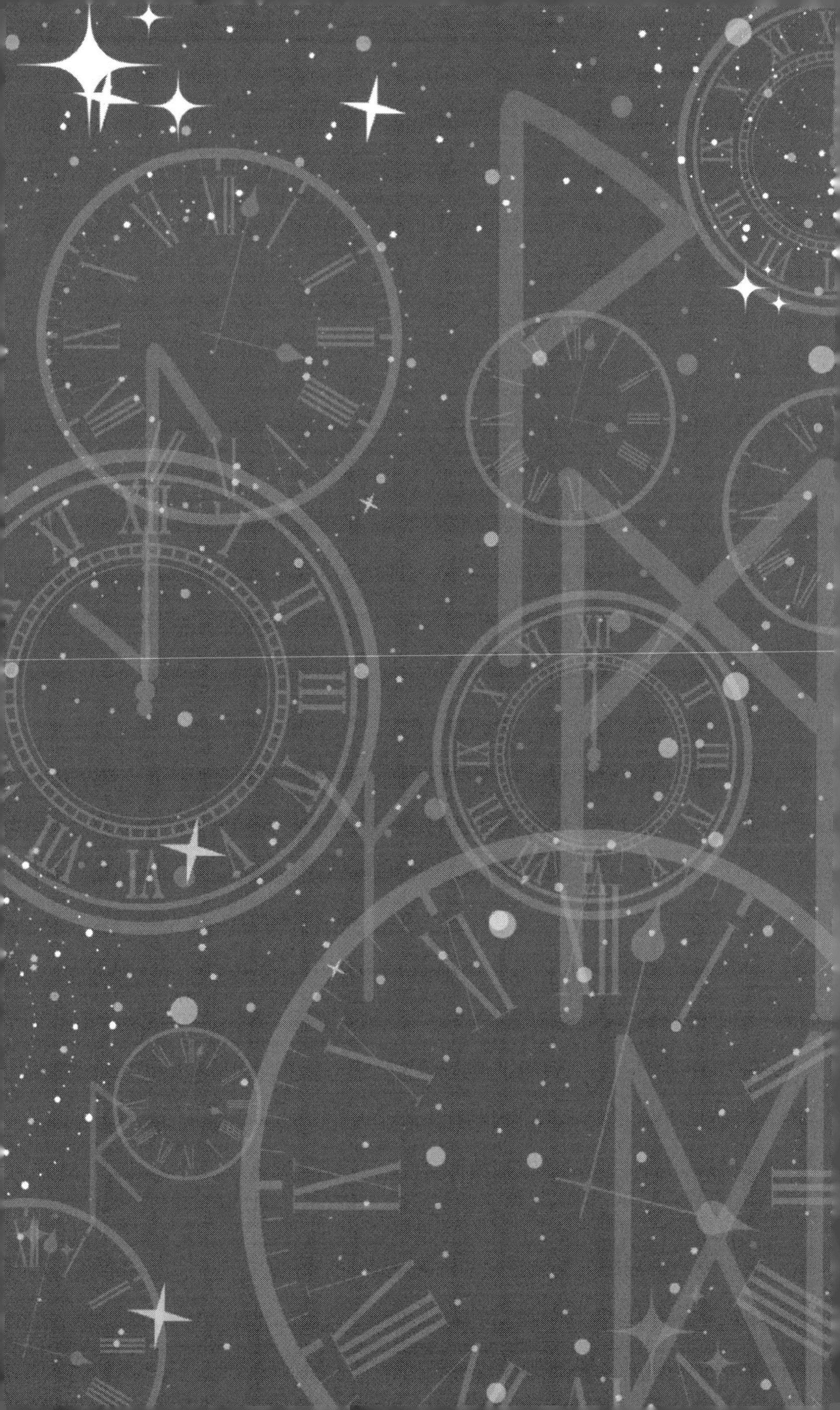

Epilogue
Thalia

"Griyf, buddy, you need to land. This is too much strain on your body."

"Not safe," his eyes search the horizon.

"We can go to my parent's house. They have the secret room and the underground tunnels."

"I said it's not safe, Thalia," Griyf is relentless.

"I know you are scared right now and so am I, but we can't fly forever. You are carrying three people; you can be doing irreparable damage. Please just head to my parents in Halaris." I glance back at Sebille and Aurora. Sebille is losing a lot of blood. She needs medical help. Griyf did his best to get us to safety, but the spear was faster.

"Fine," Griyf grumpily replies as he glides down into the city. It's not long until we are landing in the backyard of my family home. Griyf chitters to get my parents attention while I begin unlocking the runes concealing a larger entrance to the tunnels. The meeting we had prior was just a glimpse at the secrets my family carries.

"What's going on Thalia? Why aren't you in school?" my mother asks as she rushes outside. She takes sight of Sebille and gasps.

"Take Griyf and fetch Agene and Kira. Gaiwen attacked the school tonight and so did the High King. We must go," I say.

My mother hops onto Griyf and flies away.

"Where's the princess?" my father asks. "Anton?"

I shake my head. "Sage is dead. We all saw her burst into flames. I don't know where Anton is. He might have gotten away. I didn't see Meera either. I'm hoping they made it into the tunnels. Can you please help me with these runes? We don't have much time, father."

"Of course. Are you sure she's dead?"

"Can someone return after turning to ash?" I bite.

"I am not your enemy here daughter. You will do well to remember that. Did you feel your connection break?"

I'm so stupid. As guardian I should have checked. I pause my work with my runes to check the connection. The long golden thread that connected Sage and I is gone. I almost close my mind back off, but then I see something. A small thread is growing.

"The original thread is broken, but something new is taking its place. What does that mean father?"

My father breaks the last of the runes as my mother returns with Agene. Kira comes out the back door shortly after, plants in hand. The door to the tunnels opens and we all step in. The everflame comes to life as soon as the door closes and the runes reactivate. I glance over at Sebille and see Agene is tending to her.

"Father?" I ask again.

"Remember the story I told you when you were just a child of how the princess was gods blessed because of the sacrifice her parents made for her."

"Yeah. What does that have to do with the new string forming?"

"Sage is a phoenix."

FROM THE ASHES

Want to know what happens next? Stay tuned for the upcoming sequel, *From the Ashes*.

Special Edition Bonus Content

Read some scenes from Hassian's POV

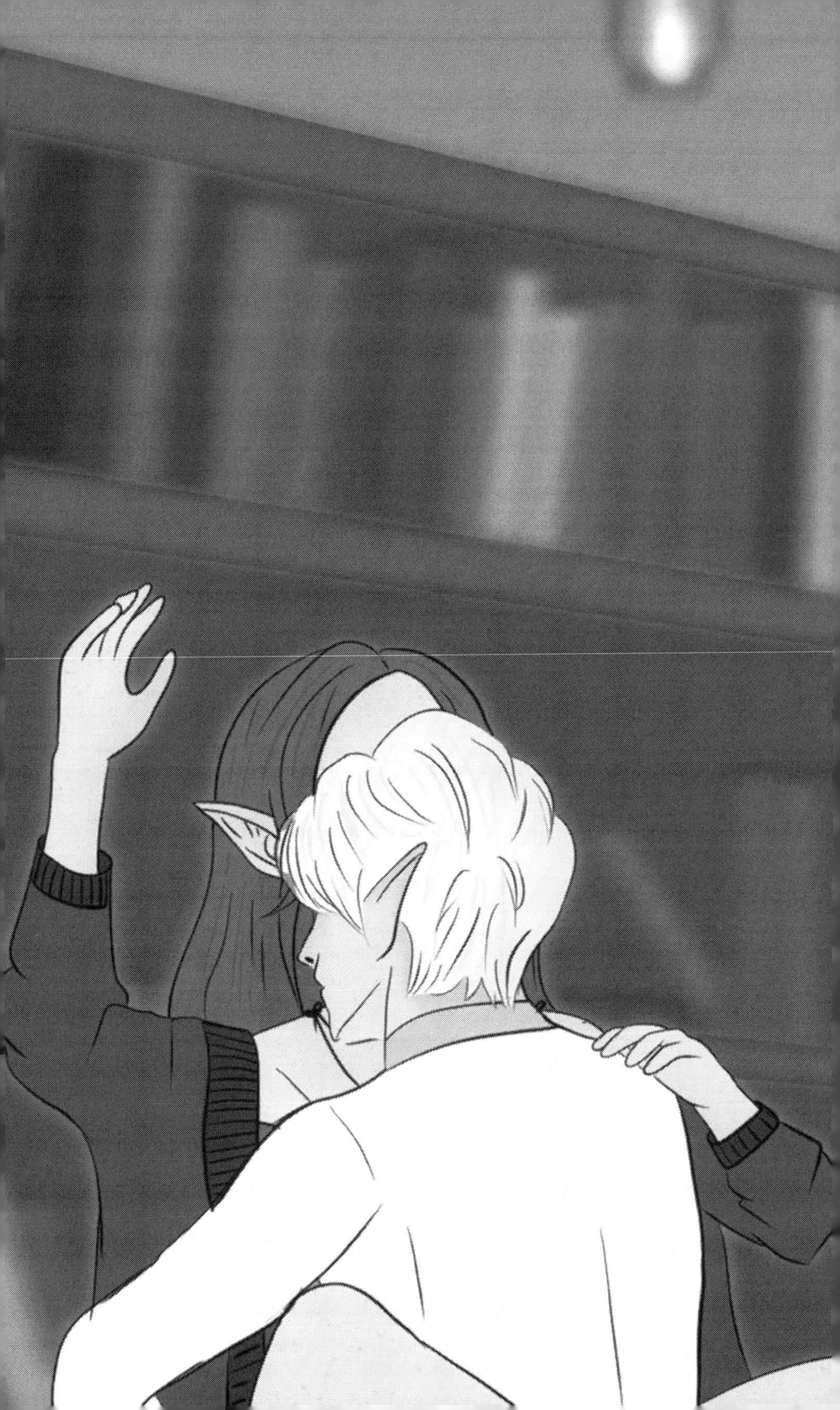

Chapter 1
Hassian

I'm leaning against one of the tall trees in the courtyard. I heard a rumor that the princess had been spotted in the capital city over the summer. The very same I was to be betrothed to before she disappeared. I'm pretending to read one of my textbooks while I watch as the first years roll in just hoping that I will catch a glimpse of her. Will she be how I imagine her in my dreams?

Dozens of students make their way across the courtyard, and I have yet to spot anyone who I think she might be. My mind grows weary of the wait, but my heart yields me and keeps me in place. I must see her. I will see her. Eventually as the majority have passed through the iron gates of the academy, I hear the sound of two fae complaining about how much they have to carry and all the walking. I cannot help but grin at the hazing that still happens to first-years.

As the voices grow closer, I cannot still the beating heart in my chest. Now that I am hearing the voice clearer, I want to hear it again and again. I dart my eyes up as I look to see who is speaking. She is the most beautiful woman I have ever seen. Her auburn hair billowing in the wind. Her freckles popping against her complexion. She must have spent a long time outdoors over the summer. I hear the sound of her laughter as she reacts to a joke her friend made and I ache to hear it again.

She turns her head to look at one of the brownies that are tending to the flowers and her eyes are a beautiful amber in the sunlight. Her long lashes brush against her cheeks as she blinks. She is breathtaking. Her friend says her name. Sage. It's her.

I see Sage get up to leave the great hall. "I'd hate to leave early as we are all catching up, but I have some place I must be," I say.

"It's whatever, Has. We will get sick of each other soon enough," Meera waves me off as I make my way out of the great hall.

I follow Sage, until she makes her way into the first-year's tower. Fuck. I can't go in there. I don't know who's on duty, but they sure as hell won't let me in those dorms. I sit in one of the alcoves and wait. Maybe she will come back out. I don't know how long I am sitting here waiting, but the flash of auburn hair crosses my vision as she walks past the alcove I am resting in.

She has clothes in hand, so I am pretty sure she is making her way to the showers. I silently follow her. I know this is wrong, but something tugs at me to be near her. I watch as she slips into the shower room, waiting briefly before I follow her in. She's exploring the room with her eyes by the time I make it inside. I watch as she undresses before she makes her way to the showers. This is wrong. I shouldn't be here, but yet I find myself walking to the other side of the room and undressing. I wait until she has rinsed out the remainder of the suds before I speak.

"You know that's basically plant cum, right?" My voice comes out deeper than usual as I crack my joke.

She lets out a shriek that could break glass, if there was any glass nearby. I watch as she desperately tries to cover her body before she turns around.

"I-" her eyes trail from my face before I watch as they make their way further south.

"Eyes up here, princess," I say, flashing my most devious smile. Her face turns beat red and it's the most alluring thing I have ever seen; the way her face heats in my presence.

"I'm sorry-"

"No, you're not, and that's okay," I interrupt. I feel my cock twitch as she blushes more.

"I am sorry. What did you just say?" she asks.

I let out a deep laugh as I press closer to her. "You know, princess. If our futures had played out the way they were meant to be between you and I; you would have been my betrothed."

"Wait, so you're-"

"Hassian Blackwell. The very same and I know you are Sage Torrin. I must admit," I trail my eyes down her body. "I am disappointed life didn't play out that way."

She scoffs, moving her arms onto her hips, exposing herself to me. She has the body of a goddess. I want to trace every inch of her with my fingers, memorize her with my lips. "You don't even know me well enough to know if you would even like me."

"I like what I see; I know that much." I move in closer until I am pressed against her warm body. "I could have learned to love the rest." My cock goes fully erect being this close to her, breathing in the same air as her.

"Yeah?" she asks as she bites her lips.

Something overtakes me and the need to assert some form of dominance over her strikes and I find myself tilting her chin up at me. I take a glance at her plump lips and I am aching with need as I press my lips to her. She kisses back, pressing into me, threatening to make me burst at the seams. I have to know she truly wants this, wants me. I pull my head back and grin as I say, "If you want more, you will have to earn it, princess, and I am sure you will."

I turn and leave her there, using my air element to bring my clothes to me. I rush into an alcove and dress. My heart is beating. Was I too forward? Was I too creepy? This burning I have for her. The kiss was all the confirmation that I needed to know she is my mate.

Chapter 2
Hassian

Classes have officially ended for the day and I am waiting near the notices. I spoke with Professor Dublin earlier to see if she needed any help with her studies. He told me she did so I spoke with the headmaster to put me on the advisor list only if it's filled up. I have a feeling my princess will be waiting until the last minute to look for one.

I watch as she says goodbye to her friend who I have now learned is named Thalia before she looks over at the notices. From the look on her face the roster has filled up. My name should be appearing very soon then. I watch as she goes over the list, backing away as she spots my name. "Absolutely not," she says as she backs right into me. Perfect timing.

"Hello, princess," I rumble.

"I was just leaving," she says as she spins around.

"No, you weren't. Did you think I didn't see you reading the notice?"

"I know damn well your name wasn't on that list when I first checked. How did your name get on that list so fast?" she asks.

Pure fucking luck is the answer you are looking for I say in my mind, but what I really say is, "You admit you were looking then?"

"Not for your name." I watch as her cheeks flush.

I laugh, "but you noticed its absence.

She groans. I want to hear that sound again, but under different circumstances. "I'm leaving."

"You need help; just accept it," I say.

"Not from you."

"Why not?" I ask raising my brow. "Is it because of last night?"

She turns flaming red at the mention of that. "N-no. I just don't think you'd be a good fit."

"Is it my size that worries you, princess?" I watch as her mouth drops open. "Judging by your reaction, I think it's just about right." I feel my cock begin to harden at the thought of it in her mouth. I know I am trying to elicit a reaction out of her, but I am not helping myself here either.

"That's exactly the problem right there," she says so fast you would think she's hosting an auction.

I laugh again. "Judging by my name being crossed off that notice, you've already agreed to this. We will meet in the library after dinner; I have weapons training before then, so it's the only time I'll have to spend with you. Unless, of course, you would like to join me. I'd much like the sight of you on your knees before me." Fuck. I need this conversation to end now before my cock breaks the seams of my pants. This fucking hurts, but my goddesses does eliciting this reaction from her feel so fucking good.

"See you in the library," Sage says before she bolts down the hall.

I hurry up and finish eating my dinner, changing into one of my better-looking outfits of my wardrobe as I race to make my way into the library. I need to beat her in there and to calm my racing heart before she sees me again. I've only just sat down and adjusted myself in my chair before the door to the library opens.

"You're late," I say as she sits down across the table from me. I pretend that I didn't just arrive a few moments ago.

"I'm literally on time."

"On-time is late; you should be here earlier. I should see you as soon as I enter this room."

"That's ridiculous. I'm not cutting my dinner and conversation with my friends short when it's not necessary."

I run a hand across my stubble. I need to shave. I should have shaved. "Fine."

"Good."

"Let's get this lesson started."

"Fine by me."

I let out a small smile before asking, " What part of casting is hardest for you?"

I think she is going to refuse me an answer, but she says, "I don't know. All of it? I can't do it, at least not of my own free will."

I hate that my princess is doubting herself and I will see to it that she sees that she can. I bend over to retrieve the plant I took for our lesson and set it in front of her. "I don't have the same affinity as you since I am an air-based fae. That doesn't mean I can't walk you through this."

"Okay. How do I do this?" she asks. Her voice is quiet, soft.

"Close your eyes," I breathe out, barely audible as the breath leaves my lungs. I am making my way behind her. "I need you to close off your mind to everything but that flower, the sound of my voice, and my touch."

"Your touch?" she asks.

"Just listen," I breathe into her ear as my hand slides over her belly. I am demonstrating where to find the core of one's magic despite this feeling very intimate in nature. I feel her let out a short breath from my touch. "Good now find the core power inside of you. For myself, it's like I'm gliding down a tall cliff side, trusting in the leap." My eyes are closed as I think how to describe my power. A gentle breeze rustles around me as I enter my magic's core. I hear the sound of movement and open my eyes to see she's made a flower bloom. "Good girl," I say as I pull my hand away. In the same instant her flower closes its bloom before shriveling up and dying. Well fuck.

"Apparently not," she mumbles.

I smile at her. "It just means we have to work on your focus, and I have a few ideas for that in mind, but I'll save those ideas for later. I want to see what my princess can do." I grip her chin, angling it up toward my face. I want so badly to kiss her right then and there. I desire everything about her. Instead, I say, "Like I said yesterday, you'll have to earn it, princess." I release her chin and leave. My Heart racing as I go.

Chapter 3
Hassian

I'm sitting in my magical artifacts class when an unfamiliar feeling of pain hits me. I wasn't touching any dark objects and I've never felt pain before so why now? I feel an inkling of fear and I don't even bother asking the professor if I can leave before I walk out of the room.

There is only one thing on my mind. One person on my mind. Sage. I think of what class she would be in right now; Professor Dublin's. I race toward that direction when I spot her wandering the halls.

"Let me see," I order.

"It's nothing. How did you even know about this the periods not even over?" Fear increases in me. She can tell me it's nothing all she wants, but until I see it; I will know no peace.

"Let me see," I say enunciating each word as I fight against a primal urge in me to grab her arm and see for myself.

"Alight. Fine, just calm down." She peels back the cloth and lets out a hissing sound. I feel the pain she feels. I know beyond a doubt she is my mate. Her pain is my pain.

I grab her wrist, pulling it closer. I ease up when I feel that I am gripping too hard. "You were reckless. You need to be more careful. Why aren't you with the healer?"

She pulls her arm from my grip to cover her cut back up. "I didn't do this on purpose. I didn't even know I could. As to why I am not with a healer, I have no idea where I'm going. I was in a state of shock. Forgive me for not thinking in my moment of panic to ask for directions."

"Come with me," I say. It comes out harsher than I intend. I turn her back in the direction she came from and walk her to the correct door.

I knock on the door and Merellee, the healer calls us in.

"Hassian, I know very well you are not a first-year. Why are you walking around with one and not in class?"

"I was just using the restroom, and she was lost looking for you. I'm going back now."

"Very well, be off, back to class. I will tend to miss?"

"Sage. Sage Torrin."

Merellee and I share a look. She is a friend of my family's. She is aware that Sage was to be my betrothed. "Oh, I understand now. She's safe with me, Hassian. Now go."

I leave the room as quickly as I can. I do not return to class. Instead, I go to the forest in the northern area of the Academy and cast until I have drained my reservoir and exhausted myself. Only then do my emotions calm down. She got hurt and I wasn't there to stop it.

I decide to speak with Professor Dublin to find out what had happened during his class. I knock on the door of his classroom.

"Come in!" He shouts. I step through the door. "Oh Hassian, what are you doing here?"

"I figured it was my obligation as Sage's tutor to find out what had happened today. How she got hurt."

"It was just emotions getting the better of her. You know how casting can be in the early years. The frustration to get it right. I must admit, I am rather impressed by it."

"Why's that?"

"She nearly drained my magic just to calm the thing down. I made it look effortless, of course, but I haven't overdone it like that in a very long time."

"It was that strong?"

Professor Dublin nods. "It brings me hope that she can really save this realm; that she is exactly what the realm has been waiting for. I know she's frustrated that her casting isn't lasting. I have theories as to why, but I need to do more research first."

"Theories?" I ask. I am rather curious now.

"Yes, normally her casting dies after a few seconds, but this held on. It cut her and took some blood, but I don't know-" Professor Dublin drifts off into his own thoughts. "Where was I? Ah, yes. I plan to speak with her caretaker to see what precisely happened when her magic awoke. I would advise against having her cast tonight." He eyes me with raised brows.

"I was planning on taking her to see the Solaris event tonight."

"That's a most excellent idea. Let her admire the realm she is to save. Show her it's not all frustration casting and textbooks." Professor Dublin stops writing and looks up at me. "That look in your eyes. Do you have feelings for her?" I don't say anything. He pauses for a moment. "How did you know she was hurt? From what I gather you study in the evenings."

"I felt it."

Professor Dublin drops his quill. "You felt her hurt?" I nod slowly. "So, you are fated? Has the bond been made yet?"

"I haven't told her. I'm not going to force it onto her. I want her know she loves me first. I want her to burn for me as I do for her."

"That's probably for the best. I do hope it all works out in the end for the both of you."

I skip my weapons training class today to set up an area for Sage and I to view the Solstice event. I gave one of the brownies a sketch I made of one of the rose bushes in exchange for an old blanket from the academy's linen closet to spread out on the grass.

It was very happy to receive such a precious gift, something handmade and garden themed. They truly are one of the purest beings in Alandria. They would never harm anyone and they only wish for something that is sentimental in a way. I am glad they decided to take up residence in the academy.

I make it to one of the more cleared out areas of the school grounds and spread the blanket over the grass. My magic reservoir has replenished a little so I cast little ripples of wind to hold the blanket in place, just in case nature decides to intervene and blow the newly acquired blanket away.

I spend the next few moments practicing how I will lay on the blanket as I invite her to lay by my side. I imagine the conversation we will have, perhaps tonight we will kiss under the dancing stars. Something not born of my heated desire, but romance. I wonder what she feels for me. Does she feel the same? Can she feel my desire for her? There is one thing I wish for in this life and it is Sage Torrin.

I barely ate anything at dinner time. Curiosity got the best of me and I wondered if my princess would arrive earlier. I am sitting in my spot waiting for her when she steps into the library early. Sweat trickles down her forehead. Did she run here? She is still so very breathtaking to me.

"Don't you dare say that I am late. I made sure to leave early just to beat you here. Do you even eat at dinner?"

I let out a laugh. If only she knew the truth of how I was so anxious to see if she would show early that I barely ate. "I eat. Don't worry, princess. I'm glad you are choosing to take these lessons seriously."

She scoffs. "Taking them seriously? Okay, I'm never coming early again."

"I would hope not; I like to draw it out." She really did set herself up for that one. I should be trying to woo her in some romantic gesture, but she brings out such a feral side of me.

"Stop that." Her face turns crimson as I laugh.

"I spoke with your professor to try to figure out what happened with your casting today. You have anger issues, princess?"

"I do not-" She cuts herself off when she sees the smirk on my face.

"I can't say I thought you would create a volatile and dangerous plant, but you did cast something that held up more than a few seconds."

"I can't tell if you are trying to insult me or if this is a poor attempt to compliment me."

"A little of both, I suppose," I say grinning. "You did good, princess, even if it wasn't what was supposed to happen. That was some powerful magic. Professor Dublin practically drained his reservoir to contain it." She really did so fucking good.

"He what?"

"That's why he had you send the students away instead of back into the classroom; there was no way he could contain another incident if there were one. Truly impressive."

"I didn't mean to burden him that way."

"Don't feel bad about that princess. He isn't upset over it. If anything, it gave him more hope of what you can accomplish when you are able to control it."

"Great, can we start our lesson now?"

"No, you were injured today, and until you are healed, we will not be casting. I do have something else planned, but first, let me see your hand."

She doesn't argue as she offers her hand to me. I can't help but trace my fingers along the stitching. I feel the tingle in my own hand. "This looks irritated. Where's the salve she gave you?" I watch as she digs through her bag to locate the salve. My free hand open and ready.

"I can apply it myself," she says as she uncaps the lid and tries to pull her hand away. My grip stays firm. I grab the salve and dip two fingers into it. Albeit it might have been done a bit sexually in hopes of arousing her. I most definitely did not need this much salve. I apply it in gentle strokes to her stitching. Watching as her face becomes more heated at the intimacy. Before I rub too much, I retrieve a cloth from my jacket and wrap it around her hand.

"Now grab your things, princess; we have plans tonight."

As I walk with Sage outside, I am feeling discomfort coming from her. I wonder how long she will ignore it before she finally speaks out. The answer would be not long at all as she lets out the most dramatic groan I have ever heard in my life.

"What's wrong, princess? Am I boring you?"

"No, I just don't understand why we must walk around. Don't your muscles ache?"

"I wanted to show you something," I say as I discreetly wipe the sweat from my palms. "How long have your muscles been bothering you?"

"Since coming out here. I don't know. I haven't had to do this much walking before"

This is a bit concerning. As fae we should be naturally more attuned to physical activity. Our bodies are capable of doing far beyond that of a human and as a fae with god's blood in her, she shouldn't be struggling really at all. "You've been using the water in the school for some time; you shouldn't be this sore."

"It's fine. I'm just adapting, but seriously, I could use a break."

I halt my movement, trying to calculate in my mind what to do. I don't want this night to end and the Solaris event will be happening really soon, so I do the first idea that comes to mind. I pick her up into my arms and I carry her the rest of the way. I ignore her protests as she fights against me for me to put her down. Eventually she relents and relaxes into me. It has to be one of the best feelings in the world. Her pressed up against me in comfort. I could spend the rest of my life with her in my arms. I can tell the connection has been amplifying since our meeting. My feelings for her are increasing at an alarming speed. I cannot rush this.

Eventually we are laying together on the blanket watching as the stars dance across the night sky. I feel the moment she falls asleep, the moment her mind becomes completely relaxed. I trail my fingers up and down her arm and I imagine what it would be like to be like this every night. I stay out there for hours until I grow weary myself. I carefully lift her into my arms and carry her to the first-year tower.

Meera is about to end her nightly duties when I walk in. "Hassian what are you doing with Sage?"

"She fell asleep watching the Solaris event. I didn't want to wake her."

She looks me up and down and her face relaxes. "I should scold you for what you are feeling toward her, but I won't. I get it. I am sort of going through something similar right now. She's room number two. Go ahead and bring her up, but come right back down. I'm serious."

"On my honor, Meera." I grin and she shakes her head before retiring to her room for the night. I carry Sage up the steps and quietly knock on her door. Thalia answers.

"What are you doing with Sage?"

"Just returning her to her room."

"Is she hurt? Is she unconscious?"

"Quiet down or you will wake her. She is fine. I took her to see the Solaris event. She fell asleep. That is all. Can I please put her to bed or do you have more questions?"

Thalia waves her arm in the direction of Sage's bed. I pull back the blankets and lay her down, taking the care to tuck in her. As I am walking away, I hear her say, "Hassian." I turn around and she is still asleep. She mumbled my name while she dreams. Thalia and I exchange a glance. The look she gives me is telling me that I better keep what I just heard to myself. I nod and make my way to my dorm.

Chapter 4
Hassian

The fall season passes and I still haven't worked up the courage to see how she truly feels about me. I spend the hours away from her, thinking about her. The headmaster will be announcing the winter solstice dance soon and I have been making every preparation to ask her. I bartered with a brownie to help me get some flowers later this evening. They didn't like the idea of cutting flowers to give to a girl, but they eventually agreed after I offered to draw them a picture before they were cut.

I painstakingly drew out variations of the flowers I had in mind to give her with my charcoal. The brownie was eventually satisfied with my exchange and assured me that they will be in my room after dinner. I spent the previous night trying to decide what I would wear when I eventually ask her. I've never been with anyone before. My mother always told me before she passed that I should wait and there might be a chance I would find my mate. She always told me she regretted not waiting. She didn't regret having me, but she regretted that she had settled for an abusive man. She never loved him; it was always out of obligation.

She told me she believed in the arrangement between Sage and I. She said Idril saw a vision of us happy together and she held onto that belief. Much as I do now. I hold onto it. I wish I could let my mother know that she was right, that Sage was the one. Perhaps in the future I can bring Sage to my mother's final resting place and they can meet.

I wipe the tear away that slides down my face at the thought of my mother. I don't often cry, but she is one of the harder topics for me. I sneak into the kitchens and steal a sandwich before I make my way up to the library. I refuse to be in the grand hall with a bunch of feral women seeking a date. I have only one person in mind and that is Sage.

Sage walks into the library and her face is aglow with a look I have never seen. "I'm surprised you were able to make it out of the great hall unscathed," she says as she plops down into her regular spot.

"Why's that?" I ask with a grin. I know very well why, but I want to hear her say it.

"Oh, you know from the multitude of women declaring that they will be your date to this ball."

"What if I say yes to one of them?" I tease. It was very much the wrong thing to say as her demeanor stiffens.

"Do what you want." I feel her mood turn to that of hurt and I know I messed up. I have to stick with my plan though. I worked too hard for this. I hope she will still be here when I return. I should have planned this better.

"Very well," I get up and leave the library. My heart begins to ache the moment I close the door. I realize I really hurt her. I hope she will forgive me when she sees what I have planned.

I am gone just long enough to change clothes and retrieve the flowers. "Sage?" I ask. The library looks empty, but I hear the sound of a sniffle.

"Over here!" She yells it out, but it sounds broken. I really fucked up.

"Turn around, Sage," I say in a stern voice. I feel like a fool now, holding these flowers and wearing this planned outfit.

"Hang on, this book just got to a good part," she says. I feel the ache in my fingers as she tightens her grip around the book.

I move closer to her. "I said," I move the hair away from her neck, "turn," goddess I want to kiss her neck and everywhere in between, instead I run a finger down the delicate area of her skin. My rings making cold contact, sending a shiver down her spine. "Around." I finish.

She slams the book closed and spins around.

"Were you crying princess?"

"No."

"Please don't lie to me," I say as I wipe a fallen tear off of her cheek. "Please don't cry over me, princess. Have I not made it obvious that you are mine from the day we met?"

"I distinctly remember a lot of teasing, not an admittance of possible feelings." I guess I should have been clearer.

"Sage, I have spent every evening with you and you alone for months. I feel I have made my intentions very, very clear." I say the last part in a whisper.

"I think I am going to need some form of proof," she breathes out. It's all I needed to let my desire win. I use my element and slide a chair across the floor to secure the library door in place. There will be no interruptions for this.

I devour Sage like she is my last meal savoring every ounce of her. Craving every quiver of her body as I bring her to release. She is the most delicious thing I have ever tasted and I wish to live in this moment forever, but we can't. She needs rest and I have a question to ask.

"Open," I say and she does. I set my fingers in her mouth. "Lick it clean." I watch as Sage sucks every last drop of herself from my fingers as she stares me in the eyes. I only pull them out when I am sure she has licked every last drop. My rings are still wet with her.

"Your rings," she says. I admire the mess she made on them.

"They're fine, princess," I say as I wave my hand to restore the books to their rightful place, return the chair, and bring the bundle of flowers to my hand. "Now, before things got away from me, I was in the middle of trying to ask my princess if she would like to go to the winter solstice ball with me."

She takes the bundle from me as she says, "I would love that very much.

I kiss her deeply. "Good. You are mine, princess. I want you to remember that and not just because of some arrangement our parents made before you were born. You are mine because from the moment I saw you. I saw my heart, my soul, my future." I kiss her again not wanting to relinquish her lips, but I must as I bid her goodnight.

She will be my undoing and I won't regret a single moment of it.

Acknowledgements

I originally started writing this story in early 2023, but I struggled to envision what would happen next. There were details I knew for certain that needed to happen, no matter how much I didn't want it to go that way. After struggling for months trying to get past certain parts, I put the story on the back burner for a while. I truly believe I needed to step back because there was somewhere else I needed to be.

After stepping away, I really started to focus more on my social media content, and that's where I met an amazing community of people: CK, Bex, Rene, Jess, Madeline, Vermilion, Sofie, Heather, Patience, and Alexus (this list could go on forever.) They have been such a light in my life and highly encouraging. They really make you feel seen and heard and that you are capable of accomplishing anything.

Another huge thank you I want to extend is to my friends in the gaming community that really helped build my confidence over the years. You all really instilled that failure doesn't necessarily mean the end and that there is always something better waiting at the end of a hard day. Thank you to all my fellow bridge sleepers, you will always be like family to me.

To my family that kept nagging me since high school asking when they would get to actually read a book of mine, here you go. It may not be the story you were hoping to read first, but I am very proud of this one. It's tremendously better than what The Hunted could have ever been.

My list of people I wish to thank is ever growing and unfortunately some of that list will never be able to read this book. To Sarah Freedlund, thank you for being one of the biggest pushers of my writing and encouraging me at a young age to go for it. Maybe one day I will write my memoir that you believe people should read. To my sister, Nina, I miss you every day. Thank you for being the inspiration for my main character. I wish phoenixes were real and you could really rise from the ashes, too. To my grandfather, Eugene, thank you for being the most selfless man I have ever known. Thank you for saving my life and seeing meaning in it.

I'd also like to thank my partner, Chris, for not minding me being on my laptop in bed writing until the early morning hours and sleeping through his first break because I stayed up too late. Thank you for listening to the in-depth lore I created for each of the characters because it seriously helps my brain so much just to talk it out.

A very special thank you to everyone who read this in its baby stages and helped me polish it up. You were the first to read this story and the hardest to hand it over to. These characters are as much a part of me as they are a part of this story, so it's very difficult to hear feedback and correct flaws.

Thank you to everyone who has taken the time to read this book. I am terribly sorry about the cliffhanger. Just remember, it's not the end, only the beginning.

ABOUT THE AUTHOR

Ashley Eileen is an indie fantasy author based in America. Growing up she moved around a lot, never staying in the same location very long. After graduating, she kept on with the rhythm of moving around and starting over. Eventually, she found a place to call home in South Carolina, where she lives with her two rescue dogs, two cats, and long-term partner. She enjoys writing more high stakes fantasy and adding a twist to some of the lore that you all may have grown up knowing. When she isn't writing she can be found reading, drawing, or diving into a board/video game.

Fate of Alandria is her debut novel and book one in her series Fate of Alandria.

Website: https://www.authorashleyeileen.com/
Tiktok: @AuthorAshleyEileen
Instagram: @AuthorAshleyEileen

Sign up for my author newsletter!

https://www.authorashleyeileen.com/newsletter

Made in the USA
Columbia, SC
04 September 2024

f5af6618-26c9-4b92-88a1-f82c0a276f19R02